RANGER'S APPRENTICE

THE RUINS OF GORLAN

&

THE BURNING BRIDGE

The Bodley Head
London

CHARACTER PROFILES

WILL is an orphan, raised as a ward by the generosity of Baron Auld at Redmont Castle. He is about to turn fifteen, and faces Choosing Day, where he and his fellow ward mates will be apprenticed to a craftmaster. He dreams of being a Knight like the father he never knew, but although he is fast and agile, he is worried that he is too small to be a Battleschool apprentice. He clashes with Horace, a tall and muscular ward mate who takes delight in taunting Will about his small size.

BARON AULD is also known as the Lord of the Redmont fief. He is tall, broad shouldered and powerfully built, although his large bulk is partly attributed to his huge appetite. He is known for his strength, kindness and humour.

HALT is a senior Ranger, mysterious and often shrouded in his mottled, grey and green Ranger's cloak. To many is ability to move almost unseen can be unnerving. Although small and slim, he projects an image of strength and power and he is known throughout the Kingdom for his courageous missions. His gruff exterior hides a softness.

HORACE is sure that he is destined to be a Knight, but his training at Battleschool is gruelling. He can be aggressive and quick to rise to anger, especially when tired. He is struggling to cope with the unwanted attention he is receiving from three school bullies but determined to resolve the matter himself. Unknown to him, he has also caught the attention of the Battleschool master who has recognised his extraordinary potential.

JENNY is a pretty blonde ward, determined to be taken in as an apprentice to Master Chubb, the rotund Head Chef. Cheerful and kind, she is well-liked by all.

ALYSS is tall, elegant and pretty with an air of self-confidence and poise that has already brought her to the attention of Lady Pauline, the head of the King's Diplomatic Service. She regards Will as a good friend.

GILAN is Halt's former apprentice and is the only Ranger who carries a sword. He is tall and humorous, in sharp contrast to his former master. For all his jokes and light-hearted manner, Gilan is serious about being a Ranger, and is the best unseen mover in the Ranger Corps.

MORGARATH is a black Lord, a former Baron of Gorlan who was driven away by the Rangers after his attempt to seize control of the Kingdom. Fifteen years later, he is restless, hungry for power and determined to take revenge.

WARGALS are rumoured to be a tribe of semi-intelligent beasts who live in the mountains. They are susceptible to influence and easily manipulated.

HAVE YOU GOT WHAT IT TAKES TO BE A RANGER?

The Rangers are an elite Special Forces Corps in the medieval Kingdom of Araluen. They are the eyes and ears of the Kingdom, the intelligence gatherers, the scouts and the troubleshooters.

Rangers are expert archers and carry two knives — one for throwing, and one for hunting. They are also highly skilled at tracking, concealment and unseen movement. Their ability to become virtually invisible has led common folk to view them with fear, thinking the Rangers must use black magic.

Occasionally, a young man who is judged to have the qualities of honesty, courage, agility and intelligence will be invited to undertake a five-year apprenticeship — to develop his natural abilities and instruct him in the almost supernatural skills of a Ranger.

If he passes his first year, he is given a bronze medallion in the shape of an oakleaf.

If he graduates, the bronze will be exchanged for the silver oakleaf of an Oakleaf Bearer — a Ranger of the Kingdom of Araluen.

Araluen, Picta and Celtica

YEAR 643 COMMON ERA

ERAK'S RANSOM (BOOK 7)

The Skandian leader has been taken by a dangerous desert tribe.
To reach him, Will faces violent sandstorms, warring tribes and
hidden danger. With him is the princess, whom Will must
keep safe at all costs.

THE KINGS OF CLONMEL (BOOK 8)

The surrounding Kingdoms have fallen prey to a religious cult
that is spreading confusion and rebellion. The only Kingdom that
is uncorrupted is Clonmel, which will fall unless the
Rangers intervene.

HALT'S PERIL (BOOK 9)

Will and Halt are on the trail of a renegade group from
the Kingdom of Clonmel, and are determined to stop them.
The battle is deadly and Will faces the prospect of
returning home alone.

THE EMPEROR OF NIHON-JA (BOOK 10)

Horace is in Nihon-Ja, protecting the Emperor from a powerful
threat. To restore order, Will must quickly form and train a
force to face the highly trained Senshi warriors, who intend to
overthrow the Emperor.

THE LOST STORIES (BOOK 11)

A collection of nine recently discovered tales that reveal the
whole story — as yet unheard — of the legends of the Rangers of
Araluen. Hear how Will became an orphan, and learn what's gone
before and what comes next for him and his loyal friends.

RANGER'S APPRENTICE: THE RUINS OF GORLAN &
RANGER'S APPRENTICE: THE BURNING BRIDGE

A BODLEY HEAD BOOK 978 0 370 33214 7

Published in Great Britain by The Bodley Head,
an imprint of Random House Children's Books
A Random House Group Company

Ranger's Apprentice: The Ruins of Gorlan
Originally published in Australia in 2004 by Random House Australia (Pty) Ltd
First published in Great Britain in 2007 by Corgi Yearling
Copyright © John Flanagan, 2004

Ranger's Apprentice: The Burning Bridge
Originally published in Australia in 2005 by Random House Australia (Pty) Ltd
First Published in Great Britain in 2007 by Corgi Yearling
Copyright © John Flanagan, 2005

This omnibus edition published 2011

1 3 5 7 9 10 8 6 4 2

The Random House Group Limited supports the Forest Stewardship Council (FSC®),
the leading international forest certification organization. Our books carrying the FSC
label are printed on FSC®-certified paper. FSC is the only forest certification scheme
endorsed by the leading environmental organizations, including Greenpeace. Our paper
procurement policy can be found at www.randomhouse.co.uk/environment
<http://www.randomhouse.co.uk/environment>

MIX
Paper from
responsible sources
FSC® C016897

Random House Children's Books, 61–63 Uxbridge Road, London W5 5SA

www.**kidsatrandomhouse**.co.uk
www.**totallyrandombooks**.co.uk
www.**randomhouse**.co.uk

Addresses for companies within The Random House Group Limited can be found at:
www.randomhouse.co.uk/offices.htm

THE RANDOM HOUSE GROUP Limited Reg. No. 954009

A CIP catalogue record for this book is available from the British Library.

Printed and bound by CPI Group (UK) Ltd, Croydon, CR0 4YY

RANGER'S APPRENTICE

THE RUINS OF GORLAN

BOOK 1

For Michael

Prologue

Morgarath, Lord of the Mountains of Rain and Night, former Baron of Gorlan in the Kingdom of Araluen, looked out over his bleak, rainswept domain and, for perhaps the thousandth time, cursed.

This was all that was left to him now — a jumble of rugged granite cliffs, tumbled boulders and icy mountains. Of sheer gorges and steep narrow passes. Of gravel and rock, with never a tree or a sign of green to break the monotony.

Even though it had been fifteen years since he had been driven back into this forbidding realm that had become his prison, he could still remember the pleasant green glades and thickly forested hills of his former fief. The streams filled with fish and the fields rich with crops and game. Gorlan had been a beautiful, living place. The Mountains of Rain and Night were dead and desolate.

A platoon of Wargals was drilling in the castle yard below him. Morgarath watched them for a few seconds, listening to the guttural, rhythmic chant that accompanied all their movements. They were stocky, misshapen beings, with features that were halfway human, but with a long, brutish muzzle and fangs like a bear or a large dog.

Avoiding all contact with humans, the Wargals had lived and bred in these remote mountains since ancient times. No one in living memory had ever set eyes upon one, but rumours and legends had persisted of a savage tribe of semi-intelligent beasts in the mountains. Morgarath, planning a revolt against the Kingdom of Araluen, had left Gorlan Fief to seek them out. If such creatures existed, they would give him an edge in the war that was to come.

It took him months but he eventually found them. Aside from their wordless chant, Wargals had no spoken language, relying on a primitive form of thought awareness for communication. But their minds were simple and their intellects basic. As a result, they had been totally susceptible to domination by a superior intelligence and willpower. Morgarath bent them to his will and they became the perfect army for him — ugly beyond nightmares, utterly pitiless and bound totally to his mental orders.

Now, looking at them, he remembered the brightly dressed knights in glittering armour who used to compete in tourneys at Castle Gorlan, their silk-gowned ladies cheering them on and applauding their skills. Mentally comparing them to these black-furred, misshapen creatures, he cursed again.

The Wargals, attuned to his thoughts, sensed his disturbance and stirred uncomfortably, pausing in what they were doing. Angrily, he directed them back to their drill and the chanting resumed.

Morgarath moved away from the unglazed window, closer to the fire that seemed utterly incapable of dispelling the damp and chill from this gloomy castle. Fifteen years, he thought to himself again. Fifteen years since he had rebelled against the newly crowned King Duncan, a youth in his twenties. He had planned it all carefully as the old king's sickness progressed, banking on the indecision and confusion that would follow his death to split the other barons and give Morgarath his opportunity to seize the throne.

Secretly, he had trained his army of Wargals, massing them up here in the mountains, ready for the moment to strike. Then, in the days of confusion and grief following the king's death, when the barons travelled to Castle Araluen for the funeral rites, leaving their armies leaderless, he had attacked, overrunning the south-eastern quarter of the Kingdom in a matter of days, routing the confused, leaderless forces that tried to oppose him.

Duncan, young and inexperienced, could never have stood against him. The Kingdom was his for the taking. The throne was his for the asking.

Then Lord Northolt, the old king's supreme army commander, had rallied some of the younger barons into a loyal confederation, giving strength to Duncan's resolve and stiffening the wavering courage of the others. The armies met at Hackham Heath, close by the Slipsunder River, and the battle swayed in the balance for five hours, with attack and counterattack and massive loss of life. The Slipsunder was a shallow river, but its treacherous reaches of quicksand and soft mud formed an impassable barrier, protecting Morgarath's right flank.

But then one of those grey-cloaked meddlers known as

Rangers led a force of heavy cavalry across a secret ford ten kilometres upstream. The armoured horsemen appeared at the crucial moment of the battle and fell upon the rear of Morgarath's army.

The Wargals, trained in the tumbled rocks of the mountains, had one weakness. They feared horses and could never stand against such a surprise cavalry attack. They broke, retreating to the narrow confines of Three Step Pass, and back to the Mountains of Rain and Night. Morgarath, his rebellion defeated, went with them. And here he had been exiled these fifteen years. Waiting, plotting, hating the men who had done this to him.

Now, he thought, it was time for his revenge. His spies told him the Kingdom had grown slack and complacent and his presence here was all but forgotten. The name Morgarath was a name of legend nowadays, a name mothers used to hush fractious children, threatening that if they did not behave, the black lord Morgarath would come for them.

The time was ripe. Once again, he would lead his Wargals into an attack. But this time he would have allies. And this time, he would sow the ground with uncertainty and confusion beforehand. This time, none of those who conspired against him previously would be left alive to aid King Duncan.

For the Wargals were not the only ancient, terrifying creatures he had found in these sombre mountains. He had two other allies, even more fearsome – the dreadful beasts known as the Kalkara.

The time was ripe to unleash them.

One

'Try to eat something, Will. Tomorrow's a big day, after all.'

Jenny, blonde, pretty and cheerful, gestured towards Will's barely touched plate and smiled encouragingly at him. Will made an attempt to return the smile but it was a dismal failure. He picked at the plate before him, piled high with his favourite foods. Tonight, his stomach knotted tight with tension and anticipation, he could hardly bring himself to swallow a bite.

Tomorrow would be a big day, he knew. He knew it all too well, in fact. Tomorrow would be the biggest day in his life, because tomorrow was the Choosing Day and it would determine how he spent the rest of his life.

'Nerves, I imagine,' said George, setting down his loaded fork and seizing the lapels of his jacket in a judicious manner. He was a thin, gangly and studious boy, fascinated by rules and regulations and with a penchant for examining and debating both sides of any question – sometimes at great length. 'Dreadful thing, nervousness. It can just freeze you up so you can't think, can't eat, can't speak.'

'I'm not nervous,' Will said quickly, noticing that Horace had looked up, ready to form a sarcastic comment.

George nodded several times, considering Will's statement. 'On the other hand,' he added, 'a little nervousness can actually improve performance. It can heighten your perceptions and sharpen your reactions. So, the fact that you are worried, if, in fact, you are, is not necessarily something to be worried about, of itself — so to speak.'

In spite of himself, a wry smile touched Will's mouth. George would be a natural in the legal profession, he thought. He would almost certainly be the Scribemaster's choice on the following morning. Perhaps, Will thought, that was at the heart of his own problem. He was the only one of the five wardmates who had any fears about the Choosing that would take place within twelve hours.

'He ought to be nervous!' Horace scoffed. 'After all, which Craftmaster is going to want him as an apprentice?'

'I'm sure we're all nervous,' Alyss said. She directed one of her rare smiles at Will. 'We'd be stupid not to be.'

'Well, I'm not!' Horace said, then reddened as Alyss raised one eyebrow and Jenny giggled.

It was typical of Alyss, Will thought. He knew that the tall, graceful girl had already been promised a place as an apprentice by Lady Pauline, head of Castle Redmont's Diplomatic Service. Her pretence that she was nervous about the following day, and her tact in refraining from pointing out Horace's gaffe, showed that she was already a diplomat of some skill.

Jenny, of course, would gravitate immediately to the

castle kitchens, domain of Master Chubb, Redmont's Head Chef. He was a man renowned throughout the Kingdom for the banquets served in the castle's massive dining hall. Jenny loved food and cooking and her easygoing nature and unfailing good humour would make her an invaluable staff member in the turmoil of the castle kitchens.

Battleschool would be Horace's choice. Will glanced at his wardmate now, hungrily tucking into the roast turkey, ham and potatoes that he had heaped onto his plate. Horace was big for his age and a natural athlete. The chances that he would be refused were virtually nonexistent. Horace was exactly the type of recruit that Sir Rodney looked for in his warrior apprentices. Strong, athletic, fit. And, thought Will a trifle sourly, not too bright. Battleschool was the path to knighthood for boys like Horace — born commoners but with the physical abilities to serve as knights of the Kingdom.

Which left Will. What would his choice be? More importantly, as Horace had pointed out, what Craftmaster would accept him as an apprentice?

For Choosing Day was the pivotal point in the life of the castle wards. They were orphan children raised by the generosity of Baron Arald, the Lord of Redmont Fief. For the most part, their parents had died in the service of the fief, and the Baron saw it as his responsibility to care for and raise the children of his former subjects — and to give them an opportunity to improve their station in life wherever possible.

Choosing Day provided that opportunity.

Each year, castle wards turning fifteen could apply to be

apprenticed to the masters of the various crafts that served the castle and its people. Ordinarily, craft apprentices were selected by dint of their parents' occupations or influence with the Craftmasters. The castle wards usually had no such influence and this was their chance to win a future for themselves.

Those wards who weren't chosen, or for whom no openings could be found, would be assigned to farming families in the nearby village, providing farm labour to raise the crops and animals that fed the castle inhabitants. It was rare for this to happen, Will knew. The Baron and his Craftmasters usually went out of their way to fit the wards into one craft or another. But it could happen and it was a fate he feared more than anything.

Horace caught his eye now and gave him a smug smile.

'Still planning on applying for Battleschool, Will?' he asked, through a mouthful of turkey and potatoes. 'Better eat something then. You'll need to build yourself up a little.'

He snorted with laughter and Will glowered at him. A few weeks previously, Horace had overheard Will confiding to Alyss that he desperately wanted to be selected for Battleschool, and he had made Will's life a misery ever since, pointing out on every possible occasion that Will's slight build was totally unsuited for the rigours of Battleschool training.

The fact that Horace was probably right only made matters worse. Where Horace was tall and muscular, Will was small and wiry. He was agile and fast and surprisingly strong but he simply didn't have the size that he knew was required of Battleschool apprentices. He'd hoped against hope for the past few years that he would have what people called his 'growing spurt' before the Choosing Day came around. But it had never happened and now the day was nearly here.

As Will said nothing, Horace sensed that he had scored a verbal hit. This was a rarity in their turbulent relationship. Over the past few years, he and Will had clashed repeatedly. Being the stronger of the two, Horace usually got the better of Will, although very occasionally Will's speed and agility allowed him to get in a surprise kick or a punch and then escape before Horace could catch him.

But while Horace generally had the best of their physical clashes, it was unusual for him to win any of their verbal encounters. Will's wit was as agile as the rest of him and he almost always managed to have the last word. In fact, it was this tendency that often led to trouble between them: Will was yet to learn that having the last word was not always a good idea. Horace decided now to press his advantage.

'You need muscles to get into Battleschool, Will. Real muscles,' he said, glancing at the others around the table to see if anyone disagreed. The other wards, uncomfortable at the growing tension between the two boys, concentrated on their plates.

'Particularly between the ears,' Will replied and, unfortunately, Jenny couldn't refrain from giggling. Horace's face flushed and he started to rise from his seat. But Will was quicker and he was already at the door before Horace could disentangle himself from his chair. He contented himself with hurling a final insult after his retreating wardmate.

'That's right! Run away, Will No-Name! You're a no-name and nobody will want you as an apprentice!'

In the anteroom outside, Will heard the parting sally and felt blood flush to his cheeks. It was the taunt he hated most, although he had tried never to let Horace know that, sensing that he would provide the bigger boy with a weapon if he did.

The truth was, nobody knew Will's second name. Nobody knew who his parents had been. Unlike his yearmates, who had lived in the fief before their parents had died and whose family histories were known, Will had appeared, virtually out of nowhere, as a newborn baby. He had been found, wrapped in a small blanket and placed in a basket, on the steps of the Ward building fifteen years ago. A note had been attached to the blanket, reading simply:

> *His mother died in childbirth.*
> *His father died a hero.*
> *Please care for him. His name is Will.*

That year, there had been only one other ward. Alyss's father was a cavalry lieutenant who had died in the battle at Hackham Heath, when Morgarath's Wargal army had been defeated and driven back to the mountains. Alyss's mother, devastated by her loss, succumbed to a fever some weeks after giving birth. So there was plenty of room in the Ward for the unknown child, and Baron Arald was, at heart, a kindly man. Even though the circumstances were unusual, he had given permission for Will to be accepted as a ward of Castle Redmont. It seemed logical to assume that, if the note were true, Will's father had died in the war against Morgarath, and since Baron Arald had taken a leading part in that war, he felt duty bound to honour the unknown father's sacrifice.

So Will had become a Redmont ward, raised and educated by the Baron's generosity. As time passed, the others had gradually joined him and Alyss until there were five in their year group. But while the others had memories of their parents or, in Alyss's case, people who had known them and who could tell her about them, Will knew nothing of his past.

That was why he had invented the story that had sustained him throughout his childhood in the Ward. And, as the years passed and he added detail and colour to the story, he eventually came to believe it himself.

His father, he knew, had died a hero's death. So it made sense to create a picture of him as a hero — a knight warrior in full armour, fighting against the Wargal hordes, cutting them down left and right until eventually he was overcome by sheer weight of numbers. Will had pictured the tall figure so often in his mind, seeing every detail of his armour and his equipment but never being able to visualise his face.

As a warrior, his father would expect him to follow in his footsteps. That was why selection for Battleschool was so important to Will. And that was why, the more unlikely it became that he would be selected, the more desperately he clung to the hope that he might.

He exited from the Ward building into the darkened castle yard. The sun was long down and the torches placed every twenty metres or so on the castle walls shed a flickering, uneven light. He hesitated a moment. He would not return to the Ward and face Horace's continued taunts. To do so would only lead to another fight between them — a fight Will knew he would probably lose. George would probably try to analyse the situation for him, looking at both sides of the question and thoroughly confusing the issue. Alyss and Jenny might try to comfort him, he knew — Alyss particularly since they had grown up together. But at the moment he didn't want their sympathy and he couldn't face Horace's taunts, so he headed for the one place where he knew he could find solitude.

The huge fig tree growing close by the castle's central tower had often afforded him a haven. Heights held no fear for Will and he climbed smoothly into the tree, keeping going long after another might have stopped, until he was in the lighter branches at the very top — branches which swayed and dipped under his weight. In the past, he had often escaped from Horace up here. The bigger boy couldn't match Will's speed in the tree and he was unwilling to follow as high as this. Will found a convenient fork and wedged himself in it, his body giving slightly to the movement of the tree as the branches swayed in the evening breeze. Below, the foreshortened figures of the watch made their rounds of the castle yard.

He heard the door of the Ward building open and, looking down, saw Alyss emerge, looking around the yard for him in vain. The tall girl hesitated a few moments then, seeming to shrug, turned back inside. The elongated rectangle of light that the open door threw across the yard was cut off as she closed the door softly behind her. Strange, he thought, how seldom people tend to look up.

There was a rustle of soft feathers and a barn owl landed on the next branch, its head swivelling, its huge eyes catching every last ray of the faint light. It studied him without concern, seeming to know it had nothing to fear from him. It was a hunter. A silent flyer. A ruler of the night.

'At least you know who you are,' he said softly to the bird. It swivelled its head again, then launched itself off into the darkness, leaving him alone with his thoughts.

Gradually, as he sat there, the lights in the castle windows went out, one by one. The torches burnt down to smouldering husks and were replaced at midnight by the change of watch. Eventually, there was only one light left burning and that, he knew, was in the Baron's study, where the Lord of Redmont was still presumably at work, poring over reports and papers. The study was virtually level with Will's position in the tree and he could see the burly figure of the Baron seated at his desk. Finally Baron Arald rose, stretched and leaned forward to extinguish the lamp as he left the room, heading for his sleeping quarters on the floor above. Now the castle was asleep, except for the guards on the walls, who kept constant watch.

In less than nine hours, Will realised, he would face the Choosing. Silently, miserably, fearing the worst, he climbed down from the tree and made his way to his bed in the darkened boys' dormitory in the Ward.

Two

'All right, candidates! This way! And look lively!'

The speaker, or more correctly the shouter, was Martin, secretary to Baron Arald. As his voice echoed around the anteroom, the five wards rose uncertainly from the long wooden benches where they had been seated. Suddenly nervous now that the day had finally arrived, they began to shuffle forward, each one reluctant to be the first through the great ironbound door that Martin now held open for them.

'Come on, come on!' Martin bellowed impatiently and Alyss finally elected to lead the way, as Will had guessed she would. The others followed the willowy blonde girl. Now that someone had decided to lead, the rest of them were content to follow.

Will looked around curiously as he entered the Baron's study. He'd never been in this part of the castle before. This tower, containing the administrative section, and the Baron's private apartments, was seldom visited by those of low rank — such as castle wards. The room was huge. The ceiling seemed to tower above him and the walls were constructed of massive stone blocks, fitted together with only the barest lines of mortar between them. On the eastern wall was a huge window space — open to the elements but with massive wooden shutters that could be closed in the event of bad weather. It was the same window he had seen through last night, he realised. Today, sunlight streamed in and fell on the huge oak table that Baron Arald used as a desk.

'Come on now! Stand in line, stand in line!' Martin seemed to be enjoying his moment of authority. The group shuffled slowly into line and he studied them, his mouth twisted in disapproval.

'In size place! Tallest this end!' He indicated the end where he wanted the tallest of the five to stand. Gradually, the group rearranged itself. Horace, of course, was the tallest. After him, Alyss took her position. Then George, half a head shorter than she and painfully thin. He stood in his usual stoop-shouldered posture. Will and Jenny hesitated. Jenny smiled at Will and gestured for him to go before her, even though she was possibly an inch taller than he was. That was typical of Jenny. She knew how Will agonised over the fact that he was the smallest of all the castle wards. As Will moved into the line, Martin's voice stopped him.

'Not you! The girl's next.'

Jenny shrugged apologetically and moved into the place Martin had indicated. Will took the last place in the line, wishing Martin hadn't made his lack of height so apparent.

'Come on! Smarten up, smarten up! Let's see you at

attention there,' Martin continued, then broke off as a deep voice interrupted him.

'I don't believe that's totally necessary, Martin.'

It was Baron Arald, who had entered, unobserved, by way of a smaller door behind his massive desk. Now it was Martin who brought himself to what he considered to be a position of attention, with his skinny elbows held out from his sides, his heels forced together so that his unmistakably bowed legs were widely separated at the knees, and his head thrown back.

Baron Arald raised his eyes to heaven. Sometimes his secretary's zeal on these occasions could be a little over-whelming. The Baron was a big man, broad in shoulder and waist and heavily muscled, as was necessary for a knight of the realm. It was well known, however, that Baron Arald was fond of his food and drink, so his considerable bulk was not totally attributable to muscle.

He had a short, neatly trimmed black beard that, like his hair, was beginning to show the traces of grey that went with his forty-two years. He had a strong jaw, a large nose and dark, piercing eyes under heavy brows. It was a powerful face, but not an unkind one, Will thought. There was a surprising hint of humour in those dark eyes. Will had noted it before, on the occasions when Arald had made his infrequent visits to the wards' quarters to see how their lessons and personal development were progressing.

'Sir!' Martin said at top volume, causing the Baron to wince slightly. 'The candidates are assembled!'

'I can see that,' Baron Arald replied patiently. 'Perhaps you might be good enough to ask the Craftmasters to step in as well?'

'Sir!' Martin responded, making an attempt to click his heels together. As he was wearing shoes of a soft, pliable leather, the attempt was doomed to failure. He marched towards the main door of the study, all elbows and knees. Will was reminded of a rooster. As Martin laid his hand on the door handle, the Baron stopped him once more.

'Martin?' he said softly. As the secretary turned an inquiring look back at him, he continued in the same quiet tone, 'Ask them. Don't bellow at them. Craftmasters don't like that.'

'Yes, sir,' said Martin, looking somewhat deflated. He opened the door and, making an obvious effort to speak in a lower tone, said, 'Craftmasters. The Baron is ready now.'

The Craftschool heads entered the room in no particular order of precedence. As a group, they admired and respected each other and so rarely stood on strict ceremonial procedure. Sir Rodney, head of the Battleschool, came first. Tall and broad-shouldered like the Baron, he wore the standard battledress of chain mail shirt under a white surcoat emblazoned with his own crest, a scarlet wolfshead. He had earned that crest as a young man, fighting the wolfships of the Skandian sea raiders who constantly harried the Kingdom's east coast. He wore a sword belt and sword, of course. No knight would be seen in public without one. He was around the Baron's age, with blue eyes and a face that would have been remarkably handsome if it weren't for the massively broken nose. He sported an enormous moustache but, unlike the Baron, he had no beard.

Next came Ulf, the Horsemaster, responsible for the care and training of the castle's mighty battlehorses. He had keen brown eyes, strong, muscular forearms and heavy wrists. He wore a simple leather vest over his woollen shirt and leggings. Tall riding boots of soft leather reached up past his knees.

Lady Pauline followed Ulf. Slim, grey-haired and elegant, she had been a considerable beauty in her youth and still had the grace and style to turn men's heads. Lady Pauline, who had been awarded the title in her own right for her work in foreign policy for the Kingdom, was head of the Diplomatic Service in Redmont. Baron Arald regarded her abilities highly and she was one of his close confidants and advisers. Arald often said that girls made the best recruits to the Diplomatic Service. They tended to be more subtle than boys, who gravitated naturally to Battleschool. And while boys constantly looked to physical means as the way of solving problems, girls could be depended on to use their wits.

It was perhaps only natural that Nigel, the Scribe-master, followed close behind Lady Pauline. They had been discussing matters of mutual interest while they waited for Martin to summon them. Nigel and Lady Pauline were close friends as well as professional colleagues. It was Nigel's trained scribes who prepared the official documents and communiqués that were so often delivered by Lady Pauline's diplomats. He also advised on the exact wording of such documents, having an extensive background in legal matters. Nigel was a small, wiry man with a quick, inquisitive face that reminded Will of a ferret. His hair was glossy black, his features were thin and his dark eyes never ceased roaming the room.

Master Chubb, the Head Chef, came in last of all. Inevitably, he was a fat, round-bellied man, wearing a cook's white jacket and tall hat. He was known to have a terrible temper that could flare as quickly as oil spilt on a fire, and most of the wards treated him with considerable caution. Florid-faced and with red, rapidly receding hair, Master Chubb carried a wooden ladle with him wherever he went. It was an unofficial staff of office. It was also used quite often as an offensive weapon, landing with a resounding crack on the heads of careless, forgetful or slow-moving kitchen apprentices. Alone among the wards, Jennifer saw Chubb as something of a hero. It was her avowed intention to work for him and learn his skills, wooden ladle or no wooden ladle.

There were other Craftmasters, of course. The Armourer and the Blacksmith were two. But only those Craftmasters who currently had vacancies for new apprentices would be represented today.

'The Craftmasters are assembled, sir!' Martin said, his voice rising in volume. Martin seemed to equate volume and the importance of the occasion in direct proportion. Once again, the Baron raised his eyes to heaven.

'So I see,' he said quietly, then added, in a more formal tone, 'Good morning, Lady Pauline. Good morning, gentlemen.'

They replied and the Baron turned to Martin once more. 'Perhaps we might proceed?'

Martin nodded several times, consulted a sheaf of notes he held in one hand and marched to confront the line of candidates.

'Right, the Baron's waiting! The Baron's waiting! Who's first?'

Will, eyes down, shifting nervously from one foot to the

other, suddenly had the strange sensation that someone was watching him. He looked up and actually started with surprise as he met the dark, unfathomable gaze of Halt, the Ranger.

Will hadn't seen him come into the room. He realised that the mysterious figure must have slipped in through a side door while everyone's attention was on the Craft-masters as they made their entrance. Now he stood, behind the Baron's chair and slightly to one side, dressed in his usual brown and grey clothes and wrapped in his long, mottled grey and green Ranger's cloak. Halt was an unnerving person. He had a habit of coming up on you when you least expected it — and you never heard his approach. The superstitious villagers believed that Rangers practised a form of magic that made them invisible to ordinary people. Will wasn't sure if he believed that — but he wasn't sure he disbelieved it either. He wondered why Halt was here today. He wasn't recognised as one of the Craftmasters and, as far as Will knew, he hadn't attended a Choosing session prior to this one.

Abruptly, Halt's gaze cut away from him and it was as if a light had been turned off. Will realised that Martin was talking once more. He noticed that the secretary had a habit of repeating statements, as if he were followed by his own personal echo.

'Now then, who's first? Who's first?'

The Baron sighed audibly. 'Why don't we take the first in line?' he suggested in a reasonable tone, and Martin nodded several times.

'Of course, my lord. Of course. First in line, step forward and face the Baron.'

After a moment's hesitation, Horace stepped forward out of the line and stood at attention. The Baron studied him for a few seconds.

'Name?' he said, and Horace answered, stumbling slightly over the correct method of address for the Baron.

'Horace Altman, sir . . . my lord.'

'And do you have a preference, Horace?' the Baron asked, with the air of one who knows what the answer is going to be before hearing it.

'Battleschool, sir!' Horace said firmly. The Baron nodded. He'd expected as much. He glanced at Rodney, who was studying the boy thoughtfully, assessing his suitability.

'Battlemaster?' the Baron said. Normally he would address Rodney by his first name, not his title. But this was a formal occasion. By the same token, Rodney would usually address the Baron as 'sir'. But on a day like today, 'my lord' was the proper form.

The big knight stepped forward, his chain mail and spurs chinking slightly as he moved closer to Horace. He eyed the boy up and down, then moved behind him. Horace's head started to turn with him.

'Still,' Sir Rodney said, and the boy ceased his movement, staring straight ahead.

'Looks strong enough, my lord, and I can always use new trainees.' He rubbed one hand over his chin. 'You ride, Horace Altman?'

A look of uncertainty crossed Horace's face as he realised this might be a hurdle to his selection. 'No, sir. I . . .'

He was about to add that castle wards had little chance to learn to ride but Sir Rodney interrupted him.

'No matter. That can be taught.' The big knight looked at the Baron and nodded. 'Very well, my lord. I'll take him for Battleschool, subject to the usual three-month probationary period.'

The Baron made a note on a sheet of paper before him and smiled briefly at the delighted, and very relieved, youth before him.

'Congratulations, Horace. Report to Battleschool tomorrow morning. Eight o'clock sharp.'

'Yes, sir!' Horace replied, grinning widely. He turned to Sir Rodney and bowed slightly. 'Thank you, sir!'

'Don't thank me yet,' the knight replied cryptically. 'You don't know what you're in for.'

Three

'Who's next then?' Martin was calling as Horace, grinning broadly, stepped back into the line. Alyss stepped forward gracefully, annoying Martin, who had wanted to nominate her as the next candidate.

'Alyss Mainwaring, my lord,' she said in her quiet, level voice. Then, before she could be asked, she continued, 'I request an appointment to the Diplomatic Service please, my lord.'

Arald smiled at the solemn-looking girl. She had an air of self-confidence and poise about her that would suit her well in the Service. He glanced at Lady Pauline.

'My lady?' he said.

She nodded her head several times. 'I've already spoken to Alyss, my lord. I believe she will be an excellent candidate. Approved and accepted.'

Alyss made a small bow of her head in the direction of the woman who would be her mentor. Will thought how alike they were — both tall and elegant in their movements, both grave in manner. He felt a small surge of pleasure for his oldest companion, knowing how much she had wanted this selection. Alyss stepped back in line and Martin, not to be forestalled this time, was already pointing to George.

'Right! You're next! You're next! Address the Baron.'

George stepped forward. His mouth opened and closed several times but nothing came out. The other wards watched in surprise. George, long regarded by them all as the official advocate for just about everything, was overcome with stage fright. He finally managed to say something in a low voice that nobody in the room could hear. Baron Arald leaned forward, one hand cupped behind his ear.

'I'm sorry, I didn't quite get that?' he said. George looked up at the Baron and, with an enormous effort, spoke in a just-audible voice.

'G-George Carter, sir. Scribeschool, sir.'

Martin, ever a stickler for the proprieties, drew breath to berate him for the truncated nature of his address. Before he could do so, and to everyone's evident relief, Baron Arald stepped in.

'Very well, Martin. Let it go.' Martin looked a little aggrieved but subsided. The Baron glanced at Nigel, his chief scribe and legal officer, with one eyebrow raised in question.

'Acceptable, my lord,' Nigel said, adding, 'I've seen some of George's work and he really does have a gift for calligraphy.'

The Baron looked doubtful. 'He's not the most forceful of speakers, though, is he, Scribemaster? That could be a problem if he has to offer legal counsel at any time in the future.'

Nigel shrugged the objection aside. 'I promise you, my lord, with proper training that sort of thing represents no problem. Absolutely no problem at all, my lord.'

The Master Scribe folded his hands together into the wide sleeves of the monk-like habit he wore as he warmed to his theme.

'I remember a boy who joined us some seven years back, rather like this one here, as a matter of fact. He had that same habit of mumbling to his shoes — but we soon showed him how to overcome it. Some of our most reluctant speakers have gone on to develop absolute eloquence, my lord, absolute eloquence.'

The Baron drew breath to comment but Nigel continued in his discourse.

'It may even surprise you to hear that, as a boy, I myself suffered from a most terrible nervous stutter. Absolutely terrible, my lord. Could barely put two words together at a time.'

'Hardly a problem now, I see,' the Baron managed to put in dryly, and Nigel smiled, taking the point. He bowed to the Baron.

'Exactly, my lord. We'll soon help young George overcome his shyness. Nothing like the rough and tumble of Scribeschool for that. Absolutely.'

The Baron smiled in spite of himself. The Scribeschool was a studious place where voices were rarely, if ever, raised and where logical, reasoned debate reigned supreme. Personally, on his visits to the place, he had found it mind-numbing in the extreme. Anything less like a rough and tumble atmosphere he could not imagine.

'I'll take your word for it,' he replied, then, to George,

he said, 'Very well, George, request granted. Report to Scribeschool tomorrow.'

George shuffled his feet awkwardly. 'Mumble-mumble-mumble,' he said and the Baron leaned forward again, frowning as he tried to make out the low-pitched words.

'What was that?' he asked.

George finally looked up and managed to whisper, 'Thank you, my lord.' He hurriedly shuffled back to the relative anonymity of the line.

'Oh,' said the Baron, a little taken aback. 'Think nothing of it. Now, next is . . .'

Jenny was already stepping forward. Blonde and pretty, she was also, it had to be admitted, a little on the chubby side. But the look suited her and at any of the castle's social functions, she was a much sought-after dance partner with the boys in the castle, both her yearmates in the Ward and the sons of castle staff as well.

'Master Chubb, sir!' she said now, stepping forward right to the edge of the Baron's desk. The Baron looked into the round face, saw the eagerness shining there in the blue eyes and couldn't help smiling at her.

'What about him?' he asked gently and she hesitated, realising that, in her enthusiasm, she had breached the protocol of the Choosing.

'Oh! Your pardon, sir . . . my . . . Baron . . . your lordship,' she hastily improvised, her tongue running away with her as she mangled the correct form of address.

'My lord!' Martin prompted her. Baron Arald looked at him, eyebrows raised.

'Yes, Martin?' he said. 'What is it?'

Martin had the grace to look embarrassed. He knew

that his master was intentionally misunderstanding his interruption. He took a deep breath, and said in an apologetic tone, 'I . . . simply wanted to inform you that the candidate's name is Jennifer Dalby, sir.'

The Baron nodded at him and Martin, a devoted servant of the thickset bearded man, saw the look of approval in his lord's eyes.

'Thank you, Martin. Now, Jennifer Dalby . . .'

'Jenny, sir,' said the irrepressible girl and he shrugged resignedly.

'Jenny, then. I assume that you are applying to be apprenticed to Master Chubb?'

'Oh, yes please, sir!' Jenny replied breathlessly, turning adoring eyes on the portly, red-haired cook. Chubb scowled thoughtfully and considered her.

'Mmmmm . . . could be, could be,' he muttered, walking back and forth in front of her. She smiled winningly at him but Chubb was beyond such feminine wiles.

'I'd work hard, sir,' she told him earnestly.

'I know you would!' he replied with some spirit. 'I'd make sure of it, girl. No slacking or lollygagging in my kitchen, let me tell you.'

Fearing that her opportunity might be slipping away, Jenny played her trump card.

'I have the right shape for it,' she said. Chubb had to agree that she was well rounded. Arald, not for the first time that morning, hid a smile.

'She has a point there, Chubb,' he put in and the cook turned to him in agreement.

'Shape is important, sir. All great cooks tend to be . . .

rounded.' He turned back to the girl, still considering. It was all very well for the others to accept their trainees in the wink of an eye, he thought. But cooking was something special.

'Tell me,' he said to the eager girl, 'what would you do with a turkey pie?'

Jenny smiled dazzlingly at him. 'Eat it,' she answered immediately.

Chubb rapped her on the head with the ladle he carried. 'I meant what would you do about cooking it?' he asked. Jenny hesitated, gathered her thoughts, then plunged into a lengthy technical description of how she would go about constructing such a masterpiece. The other four wards, the Baron, his Craftmasters and Martin listened in some awe, with absolutely no comprehension of what she was saying. Chubb, however, nodded several times as she spoke, interrupting as she detailed the rolling of the pastry.

'Nine times, you say?' he said curiously and Jenny nodded, sure of her ground.

'My mother always said: "Eight times to make it flaky and once more for love",' she said. Chubb nodded thoughtfully.

'Interesting. Interesting,' he said, then, looking up at the Baron, he nodded. 'I'll take her, my lord.'

'What a surprise,' the Baron said mildly, then added, 'Very well, report to the kitchens in the morning, Jennifer.'

'Jenny, sir,' the girl corrected him again, her smile lighting up the room.

Baron Arald smiled. He glanced at the small group before him. 'And that leaves us with one more candidate.'

He glanced at his list, then looked up to meet Will's agonised gaze, gesturing encouragement.

Will stepped forward, nervousness suddenly drying his throat so that his voice came out in barely a whisper.

'Will, sir. My name is Will.'

Four

'**W**ill? Will who?' Martin asked in exasperation, flicking through the sheets of paper with the candidates' details written on them. He had only been the Baron's secretary for five years and so knew nothing of Will's history. He realised now that there was no family name on the boy's papers and, assuming he had let this mistake slip past, he was annoyed at himself.

'What's your family name, boy?' he asked severely. Will looked at him, hesitating, hating this moment.

'I . . . don't have . . .' he began, but mercifully the Baron interceded.

'Will is a special case, Martin,' he said quietly, his look telling the secretary to let the matter go. He turned back to Will, smiling encouragement.

'What school did you wish to apply for, Will?' he asked.

'Battleschool please, my lord,' Will replied, trying to sound confident in his choice. The Baron allowed a frown to crease his forehead and Will felt his hopes sinking.

'Battleschool, Will? You don't think you're . . . a little on the small side?' the Baron asked gently. Will bit his lip. He had all but convinced himself that if he wanted this badly enough, if he believed in himself strongly enough, he would be accepted — in spite of his obvious shortcomings.

'I haven't had my growing spurt yet, sir,' he said desperately. 'Everybody says that.'

The Baron rubbed his bearded chin with thumb and forefinger as he considered the boy before him. He glanced to his Battlemaster.

'Rodney?' he said.

The tall knight stepped forward, studied Will for a moment or two, then slowly shook his head.

'I'm afraid he's too small, my lord,' he said. Will felt a cold hand clutch his heart.

'I'm stronger than I look, sir,' he said. But the Battle-master was unswayed by the plea. He glanced at the Baron, obviously not enjoying the situation, and shook his head.

'Any second choice, Will?' the Baron asked. His voice was gentle, even concerned.

Will hesitated for a long moment. He had never considered any other selection.

'Horseschool, sir?' he asked finally.

Horseschool trained and cared for the mighty battle-horses that the castle's knights rode. It was at least a link to Battleschool, Will thought. But Ulf, the Horsemaster, was shaking his head already, even before the Baron asked his opinion.

'I need apprentices, my lord,' he said, 'but this one's too

small. He'd never control one of my battlehorses. They'd stomp him into the ground as soon as look at him.'

Will could only see the Baron through a watery blur now. He fought desperately to keep the tears from sliding down his cheeks. That would be the ultimate humiliation: to be rejected from Battleschool and then to break down and cry like a baby in front of the Baron, all the Craftmasters and his wardmates.

'What skills do you have, Will?' the Baron was asking him. He racked his brain. He wasn't good at lessons and languages, as Alyss was. He couldn't form neat, perfect letters, the way George did. Nor did he have Jenny's interest in cooking.

And he certainly didn't have Horace's muscles and strength.

'I'm a good climber, sir,' he said finally, seeing that the Baron was waiting for him to say something. It was a mistake, he realised instantly. Chubb, the cook, glared at him angrily.

'He can climb, all right. I remember when he climbed up a drainpipe into my kitchen and stole a tray of sweetcakes that were cooling on the windowsill.'

Will's jaw dropped with the unfairness of it all. That had been two years ago! He was a child then and it was a mere childish prank, he wanted to say. But now the Scribemaster was talking too.

'And just this last spring he climbed up to our third floor study and turned two rabbits loose during one of our legal debates. Most disruptive. Absolutely!'

'Rabbits, you say, Scribemaster?' said the Baron and Nigel nodded emphatically.

'A male and a female rabbit, my lord, if you take my meaning?' he replied. 'Most disruptive indeed!'

Unseen by Will, the very serious Lady Pauline put one elegant hand in front of her mouth. She might have been concealing a yawn. But when she removed the hand, the corners of her mouth were slightly uptilted still.

'Well, yes,' said the Baron. 'We all know how rabbits are.'

'And, as I said, my lord, it was *spring*,' Nigel went on, in case the Baron had missed the point. Lady Pauline gave vent to an unladylike cough. The Baron looked in her direction, in some surprise.

'I think we get the picture, Scribemaster,' he said, then returned his gaze to the desperate figure who stood in front of him. Will kept his chin up and stared straight ahead. The Baron felt for the young lad in that moment. He could see the tears welling up in those lively brown eyes, held back only by an infinite determination. Willpower, he thought abstractedly, recognising the play on the boy's name. He didn't enjoy putting the boy through all this, but it had to be done. He sighed inwardly.

'Is there any one of you who could use this boy?' he said.

Despite himself, Will allowed his head to turn and gaze pleadingly at the line of Craftmasters, praying that one of them would relent and accept him. One by one, silently, they shook their heads.

Surprisingly, it was the Ranger who broke the awful silence in the room.

'There is something you should know about this boy, my lord,' he said. Will had never heard Halt speak before.

His voice was deep and soft-spoken, with the slightest burr of a Hibernian accent still noticeable.

He stepped forward now and handed the Baron a sheet of paper, folded double. Arald unfolded it, studied the words written there and frowned.

'You're sure of this, Halt?' he said.

'Indeed, my lord.'

The Baron carefully refolded the paper and placed it on his desk. He drummed his fingers thoughtfully on the desktop, then said:

'I'll have to think on this overnight.'

Halt nodded and stepped back, seeming to fade into the background as he did so. Will stared anxiously at him, wondering what information the mysterious figure had passed on to the Baron. Like most people, Will had grown up believing that Rangers were best avoided. They were a secretive, arcane group, shrouded in mystery and uncertainty, and that uncertainty led to fear.

Will didn't like the thought that Halt knew something about him — something that he felt was important enough to bring to the Baron's attention today, of all days. The sheet of paper lay there, tantalisingly close, yet impossibly far away.

He realised that there was movement around him and the Baron was speaking to the other people in the room.

'Congratulations to those who were selected here today. It's a big day for all of you so you're free to have the rest of the day off and enjoy yourselves. The kitchens will provide a banquet for you in your quarters and for the rest of the day you have free run of the castle and the village.

'Tomorrow, you'll report to your new Craftmasters first

thing in the morning. And if you'll take a tip from me, you'll make sure you're on time.' He smiled at the other four, then addressed Will, with a hint of sympathy in his voice.

'Will, I'll let you know tomorrow what I've decided about you.' He turned to Martin and gestured for him to show the new apprentices out. 'Thank you, everyone,' he said, and left the room through the door behind his desk.

The Craftmasters followed his lead, then Martin ushered the former wards to the door. They chatted together excitedly, relieved and delighted that they had been selected by the Craftmasters of their choice.

Will hung back behind the others, hesitating as he passed the desk where that sheet of paper still lay. He stared at it for a moment, as if somehow he could see through to the words written on the reverse side. Then he felt that same sensation that he had felt earlier, that someone was watching him. He looked up and found himself staring into the dark eyes of the Ranger, who remained behind the Baron's high-backed chair, almost invisible in that strange cloak of his.

Will shuddered in a sudden frisson of fear and hurried out of the room.

Five

It was long after midnight. The flickering torches around the castle yard, already replaced once, had begun to burn low again. Will had watched patiently for hours, waiting for this moment — when the light was uncertain and the guards were yawning, in the last hour of their shift.

The day had been one of the worst he could remember. While his yearmates celebrated, enjoying their feast and then spending their time in light-hearted horseplay through the castle and the village, Will had slipped away to the silence of the forest, a kilometre or so from the castle walls. There, in the dim green coolness beneath the trees, he had spent the afternoon reflecting bitterly on the events of the Choosing, nursing the deep pain of disappointment and wondering what the Ranger's paper said.

As the long day wore on, and the shadows began to lengthen in the open fields beside the forest, he came to a decision.

He had to know what was in the paper. And he had to know tonight.

Once night fell, he made his way back to the castle, avoiding villagers and castle folk alike, and secreted himself in the branches of the fig tree again. On the way, he had slipped unnoticed into the kitchens and helped himself to bread, cheese and apples. He munched moodily on these, barely tasting them, as the evening passed and the castle began to settle down for the night.

He observed the movements of the guards, getting a feeling for their timing as they went on their regular rounds. In addition to the guard troop, there was a sergeant on duty at the doorway of the tower that led to Baron Arald's quarters. But he was overweight and sleepy and there was little chance that he would pose a risk to Will. After all, he had no intention of using the door or the stairway.

Over the years, his insatiable curiosity, and a penchant for going places where he wasn't supposed to, had developed within him the skill of moving across seemingly open space without being seen.

As the wind stirred the upper branches of the trees, they created moving patterns in the moonlight — patterns that Will now used to great effect. He instinctively matched his movement to the rhythm of the trees, blending easily into the pattern of the yard, becoming part of it and so being concealed by it. In a way, the lack of obvious cover made his task a little easier. The fat sergeant didn't expect anyone to be moving across the open space of the yard. So, not expecting to see anyone, he failed to do so.

Breathless, Will flattened himself against the rough stone

of the tower wall. The sergeant was barely five metres away and Will could hear his heavy breathing, but a small buttress in the wall hid him from the man's sight. He studied the wall in front of him, craning back to look up. The Baron's office window was a long way up, and further round the tower. To reach it, he would have to climb up, then work his way across the face of the wall, to a spot beyond the point where the sergeant stood guard, then up again to the window. He licked his lips nervously. Unlike the smooth inner walls of the tower, the huge blocks of stone that comprised the tower's outer wall had large gaps between them. Climbing would be no problem. He'd have plenty of foot and hand holds all the way up. In some places, the stone would have been worn smooth by the weather over the years, he knew, and he'd have to go carefully. But he'd climbed all the other three towers at some time in the past and he expected no real difficulty with this one.

But this time, if he were seen he wouldn't be able to pass it off as a prank. He would be climbing in the middle of the night to a part of the castle where he had no right to be. After all, the Baron didn't post guards on this tower for the fun of it. People were supposed to stay away unless they had business here.

He rubbed his hands together nervously. What could they do to him? He had already been passed over in the Choosing. Nobody wanted him. He was condemned to a life in the fields already. What could be worse than that?

But there was a nagging doubt at the back of his mind: he wasn't absolutely sure that he was condemned to that life. A faint spark of hope still remained. Perhaps the Baron would relent. Perhaps, if Will pleaded with him in the morning, and explained about his father and how important it was for him to be accepted for Battleschool, there was a very faint chance that his wish would be granted. And then, once he was accepted, he could show how his eagerness and dedication would make him a worthy student, until his growing spurt happened.

On the other hand, if he were caught in the next few minutes, not even that small chance would remain. He had no idea what they would do to him if he were caught but he could be reasonably sure that it wouldn't involve being accepted into Battleschool.

He hesitated, needing some slight extra push to get him going. It was the fat sergeant who provided it. Will heard the heavy intake of breath, the shuffling of the man's studded boots against the flagstones as he gathered his equipment together, and he realised that the sergeant was about to make one of his irregular circuits of his beat. Usually, this entailed going a few metres around the tower to either side of the doorway, then returning to his original position. It was more for the purpose of staying awake than anything else but Will realised that it would bring them face to face within the next few seconds if he didn't do something.

Quickly, easily, he began to swarm up the wall. He made the first five metres in a matter of seconds, spread out against the rough stone like a giant, four-legged spider. Then, hearing the heavy footsteps directly below him, he froze, clinging to the wall in case some slight noise might alert the sentry.

In fact, it seemed that the sergeant had heard something. He paused directly below the point where Will clung, peering into the night, trying to see past the dappled, moving shadows cast by the moon and the swaying trees. But, as Will had thought the night before, people seldom look up. The sergeant, eventually satisfied that he had heard nothing significant, continued to march slowly round the tower.

That was the chance Will needed. It also gave him the opportunity to move across the tower face, so that he was directly below the window he wanted. Hands and feet finding purchase easily, he moved almost as fast as a man could walk, all the time going higher and higher up the tower wall.

At one point, he looked down and that was a mistake. Despite his good head for heights, his vision swam slightly as he saw how far he had come, and how far below him the hard flagstones of the castle yard were. The sergeant was coming back into view — a tiny figure when seen from this height. Will blinked the moment of vertigo away and continued to climb, perhaps a little more slowly and with a little more care than before.

There was a heart-stopping moment when, stretching his right foot to a new foothold, his left boot slipped on the weather-rounded edge of the massive building blocks, and he was left clinging by his hands alone, as he desperately scrabbled for a foothold. Then he recovered and kept moving.

He felt a surge of relief as his hands finally closed over the stone window ledge and he heaved himself up and into the room, swinging his legs over the sill and dropping lightly inside.

The Baron's office was deserted, of course. The three-quarter moon streamed light in through the big window.

And there, on the desk where the Baron had left it, was the single sheet of paper that held the answer to Will's future. Nervously, he glanced around the room. The Baron's huge, high-backed chair stood like a sentry behind the desk. The few other pieces of furniture loomed dark and motionless. On one wall, a portrait of one of the Baron's ancestors glared down at him, accusingly.

He shook off these fanciful thoughts and crossed quickly to the desk, his soft boots making no noise on the bare boards of the floor. The sheet of paper, bright white with the reflected moonlight, was within reach. Just look at it, read it and go, he told himself. That was all he had to do. He stretched out a hand for it.

His fingers touched it.

And a hand shot out of nowhere and seized him by the wrist!

Will shouted aloud in fright. His heart leapt into his mouth and he found himself looking up into the cold eyes of Halt the Ranger.

Where had he come from? Will had been sure there had been nobody else in the room. And there had been no sound of a door opening. Then he remembered how the Ranger could wrap himself in that strange, mottled, grey-green cloak of his and seem to melt into the background, blending with the shadows until he was invisible.

Not that it mattered how Halt had done it. The real problem was that he had caught Will, here in the Baron's office. And that meant the end to all Will's hopes.

'Thought you might try something like this,' said the Ranger in a low voice.

Will, his heart pounding from the shock of the last few moments, said nothing. He hung his head in shame and despair.

'Do you have anything to say?' Halt asked him and he shook his head, unwilling to look up and meet that dark, penetrating gaze. Halt's next words confirmed Will's worst fears.

'Well, let's see what the Baron thinks about this.'

'Please, Halt! Not . . .' Then Will stopped. There was no excuse for what he had done and the least he could do was face his punishment like a man. Like a warrior. Like his father, he thought.

The Ranger studied him for a moment. Will thought he saw a brief flicker of . . . recognition? Then the eyes darkened once more.

'What?' Halt said curtly. Will shook his head.

'Nothing.'

The Ranger's grip was like iron around his wrist as he led Will out the door and onto the wide, curving staircase that led up to the Baron's living quarters. The sentries at the head of the stairs looked up in surprise at the sight of the grim-faced Ranger and the boy beside him. At a brief signal from Halt, they stood aside and opened the doors into the Baron's apartment.

The room was brightly lit and, for a moment, Will looked around in confusion. He was sure he had seen the lights go out on this floor while he waited and watched in the tree. Then he saw the heavy drapes across the window and understood. In contrast to the Baron's sparsely furnished working quarters below, this room was a comfortable clutter of settees, footstools, carpets, tapestries and armchairs. In one of these, Baron Arald sat, reading through a pile of reports.

He looked up from the page he was holding as Halt entered with his captive.

'So you were right,' said the Baron and Halt nodded.

'Just as I said, my lord. Came across the castle yard like a shadow. Dodged the sentry as if he wasn't there and came up the tower wall like a spider.'

The Baron set the report down on a side table and leaned forward.

'He climbed the tower, you say?' he asked, a trifle incredulously.

'No rope. No ladder, my lord. Climbed it as easily as you get on your horse in the morning. Easier, in fact,' Halt said, with just the ghost of a smile.

The Baron frowned. He was a little overweight and sometimes he needed help getting on his horse after a late night. He obviously wasn't amused by Halt's reminding him of the fact.

'Well now,' he said, looking sternly at Will, 'this is a serious matter.'

Will said nothing. He wasn't sure if he should agree or disagree. Either course had its dangers. But he wished Halt hadn't put the Baron in a bad mood by referring to his weight. It certainly wouldn't make things any better for him.

'So, what shall we do with you, young Will?' the Baron continued. He rose from his chair and began to pace. Will looked up at him, trying to gauge his mood. The strong, bearded face told him nothing. The Baron stopped his pacing and fingered his beard thoughtfully.

'Tell me, young Will,' he said, facing away from the miserable boy, 'what would you do in my place? What would you do with a boy who broke into your office in the middle of the night and tried to steal an important document?'

'I wasn't stealing, my lord!' The denial burst from Will before he could contain it. The Baron turned to him, one eyebrow raised in apparent disbelief. Will continued weakly, 'I just . . . wanted to see it, that's all.'

'Perhaps so,' said the Baron, that eyebrow still raised. 'But you haven't answered my question. What would you do in my place?'

Will hung his head again. He could plead for mercy. He could apologise. He could try to explain. But then he squared his shoulders and came to a decision. He had known the consequences of being caught. And he had chosen to take the risk. He had no right now to beg for forgiveness.

'My lord . . .' he said, hesitantly, knowing that this was a decisive moment in his life. The Baron regarded him, still half turned from the window.

'Yes?' he said, and Will somehow found the resolve to go on.

'My lord, I don't know what I'd do in your place. I do know there is no excuse for my actions and I will accept whatever punishment you decide.'

As he spoke, he raised his face to look the Baron in the eye. And in doing so, he caught the Baron's quick glance to Halt. There was something in that glance, he saw. Strangely, it was almost a look of approval, or agreement. Then it was gone.

'Any suggestions, Halt?' the Baron asked, in a carefully neutral tone.

Will looked at the Ranger now. His face was stern, as it always was. The grizzled grey beard and short hair made him seem even more disapproving, more ominous.

'Perhaps we should show him the paper he was so keen to see, my lord,' he said, producing the single sheet from inside his sleeve.

The Baron allowed a smile to break through. 'Not a bad idea,' he said. 'I suppose, in a way, it does spell out his punishment, doesn't it?'

Will glanced from one man to the other. There was something going on here that he didn't understand. The Baron seemed to think that what he had just said was rather amusing. Halt, on the other hand, wasn't sharing in the joke.

'If you say so, my lord,' he replied evenly. The Baron waved a hand at him impatiently.

'Take a joke, Halt! Take a joke! Well, go on and show him the paper.'

The Ranger crossed the room and handed Will the sheet he had risked so much to see. His hand trembled as he took it. His punishment? But how had the Baron known he would deserve punishment before the actual event?

He realised that the Baron was watching him expectantly. Halt, as ever, was an impassive statue. Will unfolded the sheet and read the words Halt had written there.

The boy Will has the potential to be trained as a Ranger.
I will accept him as my apprentice.

Six

Will stared at the words on the paper in utter confusion.

His first reaction was one of relief. He wasn't to be condemned to a lifetime of farm work. And he wasn't to be punished for his actions in the Baron's study. Then that initial sense of relief gave way to a sudden, nagging doubt. He knew nothing about Rangers, beyond myth and superstition. He knew nothing about Halt — apart from the fact that the grim, grey-cloaked figure had made him feel nervous whenever he was around.

Now, it seemed, he was being assigned to spend all his time with him. And he wasn't sure that he liked the idea at all.

He looked up at the two men. The Baron, he could see, was smiling expectantly. Apparently, he felt that Will should greet his decision as good news. He couldn't see Halt's face clearly. The deep cowl of his cloak left his face in shadow.

The Baron's smile faded slightly. He appeared a little puzzled by Will's reaction to the news — or rather, his lack of any visible reaction.

'Well, what do you say, Will?' he asked, in an encouraging tone. Will drew a deep breath.

'Thank you sir . . . my lord,' he said uncertainly. What if the Baron's earlier joke about the note containing his punishment was more serious than he thought? Maybe being assigned to be Halt's apprentice was the worst punishment he could have chosen. But the Baron certainly didn't look as if he thought so. He seemed to be very pleased with the idea, and Will knew he wasn't an unkind man. The Baron gave a little sigh of pleasure as he lowered himself into an armchair. He looked up at the Ranger and gestured towards the door.

'Perhaps you might give us a few moments alone, Halt? I'd like to have a word with Will in private,' he said. The Ranger bowed gravely.

'Certainly, my lord,' he said, the voice coming from deep inside the cowl. He moved, silently as ever, past Will and out through the door that led to the corridor outside. The door closed behind him with barely a sound and Will shivered. The man was uncanny!

'Sit down, Will.' The Baron gestured to one of the low armchairs facing his own. Will sat nervously on the edge of it, as if poised for flight. The Baron noted his body language and sighed.

'You don't seem very pleased with my decision,' he said, sounding disappointed. The reaction puzzled Will. He wouldn't have thought a powerful figure like the Baron would care one way or another what an insignificant ward would think about his decisions. He didn't know how to answer, so he sat in silence, until finally the Baron continued.

'Would you prefer to work as a farmhand?' he asked. He couldn't believe that a lively, energetic boy like this could possibly prefer such a dull, uneventful life, but maybe he was wrong. Will hurriedly reassured him on that score.

'No, sir!' he said hastily. The Baron made a small, questioning gesture with his hands.

'Well then, would you prefer that I punished you somehow for what you've done?'

Will started to speak, then realised that his answer might be insulting and stopped. The Baron gestured for him to continue.

'It's just that . . . I'm not sure you haven't, sir,' he said. Then, noticing the frown that creased the Baron's forehead as he said the words, he hurried on: 'I . . . I don't know much about Rangers, sir. And people say . . .'

He let the words tail off. It was obvious that the Baron held Halt in some esteem and Will didn't think it was politic for him to point out that ordinary people feared Rangers and thought they were warlocks. He saw that the Baron was nodding, and a look of understanding had replaced the perplexed expression he had been wearing.

'Of course. People say they're black magicians, don't they?' he agreed and Will nodded, not even realising he was doing so. 'Tell me, Will, do you find Halt to be a frightening person?'

'No, sir!' Will said hastily, then, as the Baron held his gaze, he reluctantly added, 'Well . . . maybe a bit.'

The Baron leaned back, steepling his fingers together.

Now that he understood the reasons for the boy's reluctance, he berated himself mentally for not foreseeing them. After all, he had a better knowledge of the Ranger Corps than he could expect of a young boy just turned fifteen, who was subjected to the usual superstitious mutterings of the castle staff.

'The Rangers are a mysterious group of people,' he said. 'But there's nothing about them to be frightened of — unless you're an enemy of the Kingdom.'

He could see that the boy was hanging on his every word, and he added, jokingly, 'You're not an enemy of the Kingdom, are you, Will?'

'No, sir!' Will said in sudden fright and the Baron sighed again. He hated it when people didn't realise he was joking. Unfortunately, as overlord of the castle, his words were treated with great seriousness by most people.

'All right, all right,' he said reassuringly. 'I know you're not. But believe me, I thought you'd be glad of this appointment — an adventurous lad like you should take to life as a Ranger like a duck to water. It's a big opportunity for you, Will.' He paused, studying the boy closely, seeing that he was still uncertain about the whole matter. 'Very few boys are chosen to be apprentice Rangers, you know. The opportunity only comes up on rare occasions.'

Will nodded. But he still wasn't totally convinced. He thought he owed it to his dream to have one last attempt at Battleschool. After all, the Baron did seem to be in an uncommonly good mood this evening, in spite of the fact that Will had broken into his office.

'I wanted to be a warrior, sir,' he said tentatively, but the Baron shook his head immediately.

'I'm afraid your talents lie in other directions. Halt knew that when he first saw you. That's why he asked for you.'

'Oh,' said Will. There wasn't much else he could say. He felt he should be reassured by all that the Baron had said and, to a certain degree, he was. But there was still so much uncertainty to it all, he thought.

'It's just that Halt seems to be so grim all the time,' he said.

'He certainly doesn't have my sparkling sense of humour,' the Baron agreed, then, as Will looked blankly at him, he muttered something under his breath.

Will wasn't sure what he'd done to upset him, so he thought it best to change the subject. 'But . . . what does a Ranger actually do, my lord?' he asked. Once again, the Baron shook his head.

'That's for Halt to tell you himself. They're a quirky group and they don't like other people talking about them too much. Now, perhaps you should go back to your quarters and try to get some sleep. You're to report to Halt's cottage at six o'clock in the morning.'

'Yes, my lord,' Will said, rising from his uncomfortable perch on the edge of the chair. He wasn't sure if he was going to enjoy life as a Ranger's apprentice but it appeared he had no choice in the matter. He bowed to the Baron, who nodded briefly in return, then he turned away for the door. The Baron's voice stopped him.

'Will? This time, use the stairs.'

'Yes, my lord,' he replied seriously, and was a little puzzled by the way the Baron rolled his eyes to the sky and muttered to himself again. This time, Will could make out a few words. It was something about 'jokes', he thought.

He let himself out through the door. The sentries were still on duty on the landing by the stairs but Halt was gone.

Or at least, he appeared to be. With the Ranger, you could never be quite certain.

Seven

It felt strange to be leaving the castle after all these years. Will turned back at the bottom of the hill, his small bundle of belongings slung over his shoulder, and stared up at the massive walls.

Castle Redmont dominated the landscape. Built on top of a small hill, it was a massive, three-sided structure, facing roughly west and with a tower at each of the three corners. In the centre, protected by the three curtain walls, were the castle yard and the Keep, a fourth tower that soared above the others, and housed the Baron's official quarters and his private living apartments, along with those of his senior officers. The castle was built in ironstone — a rock that was almost indestructible and, in the low sun of early morning or late afternoon, seemed to glow with an inner red light. It was this characteristic that gave the castle its name — Redmont, or Red Mountain.

At the foot of the hill, and on the other side of the Tarbus River, lay Wensley Village, a cheerfully haphazard cluster of houses, with an inn and those craft shops necessary to meet the demands of day-to-day country life — a cooper, wheelwright, smithy and harness maker. The land around had been cleared for some distance, both to provide farmlands for the villagers to tend and to prevent enemies from being able to approach unseen. In times of danger, the villagers would drive their flocks across the wooden bridge that spanned the Tarbus, removing the centre span behind them, and seek shelter behind the massive ironstone walls of the castle, protected by the Baron's soldiers and the knights trained in Redmont's Battleschool.

Halt's cottage lay some distance away from both castle and village, nestling under the shelter of the trees at the edge of the forest. The sun was just rising over the trees as Will made his way to the log cabin. A thin spiral of smoke was rising from the chimney, so Will reasoned that Halt was already up and about. He stepped up onto the verandah that ran the length of one side of the house, hesitated for a moment, then, taking a deep breath, he knocked firmly on the door.

'Come in,' said a voice from inside. Will opened the door and went into the cottage.

It was small but surprisingly neat and comfortable-looking inside. He found himself in the main room, a combined living and dining area, with a small kitchen at one end, separated from the main area by a pine bench. There were comfortable chairs ranged round a fire, a well-scrubbed wooden table and pots and pans that gleamed from much polishing. There was even a vase of brightly coloured wildflowers on the mantel shelf and the early morning sun streamed cheerfully through a large window. Two other rooms led off the main room.

Halt sat in one of the chairs, his booted feet resting on the table.

'At least you're on time,' he said gruffly. 'Have you had your breakfast yet?'

'Yes, sir,' said Will, staring in fascination at the Ranger. This was the first time he had ever seen Halt without his grey-green cloak and hood. The Ranger was wearing simple brown and grey woollen clothes and soft-looking leather boots. He was older than Will had realised. His hair and beard were short and dark, but peppered with steel grey flecks. They were both roughly trimmed and Will thought they looked as if Halt had cut them himself with his hunting knife.

The Ranger stood up. He was surprisingly small in build. That was something else that Will had never realised. The grey cloak had concealed a lot about Halt. He was slim and not at all tall. In fact he was considerably shorter than average height. But there was a sense of power and whipcord strength about him so that his lack of height and bulk didn't make him any less daunting a figure.

'Finished staring?' asked the Ranger suddenly.

Will jumped nervously. 'Yes, sir! Sorry, sir!' he said.

Halt grunted. He pointed to one of the small rooms Will had noticed as he entered.

'That'll be your room. You can put your things in there.'

He moved away to the wood stove in the kitchen area and Will hesitantly entered the room he had indicated. It was small but, like the rest of the cottage, it was also clean and comfortable-looking. A small bed lay alongside one wall. There was a wardrobe for clothes and a rough table with a washing basin and jug on it. There was also, Will noticed, another vase of freshly picked wildflowers adding a bright spot of colour to the room. He put his small bundle of clothes and belongings on the bed and went back into the main room.

Halt was still busy by the stove, his back to Will. Will coughed apologetically to attract his attention. Halt continued to stir coffee into a pot on the stove.

Will coughed again.

'Got a cold, boy?' asked the Ranger, without turning around.

'Er . . . no, sir.'

'Then why are you coughing?' asked Halt, turning round to face him.

Will hesitated. 'Well, sir,' he began uncertainly, 'I just wanted to ask you . . . what does a Ranger actually *do*?'

'He doesn't ask pointless questions, boy!' said Halt. 'He keeps his eyes and ears open and he looks and listens and eventually, if he hasn't got too much cotton wool between his ears, he learns!'

'Oh,' said Will. 'I see.' He didn't, and even though he realised that this was probably no time to ask more questions, he couldn't help himself, repeating, a little rebelliously, 'I just wondered what Rangers do, is all.'

Halt caught the tone in his voice and turned to him, a strange gleam in his eye.

'Well then, I suppose I'd better tell you,' he said. 'What Rangers do, or more correctly, what Rangers' *apprentices* do, is the housework.'

Will had a sinking feeling as the suspicion struck him

that he'd made a tactical error. 'The housework?' he repeated. Halt nodded, looking distinctly pleased with himself.

'That's right. Take a look around.' He paused, gesturing around the interior of the cabin for Will to do as he suggested, then continued, 'See any servants?'

'No, sir,' Will said slowly.

'No sir indeed!' Halt said. 'Because this isn't a mighty castle with a staff of servants. This is a lowly cabin. And it has water to be fetched and firewood to be chopped and floors to be swept and rugs to be beaten. And who do you suppose might do all those things, boy?'

Will tried to think of some answer other than the one which now seemed inevitable. Nothing came to mind so he finally said, in a defeated tone, 'Would that be me, sir?'

'I believe it would be,' the Ranger told him, then rattled off a list of instructions crisply. 'Bucket there. Barrel outside the door. Water in the river. Axe in the lean-to, firewood behind the cabin. Broom by the door and I believe you can probably see where the floor might be?'

'Yes, sir,' said Will, beginning to roll up his sleeves. He'd noticed the water barrel as he approached, obviously holding the day's water supply for the cabin. He estimated that it would hold twenty or thirty buckets full. With a sigh, he realised he was going to have a busy morning.

As he walked outside, the empty bucket in one hand, he heard the Ranger say contentedly, as he poured himself a mug of coffee and sat down again:

'I'd forgotten how much fun having an apprentice can be.'

Will couldn't believe that such a small and seemingly neat cottage could generate so much cleaning and general maintenance. After he had filled the water barrel with fresh river water (thirty-one bucketsful) he chopped wood from a stack of logs behind the cabin, piling the split firewood into a neat stack. He swept out the cabin, then, after Halt decided that the rug on the living room floor needed beating, he rolled it up, carried it outside and draped it over a rope slung between two trees, beating it savagely so that clouds of dust flew from it. From time to time, Halt leaned out the window to give him encouragement, which usually consisted of curt comments such as 'You've missed a bit on the left side' or 'Put some energy into it, boy.'

When the rug had been replaced on the floor, Halt decided that several of his cooking pots didn't gleam with sufficient intensity.

'We'll have to give them a bit of a scouring,' he said, more or less to himself. Will knew by now that this translated to '*You'll* have to give them a bit of a scouring.' So, without a word, he took the pots to the river's edge and half filled them with water and fine sand, scouring and polishing the metal until it gleamed.

Halt, meanwhile, had moved to a canvas chair on the verandah, where he sat reading through a tall pile of what looked to be official communications. Passing by once or twice, Will noticed that several of the papers bore crests and coats of arms, while the vast majority were headed with a simple oakleaf design.

When Will returned from the river bank, he held the pots up for Halt's inspection. The Ranger grimaced at his distorted reflection in the bright copper surface.

'Hmmm. Not bad. Can see my own face in it,' he said, then added, without a hint of a smile, 'May not be such a good thing.'

Will said nothing. With anyone else he might have suspected it was a joke, but with Halt you simply couldn't tell. Halt studied him for a second or two, then his shoulders lifted slightly in a shrug and he gestured for Will to return the pots to the kitchen. Will was halfway through the door when he heard Halt behind him say:

'Hmmm. That's odd.'

Thinking the Ranger might be talking to him, Will paused at the door.

'I beg your pardon?' he said suspiciously. Each time Halt had found a new chore for him to attend to, he had seemed to begin the instruction with a statement like 'How unusual. The living room rug is full of dust.' Or 'I do believe the stove is in dire need of a new supply of firewood.'

It was an affectation that Will had found more than a little annoying over the day, although Halt seemed to be quite fond of it. This time, however, it seemed that he had been genuinely musing to himself as he read through a new report — one of the oakleaf-crested ones, Will noted. Now, the Ranger looked up, a little surprised that Will had addressed him.

'What's that?' he said.

Will shrugged. 'Sorry. When you said "that's odd", I thought you were talking to me.'

Halt shook his head several times, still frowning at the report in his hand. 'No, no,' he said, a trifle distractedly. 'I was just reading this . . .' His voice trailed away and he frowned thoughtfully. Will, his curiosity roused, waited expectantly.

'What is it?' he finally ventured to ask. As the Ranger turned those dark eyes on him, he instantly wished he hadn't. Halt regarded him for a second or two.

'Curious, are you?' he said at length, and when Will nodded uncomfortably, he went on in an unexpectedly milder tone. 'Well, I suppose that's a good trait for a Ranger's apprentice. After all, that's why we tested you with that paper in the Baron's office.'

'You tested me?' Will set the heavy copper kettle down by the door. 'You *expected* me to try to see what it said?'

Halt nodded. 'Would have been disappointed if you hadn't. Also, I wanted to see how you'd go about it.' Then he held up a hand to forestall the torrent of questions that were about to tumble out of Will's mouth. 'We'll discuss that later,' he said, glancing meaningfully at the kettle and the other pots. Will stooped to retrieve them, and turned back to the house once more. But curiosity still burned in him and he turned to the Ranger again.

'So what does it say?' he asked, nodding towards the report. Again there was a silence as Halt regarded him, perhaps assessing him. Then he said:

'Lord Northolt is dead. Apparently killed by a bear last week while out hunting.'

'Lord Northolt?' Will asked. The name was vaguely familiar to him but he couldn't place it.

'Former supreme commander of the King's army,' Halt told him and Will nodded, as if he had known this. But, since Halt seemed to be answering his questions, he was emboldened to continue.

'What's so odd about it? After all, bears do kill people from time to time.'

Halt nodded. 'True. But I would have thought Cordom Fief was a little far west for bears. And I would have thought Northolt was too experienced a hunter to go after one alone.' He shrugged, as if dismissing the thought. 'But then again, life is full of surprises and people do make mistakes.' He gestured towards the kitchen again, indicating that the conversation was over. 'When you've put those away, you might like to clean out the fireplace,' he said.

Will moved to do as he was told. But a few minutes later, as he walked past one of the windows to the large fireplace that took up most of one wall in the living room, he glanced out to see the Ranger tapping the report thoughtfully on his chin, his thoughts obviously a long way away.

Eight

Sometime late in the afternoon, Halt finally ran out of jobs for Will. He looked around the cabin, noting the gleaming kitchen implements, the spotless fireplace, the thoroughly swept floor and totally dust-free rug. A stack of firewood lay beside the fireplace and another stack, cut and split into shorter lengths, filled the wicker basket beside the kitchen stove.

'Hmmm. Not bad,' he said. 'Not bad at all.'

Will felt a surge of pleasure at the sparing praise, but before he could feel too pleased with himself, Halt added, 'Can you cook, boy?'

'Cook, sir?' Will asked uncertainly. Halt raised his eyes to some unseen superior being.

'Why do young people invariably answer a question with another question?' he asked. Then, receiving no reply, he continued, 'Yes, cook. Prepare food so that one might eat it. Make meals. I assume you do know what food is — what meals are?'

'Ye-es,' Will answered, careful to take any questioning inflection out of the word.

'Well, as I told you this morning, this is no grand castle. If we want to eat food here, we have to cook food here,' Halt told him. There was that word 'we' again, Will thought. Every time so far Halt had said *we must*, it had seemed to translate to mean *you must*.

'I can't cook,' Will admitted, and Halt clapped his hands and rubbed them together.

'Of course you can't! Most boys can't. So I'll have to show you how. Come on.'

He led the way to the kitchen and introduced Will to the mysteries of cooking: peeling and chopping onions, choosing a piece of beef from the meat safe, trimming it and cutting it into neat cubes, then chopping vegetables, searing the beef in a sizzling pan, and finally adding a generous dash of red wine and some of what Halt called his 'secret ingredients'. The result was a savoury-smelling stew, simmering on the top of the stove.

Now, as they waited for the dinner to be ready, they sat on the verandah in the early evening and talked quietly.

'The Rangers were founded over one hundred and fifty years ago, in King Herbert's reign. Do you know anything about him?' Halt looked sideways at the boy sitting beside him, tossing the question out quickly to see his response.

Will hesitated. He vaguely remembered the name from history lessons in the Ward, but he couldn't remember any details. Still, he decided he'd try to bluff his way through it. He didn't want to look too ignorant on his first day with his new master.

'Oh . . . yes,' he said, 'King Herbert. We learned about him.'

'Really?' said the Ranger expansively. 'Perhaps you could tell me a little about him?' He leaned back and crossed his legs, getting himself comfortable.

Will cast about desperately in his memory, trying to remember even a shred of detail about King Herbert. He'd done something . . . but what?

'He was . . .' he hesitated, pretending to gather his thoughts, '. . . the king.' That much he was sure of, and he glanced at Halt to see if he could stop now. Halt merely smiled and made a rolling gesture with his hand that meant *go on.*

'He was the king . . . a hundred and fifty years ago,' Will said, trying to sound certain of his facts. The Ranger smiled at him, gesturing for him to continue yet again.

'Ummm . . . well, I seem to recall that he was the one who founded the Ranger Corps,' he said hopefully and Halt raised his eyebrows in mock surprise.

'Really? You recall that, do you?' he said and Will had a horrible moment where he realised that Halt had merely said the Rangers were founded *during* his reign, not necessarily *by* him.

'Ahhh, well, when I say he founded the Rangers I actually mean he was the king when the Ranger Corps was founded,' he said.

'A hundred and fifty years ago?' Halt prompted.

Will nodded emphatically. 'That's right.'

'Well, that's remarkable, seeing how I just told you those facts a minute or so ago,' the Ranger said, his eyebrows coming down like thunderclouds over his eyes. Will thought it might be better if he said nothing. Finally, the Ranger said, in a milder tone:

'Boy, if you don't know something, don't try to bluff your way through it. Simply tell me "I don't know", is that clear?'

'Yes, Halt,' Will said, eyes downcast. There was a silence, then he said, 'Halt?'

'Yes?'

'About King Herbert . . . I don't really know,' Will admitted. The Ranger made a small snorting noise.

'Well, I never would have guessed,' he said. 'But I'm sure you'll remember when I tell you that he was the one who drove the northern clans back over the border into the Highlands?'

And, of course, the moment he mentioned it, Will did remember. But he thought it might be impolitic to say that he did. King Herbert was known as the 'Father of Modern Araluen'. He had banded the fifty fiefs together into a powerful union to defeat the northern clans. Will could see a way to regain a little credit in Halt's eyes now. If he mentioned the 'Father of Modern Araluen' title, maybe the Ranger would . . .

'He's sometimes known as the Father of Modern Araluen,' Halt was saying, and Will realised he'd left it too late. 'He created the union between the fifty fiefs that's still our structure today.'

'I sort of remember that now,' Will put in. He thought the addition of 'sort of' helped it sound as if he wasn't just being wise after the event. Halt looked at him, one eyebrow raised, then continued.

'At the time, King Herbert felt that to remain safe, the Kingdom needed an effective intelligence force.'

'An intelligent force?' said Will.

'Not intelligent. *Intelligence*. Although it does help if your intelligence force is also intelligent. Intelligence is knowledge of what your enemies, or your potential enemies, are up to. What they're planning. What they're thinking. If you know that sort of thing in advance, you can usually come up with a plan to stop them. That's why he founded the Rangers — to keep the Kingdom informed. To act as the eyes and ears of the Kingdom.'

'How do you do that?' Will asked, his interest aroused now. Halt noted the change in tone and a momentary gleam of approval touched his eyes.

'We keep our eyes and ears open. We patrol the Kingdom — and beyond. We listen. We observe. We report back.'

Will nodded to himself, thinking. Then he asked: 'Is that the reason why you can make yourselves invisible?'

Again, the Ranger felt that moment of approval and satisfaction. But he made sure the boy didn't notice it.

'We can't make ourselves invisible,' he said. 'People just think we can. What we do is make ourselves very hard to see. It takes years of learning and practice to do it properly — but you already have some of the skills required.'

Will looked up, surprised. 'I do?'

'When you crossed the castle yard last night, you used the shadows and the movement of the wind to conceal yourself, didn't you?'

Will nodded. 'Yes.' He'd never met anyone before who actually understood his skill for moving without being seen. Halt continued.

'We use the same principles: to blend into the background. To use it to conceal us. To become part of it.'

'I see,' said Will slowly.

'The trick is to make sure that nobody else does,' Halt told him. For a moment, Will thought the Ranger had made a joke. But when he looked up, Halt was as grim-faced as ever.

'How many Rangers are there?' he asked. Halt and the Baron had referred more than once to the Ranger Corps, but Will had only ever seen one — and that was Halt.

'King Herbert established the Corps at fifty. One for each of the fifty fiefdoms. I'm based here. My colleagues are based at the other forty-nine castles throughout the Kingdom.

'In addition to providing intelligence about potential enemies, Rangers are the law keepers,' said Halt. 'We patrol the fiefdom assigned to us and make sure that the laws are being obeyed.'

'I thought Baron Arald did that?' Will put in. Halt shook his head.

'The Baron is a judge,' he said. 'People bring their complaints to him so he can settle them. Rangers enforce the law. We take the law out to the people. If a crime has been committed, we look for evidence. We're particularly suited to that role since people often don't realise we're around. We investigate to see who's responsible.'

'What happens then?' Will asked. Halt gave a small shrug.

'Sometimes we report back to the baron of the fief and he'll have the person arrested and charged. Sometimes, if it's a matter of urgency, we just . . . deal with it.'

'What do we do?' Will asked, before he could stop himself. Halt gave him a long, considering look.

'Not too much if we've only been an apprentice for a few hours,' he replied. 'Those of us who've been Rangers for twenty years or more tend to know what to do without asking.'

'Oh,' said Will, suitably chastened. Halt continued.

'Then, in times of war, we act as special troops — guiding the armies, scouting before them, going behind enemy lines to cause the enemy grief and so on.' He glanced down at the boy. 'It's a bit more exciting than working on a farm.' Will nodded. Perhaps life as a Ranger's apprentice was going to have its appeal after all.

'What sort of enemies?' he asked. After all, Castle Redmont had been at peace for as long as he could remember.

'Enemies from within and without,' Halt told him. 'People like the Skandian sea raiders — or Morgarath and his Wargals.'

Will shivered, recalling some of the more lurid stories about Morgarath, the Lord of the Mountains of Rain and Night. Halt nodded sombrely as he saw Will's reaction.

'Yes,' he said, 'Morgarath and his Wargals are definitely people to be worried about. That's why the Rangers keep an eye on them. We like to know if they're gathering, if they're getting ready for war.'

'Still,' said Will, as much to reassure himself as for any other reason, 'the last time they attacked, the barons' armies made mincemeat out of them.'

'That's true,' Halt agreed. 'But only because they'd

been warned of the attack . . .' He paused and looked meaningfully at Will.

'By a Ranger?' the boy asked.

'Correct. It was a Ranger who brought word that Morgarath's Wargals were on their way . . . then led the cavalry across a secret ford so they could flank the enemy.'

'It was a great victory,' Will said.

'It certainly was. And all due to a Ranger's alertness and skill, and knowledge of back trails and secret paths.'

'My father died in that battle,' Will added in a quieter voice, and Halt cast a curious look at him.

'Is that so?' he said.

'He was a hero. A mighty knight,' Will continued. The Ranger paused, almost as if he were deciding whether to say something or not. Then he simply replied:

'I wasn't aware of that.'

Will was conscious of a sense of disappointment. For a moment, he'd had a feeling that Halt knew something about his father, that he could tell him the story of his heroic death. He shrugged to himself.

'That was why I was so keen to go to Battleschool,' he said finally. 'To follow in his footsteps.'

'You have other talents,' Halt told him and Will remembered the Baron saying much the same thing to him the previous night.

'Halt . . .' he said. The Ranger nodded for him to continue. 'I was sort of wondering . . . the Baron said you chose me?'

Halt nodded again, saying nothing.

'And both of you say I have other qualities — qualities that make me suitable to be a Ranger apprentice . . .'

'That's right,' Halt said.

'Well . . . what are they?'

The Ranger leaned back, linking his hands behind his head.

'You're agile. That's good in a Ranger,' he began. 'And, as we've discussed, you can move quietly. That's very important. You're fast on your feet. And you're inquisitive . . .'

'Inquisitive? How do you mean?' asked Will. Halt looked at him sternly.

'Always asking questions. Always wanting to know answers,' he explained. 'That was why I had the Baron test you with that piece of paper.'

'But when did you first notice me? I mean, when did you first think of selecting me?' Will wanted to know.

'Oh,' said Halt, 'I suppose it was when I watched you steal those cakes from Master Chubb's kitchen.'

Will's jaw dropped open with amazement.

'You watched me? But that was ages ago!' He had a sudden thought. 'Where were you?'

'In the kitchen,' said Halt. 'You were too busy to notice me when you came in.'

Will shook his head in wonder. He had been sure there was nobody in the kitchen. Then he remembered once again how Halt, wrapped in his cloak, could become virtually invisible. There was more to being a Ranger, he realised, than how to cook and clean.

'I was impressed with your skill,' said Halt. 'But there was one thing that impressed me far more.'

'What was that?' asked Will.

'Later, when Master Chubb questioned you, I saw you

hesitate. You were going to deny having stolen the cakes. Then I saw you admit it. Remember? He hit you on the head with his wooden spoon.'

Will grinned and rubbed his head thoughtfully. He could still hear the CRACK! made by the spoon hitting his head.

'I wondered if I should have lied,' he admitted. Halt shook his head very slowly.

'Oh no, Will. If you'd lied, you never would have become my apprentice.' He stood up and stretched, turning to go indoors to the stew simmering on the stove.

'Now let's eat,' he said.

Nine

Horace dropped his pack on the floor of the dormitory and fell across his bed, groaning with relief.

Every muscle in his body ached. He had no idea that he could feel so sore, so worn out. He had no idea that there were so many muscles in the human body that could feel this way. Not for the first time, he wondered if he was going to get through the three years of Battleschool training. He'd been a cadet for less than a week and already he was a total physical wreck.

When he'd applied for Battleschool Horace had a vague notion of glittering, armour-clad knights doing battle, while lesser folk stood by and watched in awed admiration. Quite a few of those lesser folk, in his mental picture, had been attractive girls – Jenny, his yearmate in the Ward, had been prominent among them. To him, Battleschool had been a place of glamour and adventure, and Battleschool cadets were people that others looked up to and envied.

The reality was something else. So far, Battleschool cadets were people who rose before the dawn and spent the hour before breakfast doing a severe course of physical training: running, lifting weights, standing in lines of ten or more to lift and hold heavy logs over their heads. Exhausted by all of this, they were then returned to their quarters, where they had the opportunity to take a brief shower — the water was cold — before making sure the dormitory and ablutions block were absolutely spotless. Quarters inspection came after that and it was painstaking. Sir Karel, the wily old knight who carried out the inspection, knew every trick in the book when it came to taking short cuts in cleaning the dormitory, making your bed and stowing your kit. The slightest infringement on the part of one of the twenty boys in the dormitory would mean all their kit would be scattered across the floor, their beds turned over, the rubbish bins emptied on the floor and they would have to turn to and start again — in the time when they should have been having breakfast.

As a consequence, new cadets only tried once to pull the wool over Sir Karel's eyes. Breakfast was nothing special. In fact, in Horace's opinion, it was downright basic. But if you missed it, it was a long, hard morning until the lunch hour which, in keeping with the spartan life in Battle-school, was only twenty minutes long.

After breakfast, there were classes for two hours in military history, the theory of tactics and so on, then the cadets were usually required to run the obstacle course — a series of obstacles designed to test speed, agility, balance and strength. There was a minimum time standard for the course. It had to be completed in under five minutes, and any cadet who failed to do so was immediately sent back to the start to try again. It was rare that anyone completed the course without falling at least once, and the course was littered with mud pools, water hazards and pits filled with nameless but unpleasant matter whose origin Horace didn't want to even think about it.

Lunch followed the obstacle course, but if you'd fallen during the run, you had to clean up before entering the mess hall — another of those famous cold showers — and that usually took half the time set aside for the meal break. As a consequence, Horace's overwhelming impressions of the first week of Battleschool were a combination of aching muscles and gnawing hunger.

There were more classes after lunch, then physical jerks in the castle yard under the eye of one of the senior year cadets. Then the class would form up and perform close order drill until the end of the school day, when they would have two hours to themselves, to clean and repair gear and prepare lessons for the following day's classes.

Unless, of course, someone had transgressed during the course of the day, or in some way caused displeasure to one of their instructors or observers. In which case, they would all be invited to load their packs with rocks and set out on a twelve-kilometre run, along a course mapped out through the surrounding countryside. Invariably, the course was nowhere near any of the level roads or tracks in the area. It meant running through broken, uneven ground, up hills and across streams, through heavily overgrown thickets where hanging vines and thick underbrush would claw at you and try to pull you down.

Horace had just completed one such run. Earlier in the

day, one of his classmates had been spotted in Tactics I, passing a note to a friend. Unfortunately, the note was not in the form of text but was an unflattering caricature of the long-nosed instructor who took the class. Equally unfortunately, the boy possessed considerable skill as a cartoonist and the drawing was instantly recognisable.

As a result, Horace and his class had been invited to fill those packs and start running.

He'd gradually felt himself pulling away from the rest of the boys as they laboured up the first hill. Even after a few days, the strict regime of the Battleschool was beginning to show results with Horace. He was fitter than he'd ever been in his life. Added to that was the fact that he had natural ability as an athlete. Though he was unaware of it, he ran with balance and grace, where the others seemed to struggle. As the run progressed, he found himself far in front of the others. He pounded on, head up and breathing evenly through his nostrils. So far, he hadn't had much chance to get to know his new classmates. He'd seen most of them around the castle or the village over the years, of course, but growing up in the Ward had tended to isolate him from the normal, day-to-day life of the castle and village. Ward children couldn't help but feel different to the others. And it was a feeling that the boys and girls with parents still living reciprocated.

The Choosing ceremony was peculiar to Ward members only. Horace was one of twenty new recruits that year, the other nineteen coming through what was considered the normal process — parental influence, patronage or recommendation from their teachers. As a result, he was regarded as something of a curiosity, and the other boys had so far made no overtures of friendship or even any real attempt to get to know him. Still, he thought, smiling with grim satisfaction, he had beaten them all in the run. None of the others were back yet. He'd shown them, all right.

The door at the end of the dormitory crashed back on its hinges and heavy boots sounded on the bare floorboards. Horace raised himself on one elbow and groaned inwardly.

Bryn, Alda and Jerome were marching towards him between the neat rows of perfectly made beds. They were second year cadets and they seemed to have decided that their life's work was to make Horace's life miserable. Quickly, he swung his legs over the side of the bed and stood up, but not quickly enough.

'What are you doing lying in bed?' Alda yelled at him. 'Who told you it was lights out?'

Bryn and Jerome grinned. They enjoyed Alda's verbal sallies. They weren't anywhere near as original. But they made up with their lack of verbal invention with a heavy reliance on the physical side of things.

'Twenty pushups!' Bryn ordered. 'Now!'

Horace hesitated a moment. He was actually bigger than any of them. If it came to a confrontation, he was sure he could beat any one of them. But they were three. And besides, they had the authority of tradition behind them. As far as he knew, it was normal practice for second year to treat first year cadets like this, and he could imagine the scorn of his classmates if he were to complain to authority about it. Nobody likes a crybaby, he told himself as he began to drop to the ground. But Bryn had seen the hesitation and perhaps even the fleeting light of rebellion in his eyes.

'Thirty pushups!' he snapped. 'Do it now!'

His muscles protesting, Horace dropped full length to the floor and began the pushups. Immediately, he felt a foot in the small of his back, bearing down on him as he tried to raise himself from the floor.

'Come on, Baby!' It was Jerome now. 'Put a bit of effort into it!'

Horace struggled through a pushup. Jerome had developed the skill of maintaining just the right amount of pressure. Any more and Horace would never have been able to complete the pushup. But the second year cadet also kept pressing down as Horace started back down again. That made the exercise all the harder. He had to maintain the same amount of upward pressure as he lowered himself, otherwise he would be driven hard against the floor. Groaning, he completed the first, then started another.

'Stop crying, Baby!' Alda yelled at him. Then he moved to Horace's bed.

'Didn't you make this bed this morning?' he yelled. Horace, struggling up again against the pressure of Jerome's foot, could only grunt in reply.

'What? What?' Alda bent so that his face was only centimetres away. 'What's that, Baby? Speak up!'

'Yes . . . sir,' Horace managed to whisper. Alda shook his head in an exaggerated movement.

'No sir, I think!' he said, standing upright again. 'Look at this bed. It's a pigsty!'

Naturally, the covers were a little rumpled where Horace had dropped across the bed. But it would have taken only a second or two to straighten them. Grinning, Bryn cottoned on to Alda's plan. He stepped forward and kicked the bed over on its side, spilling mattress, blankets and pillows onto the floor. Alda joined in, kicking the blankets across the room.

'Make the bed again!' he yelled. Then a light gleamed in his eye and he turned to the next bed in line, kicking it over as well, scattering the bedclothes and mattresses as he'd done to Horace's.

'Make them all again!' he yelled, delighted with his idea. Bryn joined him, grinning widely, as they tumbled the twenty beds, scattering blankets, pillows and mattresses around the room. Horace, struggling still through the thirty pushups, gritted his teeth. Perspiration ran into his eyes, stinging them and blurring his vision.

'Crying, are you, Baby?' he heard Jerome yell. 'Go home and cry to mummy then!'

His foot shoved viciously into Horace's back, sending him sprawling on the floor.

'Baby doesn't have a mummy,' Alda said. 'Baby's a Ward brat. Mummy ran off with a riverboat sailor.'

Jerome bent down to him again. 'Is that right, Baby?' he hissed. 'Did Mummy run away and leave you?'

'My mother is dead,' Horace grated at them. Angrily, he began to rise, but Jerome's foot was on the back of his neck, thrusting his face against the hard boards. Horace gave up the attempt.

'Very sad,' Alda said, and the other two laughed. 'Now clean this mess up, Baby, or we'll have you run the course again.'

Horace lay, exhausted, as the three older boys

swaggered out of the room, tipping footlockers over as they went, spilling his roommates' belongings onto the floor. He closed his eyes as salt perspiration stung its way into them again.

'I hate this place,' he said, his voice muffled by the rough planks of the floor.

Ten

'Time you learned about the weapons you'll be using,' said Halt.

They had eaten breakfast well before sun-up and Will had followed Halt into the forest. They'd walked for about half an hour, with the Ranger showing Will how to glide from one patch of shade to the next, as silently as possible. Will was a good student in the art of unseen movement, as Halt had already remarked, but he had a lot to learn before he reached Ranger standard. Still, Halt was pleased with his progress. The boy was keen to learn — particularly when it was a matter of field craft like this.

It was a slightly different matter when it came to the less exciting tasks like map reading and chart drawing. Will tended to skip over details that he saw as unimportant until Halt pointed out to him, with some acerbity, 'You'd find these skills would become a little more important if you were planning a route for a company of heavy cavalry and forgot to mention that there's a stream in the way.'

Now, they stopped in a clearing and Halt dropped a small bundle to the ground that had been concealed beneath his cloak.

Will regarded the bundle doubtfully. When he thought of weapons, he thought of swords and battleaxes and war maces — the weapons carried by knights. It was obvious that this small bundle contained none of those.

'What sort of weapons? Do we have swords?' Will asked, his eyes glued to the bundle.

'A Ranger's principal weapons are stealth and silence and his ability to avoid being seen,' said Halt. 'But if they fail, then you may have to fight.'

'So then we have a sword?' Will said hopefully.

Halt knelt and unwrapped the bundle.

'No. Then we have a bow,' he said and placed it at Will's feet.

Will's first reaction was one of disappointment. A bow was something people used for hunting, he thought. Everyone had bows. A bow was more a tool than a weapon. As a child, he had made his fair share of them himself, bending a springy tree branch into shape. Then, as Halt said nothing, he looked more closely at the bow. This, he realised, was no bent branch.

It was unlike any bow that Will had seen before. Most of the bow followed one long curve like a normal longbow, but then each tip curved back in the opposite direction. Will, like most of the people of the Kingdom, was used to the standard longbow — which was one long piece of wood bent into a continuous curve. This one was a good deal shorter.

'It's called a recurve bow,' said Halt, sensing his puzzlement. 'You're not strong enough to handle a full longbow yet, so the double curve will give you extra arrow speed and power, with a lower draw weight. I learned how to make one from the Temujai.'

'Who are the Temujai?' asked Will, looking up from the strange bow.

'Fierce fighting men from the east,' said Halt. 'And probably the world's finest archers.'

'You fought against them?'

'Against them . . . and with them for a time,' said Halt. 'Stop asking so many questions.'

Will glanced down at the bow in his hand again. Now that he was becoming used to its unusual shape, he could see that it was a beautifully made weapon. Several shaped strips of wood had been glued together, with their grains running in different directions. They were of differing thicknesses and it was this that achieved the double curve of the bow, as the different forces strained against each other, bending the limbs of the bow into a carefully planned pattern. Maybe, he thought, this really was a weapon, after all.

'Can I shoot it?' he asked.

Halt nodded.

'If you feel that's a good idea, go ahead,' he said.

Quickly, Will chose an arrow from the quiver that had been in the bundle alongside the bow and fitted it to the string. He pulled the arrow back with his thumb and forefinger, aimed at a tree trunk some twenty metres away and fired.

Whack!

The heavy bowstring slapped into the soft flesh on the inside of his arm, stinging like a whip. Will yelled with pain and dropped the bow as if it were red hot.

Already, a thick red welt was forming on his arm. It throbbed painfully. Will had no idea where the arrow had gone. Nor did he care.

'That hurt!' he said, looking accusingly at the Ranger.

Halt shrugged.

'You're always in a hurry, youngster,' he said. 'That may teach you to wait a little next time.'

He bent to the bundle and pulled out a long cuff made of stiff leather. He slid it onto Will's left arm so that it would protect him from the bowstring. Ruefully, Will noticed that Halt was wearing a similar cuff. Even more ruefully, he realised that he'd noticed this before, but never wondered about the reason for it.

'Now try it again,' said Halt.

Will chose another arrow and placed it on the string. As he went to draw it back again, Halt stopped him.

'Not with the thumb and finger,' he said. 'Let the arrow rest between the first and second fingers on the string . . . like this.'

He showed Will how the nock — the notch at the butt end of the arrow — actually clipped to the string and held the arrow in place. Then he demonstrated how to let the string rest on the first joint of the first, second and third fingers, with the first finger above the nock point and the others below it. Finally, he showed him how to allow the string to slip loose so that the arrow was released.

'That's better,' he said and, as Will brought the arrow back, continued, 'Try to use your back muscles, not just your arms. Feel as if you're pushing your shoulderblades together . . .'

Will tried it and the bow seemed to draw a little easier.

He found he could hold it steadier than before.

He fired again. This time, he just missed the tree trunk he'd been aiming for.

'You need to practise,' said Halt. 'Put it down for now.'

Carefully, Will laid the bow down on the ground. He was eager now to see what Halt would produce next from the bundle.

'These are a Ranger's knives,' said Halt. He handed Will a double scabbard, like the one he wore on the left-hand side of his own belt.

Will took the double scabbard and examined it. The knives were set one above the other. The top knife was the shorter of the two. It had a thick, heavy grip made of a series of leather discs set one above the other. There was a brass crosspiece between the hilt and the blade and it had a matching brass pommel.

'Take it out,' said Halt. 'Do it carefully.'

Will slid the short knife from the scabbard. It was an unusual shape. Narrow at the hilt, it tapered out sharply, becoming thicker and wider for three quarters of its length to form a broad blade with the weight concentrated towards the tip, then a steep reverse taper created a razor-sharp point. He looked curiously at Halt.

'It's for throwing,' said the Ranger. 'The extra width at the tip balances the weight of the hilt. And the combined weight of the two helps drive the knife home when you throw it. Watch.'

His hand moved smoothly and swiftly to the broad-bladed knife at his own waist. He flicked it free from the scabbard and, in one smooth action, sent it spinning towards a nearby tree.

The knife thudded home into the wood with a satisfying *thock*! Will looked at Halt, impressed with the Ranger's skill and speed.

'How do you learn to do that?' he asked.

Halt looked at him. 'Practice.'

He gestured for Will to inspect the second knife.

This one was longer. The handle was the same leather disc construction, and there was a short, sturdy cross-piece. The blade was heavy and straight, razor-sharp on one side, thick and heavy on the other.

'This is in case your enemy gets to close quarters,' said Halt. 'Although if you're any sort of an archer, he never will. It's balanced for throwing, but you can also block a sword stroke with that blade. It's made by the finest steelsmiths in the Kingdom. Look after it and keep it sharp.'

'I will,' the apprentice said softly, admiring the knife in his hands.

'It's similar to what the Skandians call a saxe knife,' Halt told him. Will frowned at the unfamiliar name and Halt went on to explain further.

'It's both weapon and tool — a sea axe, originally. But over the years the words sort of slid together to become saxe. Mind you,' he added, 'the quality of the steel in ours is a long way superior to the Skandian ones.'

Will studied the knife more closely, seeing the faint blue tint in the blade, feeling the perfect balance. With its leather and brass hilt, the knife might be plain and functional in appearance. But it was a fine weapon and, Will realised, far superior to the comparatively clumsy swords worn by Castle Redmont's warriors.

Halt showed him how to strap the double scabbard to

his belt so that his hand fell naturally to the knife hilts. 'Now,' he said, 'all you have to do is learn to use them. And you know what that means, don't you?'

Will nodded his head, grinning.

'A lot of practice,' he said.

Eleven

$\mathcal{S}$ ir Rodney leaned on the timber fence surrounding the practice area as he watched the new Battle-school cadets going through their weapons drill. He rubbed his chin thoughtfully, his eyes scanning the twenty new recruits, but always returning to one in particular — the broad-shouldered, tall boy from the Ward, whom Rodney had selected at the Choosing. He thought for a moment, searching for the boy's name.

Horace. That was it.

The drill was a standard format. Each boy, wearing a mail shirt and helmet, and carrying a shield, stood before a padded hardwood post the height of a man. There was no point practising sword work unless you were burdened with shield, helmet and armour, as would be the case in a battle, Rodney believed. He thought it was best that the boys became used to the restrictions of the armour and weight of the equipment right from the start.

In addition to shield, helmet and mail, each boy also

held a drill sword issued by the armourer. The drill swords were made of wood and bore little resemblance to a real sword, aside from the leather-bound hilt and crosspiece on each. In fact, they were long batons, made of seasoned, hardened hickory. But they weighed much the same as a slender steel blade, and the hilts were weighted to approximate the heft and balance of a real sword.

Eventually, the recruits would progress to drilling with actual swords — albeit with blunted edges and points. But that was still some months away, by which time the less suitable recruits would have been weeded out. It was quite normal for at least a third of the Battleschool applicants to drop out of the harsh training in the first three months. Sometimes it was the boy's choice. For others, it was at the discretion of his instructors or, in extreme cases, Sir Rodney himself. Battleschool was harsh and standards were strict.

The practice yard rang with the thudding of wood against the thick, sun-hardened leather padding on the practice posts. At the head of the yard, drill master Sir Karel called the standard strokes that were being practised.

Five third year cadets, under the direction of Sir Morton, an assistant drill instructor, moved among the boys, attending to the detail of the basic sword strokes: correcting a wrong movement here, changing the angle of a stroke there, making sure another boy's shield wasn't dropping too far as he struck.

It was boring, repetitive work under the hot afternoon sun. But it was necessary. These were the basic moves by which these boys might well live or die at some later date and it was vital that they should be so totally ingrained as to be instinctive.

It was that thought that had Rodney watching Horace now. As Karel called the basic cadence, Rodney had noticed that Horace was adding an occasional stroke to the sequence, and yet managing to do so without falling behind in his timing.

Karel had just begun another sequence and Sir Rodney leaned forward attentively, his eyes fixed on Horace.

'Thrust! Side cut! Backhand side! Overhand!' called the drill master. 'Overhead backhand!'

And there it was again! As Karel called for the overhead backhand cut, Horace delivered it, but then almost instantly switched to a backhanded side cut as well, allowing the first cut to bounce off the post to prepare him instantly for the second. The stroke was delivered with such stunning speed and force that, in real combat, the result would have been devastating. His opponent's shield, raised to block the overhead cut, could never have responded quickly enough to protect uncovered ribs from the rapid side cut that followed. Rodney had become aware over the past few minutes that the trainee was adding these extra strokes to the routine. He had seen it first from the corner of his eye, noticing a slight variation in the strict pattern of the drill, a quick flicker of extra movement that was there and gone almost too quickly to be noticed.

'Rest!' called Karel now and Rodney noted that, while most of the others let their weapons drop and stood flat-footed, Horace maintained his ready position, the sword tip slightly above waist height, moving on his toes in the break so as not to lose his own natural rhythm.

Apparently, someone else had noticed Horace's extra

stroke as well. Sir Morton beckoned over one of the senior cadets and spoke to him, gesturing quickly towards Horace. The first year trainee, his attention still focused on the training post that was his enemy, didn't see the exchange. He looked up, startled, as the senior cadet approached and called to him.

'You there! At post fourteen. What d'you think you're doing?'

The look on Horace's face was one of bewilderment — and worry. No first year recruit enjoyed gaining the attention of any of the drill masters or their assistants. They were all too conscious of that thirty per cent attrition rate.

'Sir?' he said anxiously, not understanding the question. The senior cadet continued.

'You're not following the pattern. Follow Sir Karel's call, understand?'

Rodney, watching carefully, was convinced that Horace's bewilderment was genuine. The tall boy made a small movement of the shoulders, almost a shrug but not quite. He was at attention now, the sword resting over his right shoulder and the shield up in the parade position.

'Sir?' he said again, uncertainly. The senior cadet was getting angry now. He hadn't noticed Horace's extra moves himself and obviously assumed the younger boy was simply following a random sequence of his own devising. He leaned forward, his face only a few centimetres away from Horace's, and said, in a voice far too loud for that small amount of separation:

'Sir Karel calls the sequence he wants performed! You perform it! Understand?'

'Sir, I . . . did,' Horace replied, very red in the face now.

He knew it was a mistake to argue with an instructor, but he also knew that he had performed every one of the strokes Karel had called.

The senior cadet, Rodney saw, was now at a disadvantage. He hadn't actually seen what Horace had done. He covered his uncertainty with bluster. 'Oh, you did, did you? Well, perhaps you might just repeat the last sequence for me. What sequence did Sir Karel call?'

Without hesitation, Horace replied. 'Sequence five, sir: Thrust. Side cut. Backhand side. Overhand. Overhead backhand.'

The senior cadet hesitated. He'd assumed that Horace had simply been in a dream, hacking away at the post any way he chose. But, as far as he could remember, Horace had just repeated the previous sequence perfectly. At least, he thought he had. The senior cadet wasn't altogether sure of the sequence himself by now, but the trainee had replied with no hesitation at all. He was conscious that all the other trainees were watching with considerable interest. It was a natural reaction. Trainees always enjoyed seeing somebody else being berated for a mistake. It tended to draw attention away from their own deficiencies.

'What's going on here, Paul?' Sir Morton, the assistant drill master, sounded none too pleased with all this discussion. He'd originally ordered the senior cadet to reprimand the trainee for lack of attention. That reprimand should have been delivered by now and the matter ended. Instead, the class was being disrupted. Senior Cadet Paul came to attention.

'Sir, the trainee *says* he performed the sequence,' he replied. Horace went to reply to the implication obvious in the emphasis the senior cadet placed on the word 'says'. Then he thought better of it and shut his mouth firmly.

'Just a moment.' Paul and Sir Morton looked around, a little surprised. They hadn't seen Sir Rodney approaching. Around them, the other trainees also came to stiff attention. Sir Rodney was held in awe by all members of Battleschool, particularly the newer ones. Morton didn't quite come to attention but he straightened a little, squaring his shoulders.

Horace bit his lip in an agony of concern. He could see the prospect of dismissal from Battleschool looming before him. First, he seemed to have alienated the three second year cadets who were making his life a misery. Then he had drawn the unwelcome attention of Senior Cadet Paul and Sir Morton. Now this — the Battlemaster himself. And to make matters worse, he had no idea what he had done wrong. He searched his memory and he could distinctly remember performing the sequence as it had been called.

'Do you remember the sequence, Cadet Horace?' said the Battlemaster.

The cadet nodded emphatically then, realising that this wasn't regarded as an acceptable response to a question from a senior officer, he said:

'Yes, sir. Sequence five, sir.'

That was the second time he had identified the sequence, Rodney noted. He would have been willing to bet that not one of the other cadets could have said which sequence from the drill manual they had just completed. He doubted that the senior cadets would have been any better informed. Sir Morton went to say something, but Rodney held up a hand to stop him.

'Perhaps you could repeat it for us now,' he said, his stern voice giving no hint of the growing interest he was feeling in this recruit. He gestured to the practice post.

'Take your position. Calling the cadence . . . begin!'

Horace performed the sequence flawlessly, calling the strokes as he went.

'Thrust! Side cut! Backhand side! Overhand! Overhead backhand!'

The drill sword thudded into the leather padding in strict timing. The rhythm was perfect. The execution of the strokes was faultless. But this time, Rodney noticed, there was no additional stroke. The lightning fast reverse side cut didn't appear. He thought he knew why. Horace was concentrating on getting the sequence correct this time. Previously, he had been acting instinctively.

Sir Karel, attracted by Sir Rodney's intervention into a standard drill session, strolled through the ranks of trainees standing by their practice posts. His eyebrows arched a question at Sir Rodney. As a senior knight, he was entitled to such informality. The Battlemaster held up his hand again. He didn't want anything to break Horace's attention right now. But he was glad Karel was here to witness what he was sure was about to happen.

'Again,' he said, in the same stern voice and, once again, Horace went through the sequence. As he finished, Rodney's voice cracked like a whip:

'Again!'

And again Horace performed the fifth sequence. This time, as he finished, Rodney snapped: 'Sequence three!'

'Thrust! Thrust! Backstep! Cross parry! Shield block! Side cut!' Horace called as he performed the moves.

Now Rodney could see that the boy was moving lightly on his toes, the sword a flickering tongue that danced out and in and across. And without realising it, Horace was calling the cadence for the moves nearly half as quickly again as the drill master had been.

Karel caught Rodney's eye. He nodded appreciatively. But Rodney wasn't finished yet. Before Horace had time to think, he called the fifth sequence again and the boy responded.

'Thrust! Side cut! Backhand side! Overhand! Overhead backhand!'

'Backhand side!' snapped Sir Rodney instantly and, in response, almost of its own will, Horace's sword flickered in that extra, deadly move. Sir Rodney heard the small sounds of surprise from Morton and Karel. They realised the significance of what they had seen. Senior Cadet Paul, perhaps understandably, wasn't quite so fast to grasp it. As far as he was concerned, the trainee had responded to an extra order from the Battlemaster. He'd done it well, admittedly, and he certainly seemed to know which end of a sword was which. But that was all the cadet had seen.

'Rest!' Sir Rodney ordered and Horace allowed the sword point to drop to the dust, hand on the pommel, standing feet apart with the sword hilt centred against his belt buckle, in the parade rest position.

'Now, Horace,' said the Battlemaster quietly, 'do you remember adding that backhand side cut to the sequence the first time?'

Horace frowned, then understanding dawned in his eyes. He wasn't sure, but now that the Battlemaster had prompted his memory, he thought that maybe he had.

'Uh . . . yes, sir. I think so. I'm sorry, sir. I didn't mean to. It just sort of . . . happened.'

Rodney glanced quickly at his drill masters. He could see they understood the significance of what had happened here. He nodded at them, passing a silent message that he wanted nothing made of this — yet.

'Well, no harm done. But pay attention for the rest of the period and just perform the strokes Sir Karel calls for, all right?'

Horace came to attention. 'Yes, sir.' He snapped his eyes towards the drill master. 'Sorry, sir!' he added, and Karel dismissed the matter with a wave of his hand.

'Pay closer attention in future.' Karel nodded to Sir Rodney, sensing that the Battlemaster wanted to be on his way. 'Thank you, sir. Permission to continue?'

Sir Rodney nodded assent. 'Carry on, drill master.' He began to turn away then, as if he'd remembered something else, he turned back, and added casually, 'Oh, by the way, could I see you in my quarters after classes are dismissed this evening?'

'Of course, sir,' said Karel, equally casually, knowing that Sir Rodney wanted to discuss this phenomenon, but didn't want Horace to be aware of his interest.

Sir Rodney strolled slowly back to the Battleschool headquarters. Behind him, he heard Karel's preparatory orders, then the repetitive 'thud, thud, thud-thud-thud' of wood on leather padding began once more.

Twelve

Halt examined the target Will had been shooting at, and nodded.

'Not bad at all,' he said. 'Your shooting is definitely improving.'

Will couldn't help grinning. That was high praise indeed from Halt. Halt saw the expression and immediately added, 'With more practice — a *lot* more practice — you might even achieve mediocrity.'

Will wasn't absolutely sure what mediocrity was but he sensed it wasn't good. The grin faded and Halt dismissed the subject with a wave of his hand.

'That's enough shooting for now. Let's go,' he said and set off, striding down a narrow path through the forest.

'Where are we going?' Will asked, half running to keep up with the Ranger's longer strides.

Halt looked up at the trees above him. 'Why does this boy ask so many questions?' he asked the trees.

Naturally, they didn't answer.

They walked for an hour before they came to a small collection of buildings buried deep in the forest.

Will was aching to ask more questions. But he'd learned by now that Halt wasn't going to answer them, so he held his tongue and bided his time. Sooner or later, he knew, he'd learn why they'd come here.

Halt led the way up to the largest of the ramshackle huts, then stopped, signalling for Will to do likewise.

'Hullo, Old Bob!' he called.

Will heard someone moving inside the hut, then a wrinkled, bent figure appeared in the doorway. His beard was long and matted and a dirty white colour. He was almost completely bald. As he moved towards them, grinning and nodding a greeting to Halt, Will caught his breath. Old Bob smelt like a stable. And a none too clean one at that.

'Morning to you, Ranger!' said Old Bob. 'Who's this you've brung to see me?'

He looked keenly at Will. The eyes were bright and very alert, despite his dirty, unkempt appearance.

'This is Will, my new apprentice,' said Halt. 'Will, this is Old Bob.'

'Good morning, sir,' said Will politely. The old man cackled.

'Calls me sir! Hear that, Ranger, calls me sir! Make a fine Ranger, this one will!'

Will smiled at him. Dirty as he might be, there was something likeable about Old Bob — perhaps it was the fact that he seemed to be in no way overawed by Halt. Will couldn't remember seeing anyone speaking to the grim-faced Ranger in quite this familiar tone before. Halt grunted impatiently.

'Are they ready?' he asked. The old man cackled again and nodded several times.

'Ready they are indeed!' he said. 'Step this way and see them.'

He led them to the back of the hut, where a small paddock was fenced off. At the far side, there was a lean-to shed. Just a roof and supporting posts. No walls. Old Bob let out a piercing whistle that made Will jump.

'There they are, see?' he said, pointing to the lean-to.

Will looked and saw two small horses trotting across the yard to greet the old man. As they came closer, he realised that one was a horse, the other was a pony. But both were small, shaggy animals, nothing like the fierce, sleek battle-horses that the Baron and his knights rode to war.

The larger of the two trotted immediately to Halt's side. He patted its neck and handed it an apple from a bin close by the fence. The horse crunched it gratefully. Halt leaned forward and said a few words into its ear. The horse tossed its head and neighed, as if it were sharing some private joke with the Ranger.

The pony waited by Old Bob until he had given it an apple to crunch as well. Then it turned one large, intelligent eye on Will.

'This 'un's called Tug,' said the old man. 'He looks about your size, don't he?'

He passed the rope bridle to Will, who took it and looked into the horse's eyes. He was a shaggy little beast.

His legs were short, but sturdy. His body was barrel shaped. His mane and tail were ragged and unbrushed. All in all, as horses went, he wasn't a very impressive sight, thought Will.

He'd always dreamt of the horse he would one day ride into battle: in those dreams, the horse was tall and majestic. It was fierce and jet black, combed and brushed until it shone like black armour.

This horse almost seemed to sense what he was thinking and butted its head gently against his shoulder.

I may not be very big, its eyes seemed to say, *but I might just surprise you.*

'Well,' said Halt. 'What do you think of him?' He was fondling the other horse's soft nose. They were obviously old friends. Will hesitated. He didn't want to offend anyone.

'He's sort of . . . small,' he said finally.

'So are you,' Halt pointed out. Will couldn't think of an answer to that. Old Bob wheezed with laughter.

'He ain't no battlehorse, are he, boy?' he asked.

'Well . . . no, he isn't,' Will said awkwardly. He liked Bob and he felt any criticism of the pony might be taken personally. But Old Bob simply laughed again.

'But he'll run any of those fine fancy-looking battle-horses into the ground!' he said proudly. 'He's a strong 'un, this 'un. He'll keep going all day, long after them fancy horses have laid down and died.'

Will looked at the shaggy little animal doubtfully.

'I'm sure he will,' he said politely.

Halt leaned against the paddock fence.

'Why don't you see?' he suggested. 'You're fast on your feet. Turn him loose and see if you can capture him again.'

Will sensed the challenge in the Ranger's voice. He dropped the rope bridle. The horse, as if realising that this was some sort of test, skipped lightly away into the centre of the small enclosure. Will ducked under the fence rails and walked softly towards the pony. He held out his hand invitingly. 'Come on, boy,' he said. 'Stand still there.'

He reached out his hand for the bridle and the little horse suddenly wheeled away. It shied to one side, then the other, then sidestepped neatly around Will and danced backwards out of reach.

He tried again.

Again, the horse evaded him easily. Will was beginning to feel foolish. He advanced on the horse and it backed away, moving closer and closer to one of the corners. Then, just when Will thought he had it, it nimbly danced to one side and was away again.

Will lost his temper now and ran after it. The horse whinnied in amusement and romped easily out of his reach. It was enjoying this game.

And so it went. Will would approach, the horse would duck and dodge and escape. Even in the close confines of the small paddock, he couldn't catch it.

He stopped. He was conscious of the fact that Halt was watching him carefully. He thought for a moment or two. There must be a way to do it. He'd never catch a horse as light on its feet and fast-moving as this one. There must be another way . . .

His gaze fell on the bin of apples outside the fence. Quickly, he ducked under the rail and seized an apple. Then he went back into the paddock and stood stock-still, holding the apple out.

'Come on, boy,' he said.

Tug's ears shot up. He liked apples. He also thought he liked this boy — he played this game well. Tossing his head approvingly, he trotted forward and took the apple delicately. Will seized hold of the bridle and the pony crunched the apple. If a horse could be said to look blissful, this one did.

Will looked up and saw Halt nodding approval.

'Well thought out,' said the Ranger. Old Bob elbowed the grey-cloaked man in the ribs.

'Clever boy, that!' he cackled. 'Clever *and* polite! That 'un'll make a good team with Tug, won't he?'

Will patted the shaggy neck and the pricked-up ears. He looked now at the old man.

'Why do you call him Tug?' he asked.

Instantly, Will's arm was nearly torn from its socket as the pony jerked its head back. Will staggered, then regained his balance. Old Bob's braying laugh rang out around the clearing.

'See if you can guess!' he said delightedly.

His laughter was infectious and Will couldn't help smiling himself. Halt glanced up at the sun, which was fast disappearing behind the trees that fringed Old Bob's clearing and the meadows beyond.

'Take him over to the lean-to and Bob can show you how to groom him and look after his tack,' he said, then added to the old man, 'We'll stay with you tonight, Bob, if that's not inconvenient?'

The old horse handler nodded his head in pleasure. 'I'll be glad of the company, Ranger. Sometimes I spend so much time with the horses that I start to think I'm one myself.' Unconsciously, he dipped a hand into the apple barrel and selected one, absentmindedly crunching into it — much as Tug had done a few minutes earlier. Halt watched him, one eyebrow raised.

'We might be just in time,' he observed dryly. 'Then, tomorrow, we'll see if Will can ride Tug as well as catch him,' he said, guessing as he said it that his apprentice would get very little sleep that night.

He was right. Old Bob's tiny cabin had only two rooms, so after their supper, Halt stretched out on the floor by the fireplace and Will bedded down in the warm, clean straw of the barn, listening to the gentle whiffling sounds of the two horses. The moon rose and fell as he lay wide awake, wondering and worrying over what the next day might bring. Would he be able to ride Tug? He'd never ridden a horse. Would he fall off the minute he tried?

Would he be hurt? Worse still, would he embarrass himself? He liked Old Bob and he didn't want to look foolish in front of him. Nor in front of Halt, he realised, with a little surprise. He was still wondering when Halt's good opinion had come to mean so much to him when he finally fell asleep.

Thirteen

'So, you saw it. What did you think?' Sir Rodney asked. Karel reached across and poured himself another tankard from the jug of beer that was on the table between them. Rodney's quarters were simple enough — even spartan when it was remembered that he was head of the Battleschool. Battlemasters in other fiefs took advantage of the position to surround themselves with the trappings of luxury, but that wasn't Rodney's style. His room was simply furnished, with a pinewood table for a desk and six straight-backed pine chairs around it.

There was a fireplace in the corner, of course. Rodney might have preferred to live in a simple style but that didn't mean he enjoyed discomfort, and winters in Castle Redmont were cold. Right now it was late summer and the thick stone walls of the castle buildings served to keep the interiors cool. When the cold weather came, those same thick walls would retain the heat of the fire. On one wall, a large bay window looked out over the Battleschool's drill field. Facing the window, on the opposite wall, was a doorway, screened by a thick curtain, leading to Rodney's sleeping quarters — a simple soldier's bed and more wooden furniture. It had been a little more ornate when his wife Antoinette was still alive, but she had died some years previously and the rooms were now unmistakably masculine in character, without any item in them that wasn't functional and with an absolute minimum of decoration.

'I saw it,' Karel agreed. 'Not sure that I believed it, but I saw it.'

'You only saw it once,' said Rodney. 'He was doing it constantly throughout the session — and I'm convinced that he was doing it unconsciously.'

'As fast as the one I saw?' Karel asked. Rodney nodded emphatically.

'If anything, faster. He was adding an extra stroke to the routines but staying in time with the call.' He hesitated, then finally said what they were both thinking. 'The boy is a natural.'

Karel inclined his head thoughtfully. Based on what he'd seen, he wasn't prepared to dispute the fact. And the Battlemaster had been watching the boy for some time during the session, he knew. But naturals were few and far between. They were those unique people for whom the skill of swordplay moved into an entirely different dimension. It became not so much a skill as an instinct to them.

They were the ones who became the champions. The sword masters. Experienced warriors like Sir Rodney and Sir Karel were expert swordsmen but naturals took the skill to a higher plane. It was as if for them, the sword in their hand became a true extension not just of their bodies, but of their personalities as well. The sword seemed to act in instant communion and harmony with the natural's mind, acting even faster than conscious thought. Naturals were possessed of unique skills in timing and balance and rhythm.

As such, they presented a heavy responsibility to those who were entrusted with their training. For those natural skills and abilities had to be carefully nurtured and developed in a long-term training programme to allow the warrior, already highly proficient as a matter of course, to develop his true potential for genius.

'You're sure?' Karel said eventually and Rodney nodded again, his gaze out the window. In his mind he was seeing the boy training, seeing those extra flickers of lightning fast movement.

'I'm sure,' he said simply. 'We'll have to let Wallace know that he'll have another pupil next semester.'

Wallace was the sword master at the Redmont Battleschool. He was the one who had the responsibility for adding the final polish to the basic skills that Karel and the others taught. In the event of an outstanding trainee — as Horace obviously was — he would give them private tuition in advanced techniques. Karel curled his bottom lip thoughtfully as he thought about the time frame Rodney had suggested.

'Not until then?' he said. The next semester was almost three months away. 'Why not get him started straight away? From what I saw, he's already mastered the basic stuff.' But Rodney shook his head.

'We haven't really assessed his personality yet,' he said.

'He seems a nice enough lad, but you never know. If he turns out to be a misfit of some kind, I don't want to give him the sort of advanced instruction that Wallace can provide.'

Once he thought of it, Karel agreed with the Battlemaster. After all, if it should turn out that Horace had to be disqualified from Battleschool because of some other failing, it might be embarrassing, not to mention dangerous, if he were already on the road to being a highly trained swordsman. Disqualified trainees often reacted with resentment.

'And another thing,' Rodney added. 'Let's keep this to ourselves – and tell Morton the same thing. I don't want the boy hearing any word of this yet. It might make him cocky and that could be dangerous for him.'

'That's true enough,' Karel agreed. He finished the last of his beer in two quick draughts, set his tankard down on the table and stood. 'Well, I'd better be getting along. I've got reports to finish.'

'Who hasn't?' the Battlemaster said with some feeling and the two old friends exchanged rueful grins. 'I never knew there was so much paper involved in running a Battleschool,' Rodney said and Karel snorted in derision.

'Sometimes I think we should forget the weapons training and just throw all the paper at the enemy – bury them in it.'

He gave an informal salute – just touching one finger to his forehead – that was in keeping with his seniority. Then he turned and headed for the door. He paused as Rodney added one last point to their discussion.

'Keep an eye on the boy, of course,' he said. 'But don't let him become aware of it.'

'Of course,' Karel replied. 'We don't want him to start thinking there's something special about him.'

At that moment, there was no chance that Horace would think there was anything special about him — at least, not in any positive sense. What he did feel was that there was something about him that attracted trouble.

Word had gone round about the strange scene at the training ground. His classmates, not understanding what had happened, all assumed that Horace had somehow annoyed the Battlemaster and now waited for the inevitable retribution. They knew that the rule during the first semester was that, when one member of a class made a mistake, the entire class paid for it. As a result, the atmosphere in their dormitory had been strained, to say the least. Horace had finally made his way out of the room, intending to head for the river to escape the condemnation and blame he could feel from the others. Unfortunately, when he did so, he walked straight into the waiting arms of Alda, Bryn and Jerome.

The three older boys had heard a garbled version of the scene at the practice yard. They assumed that Horace had been criticised for his sword work and decided to make him suffer for it.

However, they knew that their attentions would not necessarily meet with the approval of the Battleschool staff. Horace, as a newcomer, had no way of knowing that this sort of systematic bullying was totally disapproved of by Sir Rodney and the other instructors. Horace simply assumed that was the way things were supposed to be and, not knowing any better, went along with it, allowing himself to be bullied and insulted.

It was for this reason that the three second year cadets marched Horace to the riverside, where he had been heading anyway, and away from the sight of instructors. Here, they made him wade thigh deep into the river then stand to attention.

'Baby can't use his sword properly,' said Alda.

Bryn took up the refrain. 'Baby made the Battlemaster angry. Baby doesn't belong in Battleschool. Babies shouldn't be given swords to play with.'

'Baby should throw stones instead,' Jerome concluded the sarcastic litany. 'Pick up a stone, Baby.'

Horace hesitated, then glanced around. The riverbed was full of stones and he bent to get one. As he did so, his sleeve and the upper part of his jacket became soaked.

'Not a small stone, Baby,' Alda said, smiling evilly at him. 'You're a big baby so you need a big stone.'

'A great big stone,' Bryn added, indicating with his hands that he wanted Horace to pick up a large rock. Horace looked around him and saw several larger pieces in the crystal clear water. He bent and retrieved one of them. In doing so, he made a mistake. The rock he chose was easy to lift under the water, but as he brought it above the surface, he grunted with the weight of it.

'Let's see it, Baby,' Jerome said. 'Hold it up.'

Horace braced himself — the swiftly running current of the river made it difficult to keep his balance and hold the heavy rock at the same time — then he lifted it to chest height so his tormentors could see it.

'Right up, Baby,' Alda commanded. 'Right over your head.'

Painfully, Horace obeyed. The rock was feeling heavier by the second but he held it high above his head and the three boys were satisfied.

'That's good, Baby,' Jerome said and Horace, with a relieved sigh, began to let the rock down again.

'What are you doing?' demanded Jerome angrily. 'I said that's good. So that's where I want the rock to stay.'

Horace struggled and lifted the rock above his head once more, holding it at arm's length. Alda, Bryn and Jerome nodded their approval.

'Now you can stay there,' Alda told him, 'while you count to five hundred. Then you can go back to the dormitory.'

'Start counting,' Bryn ordered him, grinning at the idea.

'One, two, three . . .' began Horace, but they all shouted at him almost immediately.

'Not so fast, Baby! Nice and slowly. Start again.'

'One . . . two . . . three . . .' Horace counted and they nodded their approval.

'That's better. Now a nice slow count to five hundred and you can go,' Alda told him.

'Don't try to fudge it, because we'll know,' threatened Jerome. 'And you'll be back here counting to one thousand.'

Laughing among themselves, the three students headed back to their quarters. Horace remained in midstream, arms trembling with the weight of the rock, tears of frustration and humiliation filling his eyes. Once, he lost his balance and fell full length in the water. After that, his heavy, sodden clothing made it all the harder to hold the rock above his head but he kept at it. He couldn't be sure that they weren't concealed somewhere, watching him, and if they were, they'd make him pay for disobeying their instructions.

If this was the way of things, then so be it, he thought. But he promised himself that, first chance he got, he was going to make somebody pay for the humiliation he was undergoing.

Much later, clothes soaked, arms aching and a deep feeling of resentment burning in his heart, he crept back to his quarters. He was too late for the evening meal but he didn't care. He was too miserable to eat.

Fourteen

'**W**alk him around a little,' said Halt.

Will glanced back at the shaggy pony, who watched him with intelligent eyes.

'Come on, boy,' he said, and pulled on the halter. Instantly, Tug braced his forelegs and refused to move. Will pulled harder on the rope, leaning back in his efforts to make the stubborn little pony move.

Old Bob cackled with laughter.

'He be stronger than you!' he said.

Will felt his ears reddening with embarrassment. He pulled harder. Tug twitched his ears and resisted. It was like trying to pull a house along.

'Don't look at him,' Halt said softly. 'Just take the rope and walk away from him. He'll follow.'

Will tried it that way. He turned his back on Tug, seized the rope firmly and began walking. The pony trotted easily after him. Will looked at Halt and grinned. The Ranger nodded his head towards the far fence of the paddock. Will glanced across and saw a small saddle, placed across the top rail of the fence.

'Saddle him up,' said the Ranger.

Tug clip-clopped docilely across to the fence. Will looped the reins around the fence rail and hefted the saddle across the pony's back. He bent down to fasten the girth straps of the saddle.

'Pull them good and tight!' Old Bob advised him.

Finally, the saddle was firmly in position. Will looked eagerly at Halt. 'Can I ride him now?' he asked.

The Ranger stroked his uneven beard thoughtfully before he answered. 'If you feel that's a good idea, go ahead,' he said, finally.

Will hesitated for a moment. The phrase stirred a vague memory with him. But then eagerness overcame caution and he put one foot in the stirrup and swung himself nimbly onto the pony's back. Tug stood, unmoving.

'Get up!' Will said, drumming his heels against the pony's side.

For a moment, nothing happened. Then Will felt a small tremor of movement go through the pony's body.

Suddenly, Tug arched his muscular little back and shot straight into the air, all four feet leaving the ground at the same time. He twisted violently to one side, came down on his front legs and kicked his rear legs high into the sky. Will sailed neatly over the pony's ears, turned a complete somersault in the air and crashed on his back in the dirt. He picked himself up, rubbing his back.

Tug stood nearby, ears up, watching him intently.

Now, why did you go and do a silly thing like that? the eyes seemed to say.

Old Bob leaned against the fence, sides heaving with laughter. Will looked at Halt.

'What did I do wrong?' he asked. Halt ducked under the fence rails and walked across to where Tug stood watching the two of them expectantly. He handed the bridle back to Will, then laid one hand on his shoulder.

'Nothing, if this were an ordinary horse,' he said. 'But Tug has been trained as a Ranger horse —'

'What's the difference?' Will interrupted angrily and Halt held his hand up for silence.

'The difference is, each Ranger horse has to be asked before a rider mounts him for the first time,' said Halt. 'They're trained that way so that they can never be stolen.'

Will scratched his head. 'I've never heard of such a thing!' he said.

Old Bob smiled as he walked forward. 'Not too many folk has,' he said. 'That's why Ranger horses never get stolen.'

'Well,' said Will, 'what do you say to a Ranger horse before you mount him?'

Halt shrugged.

'It varies from horse to horse. Each one responds to a different request.' He gestured towards the larger horse. 'My horse, for example, responds to the words "permettez moi".'

'Permettez moi?' Will echoed. 'What sort of words are they?'

'They're Gallic. They mean, "Will you allow me?" His parents came from Gallica, you see,' Halt explained. Then he turned to Old Bob. 'What are the words for Tug here, Bob?'

Bob screwed up his eyes, pretending that he couldn't remember. Then his face cleared.

'Oh yes, I recall!' he said. 'This 'un here, he needs to be asked, "Do you mind" afore you get on his back.'

'Do you mind?' Will repeated and Bob shook his head.

'Don't say it to me, youngster! Say it in the horse's ear!'

Feeling a little silly, and not at all sure that the others weren't having a joke at his expense, Will stepped forward and said softly in Tug's ear:

'Do you mind?'

Tug whinnied softly. Will looked doubtfully at the two men and Bob nodded encouragement.

'Go on! Climb on now! Young Tug won't harm 'ee now.'

Very carefully, Will swung himself onto the pony's shaggy back once again. His back still ached from the previous attempt. He sat there a moment. Nothing happened. Then, he tapped his heels gently into Tug's ribs.

'Come on, boy,' he said softly.

Tug's ears twitched up and he stepped forward at an easy walk.

Still cautious, Will let him walk around the paddock once or twice, then tapped again with his heels. Tug broke into a gentle trot. Will moved easily to the rhythm of the horse's movement and Halt looked on approvingly. The boy was an instinctive rider.

The Ranger unclipped the short length of rope that held the paddock gate closed and swung the wide gate open.

'Take him out, Will,' he called, 'and see what he can really do!'

Obediently, Will turned the pony towards the gate and, as they passed through into the open ground beyond, tapped once more with his heels. He felt the muscular little body beneath him bunch momentarily, then Tug broke into a fast gallop.

The wind rushed past Will's ears as he leaned forward over the pony's neck, encouraging him to even greater speed. Tug's ears pricked upwards in response and he went even faster than before.

He was like the wind. His short legs were a blur of motion as he carried the boy at full speed towards the edge of the trees. Gently, not sure how the pony would react, Will applied pressure to the left-hand rein.

Instantly, Tug veered to the left, racing away from the trees at an angle. Will kept the gentle pressure on the rein until Tug was headed once again back towards the paddock. Will gasped in amazement as he saw how far they had come. Halt and Old Bob were tiny figures in the distance now. But they grew rapidly larger as Tug flew over the rough grass towards them.

A fallen log loomed in front of them and, before Will could make any effort to avoid it, Tug had gathered himself, steadied and leapt over the obstacle. Will let out a shout of excitement and the pony whinnied briefly in reply.

They were almost back to the paddock now and Will pulled gently on both reins. Instantly, Tug slowed to a canter, then a trot, finally coming down to walking pace as Will maintained the pressure on the reins. He brought the pony to a standstill beside Halt. Tug tossed his shaggy head and whinnied again. Will leaned forward and patted the pony on the neck.

'He's terrific!' he said breathlessly. 'He's as fast as the wind!'

Halt nodded gravely. 'Perhaps not quite as fast as the wind,' he said, 'but he can certainly cover ground.' He turned to the old man. 'You've done well with him, Bob.'

Old Bob ducked his head in appreciation and leaned forward to pat the shaggy little pony in his turn. He had spent his life breeding, training and preparing the Ranger Corps' horses and this one ranked among the best he'd seen.

'He'll keep that pace all day,' he said fondly. 'Run them fat battlehorses into the ground, this 'un will. Youngster rides him well, too, Ranger, don't 'e?'

Halt stroked his beard. 'Not too badly,' he said. Bob was scandalised.

'Not too badly? You're a hard man, Ranger! Youngster sat him light as a feather through that jump!' The old man looked up at Will, sitting astride the pony, and nodded in appreciation. ''E don't saw away at them reins like some do, neither. Got a light touch with a horse's soft mouth, 'e 'as.'

Will grinned at the old horse trainer's praise. He sneaked a quick look at Halt but the Ranger was as grave-faced as ever.

He never smiles, Will thought to himself. He went to dismount, then stopped himself hurriedly.

'Is there anything I should say to him before I get off?'

Bob laughed aloud. 'No, youngster. Once said and young Tug here will remember — as long as it's you who's riding him.' Relieved, Will climbed down. He stood beside the pony and Tug shoved him affectionately with his head. Will glanced at the apple barrel.

'Could I give him another?' he asked.

Halt nodded. 'Just one more,' he said. 'But don't go

making a habit of it. He'll be too fat to run if you feed him all the time.'

Tug snorted loudly. Apparently he and Halt were at odds over how many apples a pony should have in a day.

Will spent the rest of the day getting tips on riding technique from Old Bob, and learning how to look after and repair Tug's saddle and harness, as well as the finer points of caring for the little horse.

He brushed and curried the shaggy coat until it shone and Tug seemed to appreciate his efforts. Finally, worn out, his arms aching with the effort, he had slumped to a seat on a hay bale. Which, of course, had to be the exact moment when Halt walked into the stable.

'Come along,' he said. 'No time to be lolling around doing nothing. We'd best get moving if we're to be home before dark.'

And, so saying, he tossed a saddle across the back of his horse. Will didn't bother to protest that he hadn't been 'lolling around', as the Ranger put it. For a start, he knew it would be no use. And secondly, he was excited by the fact that they would be riding back to Halt's little cottage by the edge of the forest. It seemed that the two horses were to become a permanent part of their establishment. He realised now that Halt's horse had obviously been so before and that the Ranger had only been waiting until Will had shown his ability to ride and to bond with Tug before reclaiming him from his temporary home in Old Bob's stable.

The horses whinnied to each other from time to time as they trotted back through the dim green forest, for all the world as if they were carrying on their own conversation. Will was bursting with questions he wanted to ask. But, by now, he was wary of chattering too much in the Ranger's presence.

Finally, he could contain himself no longer.

'Halt?' he said, experimentally.

The Ranger grunted. Will took that as a sign that he could continue speaking.

'What's your horse's name?' the boy asked.

Halt looked down at him. His horse was slightly larger than Tug, although nowhere near the size of the giant battlehorses kept in the Baron's stable.

'I believe it's Abelard,' he said.

'Abelard?' Will repeated. 'What kind of name is that?'

'It's Gallic,' said the Ranger, obviously putting an end to the conversation.

They rode a few kilometres further in silence. The sun was lowering over the trees now and their shadows were long and distorted on the ground in front of them. Will studied Tug's shadow. The pony seemed to have enormously long legs and a ridiculously short body. He wanted to call Halt's attention to it but thought that such a frivolous observation would not impress the Ranger. Instead, he summoned the courage to ask another question that had been occupying his thoughts for some days.

'Halt?' he said again.

The Ranger sighed briefly.

'What now?' he asked. His tone definitely did not encourage further conversation. However, Will pressed on.

'Remember you told me how a Ranger was responsible for Morgarath's defeat?'

'Mmmm,' Halt grunted.

'Well, I was just wondering, what was the Ranger's name?' the boy asked.

'Names aren't important.' Halt said. 'I really can't remember.'

'Was it you?' Will continued, sure that it was. Halt turned that level, unsmiling gaze on him again.

'I said, names aren't important,' he repeated. There was a silence between them for some seconds, then the Ranger said: 'Do you know what is important?'

Will shook his head.

'Supper is important!' said the Ranger. 'And we'll be late for it if we don't hurry.'

He clapped his heels into Abelard's side and the horse shot away like an arrow from Halt's own bow, leaving Will and Tug far behind in a matter of seconds.

Will touched Tug's sides with his own heels and the little pony raced off in pursuit of his bigger friend.

'Come on, Tug!' Will urged. 'Let's show them how a real Ranger horse can run.'

Fifteen

$\mathbf{W}$ill rode Tug slowly through the crowded fairground that had been set up outside the castle walls. All the villagers and inhabitants of the castle itself seemed to be out and he had to ride carefully to ensure that Tug didn't step on somebody's foot.

It was Harvest Day, the day when all the crops had been gathered and stored for the winter months ahead. After a hard month of harvesting, the Baron traditionally allowed his people a holiday. Every year, at this time, the travelling fair came to the castle and set up its booths and stalls. There were fire-eaters and jugglers, singers and storytellers. There were stalls where you could attempt to win prizes by throwing soft leather balls at pyramids made from bottle-shaped pieces of wood or by throwing hoops over squares. Will sometimes thought that the squares were perhaps just a little larger than the hoops that one was given to throw and he had never actually seen anyone win one of the prizes. But it was all fun and the Baron paid for it from his own purse.

Right now, however, Will was not concerned with the fair and its attractions. There would be time later in the day for that. At the moment, he was on his way to meet his former wardmates.

By tradition, all the Craftmasters gave their apprentices the day off on Harvest Day, even though they had taken no part in the actual harvest themselves. Will had been wondering for weeks whether or not Halt would conform to the practice. The Ranger seemed to take no notice of tradition and had his own way of doing things. But, two nights before, his anxiety had been settled. Halt had gruffly told him that he could have the holiday, adding that he would probably forget everything that he had learned in the past three months.

Those three months had been a time of constant practice with his bow and the knives that Halt had given him. Three months of stalking through the fields outside the castle, moving from one scant patch of cover to the next, trying to make his way unobserved by Halt's eagle eyes. Three months of riding and caring for Tug, of forming a special bond of friendship with the little pony.

That, he thought, had been the most enjoyable part of it all.

Now, he was ready for a holiday and ready to enjoy himself a little. Even the thought that Horace would be there couldn't dim the pleasure. Maybe, he thought, a few months' hard training in Battleschool had changed Horace's aggressive manner a little.

It was Jenny who had arranged the meeting for the holiday, encouraging the others to join her with the promise of a batch of fresh mince pies that she would bring from the kitchen. She was already one of Master Chubb's prize pupils and he boasted of her artistry to anyone who would listen — giving suitable emphasis to the vital role his training had played in developing her skill, of course.

Will's stomach grumbled with pleasure at the thought of those pies. He was starving, since he had intentionally gone without breakfast so as to leave room for them. Jenny's pies were already a byword in Castle Redmont.

He had arrived at the meeting point early, so he dismounted and led Tug into the shade of an apple tree. The little pony craned his head and looked wistfully at the apples on the branches, well out of his reach. Will grinned at him and scrambled quickly up the tree, picking an apple and handing it to the pony.

'That's all you get,' he said. 'You know what Halt says about eating too much.'

Tug shook his head impatiently. That was still a matter of disagreement between him and the Ranger. Will looked around. There was no sign of the others so he sat down in the shade of the tree, leaning his back against the knobby trunk to wait.

'Why, it's young Will, isn't it?' said a deep voice close behind him.

Will scrambled hastily to his feet and touched his forehead in a polite salute. It was Baron Arald himself, seated astride his giant battlehorse and accompanied by several of his senior knights.

'Yes, sir,' said Will nervously. He wasn't used to being addressed by the Baron. 'A happy Harvest Day to you, sir.'

The Baron nodded in acknowledgement and leaned forward, slouching comfortably in his saddle. Will had to crane his neck to look up at him.

'I must say, young man, you look quite the part there,' the Baron said. 'I hardly saw you in that grey Ranger cloak. Has Halt been teaching you all his tricks already?'

Will glanced down at the grey and green mottled cloak that he was wearing. Halt had given it to him some weeks ago. He'd shown Will how the grey and green mottling broke up the shape of the wearer and helped him blend into the landscape. It was one of the reasons, he'd said, why Rangers could move unseen with such ease.

'It's the cloak, sir,' Will said. 'Halt calls it camouflage.' The Baron nodded, obviously familiar with the term, which had been a new concept to Will.

'Just make sure you don't use it to steal more cakes,' he said with mock severity and Will shook his head hurriedly.

'Oh no, sir!' he said immediately. 'Halt told me that if I did anything like that he'd tan the skin off my backsi—' He stopped awkwardly. He wasn't sure if 'backside' was the sort of word you used in the presence of someone as exalted as a Baron.

The Baron nodded again, trying not to let a wide grin break through.

'I'm sure he did,' he said. 'And how are you getting on with Halt, Will? Are you enjoying learning to be a Ranger?'

Will paused. To be honest, he hadn't had time to think if he was enjoying himself or not. His days were too busy learning new skills, practising with bow and knives and working with Tug. This was the first time in three months he'd had a moment to actually think about it.

'I suppose so,' he said hesitantly, 'Only . . .' His voice trailed off and the Baron looked at him more closely.

'Only what?' he prompted.

Will shifted from one foot to the other, wishing that his mouth didn't continually get him into these situations by talking too much. Words had a way of emerging before he'd really had time to consider whether he wanted to say them or not.

'Only . . . Halt never smiles at all,' he went on awkwardly. 'He's always so serious about things.'

He had the impression that the Baron was suppressing another grin.

'Well,' said Baron Arald, 'being a Ranger is a serious business, you know. I'm sure Halt has impressed that on you.'

'All the time,' Will said ruefully and, this time, the Baron couldn't help smiling.

'Just pay attention to what he tells you, youngster,' he said. 'You're learning a very important job there.'

'Yes, sir.' Will was a little surprised to realise that he *did* agree with the Baron. Baron Arald reached forward to gather up his reins. On an impulse, before the nobleman could ride away, Will stepped forward.

'Excuse me, sir,' he said hesitantly and the Baron turned back to him.

'Yes, Will?' he asked.

Will shuffled his feet again, then went on. 'Sir, remember when our armies fought Morgarath?'

Baron Arald's cheerful face was clouded by a thoughtful frown. 'I'll not forget that in a hurry, boy,' he said. 'What about it?'

'Sir, Halt tells me that a Ranger showed the cavalry a secret way across the Slipsunder, so they were able to attack the enemy's rear . . .'

'That's true,' said Arald.

'I've been wondering, sir, what was the Ranger's name?' Will finished, feeling himself flush with his boldness.

'Didn't Halt tell you?' the Baron asked. Will shrugged his shoulders.

'He said names weren't important. He said supper was important, but not names.'

'But you think names are important, in spite of what your master has told you?' said the Baron, seeming to frown again. Will gulped and went on.

'I think it was Halt himself, sir,' he said. 'And I wondered why he hadn't been decorated or honoured for his skill.'

The Baron thought for a moment, then spoke again.

'Well, you're right, Will,' he said. 'It was Halt. And I wanted to honour him for it but he wouldn't allow me. He said that wasn't the Rangers' way.'

'But . . .' Will began in a perplexed tone but the Baron's upraised hand stopped him from speaking any further.

'You Rangers have your own ways, Will, as I'm sure you're learning. Sometimes other people don't understand them. Just listen to Halt and do as he does and I'm sure you'll have an honourable life ahead of you.'

'Yes, sir.' Will saluted again as the Baron slapped his reins lightly on his horse's neck and turned him away towards the fairground.

'Now enough of this,' said the Baron. 'We can't chatter

all day. I'm off to the fair. Maybe this year I'll get a hoop over one of those damned squares!'

The Baron started to ride away. Then a thought seemed to strike him and he reined in for a second.

'Will,' he called back.

'Yes, sir?'

'Don't tell Halt that I told you he led the cavalry. I don't want him angry at me.'

'Yes, sir,' said Will with a grin. As the Baron rode off, he settled back down to wait for his friends.

Sixteen

Jenny, Alyss and George arrived shortly after. As she had promised, Jenny was carrying a batch of fresh pies wrapped in a red cloth. She laid them carefully on the ground under the apple tree as the others crowded round. Even Alyss, usually so poised and dignified, seemed anxious to get her hands on one of Jenny's masterpieces.

'Come on!' George said. 'I'm starving!'

Jenny shook her head. 'We should wait for Horace,' she said, looking round for him but not seeing him in the passing crowds of people.

'Oh, come on,' George pleaded, 'I've been slaving over a hot petition to the Baron all morning!'

Alyss rolled her eyes to heaven. 'Perhaps we should start,' she said. 'Otherwise he'll begin a legal argument and we'll be here all day. We can always put a couple aside for Horace.'

Will grinned. George was a different kettle of fish now to the shy, stammering boy at the Choosing. Scribeschool obviously had caused him to bloom. Jenny served out two pies each, setting two aside for Horace.

'Let's get started then,' she said. The others eagerly tucked in and soon began to chorus their praise for the pies. Jenny's reputation was well founded.

'This,' said George, standing above them and spreading his arms wide as he addressed an imaginary court, 'cannot be described as a mere pie, your honour. To describe this as a pie would be a gross miscarriage of justice, the like of which this court has never seen before!'

Will turned to Alyss. 'How long has he been like this?' he asked.

She smiled. 'They all get this way with a few months' legal training. These days, the main problem with George is getting him to shut up.'

'Oh, sit down, George,' said Jenny, blushing at his praise but delighted none the less. 'You are a complete idiot.'

'Perhaps, my fair miss. But it is the sheer magic of these works of art that has turned my brain. These are not pies, these are symphonies!' He raised his remaining half pie to the others in a mock toast.

'I give you . . . Miss Jenny's symphony of pies!'

Alyss and Will, grinning at each other and at George, raised their own pies in response, and echoed the toast. Then all four apprentices burst out laughing.

It was a pity that Horace chose that precise moment to arrive. Alone among them, he was miserable in his new situation. The work was hard and unremitting and the discipline was unwavering. He had expected that, of course, and under normal circumstances he could have handled it. But being the focus for Bryn, Alda and Jerome's spite was making his life a nightmare — literally. The three second year cadets would rouse him from his bed at all hours of the night, dragging him out to perform the most humiliating and exhausting tasks.

The lack of sleep and the worry of never knowing when they might appear to torment him further was causing him to fall behind in his classroom work. His roommates, sensing that if they showed any sympathy for him they might become targets along with him, had cast him adrift, so that he felt totally alone in his misery. The one thing he had always aspired to was rapidly becoming ashes in his mouth. He hated Battleschool but he could see no way out of his predicament without embarrassing and humiliating himself even further.

Now, on the one day when he could escape from the restrictions and the tensions of Battleschool, he arrived to find his former wardmates already busy at their feast and he was angry and hurt that they hadn't bothered to wait for him. He had no idea that Jenny had set some of the pies aside for him. He assumed that she had divided them up already and that hurt more than anything. Of all of his former wardmates, she was the one he felt closest to. Jenny was always cheerful, always friendly, always willing to listen to another's troubles. He realised that he had been looking forward to seeing her again today and now he felt that she had let him down.

He was predisposed to think badly of the others. Alyss had always seemed to hold herself aloof from him, as if he weren't good enough for her, and Will had spent his time playing tricks on him then running away and climbing into that immense tree where Horace couldn't follow. At least, that was how Horace saw things in his current vulnerable state. He conveniently forgot the times he had cuffed Will over the ear, or held him in a headlock until the smaller boy was forced to cry 'Yield!'.

As for George, Horace had never taken much notice of him. The thin boy was studious and devoted to his books and Horace had always considered him a pallid, uninteresting person. Now here he was performing for them while they laughed and ate the pies and left nothing for him and suddenly he hated them all.

'Well, this is very nice, isn't it?' he said bitterly and they turned to him, the laughter dying on their faces. As was inevitable, Jenny was the first one to recover.

'Horace! You're here at last!' she said. She started towards him but the cold look on his face stopped her.

'At last?' he said. 'I'm a few minutes late and suddenly I'm here "at last"? And just too late because you've already pigged out on all the pies.'

Which was hardly fair to poor Jenny. Like most cooks, once she had prepared a meal, she had little interest in eating it. Her real pleasure lay in watching others enjoy the results of her work — and listening to their praise. Consequently, she hadn't had any of the pies. She turned back now to the two that she had covered in a napkin to keep for him.

'No, no,' she said quickly. 'There are still some left! Look!'

But Horace's pent-up anger prevented him from acting or speaking rationally. 'Well,' he said, in a voice heavy with sarcasm, 'maybe I ought to come back later and give you time to finish them as well.'

'Horace!' Tears sprang to Jenny's eyes. She had no idea

what was wrong with Horace. All she knew was that her plan for a pleasant reunion with her old wardmates was falling in ruins.

George stepped forward now, peering curiously at Horace. The tall, thin boy cocked his head to one side, to study the apprentice warrior more closely — as if he were an exhibit or a piece of evidence in a law court.

'There's no call to be so unpleasant,' he said reasonably. But reason wasn't what Horace wanted to hear. He shoved the other boy aside angrily.

'Get away from me,' he said. 'And mind how you talk to a warrior.'

'You're not a warrior yet,' Will told him scornfully. 'You're still only an apprentice like the rest of us.'

Jenny made a small gesture with her hands, urging Will to drop the matter. Horace, who was in the act of helping himself to the remaining pies, looked up slowly. He measured Will up and down for a second or two.

'Oho!' he said. 'I see the apprentice spy is with us today!' He looked to see if the others were laughing at his wit. They weren't and it only served to make him more unpleasant.

'I suppose Halt is teaching you to slink around, spying on everyone, is he?' Horace stepped forward, without waiting for an answer, and fingered Will's mottled cloak sarcastically.

'What's this? Didn't you have enough dye to make it all one colour?'

'It's a Ranger cloak,' Will said quietly, holding down the anger that was building inside him.

Horace snorted scornfully, cramming half of one of the

pies into his mouth and spraying crumbs as he did so.

'Don't be so unpleasant,' George said. Horace rounded on the apprentice scribe, his face red.

'Watch your tongue, boy!' he snapped. 'You're talking to a warrior, you know!'

'An apprentice warrior,' Will repeated firmly, laying stress on the word 'apprentice'.

Horace went redder and looked angrily between the two of them. Will tensed himself, sensing that the bigger boy was about to launch an attack. But there was something in Will's eyes and his ready stance that made Horace think twice about it. He had never seen that look of defiance before. In the past, if he'd threatened Will, he had always seen fear. This new-found confidence unsettled him a little.

Instead, he turned back to George and gave him a heavy shove in the chest.

'How's that for unpleasant?' he said as the tall, thin boy staggered back. George's arms windmilled as he tried to save himself from falling. Accidentally, he struck Tug a glancing blow on the side. The little pony, grazing peacefully, reared suddenly against his bridle.

'Steady, Tug,' Will said and Tug quietened immediately. But now Horace had noticed him for the first time. He stepped forward and looked more closely at the shaggy pony.

'What's this?' he asked in mock disbelief. 'Has someone brought a big ugly dog to the party?'

Will clenched his fists. 'He's my horse,' he said quietly. He could put up with Horace sneering at him but he wasn't going to stand by and see his horse insulted.

Horace let out a braying laugh.

'A horse?' he said. 'That's not a horse! In the Battleschool we ride real horses! Not shaggy dogs! Looks like he needs a good bath to me, too!' He wrinkled his nose and pretended to sniff closer to Tug.

The pony glanced sideways at Will. *Who is this unpleasant clod?* his eyes seemed to say. Then Will, carefully hiding the wicked grin that was trying to show on his face, said casually:

'He's a Ranger horse. Only a Ranger can ride him.'

Horace laughed again. 'My grandmother could ride that shaggy dog!'

'Maybe she could,' said Will, 'but I'll bet you can't.'

Before he'd even finished the challenge, Horace was untying the bridle. Tug looked at Will and the boy could have sworn the horse nodded slightly.

Horace swung himself easily up onto Tug's back. The pony stood, unmoving.

'Nothing to it!' Horace crowed. Then he dug his heels into Tug's sides. 'Come on, doggy! Let's have a run.'

Will saw the familiar, preparatory bunching of muscles in Tug's legs and body. Then the pony sprang into the air off all four feet, twisted violently, came down on his front legs and shot his hindquarters high into the air.

Horace flew like a bird for several seconds. Then he crashed flat on his back in the dust. George and Alyss looked on in delighted disbelief as the bully lay there for a second or two, stunned and winded. Jenny went to step forward to see if he was all right. Then her mouth set in a determined line and she stopped. Horace had asked for it, she thought.

There was a chance then, just a chance, that the whole incident might end there. But Will couldn't resist the temptation to have one last word.

'Maybe you'd better ask your grandmother if she'll teach you to ride,' he said, straight-faced. George and Alyss managed to hide their smiles but, unfortunately, it was Jenny who couldn't stop the small giggle that escaped her.

In an instant, Horace scrambled to his feet, his face dark with rage. He looked around, saw a fallen branch from the apple tree and grabbed it, brandishing it over his head as he rushed at Tug.

'I'll show you, and your damned horse!' he yelled furiously, swinging the stick wildly at Tug. The pony danced sideways out of harm's way and, before Horace could strike again, Will was on him.

He landed on Horace's back and his weight and the force of his leap drove them both to the ground. They rolled there, grappling with each other, each trying to gain an advantage. Tug, alarmed to see his master in danger, whinnied nervously and reared.

One of Horace's wildly flailing arms caught Will a ringing blow across the ear. Then Will managed to get his right arm free and punched Horace hard in the nose.

Blood ran down the bigger boy's face. Will's arms were hard and well muscled after his three months' training with Halt. But Horace was being taught in a hard school too. He drove a fist into Will's stomach and Will gasped as the air was driven out of him.

Horace scrambled to his feet but Will, in a move that Halt had shown him, swung his own legs in a wide arc, cutting Horace's feet from under him and sending him tumbling again.

Always strike first, Halt had dinned into his brain in the hours they'd spent practising unarmed combat. Now, as the other boy crashed to the ground again, Will dived upon him, trying to pin his arms beneath his knees.

Then Will felt an iron grip on the back of his collar and he was being hauled in the air, like a fish upon a hook, wriggling and protesting.

'What's going on here, you two hooligans?' said a loud, angry voice in his ear.

Will twisted around and realised that he was being held by Sir Rodney, the Battlemaster. And the big warrior looked extremely angry. Horace scrambled to his feet and stood at attention. Sir Rodney released Will's collar and the Ranger's apprentice dropped to the ground like a sack of potatoes. Then he too came to attention.

'Two apprentices,' said Sir Rodney angrily, 'brawling like hooligans and spoiling the holiday! And, to make things worse, one of them is my *own* apprentice!'

Will and Horace shuffled their feet, eyes down, unable to meet the Battlemaster's furious gaze.

'All right, Horace, what's going on here?'

Horace shuffled his feet again and went red. He didn't answer. Sir Rodney looked at Will.

'All right, you, the Ranger's boy! What's this all about?'

Will hesitated. 'Just a fight, sir,' he mumbled.

'I can see that!' the Battlemaster shouted. 'I'm not an idiot, you know!' He paused for a moment, waiting to see if either boy had anything further to add. They were both silent. Sir Rodney sighed in exasperation. Boys! If they weren't getting under your feet, they were fighting. And if they weren't fighting, they were stealing or breaking something.

'All right,' he said finally. 'The fight's over. Now shake hands and be done with it.' He paused and, as neither boy made a move to shake hands, roared in his parade ground voice:

'Get on with it!'

Galvanised into action, Will and Horace reluctantly shook hands. But as Will looked into Horace's eyes, he saw that the matter was far from settled.

We'll finish this another time, the angry look in Horace's eyes said.

Any time you like, the apprentice Ranger's eyes replied.

Seventeen

The first snowfall of winter lay thick on the ground as Will and Halt rode slowly home from the forest.

Six weeks had passed since the Harvest Day confrontation and the situation with Horace remained unresolved. There had been little chance for the two boys to resume the argument, as their respective masters kept them busy and their paths seldom crossed.

Will had seen the apprentice warrior occasionally, but always at a distance. They hadn't spoken or even had the chance to acknowledge each other's presence. But the ill feeling was still there, Will knew, and one day it would come to a head.

Strangely, he found that the prospect didn't disturb him nearly as much as it might have a few months ago. It was not that he looked forward to renewing the fight with Horace, but he found he could face the idea with a certain amount of equanimity. He felt a deep satisfaction when he recalled that good, solid punch he had landed on

Horace's nose. He also realised, with a slight sense of surprise, that the memory of the incident was made more enjoyable by the fact that it had happened in the presence of Jenny and — this was where the surprise lay — Alyss. Inconclusive as the event might have been, there was still a lot about it to set Will thinking and remembering.

But not right now, he realised, as Halt's angry tone dragged him back to the present.

'Could we possibly continue with our tracking, or did you have something more important to do?' he inquired. Instantly, Will cast around, trying to see what Halt had pointed out. As they rode through the crisp, white snow, their horses' hooves making only the smallest of sounds, Halt had been pointing to disturbances in the even white cover. They were tracks left by animals and it was Will's task to identify them. He had sharp eyes and a good mind for the task. He normally enjoyed these tracking lessons but now his attention had wandered and he had no idea where he was supposed to be looking.

'There,' Halt said, his tone leaving no doubt that he didn't expect to have to repeat such things, as he pointed to the left. Will stood in his stirrups to see the disturbed snow more clearly.

'Rabbit,' he said promptly. Halt turned to look sidelong at him.

'Rabbit?' he asked and Will looked again, correcting himself almost immediately.

'Rabbits,' he said, stressing the plural ending. Halt insisted on accuracy.

'I should think so,' Halt muttered at him. 'After all, if

they were Skandian tracks there, you'd need to be sure you knew how many there were.'

'I suppose so,' said Will, meekly.

'You suppose so!' Halt replied sarcastically. 'Believe me, Will, there's a big difference between knowing there's one Skandian about and knowing that there are half a dozen.'

Will nodded apologetically. One of the changes that had come over their relationship lately was the fact that Halt almost never referred to him as 'boy' anymore. These days, it was always 'Will'. Will liked that. It made him feel that somehow he'd been accepted by the grim-faced Ranger. All the same, he did wish that Halt would smile once or twice when he said it.

Or even once.

Halt's low voice snapped him out of his daydreaming.

'So . . . rabbits. Is that all?'

Will looked again. In the disturbed snow, difficult to see, but there now that Halt had pointed it out to him, was another set of tracks.

'A stoat!' he said triumphantly and Halt nodded again.

'A stoat,' he agreed. 'But you should have known there was something else there, Will. Look at how deep those rabbit tracks are. It's obvious that something had frightened them. When you see a sign like that, it's a hint to look for something extra.'

'I see,' said Will. But Halt shook his head.

'No. All too often, you don't see, because you don't maintain your concentration. You'll have to work on that.'

Will said nothing. He merely accepted the criticism. He'd learned by now that Halt didn't criticise without reason. And when there was reason, no amount of excuses could save him.

They rode on in silence. Will strained his eyes at the ground around them, looking for more tracks, more animal signs. They went another kilometre or so and were starting to see some of the familiar landmarks that told him he was close to their cottage when he saw something.

'Look!' he cried, pointing to a tumbled section of snow just off the path. 'What's that?'

Halt turned to look. The tracks, if they were tracks, were like no others that Will had seen so far. The Ranger urged his horse closer to the edge of the path and looked more closely.

'Hmmm,' he said thoughtfully. 'That's one I haven't shown you yet. Don't see too many of them these days, so take a good look, Will.'

He swung easily down from the saddle and walked through the knee-deep snow towards the disturbance. Will followed him.

'What is it?' the boy asked.

'Wild boar,' said Halt briefly. 'And a big one.'

Will glanced nervously around them. He mightn't know what a wild boar's tracks looked like in the snow but he knew enough about the creatures to know they were very, very dangerous.

Halt noticed the look and made a reassuring movement with his hand.

'Relax,' he said. 'He's nowhere near us.'

'Can you tell that from the tracks?' Will asked. He stared, fascinated, at the snow. The deep ruts and furrows had obviously been made by a very large animal. And it looked as if it were a very large, very *angry* animal.

'No,' said Halt evenly. 'I can tell it from our horses. If a boar that size were anywhere in the district, those two would be snuffing and pawing and whinnying so hard we wouldn't be able to hear ourselves think.'

'Oh,' said Will, feeling a little foolish. He relaxed the grip that he'd taken on his bow. However, in spite of the Ranger's assurances, he couldn't resist taking just one more look around behind them. And as he did so, his heart began pounding faster and faster.

The thick undergrowth on the other side of the track was moving, ever so slightly. Normally, he might have passed the movement off as due to the breeze, but his training with Halt had heightened his reasoning and his observation. At the moment, there was no breeze. Not the slightest breath.

But still, the bushes continued to move.

Will's hand went slowly to his quiver. Moving slowly, so as to avoid startling the creature in the bushes, he drew an arrow and placed it on the string of his bow.

'Halt?' He tried to keep his voice down but couldn't prevent it from quaking just a little. He wondered if his bow would stop a charging boar. He didn't think so.

Halt looked round, his gaze taking in the arrow nocked to Will's bowstring and noting the direction in which Will was looking.

'I hope you're not thinking of shooting the poor old farmer who's hiding behind those bushes,' he said seriously. Yet he pitched his voice so that it carried clearly across the track to the thick clump of bushes on the other side.

Instantly, there was a scuffle of movement from the bush and Will heard a nervous voice crying out:

'Don't shoot, good sir! Please, don't shoot! It's only me!'

The bushes parted as a dishevelled and frightened-looking old man hurriedly stood up and hurried forward. His haste was his undoing, however, as his foot caught in a tangle of underbrush and he sprawled forward onto the snow. He scrambled awkwardly to his feet, hands held out, palms first, to show that he carried no weapons. As he came, he continued a nonstop babble of words:

'Only me, sir! No need for shootin', sir! Only me, I swear, and I'm no danger to the likes of you!'

He hurried forward into the centre of the track, his eyes fixed on the bow in Will's hands and the gleaming, razor-sharp tip of the arrow. Slowly, Will released the tension on the string and lowered the bow as he took a closer look at the interloper. He was skinny in the extreme. Dressed in a ragged and dirty farmer's smock, he had long, awkward arms and legs and knobby elbows and knees. His beard was grey and matted and he was going bald on top of his head.

The man stopped a few metres from them and smiled nervously at the two cloaked figures.

'Only me,' he repeated, one last time.

Eighteen

Will couldn't help smiling to himself. Anything less like a ferocious, charging wild boar, he couldn't imagine.

'How did you know he was there?' he asked Halt in a soft voice. The Ranger shrugged.

'Saw him a few minutes ago. You'll learn eventually to sense when someone's watching you. Then you know to look for them.'

Will shook his head in admiration. Halt's powers of observation were uncanny. No wonder people at the castle held him in such awe!

'Now then,' Halt said sternly, 'why are you skulking there? Who told you to spy on us?'

The old man rubbed his hands nervously together, his eyes flicking from Halt's forbidding expression to the arrow tip, lowered now but still nocked to the string on Will's bow.

'Not spying, sir! No, no! Not spying. I heard you coming and thought you was that monster porker coming back!'

Halt's eyebrows drew together. 'You thought I was a wild boar?' he asked. Again, the farmer shook his head.

'No. No. No. No,' he gabbled. 'Leastways, not once I'd saw you! But then I wasn't sure who you might be. Could be bandits, like.'

'What are you doing here?' Halt asked. 'You're not a local, are you?'

The farmer, anxious to please, shook his head once again.

'Come from over Willowtree Creek, I do!' he said. 'Been trailing that porker and hoping to find someone as could turn him into bacon.'

Halt was suddenly vitally interested. He dropped the mock severe tone in which he had been talking.

'You've seen the boar, then?' he asked and the farmer rubbed his hands again and looked fearfully round, as if nervous that the 'porker' would appear from the trees any minute.

'Seen him. Heard him. Don't want to see him no more. He's a bad 'un, sir, mark my words.'

Halt glanced back at the tracks again.

'He's certainly a big one, anyway,' he mused.

'And evil, sir!' the farmer went on. 'That 'un has a real devil of a temper in him. Why, he'd as soon tear up a man or a horse as have his breakfast, he would!'

'So what did you have in mind for him?' Halt asked, then added, 'What's your name, by the way?'

The farmer bobbed his head and knuckled his forehead in salute.

'Peter, sir. Salt Peter, they calls me, on account of I likes a little salt on my meat, I do.'

Halt nodded. 'I'm sure you do,' he said patiently. 'But what were you hoping to do about this boar?'

Salt Peter scratched his head and looked a little lost. 'Don't rightly know. Hoped maybe I'd find a soldier or a warrior or a knight to get rid of him. Or maybe a Ranger,' he added as an afterthought.

Will grinned. Halt stood up from where he'd gone down on one knee to examine the tracks in the snow. He dusted a little snow from his knee and walked back to where Salt Peter stood, nervously shifting from one foot to another.

'Has he been causing a lot of trouble?' the Ranger asked and the old farmer nodded rapidly, several times.

'That he has, sir! That he has! Killed three dogs. Tore up fields and fences, he has. And as near as anything killed my son-in-law when he tried to stop him. Like I said, sir, he's a bad 'un!'

Halt rubbed his chin thoughtfully.

'Hmmm,' he said. 'Well, there's no question that we'd better do something about it.' He looked up at the sun, sitting low to the horizon in the western sky, then turned to Will. 'How much daylight would you say is left, Will?'

Will studied the position of the sun. These days, Halt never missed an opportunity to teach him or question him or test his knowledge and developing skills. He knew it was best to consider carefully before making an answer. Halt preferred accurate replies, not fast ones.

'A little over an hour?' Will said. He saw Halt's eyebrows draw together in a frown and remembered that the Ranger also disliked being answered with a question.

'Are you asking me, or telling me?' Halt said. Will shook his head, annoyed at himself.

'A little over an hour,' he replied more confidently and, this time, the Ranger nodded agreement.

'Correct.' He turned to the old farmer again. 'Very well, Salt Peter, I want you to take a message to Baron Arald.'

'Baron Arald?' the farmer asked nervously. Halt frowned again.

'See what you've done?' he said to Will. 'You've got him answering questions with questions now!'

'Sorry,' Will mumbled, grinning in spite of himself. Halt shook his head and continued speaking to Salt Peter.

'That's right, Baron Arald. You'll find his castle a couple of kilometres along this track.'

Salt Peter peered under one hand, looking along the track as if he could see the castle already. 'A castle, you say?' he said, in a wondering voice. 'I've never seen a castle!'

Halt sighed impatiently. Keeping this old chatterbox's mind on the subject was beginning to make him short-tempered. 'That's right, a castle. Now, go to the guard at the gate . . .'

'Is it a big castle?' asked the old fellow.

'It's a *huge* castle!' Halt roared at him. Salt Peter bounded back in fright. He had a hurt look on his face.

'No need to bellow, young man,' he said huffily. 'I were only asking, is all.'

'Well then, stop interrupting me,' said the Ranger. 'We're wasting time here. Now, are you listening?'

Salt Peter nodded.

'Good,' Halt continued. 'Go to the guard on the gate and say you have a message from Halt for Baron Arald.'

A look of recognition spread across the old man's face.

'Halt?' he asked. 'Not the Ranger Halt?'

'Yes,' replied Halt wearily. 'The Ranger Halt.'

'The one who led the ambush on Morgarath's Wargals?' asked Salt Peter.

'The same,' said Halt, in a dangerously low voice. Salt Peter looked around him.

'Well,' he said. 'Where is he?'

'I'm Halt!' the Ranger thundered at him, placing his face a few centimetres from Salt Peter's as he did so. Again, the old farmer recoiled a few steps. Then he gathered his courage and shook his head in disbelief.

'No, no, no,' he said definitely. 'You can't be him. Why, the Ranger Halt is as tall as two men — and as broad. A giant of a man, he is! Brave, fierce in battle, he is. You couldn't be him.'

Halt turned away, trying to regain his temper. Will couldn't help the smile breaking out on his face again.

'I . . . am . . . Halt,' said the Ranger, spacing his words out so that Salt Peter couldn't make any mistake. 'I was taller when I was young, and a lot broader. But now I'm this size.' He thrust his glittering eyes close to the farmer's and glared at him. 'Do you understand?'

'Well, if you say so . . .' said Salt Peter. He still didn't believe the Ranger but there was a very dangerous gleam in Halt's eyes that warned him it would not be wise to disagree any further.

'Good,' said Halt icily. 'Now, tell the Baron that Halt and Will . . .'

Salt Peter opened his mouth to ask another question. Halt clamped his hand over the old man's mouth immediately and pointed to where Will stood beside Tug.

'That's Will there.' Salt Peter nodded, his eyes wide over the hand that was clamped firmly over his mouth, stopping any further questions or interruptions. The Ranger continued:

'Tell him Halt and Will are tracking a wild boar. When we find its lair, we'll return to the castle. In the meantime, the Baron should gather his men for a hunt tomorrow morning.'

He slowly took his hand down from the farmer's mouth. 'Have you got all that?' the Ranger asked. Salt Peter nodded carefully. 'Then repeat it back to me,' Halt prompted.

'Go to the castle, tell the gate guard I have a message from you . . . Halt . . . for the Baron. Tell the Baron that you . . . Halt . . . and him . . . Will . . . are tracking a wild boar to find its lair. Tell him to have his men ready for a hunt tomorrow.'

'Good,' said Halt. He gestured to Will and the two of them swung back into their saddles. Salt Peter stood uncertainly on the track, looking up at them.

'Off you go,' said Halt, pointing in the direction of the castle. The old farmer went a few paces then, when he judged he was at a safe distance, he turned around and called back at the grim-faced Ranger:

'I don't believes you, you know! Nobody grows shorter and thinner!'

Halt sighed and turned his horse away into the forest.

Nineteen

They rode slowly through the failing light, leaning sideways in their saddles to follow the trail left by the boar.

They had no trouble tracking him. The huge body had left a deep trench in the thick snow. Even without the snow, Will thought, it would have been easy. The boar was obviously in a very bad temper. It had slashed at the surrounding trees and shrubs with its tusks as it went, leaving a clear-cut path of destruction through the forest.

'Halt?' he said tentatively, when they had gone a kilometre or so into the dense trees.

'Mmmm?' said Halt, a little absently.

'Why bother the Baron? Couldn't we simply kill the boar with our bows?'

Halt shook his head.

'He's a big one, Will. You can see the size of the trail he's left. We could take half a dozen arrows to kill him, and even then he'd take time to die. With a brute like this, it's better to make sure.'

'How do we do that?'

Halt looked up for a second. 'I suppose you've never seen a boar hunt?'

Will shook his head. Halt reined in for a few seconds to explain and Will brought Tug to a stop beside him.

'Well, first,' said the Ranger, 'we'll need dogs. That's another reason why we can't simply finish him off with our bows. When we find him, he'll have most likely gone to ground in a thicket or in dense bushes where we can't get at him. The dogs will drive him out and we'll have a ring of men around the lair with boar spears.'

'And they throw them at him?' Will asked. Halt shook his head.

'Not if they have any brains,' he said. 'The boar spear is more than two metres long, with a double-sided blade and a crosspiece set behind the blade. The idea is to make the boar charge at the spearman. Then he sets the butt of the spear in the ground and lets the boar run onto it. The crosspiece stops the boar running right down the shaft and getting the spearman.'

Will looked doubtful. 'That sounds dangerous.'

The Ranger nodded. 'It is. But men like the Baron and Sir Rodney and the other knights love it. They wouldn't miss the chance of a boar hunt for worlds.'

'What about you?' asked Will. 'Will you have a boar spear?'

Halt shook his head. 'I'll be sitting right here on Abelard,' he said. 'And you'll be on Tug, in case the boar breaks through the ring of men around him. Or in case he's just wounded and gets away.'

'What do we do if that happens?' Will asked.

'We run him down before he can go to ground again,' said Halt grimly. 'And *then* we kill him with our bows.'

The following day was a Saturday and, after breakfast, the Battleschool students were free to spend the day as they pleased. In Horace's case, this usually meant trying to stay out of sight whenever Alda, Bryn and Jerome came looking for him. But lately they'd realised he was avoiding them and had taken to waiting for him outside the mess hall. As he came out onto the parade ground this morning, he saw them waiting, smiling at him. He hesitated. It was too late to turn back. With a sinking heart, he continued on towards them.

'Horace!' He was startled by a voice coming from right behind him. He turned and saw Sir Rodney watching him, a curious look in his eyes as he glanced at the three second year cadets waiting in the yard. Horace wondered if the Battlemaster knew about the treatment he was getting. He assumed he did. Horace guessed it was part of the toughening process of Battleschool.

'Sir!' he replied, wondering what he'd done wrong. Rodney's features softened and he smiled at the young man. He seemed extraordinarily pleased about something.

'Relax, Horace. It's Saturday, after all. Ever been on a boar hunt?'

'Um . . . no, sir.' In spite of Sir Rodney's invitation to relax, he remained stiffly at attention.

'Time you did then. Draw a boar spear and hunting

knife from the armoury, have Ulf assign you a horse and report back here in twenty minutes.'

'Yes, sir,' Horace replied. Sir Rodney rubbed his hands together with evident pleasure.

'Seems Halt and his apprentice have scared us up a wild boar. Time we all had a bit of fun.' He grinned encouragingly at the apprentice, then strode away eagerly to get his own equipment ready. When Horace turned back to the yard, he noticed that Alda, Bryn and Jerome were nowhere to be seen. He might have thought more about why the three bullies would disappear when Sir Rodney was around, but he had too much on his mind, wondering what he'd be expected to do in a boar hunt.

It was midmorning by the time Halt led the hunting party to the boar's lair.

The huge animal had gone to ground in a dense clump of undergrowth deep inside the forest. Halt and Will had found the hiding place just before dark the previous evening.

Now, as they approached, Halt made a signal and the Baron and his hunters dismounted, leaving their horses in the care of one of the stable hands who had accompanied them. They covered the last few hundred metres on foot. Halt and Will were the only two who remained on horseback.

There were fifteen hunters in all, each one armed with a boar spear of the type Halt had described. They spread out in a wide circle as they came closer to the boar's lair. Will was a little surprised to recognise Horace as one of the hunting group. He was the only apprentice warrior in the party. All the others were knights.

With a hundred metres to go, Halt held up his hand, signalling the hunters to stop. He urged Abelard into a gentle trot and crossed to where Will sat nervously astride Tug. The little horse was moving restlessly as he scented the presence of the boar.

'Remember,' the Ranger said quietly to Will, 'if you have to shoot, aim for a spot just behind the left shoulder. A clean shot to the heart will be your only chance to stop him if he's charging.'

Will nodded, licking his dry lips nervously. He reached forward and comforted Tug with a quick pat on the neck. The little horse tossed his head in response to his master's touch.

'And stay close to the Baron,' Halt reminded him, before moving to resume his position on the opposite side of the circle of hunters.

Halt was in the position of most danger, accompanying the hunters who were least experienced — and therefore most likely to make a mistake. If the boar broke through the ring on his side, he would be responsible for chasing it down and killing it. He had assigned Will to stay with the Baron and the more experienced of the hunters, where there was less likely to be trouble. This placed him close to Horace as well. Sir Rodney had positioned the apprentice between himself and the Baron. After all, this was the boy's first hunt and the Battlemaster didn't want to take any undue risks. Horace was there to watch and learn. If the boar charged in their direction, he was to let the Baron or Sir Rodney take care of it.

Horace glanced up once, making eye contact with Will. There was no animosity in the look. In fact, he gave the Ranger's apprentice a strained half smile. Will realised, watching Horace lick his lips over and over again, that the other boy was every bit as nervous as he was himself.

Halt signalled again and the circle began closing in on the thicket. As the circle became smaller, Will lost sight of his teacher and the other men on the far side of the boar's lair. He knew, from Tug's continued nervousness, that the boar must be inside the bushes still. But Tug was well trained and continued to move in as his rider urged him gently forward.

A deep roaring sound came from inside the thicket and Will's hair stood on end. He'd never heard the cry of an angry wild boar before. The noise was halfway between a grunt and a scream and, for a moment, the hunters hesitated.

'He's in there all right!' called the Baron, grinning at Will with excitement. 'Let's hope he comes out on our side, eh, boys?'

Will wasn't at all sure that he wanted the boar to come charging out on their side of the thicket. He thought that he'd like it very well if it went the other way.

But the Baron and Sir Rodney were both grinning like schoolboys as they readied their boar spears. They were enjoying this, just as Halt had said they would. Quickly, Will unslung his bow from across his shoulders and fitted an arrow to the string. He fingered the tip for a moment, making sure it was still razor-sharp. His throat was dry. He wasn't sure that he would be able to talk if anyone spoke to him.

The dogs plunged against their restraining leashes, setting the echoes awake in the forest with their excited baying. It was their noise that had aroused the boar. Now, as they continued to give voice, Will could hear the huge animal slashing and cutting at the trees and shrubs in its lair with its long tusks.

The Baron turned to Bert, his dog handler, and made a hand signal for the hounds to be released.

The big, powerful animals were gone almost instantly, flashing across the cleared space to the thicket and disappearing inside. They were savage, heavily built beasts, bred specifically for the purpose of hunting boar.

The noise from the thicket was indescribable. The furious baying of the dogs was joined by the blood-chilling screams of the angry boar. There was a crashing and snapping of bushes and young saplings. The very thicket seemed to shake.

Then, suddenly, the boar was in the clear.

He came out halfway round the circle, between the points where Will and Halt were stationed. With an infuriated scream, he threw off one of the dogs that still clung to him, paused a moment, then charged at the hunters with blinding speed.

The young knight directly in front of the boar's charge didn't hesitate. He dropped to one knee, bracing the butt end of his spear into the ground and presenting the gleaming point to the charging animal.

The boar had no chance to turn. His own rush carried him onto the spear head. He plunged upwards, screaming in pain and fury, trying to dislodge the killing piece of steel. But the young knight held grimly to the spear, holding it firmly against the ground and giving the enraged animal no chance to throw it free.

Will watched with wide-eyed alarm as the stout ash shaft of the spear bent like a bow under the weight of the boar's rush, then the carefully sharpened tip penetrated to the animal's heart and it was all over.

With one last screaming roar, the huge boar toppled sideways and lay dead.

The matted body was almost as large as a horse's and every inch was solid muscle. The tusks, harmless now in death, curved back over his ferocious snout. They were stained with the earth that he'd ripped up in his fury, and with the blood of at least one of the dogs.

Will looked at the massive body and shuddered. If this was a wild boar, he thought, he wasn't in any hurry to see another one.

Twenty

The other hunters crowded round the young knight who had made the kill, congratulating him and patting his back. Baron Arald started across towards him, but paused beside Tug, looking up to Will as he spoke.

'You won't see another that size in a long time, Will,' he said gruffly. 'Pity he didn't come our way. I would have liked a trophy like that for myself.' He continued on his way towards Sir Rodney, who was already with the group of warriors around the dead boar.

Consequently, Will found himself, for the first time in some weeks, face to face with Horace. There was an awkward pause, with neither boy willing to make the first move. Horace, excited by the events of the morning, his heart still pounding with the thrill of fear he'd felt when the boar first appeared, wanted to share the moment with Will. In the light of what they had just seen, their childish squabble seemed unimportant, and now he felt badly about his behaviour on that day six weeks ago. But he couldn't find the words to express his feelings and he saw no encouragement to do so in Will's set features, so with a slight shrug, he started to step past Tug to go and congratulate the young hunter. As he did so, the pony stiffened and pricked his ears, giving a warning neigh.

Will looked back at the thicket and his blood seemed to freeze in his veins.

There, standing just outside the shelter of the bushes, was another boar — even larger than the one which now lay dead in the snow.

'Look out!' he cried, as the huge beast slashed at the earth with its tusks.

It was a bad situation. The line of hunters had broken up, most of them having moved over to marvel at the size of the dead boar and to praise its killer. Only Will and Horace remained in the path of the second boar — mainly, Will realised, because Horace had hesitated for those few vital seconds.

Horace spun round at Will's shout. He looked at Will, then swung to look at the new danger. The boar lowered his head, tore at the ground again and charged. It all happened with terrifying speed. One moment the huge animal was ripping the ground with its tusks. The next, it was hurtling towards them. Placing himself between Will and the boar, Horace turned without hesitation to face it, setting his spear as Sir Rodney and the Baron had showed him.

But, as he did so, his foot slipped on an icy patch in the snow and he sprawled helplessly onto his side, the long spear falling from his grasp.

There was not a second to lose. Horace lay helpless before

those murderous tusks. Will kicked his feet clear of the stirrups and dropped to the ground, sighting and drawing back the bowstring even as he did so. He knew his small bow would have no chance of stopping the boar's maddened rush. All he could hope to do was to distract the maddened animal, to turn it away from the helpless boy on the ground.

He fired and instantly ran to one side, away from the fallen apprentice. He yelled at the top of his lungs and fired again.

The arrows stuck out of the boar's thick hide like needles in a pin cushion. They did it no serious harm, but the pain of them burnt through the animal like a hot knife. Its red, angry eyes fastened on the small, capering figure to one side and, furiously, it swung after Will.

There was no time to fire again. Horace was safe for the moment. Now Will himself was in danger. He sprinted for the shelter of a tree and ducked behind it, just in time!

The boar's enraged charge carried it straight into the trunk of the tree. Its huge body crashed against the trunk, shaking it to its roots, sending showers of snow cascading out of its upper branches.

Amazingly, the boar seemed unaffected by the crash. It backed up a few paces and charged at Will again. The boy darted round the tree trunk again, narrowly avoiding the slashing tusks as the boar thundered by.

Screaming in fury, the huge animal spun in its tracks, skidding in the snow, and came at him again. This time, it came more slowly, giving Will no chance to dart to one side at the last moment. The boar came at a trot, fury in its red eyes, tusks slashing from side to side, its hot breath steaming in the freezing winter air.

Behind him, Will could hear the shouts of the hunters but he knew they'd arrive too late to help him. He nocked another arrow, knowing that he had no chance of hitting a vital spot as the pig came at him head on.

Then there was a thud of muffled hooves on the snow and a small, shaggy shape was driving towards the furious monster.

'No, Tug!' Will screamed, in an agony of fear for his horse. But the pony charged at the huge boar, spinning in his tracks and lashing out with his rear hooves as he came within range. Tug's rear hooves caught the pig in the ribs and, with all the force of the pony's upper legs behind it, sent the boar rolling sideways in the snow.

The boar was up in an instant, even more furious than before. The pony had caught him off balance but the kick had done no serious damage. Now, the boar slashed and cut at Tug as the little pony neighed in fear and danced sideways out of the reach of those razor-sharp tusks.

'Tug! Get clear!' Will screamed again. His heart was in his throat. If those tusks caught the vulnerable tendons in the horse's lower legs, Tug would be crippled for life. He couldn't stand by and watch his horse put himself in such peril for his master. He drew and fired again and, dragging the long Ranger knife from his belt, charged across the snow at the huge, furious beast.

The third arrow struck the pig in the side. Again, he had missed a vulnerable spot and only wounded the monster. He yelled at it as he ran, screaming for Tug to get clear. The boar saw him coming, recognising the small figure that had first driven it to such fury. Its red, hate-filled eyes fastened upon him and its head lowered for a final, killing charge.

Will saw the muscles bunch in the massive hindquarters. He was too far from cover to run. He'd have to face the charge here in the open. He dropped to one knee and, hopelessly, held out the keen-bladed Ranger knife in front of him as the boar charged. Dimly, he heard Horace's hoarse cry as the apprentice warrior charged forward to help him, his spear at the ready.

Then a deep, whistling hiss cut across the sound of the boar's hooves, followed by a solid, meaty SMACK! The boar reared up in mid-stride, twisting in sudden agony, and fell, dead as a stone, in the snow.

Halt's long, heavy-shafted arrow was almost buried in its side, driven there by the full power of the Ranger's mighty longbow. He'd struck the charging monster right behind the left shoulder, driving the head of the arrow into and through the pig's massive heart.

A perfect shot.

Halt reined in Abelard in a shower of snow and hurled himself to the ground, throwing his arms around the shaking boy. Will, overcome with relief, buried his face into the rough cloth of the Ranger's cloak. He didn't want anyone to see the tears that were streaming down his face.

Gently, Halt took the knife from Will's hand.

'What on earth were you hoping to do with this?' he asked.

Will simply shook his head. He couldn't speak. He felt Tug's soft muzzle butting gently against him and looked up into the big, intelligent eyes.

Then it was all noise and confusion as the hunters

gathered around, marvelling at the size of the second boar and slapping Will on the back for his courage. He stood among them, a small figure, ashamed still of the tears that slid down his cheeks, no matter how hard he tried to stop them.

'They're cunning brutes,' said Sir Rodney, nudging the dead boar with his boot. 'We all assumed there was only one because they never left the lair together.'

Will felt a hand on his shoulder and turned to find he was looking into Horace's eyes – and the apprentice warrior was shaking his head slowly in admiration and disbelief.

'You saved my life,' he said. 'That was the bravest thing I've ever seen.'

Will tried to shrug the other boy's thanks aside but Horace pressed on. He remembered all the times in the past when he'd teased Will, when he'd bullied him. Now, acting instinctively, the smaller boy had saved him from those murderous, slashing tusks. It said something for Horace's growing maturity that he had forgotten his own instinctive action, when he had placed himself between the charging boar and the apprentice Ranger.

'But why, Will? After all, we . . .' He couldn't bring himself to finish the statement, but Will somehow knew what was in his mind.

'Horace, we may have fought in the past,' he said. 'But I don't hate you. I never hated you.'

Horace nodded once, a look of understanding coming over his face. Then he seemed to come to a decision. 'I owe you my life, Will,' he said in a determined voice. 'I'll never forget that debt. If ever you need a friend, if ever you need help, you can call on me.'

The two boys faced each other for a moment, then Horace thrust out his hand and Will took it. The circle of knights around them was silent, witnessing, but not wanting to interrupt, this important moment for the two boys. Then Baron Arald stepped forward and put his arms around them both, one either side of him.

'Well said both of you!' he said heartily and the knights chorused their assent.

The Baron grinned delightedly. It had been a perfect morning, all told. A bit of excitement. Two huge boars killed. And now two of his wards forging the sort of special bond that only came from shared danger.

'We've got two fine young men here!' he said to the group at large, and again there was that hearty chorus of assent. 'Halt, Rodney, you can both be proud of your apprentices!'

'Indeed we are, my lord,' Sir Rodney replied. He nodded approvingly at Horace. He'd seen the way the boy had turned without hesitation to face the charge. And he approved of Horace's open offer of friendship to Will. He remembered all too well seeing them fighting on Harvest Day. It seemed such childish squabbles were behind them now and he felt a deep satisfaction that he had chosen Horace for Battleschool.

Halt, for his part, said nothing. But when Will turned to look at his mentor, the grizzled Ranger met his eye, and simply nodded.

And that, Will knew, was the equivalent of three hearty cheers from Halt.

Twenty-one

In the days following the boar hunt, Will noticed a change in the way he was treated. There was a certain deference, even respect, in the way people spoke to him and looked at him as he passed. It was most noticeable among the people of the village. Being simple folk, with rather limited boundaries to their day-to-day lives, they tended to glamorise and exaggerate any event that was in any way out of the ordinary.

By the end of the first week, the events of the hunt had been so blown out of proportion that they had Will single-handedly killing both boars as they charged out of the thicket. A couple of days after that, to hear the story related, you could almost believe that he had accomplished the feat with one arrow, firing it clean through the first boar and into the heart of the second.

'I really didn't do too much at all,' he said to Halt one evening, as they sat by the fire in the warm little cottage they shared on the edge of the forest. 'I mean, it's not as if

I thought it through and decided to do it. It just sort of happened. And after all, you killed the boar, not me.'

Halt merely nodded, staring fixedly at the leaping yellow flames in the grate.

'People will think what they want to,' he said quietly. 'Never take too much notice of it.'

Nevertheless, Will was troubled by the adulation. He felt people were making too big a thing out of it all. He would have enjoyed the respect if it had been based on what had actually happened. In his heart, he felt he had done something worthwhile, and perhaps even honourable. But he was being lionised for a totally fictional account of events and, being an essentially honest person, he couldn't really take any pride in that.

He also felt a little embarrassed because he was one of the few people who had noticed Horace's original, instinctively courageous action, placing himself between the charging boar and Will and Tug. Will had mentioned this last fact to Halt. He felt that perhaps the Ranger might have an opportunity to appraise Sir Rodney of Horace's unselfish action, but his teacher had merely nodded and said briefly:

'Sir Rodney knows. He doesn't miss much. He's got a little more up top than the average bash and whacker.'

And with that, Will had to be content.

Around the castle, with the knights from the Battleschool and the various Craftmasters and apprentices, the attitudes were different. There, Will enjoyed a simple acceptance, and the recognition of the fact that he had done well. He noticed that people tended to know his name now, so that they greeted him as well as Halt when the two of them had business in the castle grounds. The Baron himself was friendlier than ever. It was a source of pride to him to see one of his castle wards acquit himself well.

The one person Will would have liked to discuss it all with was Horace himself. But as their paths seldom crossed, the opportunity hadn't arisen. He wanted to make sure that the warrior apprentice knew that Will set no store by the ridiculous stories that had swept the village, and he hoped that his former wardmate knew he had done nothing to spread the rumours.

In the meantime, Will's lessons and training proceeded at an accelerated pace. In a month's time, Halt had told him, they would be leaving for the Gathering — an annual event in the Rangers' calendar.

This was the time when all fifty Rangers came together to exchange news, to discuss any problems that might have arisen throughout the Kingdom and to make plans. Of greater importance to Will, it was also the time when apprentices were assessed, to see if they were fit to progress to the next year of their training. It was bad luck for Will that he had been in training for only seven months. If he didn't pass the assessment at this year's Gathering, he would have to wait another year, until the next opportunity arose. As a result, he practised and practised from dawn till dusk each day. The idea of a Saturday holiday was a long forgotten luxury to him. He fired arrow after arrow into targets of different sizes, in different conditions, from standing, kneeling, sitting positions. He even fired from hidden positions in trees.

And he practised with his knives. Standing to throw, kneeling, sitting, diving to the left, diving to the right. He practised throwing the larger of the two knives so that it struck its target hilt first. After all, as Halt said, sometimes you only needed to stun the person you were throwing at, so it was a good idea to know how to do it.

He practised his stealth skills, learning to stay stock-still even when he was sure that he had been discovered and learning that, all too often, people simply didn't notice him until he actually did move and gave the game away. He learned the trick that searchers would use, letting their gaze pass over a spot and then flicking back to it instantly to catch any slight movement. He learned about sweepers — the rear scouts who would follow silently behind a party on the move to catch out anyone who might have remained unseen, then broken cover when the party had gone past.

He worked with Tug, strengthening the bond and affection that had taken root so quickly between the two of them. He learned to use the little horse's extra senses of smell and hearing to give him warning of any danger and he learned the signals that the horse was trained to send to its rider.

So it was little wonder that, at the end of the day, Will had no inclination to walk up the winding path that led to Castle Redmont and find Horace so that he could discuss things with him. He accepted that, sooner or later, the chance would come. In the meantime, he could only hope that Horace was being given credit for his actions by Sir Rodney and the other members of the Battleschool.

Unfortunately for Horace, it seemed that nothing could be further than the truth.

Sir Rodney was puzzled by the muscular young apprentice. He seemed to have all the qualities that the Battleschool was looking for. He was brave. He followed orders immediately and he was still showing extraordinary skill in his weapons training. But his class work was below standard. Assignments were handed in late or sloppily finished. He seemed to have trouble paying attention to his instructors — as if he were distracted all the time. On top of that, it was suspected that he had a predilection for fighting. None of the staff had ever witnessed him fighting, but he was often seen to be sporting bruises and minor contusions, and he seemed to have made no close friends among his classmates. On the contrary, they took pains to steer clear of him. It all served to create a picture of an argumentative, anti-social, lazy recruit who had a certain amount of skill at arms.

All things considered, and with a great deal of reluctance, the Battlemaster was beginning to feel that he would have to expel Horace from Battleschool. All the evidence seemed to point in that direction. Yet his instincts told him he was wrong. That there was some other factor he wasn't aware of.

In point of fact, there were three other factors: Alda, Bryn and Jerome. And even as the Battlemaster was considering the future of his newest recruit, they had Horace surrounded once more.

It seemed that each time Horace managed to find a place where he could escape their attentions, the three older students tracked him down. Of course, this wasn't difficult for them, as they had a network of spies and informants among the other younger boys who were afraid of them, both in and outside the Battleschool. This time, they had cornered Horace behind the armoury, in a quiet spot that he had discovered a few days before. He was hemmed in against the stone wall of the armoury building, the three bullies standing in a half circle before him. Each of them carried a thick cane and Alda had a piece of heavy sacking folded over one arm.

'We've been looking for you, Baby,' said Alda. Horace said nothing. His eyes shifted from one to the other, as he wondered which of them would be the first to make a move.

'Baby's made a fool of us,' Bryn said.

'Made a fool of the entire Battleschool.' That was Jerome. Horace frowned, puzzled by their words. He had no idea what they were talking about. Alda's next statement made it clear.

'Baby had to be rescued from the big, bad boar,' he said.

'By a little, creeping apprentice sneaker,' Bryn added, the sneer heavy in his tone.

'And that makes us all look bad.' Jerome shoved him against the shoulder as he spoke, pushing him back against the rough stone of the wall. His face was red and angry and Horace knew he was building himself up for something. His hands bunched into fists at his side. Jerome saw the action.

'Don't threaten me, Baby! Time you learned a lesson.' He stepped forward threateningly. Horace turned to face him and, in the same instant, knew he had made a mistake. Jerome's move was a feint. The real attack came from Alda, who whipped a heavy hessian sack over

Horace's head before he could resist, pulling a drawcord tight so that he was contained from the waist up, blinded and helpless.

He felt several loops of the drawcord falling over his shoulders to fasten it, then the blows began.

He staggered blindly, helpless to defend himself as the three boys rained blows down on him from the heavy canes they had been carrying. He blundered into the wall and fell, unable to break his fall with his arms immobilised by his side. The blows continued, falling on his unprotected head, his arms and his legs as the three boys continued their mindless litany of hate.

'Call for the sneaker to save you now, Baby.'

'This is for making us all look like fools.'

'Learn respect for your Battleschool, Baby.'

On and on it went as he writhed on the ground, trying in vain to escape the blows. It was the worst beating they had ever given him and they continued until, gradually, mercifully, he fell still, semi-conscious. They each hit him a few more times, then Alda dragged the sack clear. Horace drew in one giant shuddering breath of fresh air. He ached and hurt viciously in every part of his body. From a long distance away, he heard Bryn's voice.

'Now let's teach the sneaker the same lesson.' The others laughed and he heard them moving away. He groaned softly, longing for the release of unconsciousness, wanting to let himself sink into its dark, welcoming arms so that the pain would go away, at least for a while.

Then the full import of Bryn's words struck him. They were going to give the same treatment to Will — for the ridiculous reason that they felt his action in saving Horace had somehow belittled them and their Battleschool. With a gigantic effort, he pushed the welcoming folds of darkness back and struggled to his feet, moaning with the pain, chest heaving, head spinning, as he supported himself against the wall. He remembered his promise to Will: *If you ever need a friend, you can call on me.*

It was time to make good on the promise.

Twenty-two

Will was in the open meadow behind Halt's cottage, practising. He had four targets set up at different ranges and was alternating his shots at random between the four of them, never firing at the same one twice in a row. Halt had set the exercise for him before he had gone to the Baron's office to discuss a despatch that had come in from the King.

'If you fire twice at the same target,' he had said, 'you'll begin to rely on the first shot to determine your direction and elevation. That way, you'll never learn to shoot instinctively. You'll always need to fire a sighting shot first.'

Will knew his teacher was right. But that didn't make the exercise any easier. To add to the difficulty, Halt had stipulated that he should let no more than five seconds elapse between each shot.

Frowning in concentration, he let the last five arrows of a set go. One after the other, in rapid succession, they flashed across the meadow, thudding into the targets. Will, his quiver empty for the tenth time that morning, stopped to survey the results. He nodded in satisfaction. Every arrow had hit a target, and most of them were clustered in the inner ring or the bullseye itself. It was shooting of an exceptionally high quality and it proved to him the value of constant practice. He wasn't to know it, of course, but there were already few archers in the Kingdom, outside of the Ranger Corps, who could have matched him. Even the archers in the King's army weren't trained to shoot with such individual speed and accuracy. They were trained to fire as a group, sending a mass of arrows against an attacking force. As a result, their training concentrated more on co-ordinated actions, so that all arrows were fired simultaneously.

He had just set the bow down, preparatory to recovering his arrows, when the sound of a footstep behind him made him turn. He was a little surprised to see three Battleschool apprentices watching him, their red surcoats marking them as second year trainees. He didn't recognise any of them, but he nodded a friendly greeting.

'Good morning,' he said. 'What brings you down here?'

It was unusual to find Battleschool apprentices this far from the castle. He noted the thick canes that they all carried and decided they must have set out for a walk. The closest of them, a handsome, blond-haired boy, smiled and said:

'We're looking for the Ranger's apprentice.'

Will couldn't help smiling in return. After all, the Ranger cloak that he wore marked him unmistakably as an apprentice Ranger. But perhaps the Battleschool apprentice was only being polite.

'Well, you've found him,' he said. 'What can I do for you?'

'We've brought a message from the Battleschool for you,' the boy replied.

Like all Battleschool trainees, he was tall and well muscled, as were his companions. They moved closer to him now and Will instinctively backed off a pace. They were a little too close, he felt. Closer than they needed to be to pass on a message.

'It's about what happened at the boar hunt,' said one of the others. This one was red-haired, with a heavy dusting of freckles, and a nose that showed distinct signs of having been broken — probably in one of the training combats that Battleschool students were always practising. Will shrugged uncomfortably. There was something in the air he didn't like. The blond boy was smiling still. But neither the redhead nor their third companion, an olive-skinned boy who was the tallest of the three, looked as if they thought there was anything to smile about.

'You know,' Will said, 'people are talking a lot of nonsense about that. I didn't do much.'

'We know,' the red-haired boy snapped angrily, and again Will took a pace back as they all moved a little closer. Halt's training was ringing alarm bells in his mind now. *Never let people get too close to you*, he'd been told. *If they try to, be on your guard, no matter who they are or how friendly you think they are.*

'But when you go swanking around telling everyone you saved a big, clumsy Battleschool apprentice, you make us look foolish,' the tall boy accused. Will looked at him, frowning.

'I never said that!' he protested. 'I . . .'

And at that moment, while he was distracted by Bryn, Alda made his move, stepping quickly forward with the sack held open to throw it over Will's head. It was the same tactic they had used so successfully with Horace, but Will was already on his guard and, as the other boy moved, he sensed the attack and reacted.

Unexpectedly, he dived forward towards Alda, rolling in a somersault that took him under the sack, then letting his legs sweep round, scything Alda's legs from under him so that the bigger boy was sent sprawling on the grass. But there were three of them and that was too many for him to keep track of. He'd evaded Alda and Bryn but as he rolled to his feet, completing the movement, Jerome brought his cane round in a ringing crack across the back of his shoulders.

With a cry of pain and shock, Will staggered forward, as Bryn now brought his cane round and hit him across the side. By then, Alda had regained his feet, furious with the way Will had evaded him, and he struck Will across the point of the shoulder.

The pain was excruciating and, with a sob of agony, Will dropped to his knees.

Instantly, the three Battleschool apprentices crowded forward, ringing him, trapping him between them, the heavy canes raised to continue the beating.

'That's enough!'

The unexpected voice stopped them. Will, crouched on the ground, waiting for the beating to begin, arms over his head, looked up and saw Horace, bruised and battered, standing a few metres away. He held one of the wooden

Battleschool drill swords in his right hand. One eye was blackened and there was a trickle of blood running from his lip. But in his eyes there was a look of hatred and sheer determination that, for a moment, made the three older boys hesitate. Then they realised that there were three of them and Horace's sword was, after all, no more of a weapon than the canes they carried. Forgetting Will for the moment, they fanned out and moved to encircle Horace, the heavy canes raised to strike.

'Baby followed us,' said Alda.

'Baby wants another beating,' Jerome agreed.

'And Baby's going to get it,' said Bryn, smiling confidently. But then a yell of fright was torn from his lips as a sudden, jarring force slammed against the cane, whipping it from his grasp and sending it spinning to land several metres away.

A similar yell to his right told him that the same thing had happened to Jerome.

Confused, Bryn looked around to where the two canes lay. With a sinking feeling, he saw that each one was transfixed by a black-shafted arrow.

'I think one at a time is fairer, don't you?' said Halt.

Bryn and Jerome felt a surge of terror as they looked up to see the grim-faced Ranger standing in the shadows ten metres away, another arrow already nocked to the string of his massive longbow.

Only Alda showed any sign of rebellion. 'This is Battleschool business, Ranger,' he said, trying to bluster his way through the situation. 'You'd best stay out of it.'

Will, slowly regaining his feet, saw the dark anger that burned deep in Halt's eyes at the arrogant words. For a moment, he almost felt sorry for Alda, then he felt the throbbing pain in his back and shoulders and any thoughts of sympathy were instantly blotted out.

'Battleschool business, is it, sonny?' Halt said in a dangerously low voice. He moved forward, covering the ground between him and Alda in a few deceptively swift, gliding steps. Before Alda knew it, Halt was barely a metre away. Still, the apprentice remained defiant. The dark look on Halt's face was unsettling, but seen close to, Alda realised that he was a good head taller than the Ranger and his confidence flowed back. All these years he had been nervous of the mysterious man who now stood before him. He had never realised what a puny figure he really was.

Which was Alda's second mistake of the day. Halt was small. But puny was not a word that entered into it. In addition, Halt had spent a lifetime fighting far more dangerous adversaries than a second year Battleschool apprentice.

'I seem to notice that there was a Ranger apprentice being attacked,' Halt was saying softly. 'I think that makes it Rangers' business as well, don't you?'

Alda shrugged, confident now that, whatever the Ranger might do, he could more than handle it.

'Make it your business if you like,' he said, a sneer entering his voice. 'I really don't care one way or the other.'

Halt nodded several times as he digested that speech. Then he replied. 'Well then, I think I *will* make it my business — but I won't be needing this.'

As he said it, he replaced the arrow in his quiver and lightly tossed the bow to one side, turning away as he did so. Inadvertently, Alda's eyes followed the action and instantly he felt a searing pain as Halt stamped backwards with the edge of his boot, catching the apprentice's foot between arch and ankle and driving into it. As Alda doubled over to clasp his injured foot, the Ranger pivoted on his left heel and his right elbow slammed upwards into Alda's nose, jerking him upright again and sending him staggering back, eyes streaming with the pain. For a second or two, Alda's sight was blurred by the reflex tears and he felt a slight pricking sensation under his chin. As his eyes cleared, he found the Ranger's eyes were only a few centimetres from his own. There was no anger there. Instead, there was a look of utter contempt and disregard that was somehow far more frightening.

The pricking sensation became a little more pronounced and, as he tried to look down, Alda gave a gasp of fear. Halt's larger knife, razor edged and needle pointed, was just under his chin, pressing lightly into the soft flesh of his throat.

'Don't *ever* talk to me like that again, boy,' the Ranger said, so softly that Alda had to strain to hear the words. 'And don't ever lay a hand on my apprentice again. Understand?'

Alda, all his arrogance gone, his heart pounding in terror, could say nothing. The knife pricked a little harder against his throat and he felt a warm trickle of blood sliding down under his collar. Halt's eyes blazed suddenly, like the coals of a fire in a sudden draught.

'Understand?' he repeated and Alda croaked a reply.

'Yes . . . sir.'

Halt stepped back, re-sheathing the knife in one fluid movement. Alda sank to the ground, massaging his injured ankle. He was sure there was damage to the tendons. Ignoring him, Halt turned to face the other two second year apprentices. Instinctively, they had moved closer together and were watching him fearfully, uncertain as to what he was going to do next. Halt pointed to Bryn.

'You,' he said, his words edged with contempt, 'pick up your cane.'

Fearfully, Bryn moved to where his cane lay on the ground, Halt's arrow still embedded halfway along its length. Without taking his eyes off the Ranger, fearing some trick, he stooped at the knees, his hand scrabbling on the grass until it touched the cane. Then he stood again, holding it uncertainly in his left hand.

'Now give me back my arrow,' the Ranger ordered and the tall, swarthy boy struggled to remove the arrow, stepping close enough to hand it to Halt, tensed in every muscle as he waited for some unexpected move from the Ranger. Halt, however, merely took the arrow and replaced it in his quiver. Brynn stepped hurriedly back out of reach. Halt gave a small, contemptuous laugh. Then he turned to Horace.

'I take it these are the three who gave you those bruises?' he asked. Horace said nothing for a moment, then realised that his continued silence was ridiculous. There was no reason why he should shield the three bullies any further. There never had been a reason.

'Yes, sir,' he said decisively. Halt nodded, rubbing his chin.

'I rather thought so,' he said. 'Well then, I've heard rumours that you're pretty good with a sword. How about a practice bout with this hero in front of me?'

A slow grin spread over Horace's face as he understood what the Ranger was suggesting. He started forward. 'I think I'd like that.'

Bryn backed away a pace. 'Just a moment!' he cried. 'You can't expect me to . . .'

He got no further. The Ranger's eyes glittered with that dangerous light once more and he took a half step forward, his hand dropping to the hilt of the saxe knife again.

'You've got a cane. So has he. Now get on with it,' he ordered, his voice very low and dangerous.

Realising he was trapped, Bryn turned to face Horace. Now that it was a matter of one on one, he felt far less confident about dealing with the younger boy. Everyone had heard of Horace's almost uncanny natural swordsmanship.

Deciding that attack might be the best defence, Bryn stepped forward and aimed an overhead slash at Horace. Horace parried it easily. He parried Bryn's next two strokes with equal ease. Then, as he blocked Bryn's fourth stroke, he flicked his wooden blade down the length of the other boy's cane in the instant before the two weapons disengaged. There was no crosspiece to protect Bryn's hand from the movement and the hardwood drill sword slammed painfully into his fingers. With a cry of agony, he dropped the heavy stick, leaping back and wringing his injured hand painfully under his arm. Horace stood, ready to resume.

'I didn't hear anybody call stop,' Halt said mildly.

'But . . . he's disarmed me!' Bryn whined.

Halt smiled at him. 'So he has. But I'm sure he'll let you pick up your cane and start again. Go ahead.'

Bryn looked from Halt to Horace and back again. He saw no pity in either face.

'I don't want to,' he said in a very small voice. Horace found it hard to reconcile this cringing figure with the sneering bully who had been making his life hell for the past few months. Halt appeared to consider Bryn's statement.

'We'll note your protest,' he said cheerfully. 'Now continue, please.'

Bryn's hand throbbed painfully. But even worse than the pain was the fear of what was to come, the certainty that Horace would punish him without mercy. He bent down and reached fearfully for the cane, his eyes fixed on Horace. The younger boy waited patiently until Bryn was ready, then made a sudden feint forward.

Bryn yelped in fear and threw the cane aside. Horace shook his head in disgust.

'Who's the baby now?' he asked. Bryn wouldn't meet his gaze. He shrank away, his eyes cast down.

'If he's going to be a baby,' Halt suggested, 'I suppose you'll just have to paddle him.'

A grin spread over Horace's face. He sprang forward and grabbed Bryn by the scruff of his neck, spinning him round. Then he proceeded to whack the older boy's backside with the flat of the drill sword, over and over again, following him round the clearing as Bryn tried to pull away from the remorseless punishment. Bryn howled and hopped and sobbed but Horace's grip was firm on his collar and there was no escape. Finally, when Horace felt he had repaid all the bullying, the insults and the pain that he had suffered, he let go.

Bryn staggered away and dropped to his hands and knees in the dirt, sobbing with pain and fear.

Jerome had watched the proceedings in horror, knowing his turn was coming. He began to edge away, hoping to escape while the Ranger's attention was distracted.

'Take one more step and I'll put an arrow through you.'

Will tried to model his voice on the quiet, threatening tone Halt had used. He had retrieved several of his arrows from the nearest target and now he had one of them ready, laid on the bowstring. Halt glanced round approvingly.

'Good idea,' he said. 'Aim for the left calf. It's a very painful wound.' He glanced over to where Bryn lay, sobbing, on the ground at Horace's feet. 'I think he's had enough,' he said. Then he jerked a thumb at Jerome.

'Your turn,' he said briefly. Horace retrieved the cane that Bryn had dropped and moved towards Jerome, holding it out to him. Jerome backed away.

'No!' Jerome yelled, wide-eyed. 'It's not fair! He . . .'

'Well, of course it's not *fair*,' Halt agreed in a reasonable tone. 'I gather you think three against one is fair. Now get on with it.'

Will had often heard the saying that a cornered rat will eventually show fight. Jerome proved it now. He went onto the attack and to his surprise, Horace gave ground before the rain of blows aimed at him. The bully's confidence began to grow as he advanced. He failed to notice that Horace was blocking every stroke with consummate ease, almost with contempt. Jerome's best strokes never even looked like breaking through Horace's defence. The second year apprentice might as well have been hitting a stone wall.

Then, Horace stopped retreating. He stood fast, blocking Jerome's latest stroke with an iron wrist. They stood chest to chest for a few seconds and then Horace began to push Jerome back. His left hand gripped Jerome's right wrist, keeping their weapons locked together. Jerome's feet skidded on the soft grass as Horace forced him backwards, further and further. Then he gave a final heave and sent Jerome sprawling on the ground.

Jerome had seen what happened to Bryn. He knew that surrender wasn't an option. He scrambled to his feet and defended desperately as Horace began his own attack. Jerome was driven back by a whirlwind of forehands, backhands, side and overhead cuts. He managed to block some of the strokes but the blistering speed of Horace's attack defeated him. Blows rained on his shins, elbows and shoulders almost at will. Horace seemed to concentrate on the bony spots that would hurt most. Occasionally, he used the rounded point of the sword to thrust into Jerome's ribs — just hard enough to bruise, without breaking bones.

Finally, Jerome had had enough. He wheeled away from the onslaught, dropped the cane and fell to the ground, hands clasped protectively over his head. His backside was raised invitingly in the air and Horace paused and looked a question at Halt. The Ranger made a little gesture towards Jerome.

'Why not?' he said. 'An opportunity like that doesn't come every day.'

But even he winced at the thundering kick in the backside that Horace delivered. Jerome, nose down in the dirt, skidded at least a metre from the force of it.

Halt retrieved the cane that Jerome had dropped. He

studied it for a moment, testing its weight and balance.

'Really not much of a weapon,' he said. 'You have to wonder why they chose it.' Then he tossed the cane to Alda. 'Get busy,' he ordered.

The blond boy, still crouched on the grass nursing his injured ankle, looked at the cane in disbelief. Blood streamed down his face from his shattered nose. He'd never be quite so good looking again, Will thought.

'But . . . but . . . I'm injured!' he protested, hobbling awkwardly to his feet. He couldn't believe that Halt would require him to go through the punishment he'd just witnessed.

Halt paused, studying him as if that fact hadn't occurred to him. For a moment, a ray of hope shone in Alda's mind.

'So you are,' the Ranger said. 'So you are.' He looked a little disappointed and Alda began to believe that Halt's sense of fair play would spare him the sort of punishment that had been handed out to his friends. Then the Ranger's face cleared.

'But just a minute,' he said, 'so is Horace. Isn't that right, Will?'

Will grinned. 'Definitely, Halt,' he said and Alda's brief hope vanished without trace.

Halt now turned to Horace, asking with mock concern, 'Are you sure you're not too badly injured to continue, Horace?'

Horace smiled. It was a smile that never reached his eyes. 'Oh, I think I can manage,' he said.

'Well, that's settled then!' Halt said cheerfully. 'Let's continue, shall we?'

And Alda knew there was to be no escape for him either. He faced up to Horace and the final duel began.

Alda was the best swordsman of the three bullies, and at least he gave Horace some competition for a few minutes. But as they felt each other out with stroke and counter-stroke, thrust and parry, he quickly realised that Horace was his master. His only chance, he felt, was to try something unexpected.

He disengaged, then changed his grip on the cane, holding it in both hands like a quarterstaff and launching a series of rapid left and right hooking blows with it.

For a second, Horace was caught by surprise and he fell back. But he recovered with cat-like speed and aimed an overhead blow at Alda. The second year student attempted the standard quarterstaff parry, holding the staff at either end, to block the sword stroke with the middle section. In theory, it was the right tactic. In practice, the hardened hickory drill sword simply sheared through the cane, leaving Alda holding two useless, shortened sticks. Totally unnerved, he let them drop and stood defenceless before Horace.

Horace looked at his long-time tormentor, then at the sword in his hand.

'I don't need this,' he muttered, and let the sword drop.

The right-hand punch that he threw travelled no more than twenty centimetres to the point of Alda's jaw. But it had his shoulder and body weight and months of suffering and loneliness behind it — the loneliness that only a victim of bullying can know.

Will's eyes widened slightly as Alda came off his feet and hurtled backwards, to come crashing down in the dirt beside his two friends. He thought about the times in the past when he had fought with Horace. If he'd known the other boy was capable of throwing a punch like that, he never would have done so.

Alda didn't move. Odds were, he wouldn't move for some time, Will thought. Horace stepped back, shaking his bruised knuckles and heaving a sigh of satisfaction.

'You have no idea how good that felt,' he said. 'Thank you, Ranger.'

Halt nodded acknowledgement. 'Thank you for taking a hand when they attacked Will. And by the way, my friends call me Halt.'

Twenty-three

In the weeks following his final encounter with the three bullies, Horace noticed a definite change in life at the Battleschool.

The most important factor in the change was that Alda, Bryn and Jerome were all expelled from the school — and from the castle and its neighbouring village. Sir Rodney had been suspicious for some time that there had been a problem among the ranks of his junior students. A quiet visit from Halt alerted him as to where it lay and the resultant investigation soon brought to light the full story of the way Horace had been victimised. Sir Rodney's judgement was swift and uncompromising. The three second year students were given a half day to prepare and pack. They were supplied with a small amount of money and a week's supplies and were transported to the fief's boundaries, where they were told, in no uncertain terms, not to return.

Once they were gone, Horace's lot improved considerably. The daily routine of the Battleschool was still as harsh and challenging as ever. But without the added burden that Alda, Bryn and Jerome had laid upon him, Horace found he could easily cope with the drills, the discipline and the studies. He rapidly began to achieve the potential that Sir Rodney had seen in him. In addition, his room-mates, without the fear of incurring the bullies' vengeance, began to be more welcoming and friendly.

In short, Horace felt things were definitely looking up.

His only regret was that he hadn't been able to thank Halt properly for the improvement in his life. After the events in the meadow, Horace had been placed in the infirmary for several days while his bruises and contusions were attended to. By the time he was released, he found that Halt and Will had already left for the Rangers' Gathering.

'Are we nearly there?' Will asked, for perhaps the tenth time that morning.

Halt gave vent to a small sigh of exasperation. Other than that, he made no reply. They had been on the road now for three days and it seemed to Will that they must be close to the Gathering Ground. Several times in the past hour, he had noticed an unfamiliar scent on the air. He mentioned it to Halt, who said briefly, 'It's salt. We're getting close to the sea,' then refused to elaborate any further. Will glanced sidelong at his teacher, hoping that perhaps Halt might deign to share a little more information with him, but the Ranger's keen eyes were scanning the ground in front of them. From time to time, Will noticed, he looked up into the trees that flanked the road.

'Are you looking for something?' Will asked and Halt turned in his saddle.

'Finally, a useful question,' he said. 'Yes, as a matter of fact, I am. The Chief Ranger will have sentries out around the Gathering Ground. I always like to try to fool them as I'm approaching.'

'Why?' asked Will and Halt allowed himself a tight little grin.

'It keeps them on their toes,' he explained. 'They'll try to slip behind us and follow us in, just so they can say they've ambushed me. It's a silly game they like to play.'

'Why is it silly?' asked Will. It sounded exactly like the sort of skill exercises that he and Halt practised regularly. The grizzled Ranger turned in his saddle and fixed Will with an unblinking stare.

'Because they never succeed,' he said. 'And this year they'll be trying even harder because they know I'm bringing an apprentice. They'll want to see how good you are.'

'Is this part of the testing?' Will asked and Halt nodded.

'It's the start of it. Do you remember what I told you last night?'

Will nodded. For the past two nights, around the camp fire, Halt's soft voice had given Will advice and instructions on how to conduct himself at the Gathering. Last night, they'd devised tactics for use in case of an ambush — just the sort of thing that Halt had mentioned now.

'When will we . . .' he began, but suddenly Halt was alert. He held up a warning finger for silence and Will stopped speaking instantly. The Ranger's head was turned slightly. The two horses continued without hesitation.

'Hear it?' Halt asked.

Will craned his head too. He thought that, just maybe, he could hear soft hoof beats behind them. But he wasn't sure. The gait of their own horses masked any real sound from the trail behind. If there was someone there, his horse was moving in step with their own.

'Change gait,' Halt whispered. 'On three. One, two, three.'

Simultaneously, they both nudged their left toes into the horses' shoulders. It was just one of many signals to which Tug and Abelard were trained to respond.

Instantly, both horses hesitated in their stride. They seemed to skip a pace, then continued in their even gait.

But the hesitation had changed the pattern of their hoof beats and for an instant, Will could hear another set of horse's hooves behind them, like a slightly delayed echo. Then the other horse changed gait as well to match their own and the sound was gone.

'Ranger horse,' Halt said softly. 'It'll be Gilan, for sure.'

'How can you tell?' Will asked.

'Only a Ranger horse could change his pace as quickly as that. And it'll be Gilan because it's always Gilan. He loves trying to catch me out.'

'Why?' asked Will and Halt looked sternly at him.

'Because he was my last apprentice,' he explained. 'And for some reason, former apprentices just love to catch their former masters with their breeches down.' He looked accusingly at his current apprentice. Will was about to protest that he would never behave in such a fashion after he graduated, then realised that he probably would, and at the very first opportunity. The protest died unspoken.

Halt signalled for silence, and scanned the trail ahead of them. Then he pointed. 'That's the spot there,' he said. 'Ready?'

There was a large tree close to the side of the trail, with branches hanging out just above head height. Will studied it for a moment, then nodded. Tug and Abelard continued their even pacing towards the tree. As they came closer, Will kicked his feet from the stirrups and rose to stand, crouching, on Tug's back. The horse didn't vary his pace as his master shifted position.

As they passed under the branches, Will reached up and seized the lowest one, swinging himself up onto it. The instant his weight left Tug's back, the little horse began to pace more vigorously, forcing his hooves into the ground with each step so that there would be no sign to a tracker behind them that his load had suddenly lightened.

Silently, Will climbed higher into the tree until he found a spot where he had a solid perch and a clear view. He could see Halt and the two horses moving slowly down the trail.

As they reached the next bend, Halt urged Tug to keep going, then halted Abelard and swung down from the saddle. He dropped to his knees, seeming to study the ground for signs of tracks.

Now Will could hear the other horse behind them. He looked back the way they had come but another bend hid their follower from sight.

Then, the soft hoof beats ceased.

Will's mouth was dry and his heart beat faster and faster

inside his ribcage. He was sure the sound must be audible to anyone within fifty metres or so. But his training asserted itself and he stood motionless on the tree branch, among the leaves and dappled shadows, watching the trail behind them.

A movement!

He saw it from the corner of his eye, then it was gone. He peered closely at the spot for a second or two, then remembered Halt's lessons: *Don't focus your attention on one spot. Keep a wide focus all the time and keep scanning. You'll see him as a movement, not as a figure. Remember, he's a Ranger too and he's been trained in the art of not being seen.*

Will widened his focus and scanned the forest behind them. Within seconds, he was rewarded by another sign of movement. A branch swung back into place as an unseen figure passed silently by.

Then, ten metres further on, a bush swayed slightly. Then he saw a clump of tall grass springing slowly back into position from where a passing foot had crushed it momentarily.

Will stayed stock-still. He marvelled at the fact that their pursuer could move through the forest without his seeing him. Obviously, the other Ranger had left his horse behind and was stalking Halt on foot. Will's eyes swivelled for a quick glance at Halt. His teacher still seemed to be preoccupied with some sign on the ground.

Another movement came from the forest. The unseen Ranger had passed Will's hiding place now and was moving back towards the trail, intent on surprising Halt from behind.

Suddenly, a tall figure in a grey-green cloak seemed to rise out of the ground in the middle of the trail, some twenty metres behind the kneeling figure of Halt. Will blinked. One moment the figure hadn't been there. Next, he seemed to materialise out of thin air. Will's hand began to move towards the quiver of arrows slung over his back, then he halted the movement. Halt had told him the night before: *Wait until we're talking. If he's not talking, he'll hear the slightest movement you make.*

Will gulped, hoping that the tall figure hadn't heard the movement of his hand towards the quiver. But it seemed that he'd stopped in time. Below him, he heard a cheerful voice call out.

'Halt, Halt!'

Halt turned and rose slowly to his feet, brushing the dirt from his knees as he rose. He put his head on one side and studied the figure in the middle of the trail, who was leaning easily on a longbow identical to Halt's own.

'Well, Gilan,' he called, 'I see you're still making that old joke.'

The tall Ranger shrugged and replied cheerfully, 'The joke appears to be on you this year, Halt.'

As Gilan spoke, Will's hand moved quickly but quietly to his quiver and selected an arrow, laying it ready on the bowstring. Halt was speaking again now.

'Really, Gilan? And what joke would that be, I wonder?'

The amusement was evident in Gilan's voice as he replied to his old master.

'Come now, Halt. Admit it. For once I've got the best of you — and you know how many years I've been trying.'

Halt rubbed one hand over his grizzled beard thoughtfully.

'It beats me why you keep on trying, Gilan, as a matter of fact.'

Gilan laughed. 'You should know how much pleasure it gives an ex-apprentice to get the better of his master, Halt. Now come on. Admit it. This year, I've won.'

As the tall figure spoke, Will carefully drew back the arrow, sighting on a tree trunk some two metres to Gilan's left. Halt's instructions echoed in his ears: *Choose a target close enough to startle him when you shoot. But for pity's sake not too close. If he moves, I don't want you putting an arrow through him!*

Halt hadn't moved from his position in the centre of the trail. Gilan was now shifting his weight uneasily from one foot to another. Halt's unperturbed manner was beginning to bother him. It appeared that, all of a sudden, he wasn't totally sure that Halt was merely trying to bluff his way out of the trap.

Halt's next words added to his suspicions.

'Ah yes . . . apprentices and masters. They're a strange combination, all right. But tell me, Gilan, my old apprentice, aren't you forgetting something this year?'

Perhaps it was the way Halt laid a little extra stress on the word 'apprentice', but suddenly Gilan became aware that he had made a mistake. His head began to turn, searching for the apprentice that he'd forgotten.

As he began the movement, Will released his arrow.

The shaft hissed through the air past the tall Ranger and thudded, quivering, into the tree that Will had selected. Gilan jerked back with shock, then his eyes swung into the branches of the tree where Will stood concealed. Will marvelled that, even caught by surprise as he was, Gilan was still able to react so quickly in identifying the direction from which his attacker had shot.

Gilan shook his head ruefully. His keen eyes could make out the small grey and green clad figure concealed in the shadows of the tree's foliage.

'Come down, Will,' Halt called. 'And meet Gilan, one of our more careless Rangers.' He shook his head at Gilan. 'I told you when you were a boy, didn't I? Never be too hasty. Don't rush into things.'

Gilan nodded, somewhat crestfallen. He looked even more so when Will dropped to the ground from the lowest branch and the tall Ranger saw how small and young the apprentice was.

'It appears,' he said, 'that I was so intent on catching myself an old grey fox that I overlooked the small monkey hiding in the trees.' He grinned at his own mistake.

'Monkey, is it?' Halt said gruffly. 'I'd say he's made a monkey out of you today. Will, this is Gilan, my former apprentice and now Ranger of Meric Fief — although what they did to deserve him is beyond me.'

Gilan's grin widened and he held out his hand to Will.

'And just as I was thinking I'd finally got the better of you, Halt,' he said cheerfully. 'So you're Will,' he continued, shaking hands firmly. 'I'm pleased to meet you. That was a neat piece of work, young fellow.'

Will grinned at Halt and the older Ranger made a slight, meaningful movement of his head. Will remembered the final instructions that Halt had given him the night before:

Once you best a man, never gloat. Be generous and find something in his actions to praise. He won't enjoy being bested but he'll make a good face of it. Show him you appreciate it. Praise can win you a friend. Gloating will only ever make enemies.

'Yes, I'm Will,' he said. Then he added, 'Could you perhaps teach me how you move like that? It was brilliant.'

Gilan laughed ruefully. 'Not too brilliant, I think. You obviously saw me coming from a long way away.'

Will shook his head, remembering how hard he'd tried to spot Gilan. Now that he thought of it, his praise and his request were more genuine than he'd realised.

'I saw you when you arrived,' he said. 'And I saw where you'd been. But I never once saw you from the time you rounded that bend. I wish I could move like that.'

Gilan's face showed his pleasure at Will's obvious sincerity.

'Well, Halt,' he said, 'I see this young fellow doesn't merely have talent. He has excellent manners as well.'

Halt regarded the two of them: his current apprentice and his former student. He nodded to Will, approving his tactful words.

'Unseen movement was always Gilan's best skill,' he said. 'You'd do well if he agreed to tutor you.' He moved towards his ex-apprentice and placed his arm around the taller man's shoulders. 'It's good to see you again.'

They embraced each other warmly. Then Halt held the other man at arm's length, studying him carefully.

'You get lankier every year,' he said finally. 'When are you going to put some meat on those bones?'

Gilan smiled. It was obviously an old joke between them.

'You appear to have enough for both of us,' he said. He poked Halt in the ribs, none too gently. 'Is that the beginnings of a pot belly I see there?' He grinned at Will. 'I'll wager he's sitting around the cabin letting you do all the housework these days?'

Before Halt or Will could reply, he turned away and let out a whistle. A few seconds later, his horse trotted round the bend in the road. As the tall young Ranger moved towards his horse and mounted, Will noticed a sword hanging in a scabbard from the saddle. He turned to Halt, puzzled.

'I thought we weren't allowed to have swords?' he said quietly. Halt frowned for a moment, not understanding, then followed Will's gaze and realised what had prompted the question.

'It's not that we're not allowed,' he explained, as they both mounted. 'It's a matter of priorities. It takes years to become a good swordsman and we don't have the time. We have other skills to develop.'

He saw the next question forming on Will's lips and went on. 'Gilan's father is a knight, so Gilan had already been training with the sword for some years before he joined the Rangers. He was considered a special case and he was allowed to continue that training when he was apprenticed to me.'

'But I thought . . .' Will began and then hesitated. Gilan was trotting his horse towards them and he wasn't sure if it would be polite to ask his next question in front of him.

'Never say that in front of Halt,' Gilan said, overhearing Will's last words. 'He'll simply reply, "You're an apprentice. You're not ready to think" or "If you thought about it, you wouldn't ask".'

Will had to smile. Halt had used those exact words to him on more than one occasion and Gilan's impersonation of the older Ranger was uncanny. Now, however, both men were looking expectantly at him, waiting to hear the question he had been about to ask, so he plunged ahead.

'If Gilan's father was a knight, wasn't he automatically eligible for Battleschool? Or did they think he was too small as well?'

Halt and Gilan exchanged a look. Halt raised one eyebrow, then gestured for Gilan to reply.

'I could have gone to Battleschool,' he said. 'But I chose to join the Rangers.'

'Some of us do, you know,' Halt put in mildly. Will thought this over. He had always assumed that the Rangers did not come from the ranks of the Kingdom's nobles. Apparently he was wrong.

'But I thought . . .' he began and instantly realised his mistake. Halt and Gilan looked at him, then looked at each other, and said in chorus:

'You're an apprentice. You're not ready to think.'

Then they wheeled their horses and trotted off. Will hurriedly retrieved Tug and cantered after them. As he caught up, the two Rangers edged their horses to either side, allowing him space to ride between them. Gilan grinned once at him. Halt was as grim as ever. But as they continued in a companionable silence, Will became aware of the comforting realisation that he was now a part of an exclusive, tightly knit group.

It was a warm sense of belonging, as if, somehow, he had arrived home for the first time in his life.

Twenty-four

'Something's happened,' Halt said quietly, signalling for his two companions to rein in their horses.

The three riders had cantered the last half a kilometre to the Gathering Ground. Now, as they crested a slight rise, the open space among the trees lay just below them, a hundred metres away. Small, one-man tents stretched in ordered ranks, and the smoke of cooking fires scented the air. An archery range had been set up to one side of the open space and several dozen horses, all small and shaggy Ranger horses, were grazing close to the trees.

Even from where they sat on their horses, they could make out an air of urgency and activity throughout the camp. In the centre of the tent lines was a larger pavilion, easily four metres by four metres and with enough headroom for a tall man to stand. The sides were currently rolled up and Will could see a group of green and grey clad men standing round a table, apparently deep in conversation. As they watched, one of the group detached himself, running to a horse waiting just outside the entrance. He mounted and spun the horse on its back legs, setting out through the camp at a gallop, heading for the narrow track through the trees at the far side.

He had barely disappeared into the deep shadows under the trees when another rider appeared from the opposite direction, galloping through the lines and reining in outside the large tent. His horse had barely stopped before he swung down and headed in to join the group inside.

'What is it?' Will asked. Frowning, he realised that several of the small tents were being struck and rolled up by their owners.

'Not sure,' Halt replied. He gestured to the tent lines. 'See if you can find us a decent camp site. I'll see what's going on.'

He urged Abelard forward, then turned and called back: 'Don't pitch the tents yet. From the looks of things, we may not be needing them.' Then Abelard's hooves were drumming on the turf as he galloped towards the centre of the camp.

Will and Gilan found a camp site under a large tree, reasonably close to the central gathering area. Then, uncertain as to what they should do next, they sat on a log, waiting for Halt's return. As a senior Ranger in the Corps, Halt had access to the larger pavilion, which Gilan explained was the command tent. The Corps Commandant, a Ranger named Crowley, would meet with his staff there each day to organise activities and to collate and evaluate the reports and information that individual Rangers brought to the Gathering.

Most of the tents near the two younger Rangers were unoccupied, but there was a thin gangly Ranger outside one, pacing impatiently back and forth, looking every bit as confused as Gilan and Will. Seeing them on the log, he moved over to join them.

'Any news?' he said immediately, and his face fell when Gilan answered.

'We were just about to ask you the same question.' He held out his hand in greeting. 'It's Merron, isn't it?' he said and they shook hands.

'That's right. And you're Gilan if I remember correctly.' Gilan introduced Will, and the newcomer, who appeared to be in his early thirties, looked at him speculatively.

'So you're Halt's new apprentice,' he said. 'We wondered what you'd be like. I was going to be one of your assessors, you know.'

'Going to be?' Gilan asked quickly, and Merron looked at him.

'Yes. I doubt we'll continue with the Gathering now.' He hesitated, then added, 'You mean you haven't heard?' The two newcomers shook their heads.

'Morgarath is up to something again,' he said quietly and Will felt a shiver of fear up his spine at the mention of that evil name.

'What's happened?' Gilan asked, his eyes narrowing. Merron shook his head, stirring the dirt in front of him with the toe of his boot in a frustrated gesture.

'There's no clear news so far. Only garbled reports. But it looks as if a force of Wargals broke out of Three Step Pass some days ago. They overran the sentries there and headed north.'

'Was Morgarath with them?' Gilan asked. Will remained wide-eyed and silent. He couldn't bring himself to ask any questions, couldn't bring himself to actually mention Morgarath's name.

Merron shrugged in reply. 'We don't know. Don't think so at this stage, but Crowley has been sending scouts out for the past two days. Could be it's just a raid. But if it's more than that, it could mean the start of another war. If so, it's a bad time to lose Lord Lorriac.'

Gilan looked up, concern in his voice. 'Lorriac is dead?' he asked and Merron nodded.

'A stroke apparently. Or his heart. He was found dead a few days ago, with not a mark on him. Staring straight ahead. Stone cold dead.'

'But he was in his prime!' Gilan said. 'I saw him only a month ago and he was as healthy as a bull.'

Merron shrugged. He had no explanation. He only knew the facts of the matter. 'I suppose it can happen to anyone,' he said. 'You just never know.'

'Who's Lord Lorriac?' Will asked Gilan quietly. The young Ranger shook his head thoughtfully as he answered.

'Lorriac of Steden. He was the leader of the King's heavy cavalry. Probably our best cavalry commander. As Merron said, if there's war, he'll be sorely missed.'

A cold hand of fear closed around Will's heart. All his life people had spoken in whispers of Morgarath, if they had spoken of him at all. The Great Enemy had assumed the proportions almost of a myth — a legend from the old, dark days. Now the myth was becoming reality once more — a confronting, terrifying reality. He looked at Gilan for reassurance but the young Ranger's handsome face showed nothing but doubt and concern for the future.

It was a most an hour before Halt rejoined them. As it was after midday, Will and Gilan had prepared a meal of bread, cold meat and dried fruit. The grey-haired Ranger slid down from Abelard's saddle and accepted a plate from Will, eating the food in quick bites.

'The Gathering's over,' he said shortly, between mouthfuls. Seeing the senior Ranger's arrival, Merron had drifted back to join their group. He and Halt greeted each other briefly then Merron posed the question that was on all their minds.

'Is it war?' he asked anxiously and Halt shook his head.

'We don't know for certain. Latest reports show that Morgarath is still in the mountains.'

'Then why did the Wargals break out?' Will asked. Everyone knew that Wargals only did the will of Morgarath. They never would have performed such a radical act without his direction. Halt's face was grim as he answered.

'They're only a small party — perhaps fifty of them. They were intended to act as a diversion. While our guards were busy chasing the Wargals, Crowley thinks that the two Kalkara slipped out of the Mountains and are holed up somewhere on the Solitary Plain.'

Gilan gave a low whistle. Merron actually took a step back in surprise. Both the younger Rangers' faces showed their utter horror at the news. Will had no idea what the Kalkara might be but, judging from Halt's expression and the reactions of Gilan and Merron, they were obviously not good news.

'You mean they still exist?' Merron said, 'I thought they died out years ago.'

'Oh, they still exist all right,' Halt said. 'There are only two of them left, but that's enough to worry about.'

There was a long silence between them. Finally, hesitantly, Will had to ask:

'What are they?'

Halt shook his head sadly. It was not a subject that he wanted to discuss with someone as young as Will. But, knowing what lay ahead of them all, he had no choice. The boy had to know.

'When Morgarath was planning his rebellion, he wanted more than an ordinary army. He knew that if he could terrify his enemies, his task would be far easier. So over the years, he made several expeditions into the Mountains of Rain and Night, searching.'

'Searching for what?' Will asked, although he had the uncomfortable feeling that he knew what the answer would be.

'For allies he could use against the Kingdom. The Mountains are an ancient, undisturbed part of the world. They've remained unchanged for centuries and there were rumours that strange beasts and ancient monsters still lived there. The rumours turned out to be all too true.'

'Like the Wargals,' Will put in and Halt nodded.

'Yes. Like the Wargals. And he very quickly enslaved them and bent them to his will,' he said with a touch of bitterness in his voice. 'But then he found the Kalkara. And they're worse than Wargals. Much, much worse.'

Will said nothing. The thought of beasts that were worse than Wargals was a disturbing one, to say the least.

'There were three of them. But one was killed about eight years ago, so we know a little more about them. Think of a creature somewhere between an ape and a bear, that walks upright, and you'll have an idea of what a Kalkara looks like.'

'So does Morgarath control them with his mind, like the Wargals?' Will asked and Halt shook his head.

'No. They're more intelligent than Wargals. But they are totally obsessed with silver. They worship it and hoard it and Morgarath apparently gives it to them in large amounts so they'll do his bidding. And they do it well. They can be incredibly cunning while they stalk their prey.'

'Prey?' Will asked. 'What sort of prey?'

Halt and Gilan exchanged a glance and Will could see that his mentor was reluctant to talk about the subject. For a moment, he thought Halt was going to begin another of his dissertations on Will's endless questions. But then he realised this was a far more serious matter than idle curiosity as the grizzled Ranger replied quietly.

'The Kalkara are assassins. Once they've been given a specific victim, they will do anything in their power to reach that person and kill them.'

'Can't we stop them?' Will asked, his gaze shifting briefly to Halt's massive longbow and the bristling quiver of black arrows.

'They're very difficult to kill. They have a thick hair covering that's matted and bonded together so that it's almost like scales. An arrow will hardly penetrate. A battleaxe or a broadsword is best against them. Or a good thrust with a heavy spear might do the job.'

Will felt a moment of relief. These Kalkara had started to sound almost invincible. But there were plenty of accomplished knights in the Kingdom who would doubtless be able to account for them.

'So was it a knight who killed the one eight years ago?' he asked. Halt shook his head.

'Not *a* knight. Three. It took three fully armed knights to kill it, and only one of them survived the battle. What's more, he was crippled for life,' Halt finished grimly.

'Three men? All of them knights?' Will said incredulously. 'But how —'

Gilan interrupted him before he could finish. 'The problem is, if you get close enough to use a sword or spear, the Kalkara can usually stop you before you have a chance.'

As he spoke, his fingers drummed lightly on the hilt of the sword that he wore at his waist.

'How does it stop you?' Will asked, the momentary feeling of relief instantly dispelled by Gilan's words. This time it was Merron who answered.

'His eyes,' the gangly Ranger said. 'If you look into his eyes, you are frozen helpless — the way a snake freezes a bird with its gaze before it kills it.'

Will looked from one to the other of the three men, uncomprehending. What Merron was saying seemed too far-fetched to be true. Yet Halt wasn't contradicting him.

'Freezes you . . . how can it do that? Are you talking about magic here?'

Halt shrugged. Merron looked away uncomfortably. None of them liked discussing this subject.

'Some people call it magic,' Halt finally said. 'I think it's more likely a form of hypnotism. Either way, Merron is right. If a Kalkara can make you look into his eyes, you become paralysed by sheer terror, unable to do anything to save yourself.'

Will glanced around anxiously, as if expecting any moment to see an ape-bear creature charging out of the silent trees. He could feel panic growing in his chest. Somehow, he'd come to think of Halt as invincible. Yet here he was, seeming to admit that there was no defence against these vile monsters.

'Isn't there anything you can do?' he asked in a hopeless voice. Halt shrugged.

'Legend has it that they are particularly vulnerable to fire. Problem is, as before, getting close enough to do any damage. Carrying a naked flame makes it a little difficult to stalk a Kalkara. They tend to hunt at night and they can see you coming.'

Will found it difficult to believe what he was hearing. Halt seemed so matter of fact about it all, and Gilan and Merron were obviously disturbed by his news.

There was an awkward silence, which Gilan broke by asking, 'What makes Crowley think that Morgarath is using them?'

Halt hesitated. He'd been told Crowley's thoughts in private council. Then he shrugged. They'd all need to know about it sooner or later and they *were* all members of the Ranger Corps, even Will.

'He's already used them twice in the past year — to kill Lord Northolt and Lord Lorriac.' The three younger men all exchanged puzzled glances, so he went on.

'Northolt was thought to be killed by a bear, remember?' Will nodded slowly. He remembered now. On his first day as Halt's apprentice, the Ranger had received news of the supreme commander's death. 'I thought at the time that Northolt was too skilled a hunter to be killed that way. Crowley evidently agrees.'

'But what about Lorriac? Everyone said it was a stroke.' It was Merron who asked this question. Halt glanced at him briefly, then answered.

'You'd heard that, had you? Well, his physician was most surprised. Said he'd never seen a healthier man. On the other hand . . .' He paused, and Gilan finished the thought.

'It could have been the work of the Kalkara.'

Halt nodded. 'Exactly. We don't know the full effects of the freezing stare they've developed. Maintained over a long enough time, the terror could well be enough to stop a man's heart. And there were vague reports that a large, dark animal was seen in the area.'

Again, silence settled over the small group under the trees. Around them, Rangers bustled to and fro, striking camp and saddling their horses. Halt finally roused them all from their thoughts.

'We'd best be moving. Merron, you'll need to return to your fief. Crowley wants the army alerted and mobilised. Orders will be distributed in a few minutes.'

Merron nodded and turned away towards his camp site. He paused and turned back. Something in Halt's voice, the way he had said '*you'll* need to return to your fief', had made him think.

'What about you three?' he said. 'Where are you going?'

Even before Halt answered, Will knew what he was going to say. But that didn't make it any less terrifying or blood-chilling when the words were said.

'We're going after the Kalkara.'

Twenty-five

The camp buzzed with activity as tents came down and Rangers repacked their equipment and tied on their saddle bags. Already, the first few riders had departed, heading back to their own fiefs.

Will was fastening the ties on their saddle packs, having replaced the few items they had taken out. Halt sat a few metres away, frowning thoughtfully as he studied a map of the area surrounding the Solitary Plain. The Plain itself was a vast, unmapped area, with no roads and few features indicated. A shadow fell across him and he looked up. Gilan stood there, a worried look on his face.

'Halt,' he said in a low, concerned voice. 'Are you sure about this?'

Halt met his gaze steadily. 'Very sure, Gilan. It simply has to be done.'

'But he's only a boy!' Gilan protested, looking to where Will was tying a pack roll in place behind Tug's saddle. Halt let go a long breath, his eyes dropping from Gilan's.

'I know that. But he's a Ranger. Apprentice or not, he's a member of the Corps, like all of us.' He saw that Gilan was about to protest further, out of concern for Will, and he felt a surge of affection for his old apprentice.

'Gilan, in an ideal world, I wouldn't put him at risk like this. But this isn't an ideal world. Everyone's going to have to play his part in this campaign, even boys like Will. Morgarath is preparing for something big. Crowley's agents have got wind that, on top of everything else, he's been in touch with the Skandians.'

'The Skandians? What for?'

Halt shrugged. 'We don't know the details but my bet is he's hoping to form an alliance with them. They'll fight anyone for money. And apparently, they'll fight *for* anyone as well,' he added, his distaste for mercenaries obvious in his voice. 'The point is, we're short-handed enough while Crowley tries to raise the army. Normally, I wouldn't go after the Kalkara with a force of less than five senior Rangers. But he simply can't spare them for me. So I've had to settle for the two I trust most — you and Will.'

Gilan grinned crookedly. 'Well, thanks for that, anyway.' He was touched by Halt's confidence. He still looked up to his old mentor. Most of the Ranger Corps did.

'Besides, I thought that rusty old sword of yours might come in handy if we run into those horrors,' Halt said. The Ranger Corps had chosen wisely when they allowed Gilan to continue his training with the weapon. Although very few people knew it, Gilan was one of the finest swordsmen in Araluen.

'As for Will,' Halt continued, 'don't underestimate him.

He's very resourceful. He's quick and brave and a damn good shot already. Best of all, he thinks quickly. My real thinking is that if we get on the trail of the Kalkara, we can send him for reinforcements. That'll help us and keep him out of harm's way.'

Gilan scratched his chin thoughtfully. Now that Halt had explained it, it seemed the only logical course for them to take. He met the older man's eyes and nodded his understanding of the situation. Then he turned to organise his own kit, only to find that Will had already repacked it and tied it to his saddle. He smiled at Halt.

'You're right,' he said. 'He does think for himself.'

The three of them rode out a little while later, while the other Rangers were still receiving their orders. Mobilising the Araluen army would be no small task, and it would be the Rangers' job to co-ordinate it, then be ready to guide the individual forces from the fifty fiefs to their assembly point at the Plains of Uthal. With both Gilan and Halt assigned to searching for the Kalkara, other Rangers had to be tasked with co-ordinating the forces from their fiefs as well.

There was little said between the three companions as Halt led the way to the south-east. Even Will's natural curiosity was subdued by the magnitude of the task ahead of them. As they rode in silence, his mind's eye kept conjuring images of savage bear-like creatures with the features of apes — creatures that might well prove to be invincible, even for someone of Halt's skill.

Eventually, however, as monotony set in, the horrific images receded and he began to wonder what plan, if any, Halt had in mind.

'Halt,' he said, a little breathlessly, 'where do you hope to find the Kalkara?'

Halt looked at the serious young face beside him. They were travelling at the Rangers' forced march pace — forty minutes in the saddle, riding at a steady canter, then twenty minutes on foot, leading the horses and allowing them to travel unburdened, while the men ran at a steady trot.

Every four hours, they would pause for one hour's rest, when they ate a quick meal of dried meat, hard bread and fruit, then rolled into their cloaks to sleep.

They had been travelling for some time now and Halt judged that it was time to rest. He led Abelard off the road and into the shelter of a grove of trees. Will and Gilan followed, dropping the reins and allowing their horses to graze.

'The best way I can think of,' Halt said, in answer to Will's question, 'is to start at their lair and see if they're in the vicinity.'

'Do we know where that is?' Gilan asked.

'Best intelligence we have is that it's somewhere on the Solitary Plain, beyond the Stone Flutes. We'll scout around that area and see what we can find. If they're in the area, we should find that the odd sheep or goat is going missing from villages nearby. Although getting the villagers themselves to talk will be another matter. Plains people are a close-mouthed bunch at the best of times.'

'What's this Plain you're talking about?' Will asked,

through a mouthful of hard bread. 'And what on earth is a Stone Flute?'

'The Solitary Plain is a vast flat area — very few trees, mainly covered in rock outcrops and long grass,' Halt told him. 'The wind seems to always be blowing, no matter what time of year you go there. It's a dismal, depressing place and the Stone Flutes are the most dismal part of it.'

'But what are —' Will began but Halt had only paused briefly.

'The Stone Flutes? Nobody really knows. They're a circle of standing stones built by the ancients, smack in the middle of the windiest part of the Plain.

'Nobody has ever worked out their original purpose but they're arranged in such a way that the wind is deflected round the circle, and through a series of holes in the stones themselves. They create a constant keening sound, although why anyone thought they sounded like flutes is beyond me. The sound is eerie and discordant and you can hear it from kilometres away. After a few minutes, it sets your teeth on edge — and it goes on and on for hours.'

Will was silent. The thought of a dismal, windswept plain and stones that emitted a nonstop, keening wail seemed to take the last vestige of warmth from the late afternoon sun. He shivered involuntarily. Halt saw the movement and leaned forward to clap him on the shoulder encouragingly.

'Cheer up,' he said. 'Nothing's ever as bad as it sounds. Now let's get some rest.'

They reached the outskirts of the Solitary Plain by noon the second day. Halt was right, Will thought, it was a vast, depressing place. The featureless ground stretched out before them for kilometre after kilometre, covered in tall, grey grass, made rank and dry by the constant wind.

The wind itself almost seemed to be a living presence. It rubbed on their nerves, blowing constantly and unvaryingly from the west, bending the tall grass before it as it swept across the flat ground of the Solitary Plain.

'Now you can see why they call it the Solitary Plain?' Halt said to the two of them, reining Abelard in so they could come abreast of him. 'When you ride out into this damned wind, you feel as if you're the only person left alive on earth.'

It was true, Will thought. He felt small and insignificant against the emptiness of the Plain. And with the feeling of insignificance came an accompanying feeling of impotence. The wasteland they were riding across seemed to hint at the presence of arcane forces — forces far greater than his own capabilities. Even Gilan, normally cheerful and ebullient, seemed affected by the heavy, depressing atmosphere of the place. Only Halt seemed unchanged, remaining grim and taciturn as ever.

Gradually, as they rode, Will became aware of a disquieting sensation. Something was lurking, just outside the range of his conscious perception. Something that made him feel uneasy. He couldn't isolate it, couldn't even tell where it was coming from or what form it took. It was just there, ever present. He shifted in his saddle, standing in the stirrups to scan the featureless horizon in the hope that he might see the source of it all. Halt noticed the movement.

'You've noticed them,' he said. 'It's the Stones.'

And now that Halt said it, Will realised that it had been a sound — so faint and so continuous that he couldn't isolate it as such — that had been creating the sense of unease in his mind, and the tight cramping of fear in the pit of his stomach. Or perhaps it was just that as Halt said it, they came into proper earshot of the Stone Flutes. Because now he could isolate it. It was an unmelodic series of musical notes, all being played at once but creating a harsh, discordant sound that jangled the nerves and unsettled the mind. His left hand crept unobtrusively to the hilt of his saxe knife as he rode, and he drew comfort from the solid, dependable touch of the weapon.

They went on through the afternoon, never seeming to advance across the empty featureless Plain. With each pace, the horizons behind and before them seemed to neither recede nor draw closer. It was as if they were marking time in the empty world. The constant keening sound of the Stone Flutes was with them all day, growing gradually stronger as they travelled. It was the only sign that they were making progress. The hours passed and the sound continued and Will found it no easier to bear. It wore at his nerves, keeping him constantly on edge. As the sun began to sink at the western rim, Halt reined Abelard in.

'We'll rest for the night,' he announced. 'It's almost impossible to maintain a constant course in the dark. Without any significant land features to set a course by, we could easily wind up going round in circles.'

Gratefully, the others dismounted. Fit as they were, the hours spent at forced march pace had left them bone weary. Will began scouting around the few stunted bushes that grew on the Plain, searching for firewood. Halt, realising what was in his mind, shook his head.

'No fire,' he said. 'We'd be visible for miles and we have no idea who might be watching.'

Will paused, letting the small bundle he had gathered fall to the ground. 'You mean the Kalkara?' he said. Halt shrugged.

'Them, or Plains people. We can't be sure that some of them aren't in league with the Kalkara. After all, living cheek by jowl with creatures like that, you might well end up co-operating with them, just to ensure your own safety. And we don't want them getting word that there are strangers on the Plain.'

Gilan was unsaddling Blaze, his bay horse. He dropped the saddle to the ground and rubbed the horse down with a handful of the ever-present dry grass.

'You don't think we've been seen already?' he asked. Halt considered the question for a few seconds before answering.

'We might have been. There are just too many unknowns here — like where the Kalkara actually have their lair, whether or not the Plains people are their allies, whether or not any of them have seen us and reported our presence. But until I *know* we have been seen, we'll assume we haven't. So, no fire.'

Gilan nodded reluctantly. 'You're right, of course,' he said. 'It's just I'd happily kill someone for a cup of coffee.'

'Light a fire to brew it,' Halt told him, 'and you might end up having to do just that.'

Twenty-six

It was a cold, cheerless camp. Tired from the hard pace they had been keeping up, the Rangers ate a cold meal — bread, dried fruit and cold meat once more, washed down with cold water from their canteens. Will was beginning to hate the sight of the virtually tasteless hard rations they carried. Then Halt took the first watch as Will and Gilan rolled themselves into their cloaks and slept.

It wasn't the first rough camp that Will had endured since his training period began. But this was the first time there wasn't the slight comfort of a crackling fire, or at least a bed of warm coals, to sleep by. He slept fitfully, uncomfortable dreams chasing through his subconscious — dreams of fearful creatures, strange and terrifying things that stayed just outside his consciousness, but close enough to the surface that he felt their presence, and was unsettled by them.

He was almost glad when Halt shook him gently awake for his watch.

The wind was scudding clouds across the moon. The moaning song of the Stones was stronger than ever. Will felt a weariness of spirit and wondered if the Stones had been designed to wear people down like this. The long grass around them hissed a counterpoint to the far-off keening. Halt pointed to a spot in the heavens, indicating an angle of elevation for Will to remember.

'When the moon reaches that angle,' he told the apprentice, 'turn over the watch to Gilan.'

Will nodded, rousing himself and standing to stretch his stiff muscles. He picked up his bow and quiver and walked to the bush Halt had selected as a vantage point. Rangers on watch never stayed in the open by the camp site but always moved away ten or twenty metres, and found a place of concealment. That way, strangers coming upon the camp site would be less likely to see them. It was one of the many skills Will had learned in his months of training.

He took two arrows from the quiver and held them between the fingers of his bow hand. He would hold them thus for the four hours of his watch. If he needed them, there would be no excessive movement as he took an arrow from his quiver — movement that might alert an attacker. Then he flipped the cowl of his cloak over his head so he would merge with the irregular shape of the bush. His head and eyes scanned constantly from side to side as Halt had taught him, changing focus constantly, from close to the camp site and out to the dim horizon around them. That way, his vision would not become fixated on one distance and one area and he'd stand a better chance of seeing movement. From time to time, he turned slowly through a complete circle, scanning the entire ground around them, moving slowly to keep his own movement as imperceptible as possible.

The keening of the Stones and the hissing of wind through the grass formed a constant background. But he began to hear other noises as well — the rustling of small animals in the grass, and other, less explicable, sounds. With each one, his heart raced a little faster, wondering if this might be the Kalkara, creeping in on the sleeping figures of his friends. Once, he was convinced that he could hear the breath of a heavy animal. Fear rose up in him, clutching at his throat, until he realised that, with his senses tuned to the utmost degree, he could actually hear his companions breathing quietly in their sleep.

He knew that, from any more than five metres away, he would be virtually invisible to the human eye, thanks to the cloak, the shadows and the shape of the bush around him. But he wondered if the Kalkara depended on sight alone. Perhaps they had other senses that would tell them that there was an enemy concealed in the bush. Perhaps, even now, they were moving closer, concealed by the long shifting grass, ready to strike . . .

His nerves, already stretched beyond endurance by the Stone Flutes' dismal song, urged him to spin round and identify the source of each new sound as he heard it. But he knew that to do so would be to reveal himself. He forced himself to move slowly, turning carefully until he faced the direction from which he thought the sound had come, assessing each new risk before discarding it.

In the long hours of tense watching, he saw nothing but the racing clouds, the fleeting moon and the undulating sea of grass that surrounded them. By the time the moon reached the preordained elevation, he was physically and mentally drained. He woke Gilan to take over the watch, then rolled back into his cloak again.

This time there were no dreams. Exhausted, he slept soundly until the grey light of dawn.

They saw the Stone Flutes by midmorning — a grey and surprisingly small circle of granite monoliths that stood at the top of a rise in the Plain. Their elected course took the riders a kilometre or so to one side of the Stones and Will was content to go no closer. The depressing song was now louder than ever, ebbing and flowing on the tide of the wind.

'Next flute player I meet,' said Gilan with grim humour, 'I'm going to split his lip for him.'

They continued on their way, the kilometres passing behind them, hour after hour, one the same as the next, with nothing new to see and always with the faint howl of the Stones at their back, keeping their nerves on edge.

The Plainsman rose suddenly from the grass some fifty metres away from them. Small, dressed in grey rags and with long hair hanging unkempt to his shoulder, he glared at them through mad eyes for several seconds.

Will's heart had barely recovered from the shock of his sudden appearance when he was off, bent double and running through the grass, seeming to sink into it. Within seconds, he had disappeared, swallowed by the grass. Halt was about to urge Abelard in pursuit but he stopped. The arrow he had selected instantly and laid on the bowstring remained undrawn. Gilan was also ready to shoot, his reactions every bit as sharp as Halt's. He too held his shot, looking curiously at his senior.

Halt shrugged. 'May mean nothing,' he said. 'Or maybe he's off to tell the Kalkara. But we can hardly kill him on suspicion.'

Gilan let out a short bark of laughter, more to release the tension he felt as a result of the man's unexpected appearance.

'I suppose there's no difference,' he said, 'whether we find the Kalkara or they find us.' Halt's eyes fixed on him for a moment, without any sign of answering humour.

'Believe me, Gilan,' he said, 'there's a big difference.'

They had abandoned the forced march pace now and rode slowly through the tall grass. Behind them, the sound of the Stones began to fade a little, much to Will's relief. Now, he realised, the wind was carrying it away from them.

Some time passed following the sudden appearance of the Plain dweller, with no further sign of life. A question had been nagging at Will all through the afternoon.

'Halt?' he said experimentally, not sure if Halt would order him to silence. The Ranger looked at him, eyebrows raised in a sign that he was prepared to answer questions, so Will continued. 'Why do you think Morgarath has enlisted the Kalkara? What does he stand to gain?'

Halt realised that Gilan was waiting for his answer as well. He marshalled his thoughts before he replied. He was a little reluctant to verbalise them, as so much of the answer depended on guesswork and intuition.

'Who knows why Morgarath ever does anything?' he answered slowly. 'I can't give you a definite answer. All I can tell you is what I assume — and what Crowley thinks as well.'

He glanced quickly at his two companions. It was obvious from their expectant expressions that they were prepared to accept his assumptions as ironclad fact. Sometimes, he thought wryly, a reputation for being right all the time could be a heavy burden.

'There's a war coming,' he went on. 'That much is already obvious. The Wargals are on the move and we've heard that Morgarath has been in contact with Ragnak.' He saw the puzzled expression flit across Will's face. Gilan, he knew, understood who Ragnak was. 'Ragnak is the Oberjarl, or supreme lord, if you like, of the Skandians — the sea wolves.' He saw the quick flash of comprehension and went on.

'This is obviously going to be a bigger war than we've fought before and we're going to need all our resources — and our best commanders to lead us. I think that's what Morgarath has in mind. He's seeking to weaken us by having the Kalkara kill our leaders. Northolt, the supreme army commander, and Lorriac, our best cavalry commander, have gone already. Certainly there will be other men who will step into those positions but there will inevitably be some confusion in the changeover period, some loss of cohesion. I think that's what's behind Morgarath's plan.'

Gilan said thoughtfully. 'There's another aspect as well.

Both those men were instrumental in his defeat last time. He's destroying our command structure and getting revenge at the same time.'

Halt nodded. 'That's true, of course. And to a twisted mind like Morgarath's, revenge is a powerful motive.'

'So you think there'll be more killings?' Will asked and Halt met his gaze steadily.

'I think there'll be more attempts. Morgarath has sent them out twice with targets and they've succeeded. I don't see any reason why they won't go after others. Morgarath has reason to hate a lot of people in the Kingdom. The King himself, perhaps. Or maybe Baron Arald — he caused Morgarath some grief in the last war.'

And so did you, Will thought, with a sudden flash of fear for his teacher. He was about to voice the thought that Halt might be a target, then realised that Halt was probably well aware of the fact himself. Gilan was asking the older Ranger another question.

'One thing I don't understand. Why do the Kalkara keep returning to their hideout? Why not just move from one victim to the next?'

'I suppose that's one of the few advantages we do have,' Halt told them. 'They're savage and merciless and more intelligent than Wargals. But they're not human. They are totally single-minded. Show them a victim and they'll hunt him down and kill him or die themselves in the attempt. But they can only keep track of one victim at a time. Between killings, they'll return to their lair. Then Morgarath — or one of his underlings — will prime them for their next victim and they'll head out again. Our best hope is to intercept them on the way if they've been given a new target. Or kill them in their lair if they haven't.'

Will looked for the thousandth time at the featureless grass plain that lay before them. Somewhere out there, the two fearsome creatures were waiting, perhaps with a new victim already in mind. Halt's voice interrupted his train of thought.

'Sun's going down,' he said. 'We may as well camp here.'

They swung down stiffly from their saddles, easing the girths to make their horses more comfortable.

'That's one thing about this blasted place,' Gilan said, looking around them. 'One spot is as good as another to camp. Or as bad.'

Will woke from a dreamless sleep to the touch of Halt's hand on his shoulder. He tossed back the cloak, glanced at the scudding moon overhead and frowned. He couldn't have been asleep for more than an hour. He started to say so, but Halt stopped him, placing a finger to his lips for silence. Will looked around and realised Gilan was already awake, standing above him, his head turned to the north-east, back the way they had come, listening.

Will came to his feet, moving carefully to avoid making any undue noise. His hands had automatically gone to his weapons but he relaxed as he realised there was no immediate threat. The other two were listening intently. Then Halt raised a hand and pointed to the north.

'There it is again,' he said softly.

Then Will heard it, above the moaning of the Stone

Flutes and the soughing of the wind through the grass, and the blood froze in his veins. It was a high-pitched, bestial howl that ululated and climbed in pitch. An inhuman sound carried to them on the wind from the throat of a monster.

Seconds later, another howl answered the first. Slightly deeper in pitch, it seemed to come from a position a little to the left of the first. Without needing to be told, Will knew what the sounds meant.

'It's the Kalkara,' Halt said grimly. 'They have a new target and they're hunting.'

Twenty-seven

The three companions spent a sleepless night as the hunting cries of the Kalkara dwindled to the north. When they first heard the sounds, Gilan had moved to saddle Blaze, the bay horse snorting nervously at the fearsome howling of the two beasts. Halt, however, gestured for him to stop.

'I'm not going after those things in the dark,' he said briefly. 'We'll wait till first light, then look for their tracks.'

The tracks were easy enough to find, as the Kalkara obviously made no attempt to conceal their passing. The long grass had been crushed by the two heavy bodies, leaving a clear trail pointing east-north-east. Halt found the trail left by the first of the two monsters, then a few minutes later, Gilan found the second, about a quarter of a kilometre to the left and travelling parallel — close enough to provide support in case of an attack, but distant enough to avoid any trap set for its brother.

Halt considered the situation for a few moments, then came to a decision.

'You stay with the second one,' he told Gilan. 'Will and I will follow this one. I want to make sure they both keep heading in the same direction. I don't want one of them doubling back to come behind us.'

'You think they know we're here?' Will asked, working hard to keep his voice sounding steady and disinterested.

'They could. There's been time for that Plainsman we saw to have warned them. Or maybe it's just coincidence and they're heading out on their next mission.' He glanced at the trail of crushed grass, moving irrevocably in one constant direction. 'They certainly seem to have a purpose.' He turned to Gilan again. 'In any event, keep your eyes peeled and pay close attention to Blaze. The horses will sense these beasts before we will. We don't want to run into an ambush.'

Gilan nodded and swung Blaze away to return to the second trail. At a hand signal from Halt, the three Rangers began riding forward, following the direction the Kalkara had taken.

'I'll watch the trail,' Halt told Will. 'You keep an eye on Gilan, just in case.'

Will turned his attention to the tall Ranger, some two hundred metres away and keeping pace with them. Blaze was only visible from the shoulders up, his lower half masked by the long grass. From time to time, undulations in the intervening ground took both rider and horse out of sight and the first time this happened, Will reacted with a cry of alarm as Gilan simply seemed to disappear into the ground. Halt turned quickly, an arrow already at half draw, but at that moment, Gilan and Blaze reappeared, seemingly unconscious of the moment of panic they'd caused.

'Sorry,' Will muttered, annoyed that he'd allowed his nerves to get the better of him. Halt regarded him shrewdly.

'That's all right,' he said steadily. 'I'd rather you let me know any time you even think there's a problem.' Halt knew only too well that, having called a false alarm once, Will might be reluctant to react next time — and that could be fatal for all of them.

'Tell me every time you lose sight of Gilan. And tell me again when he reappears,' he said. Will nodded, understanding his teacher's reasoning.

And so they rode on, the keening cry of the Flutes swelling in their ears again as they approached the stone circle. This time, they would pass much closer, Will realised, as the Kalkara seemed to be heading straight for the site. As they rode, their passage was marked by intermittent reports from Will.

'He's gone . . . still gone . . . All right. I see him again.' The dips and rises in the ground were virtually invisible under the waving cover of tall grass. In fact, Will was never sure whether it was Gilan passing through a depression or he and Halt. Often it was a combination of both.

There was one bad time Gilan and Blaze sank from sight and didn't reappear within the customary few seconds.

'I can't see him . . .' Will reported. Then: 'Still gone . . . still gone . . . no sign of him . . .' His voice began to rise in pitch as the tension grew within him. 'No sign of them . . . *still* no sign . . .'

Halt brought Abelard to a stop, his bow ready once again, his eyes searching the ground to their left as they waited for Gilan to reappear. He let go a piercing whistle, three ascending notes. There was a pause, then an answering whistle, this time the same three notes in descending order, came clearly to them. Will heaved a sigh of relief and just at that moment Gilan reappeared, large as life. He faced them and made a large gesture with both arms raised in an obvious question: *What's the problem?*

Halt made a negative gesture and they moved on.

As they approached the Stone Flutes, Halt became more and more watchful. The Kalkara that he and Will were trailing was heading straight towards the circle. He reined in Abelard and shaded his eyes, studying the dismal grey rocks intently, looking for movement or any sign that the Kalkara might be lying in wait to ambush them.

'It's the only decent cover for miles around,' he said. 'Let's not take the chance that the damn thing could be lurking in there waiting for us. We'll go a little carefully, I think.'

He signalled for Gilan to join them and explained the situation. Then they split up to form a wide perimeter around the Stones, riding in slowly from three different directions, checking their horses for any possible sign of reaction as they came closer. But the site was empty, although close in, the jangling moan of the wind through the flute holes was close to unbearable. Halt chewed his lip reflectively, staring out across the sea of grass at the two undeviating trails left by the Kalkara.

'This is taking us too long,' he said finally. 'As long as we can see their trails for a couple of hundred metres ahead, we'll move faster. Slow down when you come to a rise or any time when the trail isn't visible for more than fifty metres.'

Gilan nodded his understanding and resumed his wide position. They urged their horses on now in a canter, the easy lope of the Ranger horse that would eat the kilometres ahead of them. Will maintained his watch on Gilan and whenever the visible trail diminished, either Halt or Gilan would whistle and they would slow to a walk until the ground opened up again before them.

As night fell, they camped once again. Halt still refused to follow the two killers in the dark, even though the moon meant their trail was easily visible.

'Too easy for them to double back in the dark,' he said. 'I want plenty of warning when they finally come at us.'

'You think they will?' asked Will, noticing that Halt had said *when*, not *if*. The Ranger glanced at his young pupil.

'Always assume an enemy knows you're there and that he will attack you,' he said. 'That way, you tend to avoid unpleasant surprises.' He dropped a hand on Will's shoulder to reassure the boy. 'It can still be unpleasant but at least it's not a surprise.'

In the morning, they resumed the trail once more, moving at the same brisk pace, slowing only when they had no clear sight of the lie of the land ahead of them. By early afternoon, they had reached the edge of the Plain and rode once again into the wooded country to the north of the Mountains of Rain and Night.

Here, they found, the two Kalkara had joined company, no longer keeping the wide separation they had maintained on the open ground of the Plain. But their chosen path remained the same, just east of north. The three Rangers followed this course for another hour before Halt reined in Abelard, and signalled the others to dismount for a conference. They grouped around a map of the Kingdom that he rolled out on the grass, using arrows as weights to stop the edges re-rolling.

'Judging from their tracks, we've made up some time on them,' he said. 'But they're still a good half day ahead of us. Now, this is the direction they're following . . .'

He took another arrow and laid it on the map, orientating it so that it pointed to the direction the Kalkara had been following for the past two days and nights.

'As you can see, if they keep going in this direction, there are only two places of any significance that they could be heading for.' He pointed to a place on the map. 'Here — the Ruins of Gorlan. Or further north, Castle Araluen itself.'

Gilan drew in breath sharply. 'Castle Araluen?' he said. 'You don't think they'd dare try for King Duncan?'

Halt looked at him and shook his head. 'I simply don't know,' he replied. 'We don't know nearly enough about these beasts and half of what we think we know is probably myth and legend. But you've got to admit, it would be a bold stroke — a masterstroke — and Morgarath has never been averse to that sort of thing.'

He let the others digest the thought for a few moments, then traced a line from their current position to the north-west. 'Now I've been thinking. Look, here's Castle Redmont. Perhaps a day's ride away — and then another day to here.'

From Redmont, he traced a line north-east, to the Ruins of Gorlan marked on the map.

'One person, riding hard, and using two horses, could make it in less than a day to Redmont, and then lead the Baron and Sir Rodney here, to the Ruins. If the Kalkara keep moving at the pace they are, we might just be able to intercept them there. It'll be close, but it's possible. And with two warriors like Arald and Rodney on hand, we'll stand a far better chance of stopping the damn things once and for all.'

'One moment, Halt,' Gilan interrupted. 'You said *one* person, riding *two* horses?'

Halt met Gilan's gaze with his own. He could see that the young Ranger had already divined what he had in mind.

'That's right, Gilan,' he said. 'And the lightest one among us will travel fastest. I want you to turn Blaze over to Will. If he alternates between Tug and your horse, he can do it in the time.'

He saw the reluctance on Gilan's face and understood it perfectly. No Ranger would like the idea of handing his horse over to someone else — even another Ranger. But at the same time Gilan understood the logic behind the suggestion. Halt waited for the younger man to break the silence, while Will watched the two of them, eyes wide with alarm at the thought of the responsibility that was about to be loaded onto him.

Finally, reluctantly, Gilan broke the silence.

'I suppose it makes sense,' he said. 'So what do you want me to do?'

'Follow behind me on foot,' Halt said briskly, rolling the chart up and replacing it in his saddlebag. 'If you can get hold of a horse anywhere, do so and catch up with me. Otherwise, we'll rendezvous at Gorlan. If we miss the

Kalkara there, Will can wait for you — with Blaze. I'll keep following the Kalkara until you all catch up with me.'

Gilan nodded his acquiescence and Halt felt a surge of fondness for him as he did. Once Gilan saw the sense of his proposal, he wasn't the kind to raise arguments or objections. He did say, rather ruefully:

'I thought you said my sword might come in handy?'

'I did,' replied Halt, 'but this gives me a chance to bring in a force of fully armoured knights, with axes and lances. And you know that's the best way to fight the Kalkara.'

'True,' said Gilan, then, taking Blaze's bridle, he knotted the reins together and threw them over the bay's neck. 'You may as well start out on Tug,' he said to Will. 'That'll give Blaze a chance to rest. He'll follow behind you without a lead rein and so will Tug when you're riding Blaze. Tie the reins up like this on Tug's neck so they don't dangle down and snag anything.'

He began to turn back to Halt, then remembered something. 'Oh yes, before you mount him the first time, remember to say "Brown Eyes".'

'Brown eyes,' Will repeated and Gilan couldn't help grinning.

'Not to me. To the horse.' It was an old Ranger joke and they all smiled. Then Halt brought them back to the business at hand.

'Will? You're confident you can find your way to Redmont?'

Will nodded. He touched the pocket where he kept his own copy of the chart, and glanced at the sun for direction.

'North-west,' he said tightly, indicating the direction he had chosen. Halt nodded, satisfied.

'You'll strike the Salmon River before dusk, that will give you a good reference point. And the main highway is just a little way west of the river. Keep to a steady canter all the way. Don't try to race the horses — you'll just tire them out that way and you'll be slower in the long run. Travel safely now.'

Halt swung up into Abelard's saddle and Will mounted Tug. Gilan pointed to Will and spoke in Blaze's ear.

'Follow, Blaze. Follow.' The bay horse, intelligent as all Ranger horses were, tossed its head as if in acknowledgement of the order. Before they parted, Will had one more question that had been bothering him.

'Halt,' he said, 'the Ruins of Gorlan . . . what exactly are they?'

'It's ironic, isn't it?' Halt replied. 'They're the ruins of Castle Gorlan, Morgarath's former fiefdom.'

Twenty-eight

The ride to Castle Redmont soon settled into a blur of weariness. The two horses maintained the steady lope for which they had been bred. The temptation, of course, was to urge Tug into a wild gallop, with Blaze following behind. But Will knew that such a course would be self-defeating. He was moving at the horses' best speed. As old Bob, the horse trainer, had told him, Ranger horses could maintain a canter all day without tiring.

It was a different matter for the rider. Added to the physical effort of moving constantly to the rhythm of whichever horse he was riding — and the two had distinctly different gaits, due to their difference in size — was the equally debilitating mental strain.

What if Halt were wrong? What if the Kalkara had suddenly veered to the west and were heading now on a course that would intercept his? What if he made some terrible mistake and failed to reach Redmont in time?

That last fear, the fear of self-doubt, was the hardest

one of all to deal with. In spite of the hard training he had undergone over the past months, he was still little more than a boy. What was more, he had always had Halt's judgement and experience to rely on in the past. Now he was alone — and he knew how much depended on his ability to carry out the task he had been set.

The thoughts, the doubts, the fears crowded his tired mind, tumbling over each other, jostling for position. The Salmon River came and went beneath the steady rhythm of his horses' hooves. He paused to water the horses briefly at the bridge then, once on the King's Highway, he made excellent time, with only short halts at regular intervals to change his mount.

The day's shadows lengthened and the trees over-hanging the road grew dark and menacing. Each noise from the darkening trees, each vaguely seen movement in the shadows, brought his heart to his mouth with a lurch.

Here, an owl hooted and stooped to fasten its claws round an unwary mouse. There, a badger prowled, hunting its prey like a grey shadow in the undergrowth of the forest. With each movement and noise, Will's imagination worked overtime. He began to see great black figures — much as he imagined a Kalkara would look — in every patch of shadow, in every dark clump of bushes that stirred with the light breeze. Reason told him that there was almost no chance that the Kalkara would be seeking him out. Imagination and fear replied that they were abroad somewhere — and who was to say they weren't close by?

Imagination and fear won.

And so the long, fear-filled night passed, until the low light of dawn found a weary figure hunched in the saddle of a sturdy, barrel-chested horse that drove steadily onwards to the north-west.

Dozing in the saddle, Will snapped awake with a start, feeling the first warmth of the sun's rays upon him. Gently, he reined Tug in and the little horse stood, head down, sides heaving. Will realised he had been riding far longer than he should have been, his fear having driven him to keep Tug running through the darkness, long after he should have rested him. He dismounted stiffly, aching in every joint, and paused to rub the horse's soft nose affectionately.

'Sorry, boy,' he said. Tug, reacting to the touch and the voice that he now knew so well, tossed his head and shook his shaggy mane. If Will had asked it, he would have continued, uncomplaining, until he dropped. Will looked around. The cheerful light of early morning had dispelled all the dark fears of the night before. Now, he felt slightly foolish as he remembered those moments of choking panic. Stiffly, he dismounted, then loosened the girth straps on the saddle. He gave his horse ten minutes respite, until Tug's breathing seemed to settle and his sides ceased heaving. Then, marvelling at the recuperative powers and endurance of the Ranger horse breed, he tightened the girths on Blaze's saddle and swung astride the bay, groaning softly as he did so. Ranger horses might recover quickly. Ranger apprentices took a little longer.

It was late morning when Castle Redmont finally came in sight.

Will was riding Tug again, the small horse seemingly none the worse for the hard night he'd put in, as they crested the last row of hills and the green valley of Arald's barony stretched out before them.

Exhausted, Will stopped for a few seconds, leaning tiredly on the pommel. They'd come so far, so quickly. He looked with relief on the familiar sight of the castle — and the tidy little village that nestled contentedly in its shadow. Smoke was rising from chimneys. Farmers were walking slowly home from their fields for their midday meal. The castle itself stood solid and reassuring in its bulk at the crest of the hill.

'It all looks so . . . normal,' Will said to his horse.

Somehow, he realised, he had been expecting to find things changed. The Kingdom was about to go to war again for the first time in fifteen years, but here life went on as normal.

Then, realising he was wasting time, he urged Tug forward until he was stretched out in a gallop, both boy and horse eager to finish this final leg of their journey.

People looked up in surprise at the rapid passing of the small, green and grey clad figure, hunched low over the neck of his dusty horse, with a larger bay horse following behind. One or two of the villagers recognised Will and called a greeting. But their words were lost in the rattle of hooves.

The rattle turned to an echoing drumming as they swept across the lowered drawbridge into the foreyard of the castle itself. Then the drumming became an urgent clattering on the cobblestones of the yard. Will drew back lightly on the reins and Tug slid to a halt by the entrance to Baron Arald's tower.

The two men at arms on duty there, surprised by his sudden appearance and breakneck pace, stepped forward and barred his path with their crossed pikes.

'Just a moment, you!' said one of them, a corporal. 'Where do you think you're off to in such a clatter and a rush?'

Will opened his mouth to reply but before words could form, an angry voice boomed from behind him.

'What the hell do you think you're doing, you idiot? Don't you recognise a King's Ranger when you see one?'

It was Sir Rodney, striding across the courtyard on his way to see the Baron. The two sentries stiffened to attention as Will turned, gratefully, to the Battlemaster.

'Sir Rodney,' he said, 'I have an urgent message from Halt for Lord Arald and yourself.'

As Halt had observed to Will after the boar hunt, the Battlemaster was a shrewd man. He took in Will's dishevelled clothing, the two dusty horses, standing, heads drooping tiredly, and realised this was no time for a lot of foolish questions. He jerked a thumb at the doorway.

'Best come in and tell us then.' He turned to the sentries. 'Have these horses looked after. Feed and water them.'

'Not too much of either, please, Sir Rodney,' Will said quickly. 'Just a small amount of grain and water, and maybe you could have them rubbed down. I'll be needing them again soon.'

Rodney's eyebrows rose at that. Will and the horses looked as if they could use a long rest.

'Something must be urgent,' he said, adding to the corporal, 'See to the horses then. And have food brought to Baron Arald's study — and a jug of cold milk.'

The two knights whistled in astonishment as Will told them the news. Word had already come that Morgarath was mustering his army and the Baron had sent out messengers to assemble his own troops — both knights and men at arms. But the news of the Kalkara was something else entirely. No hint of that had reached Castle Redmont.

'You say Halt thinks they may be going after the King?' Baron Arald asked as Will finished speaking. Will nodded, then hesitated before he added:

'Yes, my lord. But I think there's another possibility.'

He was loath to go further but the Baron gestured for him to continue and he finally gave voice to the suspicion that had been building inside him through the long night and day.

'Sir . . . I think maybe there's a chance that they're after Halt himself.'

Once the suspicion was voiced, and the fear was out in the open to be examined and evaluated, he felt the better for it. Somewhat to his surprise, Baron Arald didn't dismiss the idea. He stroked his beard thoughtfully as he digested the words.

'Go on,' he said, wanting to hear Will's reasoning.

'It's just that Halt felt Morgarath might be looking for revenge — looking to punish those who fought him last time. And I thought, probably Halt did him the most harm of all, didn't he?'

'That's true enough,' said Rodney.

'And I thought, maybe the Kalkara knew we were following them — the Plainsman had plenty of time to find them and tell them. And maybe they were leading Halt on, until they found a place for an ambush. So while he thinks he's hunting them, he's actually the one being hunted.'

'And the Ruins of Gorlan would be an ideal place for it,' Arald agreed. 'In that tumble of rocks, they could be on him before he had a chance to use that longbow of his. Well, Rodney, there's no time to waste. You and I will go immediately. Half armour, I think. We'll move faster that way. Lances, axes and broadswords. And we'll take two horses each — we'll follow Will's example there. We'll leave in an hour. Have Karel gather another ten knights and follow us as soon as he can.'

'Yes, my lord,' the Battlemaster replied.

Baron Arald turned back to Will.

'You've done a good job, Will. We'll take care of this now. As for you, you look as if you could use eight hours' solid sleep.'

Wearily, aching in every muscle and joint, Will drew himself erect.

'I'd like to come with you, my lord,' he said. He sensed that the Baron was about to disagree and added hurriedly, 'Sir, none of us know what is going to happen and Gilan is out there somewhere on foot. Besides . . .' He hesitated.

'Go on, Will,' the Baron said quietly and, when the boy looked up, Arald saw the steel in his eyes.

'Halt is my master, sir, and he's in danger. My place is with him,' Will said.

The Baron assessed him shrewdly, then came to a decision.

'Very well. But at least you can get an hour's rest. There's a cot in that annexe over there.' He indicated a curtained-off section of the study. 'Why don't you use it?'

'Yes, sir,' said Will gratefully. His eyes felt as if he'd had handfuls of sand rubbed into them. He had never been happier to obey an order in his life.

Twenty-nine

Through that long afternoon, Will felt as if he had lived his entire life in the saddle, his only respite being the hourly changes from one horse to another.

A brief pause to dismount, loosen the girth straps of the horse he had been riding, tighten those on the horse which had been following, then he would remount and ride on. Again and again, he marvelled at the amazing endurance shown by Tug and Blaze as they maintained their steady canter. He even had to rein them in a little, to keep pace with the battlehorses ridden by the two knights. Big, powerful and trained for war as they might be, they couldn't match the constant pace of the Ranger horses, in spite of the fact that they were fresh when the small party had left Castle Redmont.

They rode without speaking. There was no time for idle talk and, even if there had been, it would have been difficult to hear one another above the drumming thunder of the four heavy battlehorses, the lighter rattle of Tug and

Blaze's hooves and the constant clank of equipment and weapons that accompanied them as they rode.

Both men carried long war lances — hard ash poles more than three metres in length, tipped with a heavy iron point. In addition, each had a broadsword strapped to his saddle — huge, two-handed weapons that dwarfed the swords they normally wore in day-to-day use — and Rodney had a heavy battleaxe slung at the rear right pommel of his saddle. It was the lances on which they would place greatest trust, however. They would keep the Kalkara at a distance, and so reduce the chance that the knights might be frozen by the terrifying stare of the two beasts. Apparently, the hypnotic gaze was only effective at close quarters. If a man couldn't see the eyes clearly, there was little chance of their paralysing him with their gaze.

The sun was dropping fast behind them, throwing their shadows out before them, long and distorted by the low angle light. Arald glanced over his shoulder at the sun's position and called to Will.

'How long before dusk, Will?'

Will turned in his saddle and frowned at the descending ball of light before answering.

'Less than an hour, my lord.'

The Baron shook his head doubtfully. 'It'll be a close run thing to get there before full dark then,' he said. He urged his battlehorse onward, increasing speed a little. Tug and Blaze matched the increase without effort. None of them wanted to be hunting the Kalkara in the dark.

The hour's rest at the castle had done wonders for Will. But it seemed that it had happened in another lifetime now. He thought over the cursory briefing that Arald had given as they mounted to leave Redmont. If they found the Kalkara at the Ruins of Gorlan, Will was to hold back while the Baron and Sir Rodney charged the two monsters. There were no complex tactics involved, just a headlong charge that might take the two killers by surprise.

'If Halt's there, I'm sure he'll take a hand too. But I want you well back out of harm's way, Will. That bow of yours won't make any impression on a Kalkara.'

'Yes, sir,' Will had said. He had no intention of getting close to the Kalkara. He was more than content to leave things to the two knights, protected by their shields, helmets and half armour of chain mail shirts and leggings. However, Arald's next words quickly dispelled any overconfidence he might have had in their ability to deal with the beasts.

'If the damn things get the better of us, I'll want you to ride for more help. Karel and the others will be somewhere behind us. Find them, then go after the Kalkara with them. Track those beasts down and kill them.'

Will had said nothing to that. The fact that Arald even contemplated failure, when he and Rodney were the two foremost knights within a two hundred kilometre radius, spoke volumes of his concern about the Kalkara. For the first time, Will realised that in this contest, the odds were heavily against them.

The sun was trembling on the brink of the world, the shadows at their longest, and they still had several kilometres to go. Baron Arald raised a hand and brought the party to a stop. He glanced at Rodney and jerked a thumb at the bundle of pitch-soaked torches each man carried behind his saddle.

'Torches, Rodney,' he said briefly. The Battlemaster demurred for a moment.

'Are you sure, my lord? They'll give away our position if the Kalkara are watching.'

Arald shrugged. 'They'll hear us coming anyway. And among the trees we'll move too slowly without the light. Let's take the chance.'

He was already striking his flint and steel together, igniting a spark that set his small pile of tinder smoking, then flaring into flame. He held the torch in the flame and the thick, sticky pine pitch with which it was impregnated suddenly caught and burst into yellow flame. Rodney leaned towards him with another torch and lit it in the Baron's flame. Then, holding the torches high, their lances held in place by leather thongs looped around their right wrists, they resumed their gallop, thundering into the darkness beneath the trees as they finally left the broad road they had been following since noon.

It was another ten minutes before they heard the screaming.

It was an unearthly sound that twisted the stomach into knots of fear and turned the blood cold. Involuntarily, the Baron and Sir Rodney reined in as they heard it. Their horses plunged wildly against the reins. It came from straight ahead of them and rose and fell, until the night air quaked with the horror of it.

'Good God in heaven!' the Baron exclaimed. 'What is that?' His face was ashen as the hellish sound soared through the night towards them, to be answered immediately by another, identical howl.

But Will had heard the terrible noise before. He felt the blood leave his face now as he realised his fears were being proven correct.

'It's the Kalkara,' he said. 'They're hunting.'

And he knew there was only one person out there that they could be after. They had turned back and were hunting Halt.

'Look, my lord!' Rodney said, pointing to the rapidly darkening night sky. Through a break in the tree cover, they saw it, a sudden flare of light reflecting in the sky, evidence of a fire in the near distance.

'That's Halt!' the Baron said. 'Bound to be. And he'll need help!'

He rammed his spurs into the tired Battlehorse's flanks, urging the beast forward into a lumbering gallop, the torch in his hand streaming flame and sparks behind him as Sir Rodney and Will galloped in his tracks.

It was an eerie sensation, following those flaming, spitting torches through the trees, their elongated tongues of flame blowing back behind the two riders, casting weird and terrifying shadows among the trees, while ahead of them, the glow of the large fire, presumably lit by Halt, grew stronger and nearer with each stride.

They broke out of the trees with virtually no warning, and before them was a scene from nightmares.

There was a short space of open grass, then the ground beyond was a litter of tumbled rocks and boulders. Giant pieces of masonry, still held together by mortar, lay scattered on their sides and edges, sometimes half buried in the soft grassy earth. The ruined walls of Castle Gorlan surrounded the scene on three sides, nowhere rising to more than five metres in height, destroyed and cast down by a vengeful Kingdom after Morgarath had been driven south to the Mountains of

Rain and Night. The resulting chaos of rocks and sections of tumbled wall was like the playground of a giant child — scattered in all directions, piled carelessly on top of one another, leaving virtually no clear ground at all.

The whole scene was illuminated by the leaping, twisting flames of a bonfire some forty metres in front of them. And beside it, a horrific figure crouched, screaming hatred and fury, plucking uselessly at the mortal wound in its chest that had finally brought it down.

Over two and a half metres tall, with shaggy, matted, scale-like hair covering its entire body, the Kalkara had long, talon-clad arms that reached to beneath its knees. Relatively short, powerful hind legs gave it the ability to cover the ground at a deceptive speed in a series of leaps and bounds. All of this the three riders took in as they emerged from the trees. But what they noticed most was the face — savage and ape-like, with huge, yellowed canine teeth and red, glowing eyes filled with hatred and the blind desire to kill. The face turned towards them now and the beast screamed a challenge, tried to rise, and stumbled back into a half crouch again.

'What's wrong with it?' Rodney asked, reining in his horse. Will pointed to the cluster of arrows that protruded from its chest. There must have been eight of them, all placed within a hand's breadth of each other.

'Look!' he cried. 'Look at the arrows!'

Halt, with his uncanny ability to aim and fire in a blur of movement, must have sent a volley of arrows, one after the other, to smash into the armour-like matted hair, each one widening a gap in the monster's defences until the final arrow had penetrated deep into its flesh. Its black blood ran in sheets down its torso and again it screamed its hatred at them.

'Rodney!' yelled Baron Arald. 'With me! Now!'

Dropping the lead rein to his spare horse, he tossed the flaming torch to one side, couched his lance and charged. Rodney was a half second behind him, the two battle-horses thundering across the open space. The Kalkara, its lifeblood saturating the ground at its feet, rose to meet them, in time to take the two lance points, one after the other, in the chest.

It was all but dead. Even so, the weight and strength of the monster checked the onward rush of the battlehorses. They reared back on their haunches as both knights leaned forward in the stirrups to drive the lance points home. The sharp iron penetrated, smashing through the matted hair. Then the force of the charge drove the Kalkara from its feet and hurled it backwards, into the flames of the fire behind it.

For an instant nothing happened. Then there was a blinding flash, and a pillar of red flame that reached ten metres into the night sky. And quite simply, the Kalkara disappeared.

The two battlehorses reared in terror, Rodney and the Baron only just managing to retain their seats. They backed away from the fire. There was a terrible reek of charred hair and flesh filling the air. Vaguely, Will remembered Halt discussing the way to deal with a Kalkara. He had said that they were rumoured to be particularly susceptible to fire. Some rumour, he thought heavily, trotting Tug forward to join the two knights.

Rodney was rubbing his eyes, still dazzled by the enormous flash.

'What the devil caused that?' he asked. The Baron gingerly retrieved his lance from the fire. The wood was charred and the point blackened.

'It must be the waxy substance that mats their hair together into that hard shell,' he replied, in a wondering tone of voice. 'It must be highly flammable.'

'Well, whatever it was, we did it,' Rodney replied, a note of satisfaction in his voice. The Baron shook his head.

'Halt did it,' he corrected his Battlemaster. 'We merely finished him off.'

Rodney nodded, accepting the correction. The Baron glanced at the fire, still pouring a torrent of sparks into the air, but settling back now from the huge explosion of red flame.

'He must have lit this fire when he sensed they were circling back on him. It lit up the area so he had light to shoot by.'

'He shot all right,' Sir Rodney put in. 'Those arrows must have all struck within a few square centimetres.'

They looked around, searching for some sign of the Ranger. Then, below the ruined walls of the castle, Will caught sight of a familiar object. He dismounted and ran to retrieve it and his heart sank as he picked up Halt's powerful longbow, smashed and splintered into two pieces.

'He must have fired from over here,' he said, indicating the point below the ruined wall where he had found the bow. They looked up, imagining the scene, trying to re-create it. The Baron took the shattered weapon from Will as he remounted Tug.

'And the second Kalkara reached him as he killed its brother,' he said. 'The question is, where is Halt now? And where is the other Kalkara?'

That was when they heard the screaming start again.

Thirty

Inside the ruined, overgrown courtyard, Halt crouched among the tumbled masonry that had once been Morgarath's stronghold. His leg, numb where the Kalkara had clawed him, was beginning to throb painfully and he could feel the blood seeping past the rough bandage he had thrown around it.

Somewhere close by, he knew the second Kalkara was searching for him. He heard its shuffling movements from time to time and once even its rasping breath as it moved close to his hiding place between two fallen sections of wall. It was only a matter of time before it found him, he knew. And when that happened, he was finished.

He was wounded and unarmed. His bow was gone, smashed in that first terrifying charge when he had fired arrow after arrow into the first of the two monsters. He knew the power of his bow and the penetrative qualities of his razor-sharp, heavy arrowheads. He couldn't believe that the monster had continued to absorb that hail of arrows and still come on, seemingly undaunted. By the time it faltered, it was already too late for Halt to turn his attention to its companion. The second Kalkara was almost upon him, its massive, taloned paw smashing the bow from his grasp, so that he barely had time to scramble for safety onto the ruined wall.

As it clawed its way after him, he had drawn his saxe knife and struck at the terrible head. But the beast was too fast for him and the heavy knife glanced off one of its armoured forearms. At the same time, he found himself confronted by its red, hate-filled eyes and felt his mind leaving him, his muscles freezing in terror as he was drawn to the horrific beast before him. It took an immense effort to wrench his eyes away from the creature's gaze, and he staggered back, losing the saxe knife as the bear-like claws swiped at him and ripped down the length of his thigh.

Then he had run, unarmed and bleeding, trusting to the maze-like confusion of the ruins to evade the monster behind him.

He had sensed the change in the Kalkara's movements around late afternoon. Their steady and previously undeviating path to the north-east suddenly changed as the two beasts abruptly separated, each turning through ninety degrees and moving in different directions into the forest that surrounded them. Their trails, up until then so easy to follow, also showed signs of concealment, so that only a tracker as skilled as a Ranger would have been able to follow them. For the first time in years, Halt felt a cold stone of fear in his belly as he realised that the Kalkara were now hunting him.

The Ruins were close by and he elected to make a stand there, rather than in the woods. Leaving Abelard safely out of harm's way, he made his way on foot to the Ruins. He knew the Kalkara would come after him once night fell, so he prepared as best he could, gathering deadfall wood to form the bonfire. He even found half a jar of cooking oil in the ruins of the kitchen. It was rancid and foul smelling but it would still burn. He poured it over the pile of wood and moved back to a spot where he could place the wall at his back. He had fashioned a supply of torches and kept them burning as darkness fell and he waited for the implacable killers to come for him.

He sensed them before he saw them. Then he made out the two shambling forms, darker patches against the darkness of the trees. They saw him immediately, of course. The flickering torch jammed into the wall behind him made sure of that. But they missed the pile of oil-soaked wood — and that was what he had been counting on. As they screamed their hunting cries, he tossed the burning torch into the pile and the flames leapt up instantly, flaring yellow in the darkness.

For a moment, the beasts hesitated. Fire was their one nemesis. But they saw the Ranger was nowhere near the flames and they came on — straight into the hail of arrows that Halt met them with.

If they'd had another hundred metres to cover, he might have managed to stop them both. He still had over a dozen arrows in his quiver. But time and distance were against him and he had barely escaped with his life. Now, he huddled beneath two pieces of masonry that formed an A-shaped refuge, hidden in a shallow indentation in the ground, his cloak concealing him, as it had for years. His only hope now was that Will would arrive with Arald and Rodney. If he could evade the creature until help came, he might have a chance.

He tried not to think of the other possibility — that Gilan would arrive before them, alone and armed only with his bow and sword. Now that he had seen the Kalkara close up, Halt knew that one man had little chance of standing against one. If Gilan arrived before the knights, he and Halt would both die here.

The creature was quartering the old courtyard now like a hunting dog in search of game, adopting a methodical search pattern, back and forth, examining every space, every cranny, every possible hiding place. This time, he knew, it would find him. His hand touched the hilt of his small throwing knife, the only weapon left to him. It would be a puny, almost useless defence, but it was all he had left.

Then he heard it: the unmistakable heavy drumming of battlehorses' hooves. He looked up, watching the Kalkara through a small gap between the rocks that concealed him. It had heard them too. It was standing erect, its face turned towards the sound outside the ruined walls.

The horses stopped, and he heard the ringing scream of the mortally wounded Kalkara outside as it challenged these new enemies. The hoofbeats rose again, gaining speed and momentum. Then there was a scream and a gigantic red flash that towered for a moment into the sky. Dimly, Halt reasoned that the first Kalkara must have been thrust into the fire. He began to inch back, wriggling out of his hiding place. Perhaps he could outflank the remaining Kalkara, moving to the side and scaling the wall before it noticed him. The chances seemed good. Its attention was drawn now to whatever was happening outside. But even as he had the thought, he realised it was no option. Though the Kalkara had apparently forgotten him for the moment, it was moving stealthily towards the tumbled masonry that formed a rough stairway to the top of the wall.

In a few more minutes, it would be in position to drop on his unsuspecting friends on the other side, taking them by surprise. He had to stop it.

Halt was clear of the hiding place now, the small knife sliding free of the sheath almost of its own volition as he ran across the courtyard, dodging and weaving among the scattered rubble. The Kalkara heard him before he had gone half a dozen paces and it turned back on him, terrifying in its silence as it loped, ape-like, to cut him off before he could warn his friends.

Halt stopped suddenly, stock-still, eyes locked on the shambling figure coming at him.

In another few metres, its hypnotic gaze would seize control of his mind. He felt the irresistible urge to look into those red eyes growing stronger. Then he closed his own eyes, his brow furrowed in fierce concentration, and brought his knife hand up, back and forward in one smooth, instinctive memory throw, seeing the target moving in his mind's eye, mentally aligning the throw and the spin of the knife to the point in space where knife and target would arrive simultaneously.

Only a Ranger could have made that throw — and only one of a handful of them. It took the Kalkara in its right eye and the beast screamed in pain and fury as it stopped to clutch at the sudden lance of agony that began in its eye and seared all the way to the pain sensors in its brain. Then Halt was running past it for the wall, scrambling up the rocks.

Will saw him as a shadowy figure as he scrambled onto the top of the ruined wall. But shadowy or not, there was something unmistakable about it.

'Halt!' he cried, pointing so that the two knights saw him as well. All three of them saw the Ranger pause, look back and hesitate. Then a huge shape began to appear a few metres behind him as the Kalkara, whose wound was painful but nowhere near mortal, came after him.

Baron Arald went to remount. Then, realising that no horse could pick its way through the tumble of rocks and masonry beside the wall, he dragged his huge broadsword from its saddle scabbard and ran towards the ruins.

'Get back, Will!' he shouted as he advanced and Will nervously edged Tug back to the fringe of the trees.

On the wall, Halt heard the shout and saw Arald running forward. Sir Rodney was close behind him, a huge battleaxe whirring in circles around his head.

'Jump, Halt! Jump!' the Baron shouted and Halt needed no further invitation. He leapt the three metres from the wall, rolling to break his fall as he landed. Then he was up on his feet, running awkwardly to meet the two knights as the wound in his leg re-opened.

Will watched, his heart in his mouth, as Halt ran towards the two knights. The Kalkara hesitated a moment then, screaming a bloodcurdling challenge, it leapt after him. But, whereas Halt had rolled to recover, the Kalkara simply transformed the three-metre drop into a huge, bounding leap, its unbelievably powerful rear legs driving it up and forward, covering the ground between it and Halt in that one movement. The massive arm swung, catching Halt a glancing blow and sending him rolling forward, unconscious. But the beast had no time to finish him off, as Baron Arald stepped up to meet it, the broadsword humming in a deadly arc for its neck.

The Kalkara was wickedly fast and it ducked the killing blow, then slammed its talons into Arald's exposed back before he could recover from the stroke. They slashed the chain mail as if it were wool and Arald grunted in pain and surprise as the force of the blow drove him to his knees, the broadsword falling from his hands, blood streaming from half a dozen deep slashes in his back.

He would have died then and there had it not been for Sir Rodney. The Battlemaster whirled the heavy war axe as if it were a toy, and crashed it into the Kalkara's side.

The armour of wax-matted hair protected the beast, but the sheer force of the blow staggered it so that it reeled back from the knight, screaming in fury and frustration. Sir Rodney advanced, placing himself protectively between the Kalkara and the prone figures of Halt and the Baron, his feet set, the axe drawing back for another crushing blow.

And then, strangely, he let the weapon fall from his grasp and stood before the monster, totally at its mercy as the power of the Kalkara's gaze, now channelled through its one good eye, robbed him of his will and his ability to think.

The Kalkara screamed its victory to the night sky. Black blood streamed down its face. Never in its life had it felt such pain as these three puny men had inflicted on it. And now they would die for presuming to stand against it. But the primitive intelligence that drove it wanted its moment of triumph and it screamed again and again over the three helpless men.

Will watched, horrified. A thought was forming, an idea was lurking somewhere at the edge of his mind. He looked to one side, saw the flickering torch that Baron Arald had discarded. Fire. The one weapon that could defeat the Kalkara. But he was forty metres away . . .

He whipped an arrow from his quiver, slipping from the saddle and running lightly to the flickering torch. A good supply of sticky, melted pitch had run down the handle of the torch and he quickly rolled the arrowhead in the soft, clinging stuff, forming a huge gobbet of it on the arrow. Then he placed it in the flame until it flared to life.

Forty metres away, the huge evil creature was satisfying its need for triumph, its screams rolling and echoing through the night as it stood over the two bodies — Halt unconscious, Baron Arald in a daze of pain. Sir Rodney still stood, frozen in place, hands dangling helplessly by his side as he waited for his death. Now the Kalkara raised one massive, taloned paw to strike him down and all the knight could feel was the paralysing terror of its gaze.

Will brought the arrow back to full draw, wincing at the pain as the flames singed against his bow hand. He raised his aim point a little to allow for the extra weight of the pitch, and released.

The arrow soared in a spark-trailing arc, the wind of its

passage subduing the flame to a mere coal. The Kalkara saw the flash of light coming and turned to look, sealing its own fate as the arrow struck it square in its massive chest.

It barely penetrated into the hard, scale-like hair. But as the arrow came to a halt, the little flame flared again, the bonding material in the hair around it caught, and the flame began to spread with incredible speed.

Now the Kalkara's screams had terror in them as it felt the touch of fire — the one thing in life it feared.

The monster beat at the flames on its chest with its paws but that served only to spread the fire to its arms. There was a sudden rush of red flame and in seconds the Kalkara was engulfed, burning from head to toe, rushing blindly in circles in a vain attempt to escape. The screams were nonstop, piercing, reaching higher and higher into a scale of agony that the mind could barely comprehend as the rush of flames grew fiercer with each second.

And then the screaming stopped and the creature was dead.

Thirty-one

The inn at Wensley Village was full of music and laughter and noise. Will sat at a table with Horace, Alyss and Jenny, while the innkeeper plied them with a succulent dinner of roast goose and farm fresh vegetables, followed by a delicious blueberry pie whose flaky pastry won even Jenny's approval.

It had been Horace's idea to celebrate Will's return to Castle Redmont with a feast. The two girls had agreed immediately, eager for a break in their day-to-day lives, which now seemed rather humdrum compared to the events that Will had been part of.

Naturally, word of the battle with the Kalkara had gone round the village like wildfire — an appropriate simile, Will thought as it occurred to him. As he entered the inn with his friends that evening, an expectant hush had fallen over the room and every eye had turned towards him. He was grateful for the deep cowl on his cloak, which concealed his rapidly reddening features. His three companions sensed his embarrassment. Jenny, as ever, was the quickest to react, and to break the silence that filled the inn.

'Come on, you solemn lot!' she cried to the musicians by the fireplace. 'Let's have some music in here! And some chatter if you please!' She added the second suggestion with a meaningful glace at the other occupants in the room.

The musicians took their cue from her. Jenny was a difficult person to refuse. They quickly struck up a popular local folk tune and the sound filled the room. The other villagers gradually realised that their attention was making Will uncomfortable. They remembered their manners and began talking among themselves again, only occasionally casting glances his way, marvelling that one so apparently young could have been part of such momentous events.

The four former wardmates took their seats at a table at the back of the room, where they could talk without interruption.

'George sent his apologies,' Alyss said as they took their seats. 'He's snowed under with paperwork — the entire Scribeschool is working day and night.'

Will nodded his understanding. The impending war with Morgarath, and the need to mobilise troops and call in old alliances, must have created a mountain of paperwork.

So much had happened in the ten days since the battle with the Kalkara.

Making camp by the ruins, Rodney and Will had tended to the wounds of Baron Arald and Halt, finally settling the two men into a restful sleep. Soon after first light, Abelard trotted into the camp, anxiously searching for his master. Will had only just managed to soothe the horse when a leg-weary Gilan arrived, riding a sway-backed plough horse.

The tall Ranger gratefully reclaimed Blaze. Then, after being reassured that his former master was in no danger, he set off almost immediately for his own fief, after Will promised to return the plough horse to its owner.

Later in the day, Will, Halt, Rodney and Arald had returned to Castle Redmont, where they were all plunged into the nonstop activity of preparing the castle's fighting men for war. There were a thousand and one details to be handled, messages to be delivered and summonses sent out. With Halt still recuperating from his wound, a great deal of this work had fallen to Will.

In times like these, he realised, a Ranger had little chance for relaxation, which made this evening such a welcome diversion. The innkeeper bustled importantly to their table and set down four glass tankards and a jug of the non-alcoholic beer he brewed from ginger root before them.

'No charge for this table tonight,' he said. 'We're privileged to have you in our establishment, Ranger.'

He moved away, calling to one of his serving boys to come and attend the Ranger's table, 'And be quick smart about it!' Alyss raised one eyebrow in amazement.

'Nice to be with a celebrity,' she said. 'Old Skinner usually holds onto a coin so tight the king's head suffocates.'

Will made a dismissive gesture. 'People exaggerate things,' he said. But Horace leaned forward, his elbows on the table.

'So tell us about the fight,' he said, eager for details. Jenny looked wide-eyed at Will.

'I can't believe how brave you were!' she said admiringly. 'I would have been terrified.'

'Actually, I was petrified,' Will told them with a rueful grin. 'The Baron and Sir Rodney were the brave ones.

They charged in and took those creatures on at close quarters. I was forty or fifty metres away the whole time.'

He described the events of the battle, without going into too much detail in his description of the Kalkara. They were dead and gone now, he thought, and best forgotten as soon as possible. Some things didn't need dwelling on. The three others listened, Jenny wide-eyed and excited, Horace eager for details of the fight and Alyss, calm and dignified as ever, but totally engrossed in his story. As he described his solo ride to summon help, Horace shook his head in admiration.

'Those Ranger horses must be a breed apart,' he said. Will grinned at him, unable to resist the jibe that rose to his mind.

'The trick is staying on them,' he said, and was pleased to see a matching grin spread over Horace's face as they both remembered the scene at the Harvest Day Fair. He realised, with a small glow of pleasure, that his relationship with Horace had evolved into a firm friendship, with each viewing the other as an equal. Eager to slip out of the spotlight, he asked Horace how life was progressing in Battleschool. The grin on the bigger boy's face widened.

'A lot better these days, thanks to Halt,' he said and, as Will adroitly plied him with more questions, he described life in the Battleschool for them, joking about his mistakes and shortcomings, laughing as he described the many punishment details he attracted. Will noticed how Horace, once inclined to be boastful and a little arrogant, was far more self-effacing these days. He suspected that Horace was doing better as an apprentice warrior than he let on.

It was a pleasant evening, all the more so after the strain

and terror of the hunt for the Kalkara. As the servers cleared their plates, Jenny smiled expectantly at the two boys.

'Right! Now who's going to dance with me?' she said brightly and Will was just too slow in responding, Horace claiming her hand and leading her to the dance floor. As they joined the dancers, Will glanced uncertainly at Alyss. He was never quite sure what the tall girl was thinking. He thought that perhaps it might be good manners to ask her to dance as well. He cleared his throat nervously.

'Um . . . would you like to dance too, Alyss?' he said awkwardly. She favoured him with the barest trace of a smile.

'Perhaps not, Will. I'm no great shakes as a dancer. I seem to be all legs.'

In fact, she was an excellent dancer but, a diplomat to the core, she sensed that Will had only asked her out of politeness. He nodded several times and they lapsed into silence — but a friendly sort of silence.

After some minutes, she turned towards him, placing her chin on her hand to consider him closely.

'A big day for you tomorrow,' she said and he flushed. He had been summoned to appear before the Baron's entire court the following day.

'I don't know what that's all about,' he muttered. Alyss smiled at him.

'He possibly wants to thank you in public,' she said. 'I'm told barons tend to do that to people who have saved their lives.'

He began to say something but she laid one soft cool hand over his and he stopped. He looked into those calm, smiling grey eyes. Alyss had never struck him as pretty.

But now he realised that her elegance and grace and those grey eyes, framed by her fine blonde hair, created a natural beauty that far surpassed mere prettiness. Surprisingly, she leaned closer to him and whispered.

'We're all proud of you, Will. And I think I'm proudest of all.'

And she kissed him. Her lips on his were incredibly, indescribably soft.

Hours later, before he finally fell asleep, he could still feel them.

Thirty-two

Will stood, transfixed by stage fright, just inside the massive doors to the Baron's audience hall.

The building itself was enormous. It was the main room of the castle, the room where the Baron conducted all his official business with the members of his court. The ceiling seemed to stretch upwards forever. Shafts of light poured down into the room from windows set high in the massive walls. At the far end of the room, seeming to be an immense distance away, the Baron sat, wearing his finest robes, on a raised, throne-like chair.

Between him and Will was the biggest crowd Will had ever seen. Halt propelled his apprentice gently forward with a shove in the back.

'Get on with it,' he muttered.

There were hundreds of people in the Great Hall and every eye was turned towards Will. All of the Baron's Craftmasters were there, in their official robes. All of his knights and all the ladies of the court — every one in their best and finest clothes. Further down the hall were the men at arms from the Baron's army, the other apprentices and the trademasters from the village. He saw a flutter of colour as Jenny, uninhibited as ever, waved a scarf at him. Alyss, standing beside her, was a little more discreet. She unobtrusively kissed her fingertips to him.

He stood awkwardly, shifting his weight from one foot to another. He wished that Halt had let him wear his Ranger's cloak, so he could blend into the background and disappear.

Halt shoved him again.

'Get a move on!' he hissed.

Will turned to him. 'Aren't you coming with me?' he asked. Halt shook his head.

'Not invited. Now get going!'

He shoved Will once more, then limped, favouring his injured leg, to a seat. Finally, realising he had no other course to follow, Will began to walk down the long, long aisle. He heard the muttering voices as he went. Heard his name being whispered from one mouth to another.

And then the clapping started.

It began with one knight's lady and rapidly spread throughout the entire hall as everyone joined in. It was deafening, a thundering, echoing roar of applause that continued until he reached the foot of the Baron's chair.

As Halt had instructed him, he dropped to one knee and bowed his head forward.

The Baron stood up and raised his hand for silence and the clapping died away to echoes.

'Stand up, Will,' he said softly, and reached out a hand to help the boy to his feet.

In a daze, Will obeyed. The Baron rested a hand on his shoulder and turned him to face the huge throng before them. His deep voice carried effortlessly to the farthest corner of the hall when he spoke.

'This is Will. Apprentice to the Ranger Halt of this fiefdom. See him now and know him, all of you. He has proven his fidelity, courage and initiative to this fief and to the Kingdom of Araluen.'

There was a murmur of appreciation from the people watching. Then the clapping began again, this time accompanied by cheering. Will realised the cheers had begun in the section of the crowd where the Battleschool apprentice warriors stood. He could make out Horace's grinning face, leading the chorus.

The Baron held up a hand for silence, wincing as the movement brought pain to his cracked ribs and the carefully bandaged and sutured gashes in his back. The cheering and clapping slowly died away.

'Will,' he said, in a voice that echoed to the farthest corners of the massive room, 'I owe you my life. There can be no thanks adequate for that. However, it is in my power to grant you a wish that you once made of me . . .'

Will looked up at him, frowning.

'A wish, sir?' he said, more than a little puzzled by the Baron's words.

The Baron nodded. 'I made a mistake, Will. You asked me if you could train as a warrior. It was your wish to become one of my knights and I refused you.

'Now, I can rectify that mistake. It would do me honour to have one so brave and resourceful as one of my knights. Say the word now and you have my permission to transfer to the Battleschool as one of Sir Rodney's apprentices.'

Will's heart pounded in his ribs. He thought how, all his life, he had yearned to be a knight. He remembered his deep and bitter disappointment on the day of the Choosing, when Sir Rodney and the Baron had refused his request.

Sir Rodney stepped forward, and the Baron gestured for him to speak.

'My lord,' said the Battlemaster, 'it was I who refused this boy as an apprentice, as you know. Now, I want all here to know that I was wrong to do so. I, my knights and my apprentices all agree that there could be no more worthy member of the Battleschool than Will!'

There was a great roar of approval from the assembled knights and apprentice warriors. With a slithering clash of steel they unsheathed their swords and clashed them together above their heads, shouting Will's name. Again, Horace was one of the first to do so, and the last to stop.

Gradually, the tumult died down and the knights resheathed their swords. At a sign from Baron Arald, two pages stepped forward, bearing with them a sword and a beautifully enamelled shield which they laid at Will's feet. The shield was painted with a representation of a fierce boar's head.

'This will be your coat of arms when you graduate, Will,' said the Baron gently, 'to remind the world of the first time we learned of your courage and loyalty to a comrade.'

The boy went down on one knee and touched the smooth, enamelled surface of the shield. He drew the sword slowly and reverently from its scabbard. It was a beautiful weapon, a masterpiece of the swordsmith's art.

The blade was razor keen, and slightly blued. The hilt and crosspiece were inlaid with gold and the boar's head symbol was repeated on the pommel. The sword itself seemed to have a life of its own. Perfectly balanced, it seemed light as a feather in his grasp. He glanced from the beautiful, jewelled sword to the plain leather grip of his Ranger knife.

'They're a knight's weapons, Will,' the Baron urged. 'But you've proved over and again that you're worthy of them. Just say the word and they're yours.'

Will slid the sword back into its scabbard and stood slowly up. Here was everything he had ever wished for. And yet . . .

He thought of the long days in the forest with Halt. The fierce satisfaction that he felt when one of his arrows struck home, exactly where he had aimed it, exactly as he had seen it in his mind before releasing it. He thought of the hours spent learning to track animals and men. Learning the art of concealment. He thought of Tug, of the pony's courage and devotion.

And he thought of the sheer pleasure that came when he heard Halt's simple 'Well done' as he completed a task to his satisfaction. And suddenly, he knew. He looked up at the Baron and said in a firm voice:

'I am a Ranger, my lord.'

There was a murmur of surprise from the crowd.

The Baron stepped closer and said in a low voice, 'Are you sure, Will? Don't turn this down just because you think Halt might be offended or disappointed. He insisted that this is up to you. He's already agreed to abide by your decision.'

Will shook his head. He was more certain than ever.

'I thank you for the honour, my lord.' He glanced at the Battlemaster, and saw, to his surprise, that Sir Rodney was smiling and nodding his head in approval. 'And I thank the Battlemaster and his knights for their generous offer. But I am a Ranger.' He hesitated. 'I mean no offence by this, my lord,' he finished awkwardly.

A huge smile creased the Baron's features and he gripped Will's hand in his enormous grip.

'And I take none, Will. None at all! Your loyalty to your craft and your Craftmaster does honour to you and to all of us who know you!' He gave Will's hand one final, firm shake and released him.

Will bowed and turned away to walk down that long, long aisle again. Again, the cheering started and this time, he kept his head high as the cheers rolled around him and echoed to the rafters of the Great Hall. Then, as he neared the massive doors once more, he saw a sight that stopped him in his tracks, stunned with surprise.

For, standing a little aside from the crowd, wrapped in his grey and green mottled cloak, his eyes shadowed by the cowl, was Halt.

And he was smiling.

Epilogue

ater that afternoon, after all the noise and cele-brations had died down, Will sat alone on the tiny verandah of Halt's small cottage. In his hand, he held a small bronze amulet, shaped like an oak leaf, with a steel chain threaded through a ring at the top.

'It's our symbol,' his teacher had explained as he handed it to him after the events at the castle. 'The Rangers' equivalent of a coat of arms.'

Then he had fumbled inside his own collar and produced an identically shaped oak leaf, on a chain around his neck. The shape was identical, but the colour was different. The oak leaf Halt wore was made of silver.

'Bronze is the apprentice colour,' Halt had told him. 'When you finish your training, you'll receive a silver oak leaf like this one. We all wear them in the Ranger Corps, either silver or bronze.' He had looked away from the boy for a few minutes, then had added, his voice a little husky, 'Strictly speaking, you shouldn't receive it until you've passed your first Assessment. But I doubt anyone will argue about it, the way things have turned out.'

Now the curiously shaped piece of metal gleamed dully in Will's hand as he thought of the decision he'd made. It seemed so strange to him that he had voluntarily given up the one thing that he had spent most of his life hoping for: the chance to go through Battleschool and take his place as a knight in Castle Redmont's army.

He twirled the bronze oak leaf on its chain around his index finger, letting it wind right up to the finger, then spiral loose again. He sighed deeply. Life could be so complicated. Deep within himself, he felt he had made the right decision. And yet, way down deeper still, there was a tiny thread of doubt.

With a start, he realised that there was someone standing beside him. It was Halt, he recognised as he turned quickly. The Ranger stooped and sat beside the boy on the rough pine planking of the narrow verandah. Before them, the low sun of the late afternoon filtered through the luminous green leaves of the forest, the light seeming to dance and gyrate as the light breeze stirred the leaves.

'A big day,' he said softly and Will nodded.

'And a big decision that you made,' the Ranger said, after several more minutes' silence between them. This time, Will turned to face him.

'Halt, did I make the right decision?' he asked finally, the anguish clear in his voice. Halt placed his elbows on his knees and leaned forward a little, squinting into the dappled glare through the trees.

'As far as I'm concerned, yes. I chose you as an apprentice and I can see all the potential you have to be a

Ranger. I've even come to almost enjoy having you around and getting under my feet,' he added, with the barest hint of a smile. 'But my feelings, my wishes, aren't important in this. The right decision for you is the one you want most.'

'I always wanted to become a knight,' Will said, then realised, with a sense of surprise, that he'd phrased the statement in the past tense. And yet he knew that a part of him still wanted it.

'It is possible, of course,' said Halt quietly, 'to want to do two different things at the same time. Then it just becomes a choice of knowing which one you want most.'

Not for the first time, Will felt that Halt had some way of reading his mind.

'If you can sum it up in one thought, what's the main reason you feel a little disappointed that you refused the Baron's offer?' Halt continued.

Will considered the question. 'I guess . . .' he said slowly, 'I feel that by turning down Battleschool, I'm somehow letting my father down.'

Halt's eyebrows shot up in surprise. 'Your father?' he repeated and Will nodded.

'He was a mighty warrior,' he told the Ranger, 'A knight. He died at Hackham Heath, fighting the Wargals — a hero.'

'You know all this, do you?' Halt asked him and Will nodded. This was the dream that had sustained him through the long, lonely years of never knowing who he was or what he was meant to be. The dream had become reality for him now.

'He was a man any son would be proud of,' he said finally, and Halt nodded.

'That's certainly true.'

There was something in his voice that made Will hesitate. Halt wasn't simply agreeing out of politeness. Will turned quickly to him, realising the full implications of the Ranger's words.

'You knew him, Halt? You knew my father?'

There was a light of hope in the boy's eyes that cried out for the truth and the Ranger nodded soberly.

'Yes. I did. I didn't know him for long. But I think I could say I knew him well. And you're right. You can be extremely proud of him.'

'He was a mighty warrior, wasn't he?' said Will.

'He was a soldier,' Halt agreed, 'and a brave fighter.'

'I knew it!' Will said happily, 'He was a great knight!'

'A sergeant,' Halt said softly, and not unkindly.

Will's jaw hung open, the next words he had been about to say frozen in his throat. Finally, he managed, in a confused voice:

'A sergeant?'

Halt nodded. He could see the disappointment in the boy's eyes and he put an arm around his shoulders.

'Don't judge a man's quality by his position in life, Will. Your father, Daniel, was a loyal and brave soldier. He didn't have the opportunity to go to Battleschool because he began life as a farmer. But, if he had, he would have been one of the greatest of knights.'

'But he . . .' the boy began sadly. The Ranger stopped him, continuing in that same kind, soft, compelling voice.

'Because without taking any of the vows or the special training that knights have, he lived up to the highest ideals of knighthood and chivalry and valour. It was actually a few days after the battle at Hackham Heath, while

Morgarath and his Wargals were fighting their way back to Three Step Pass. A sudden counterattack took us by surprise and your father saw a comrade surrounded by a troop of Wargals. The man was on the ground and was within a second of being cut to pieces when your father took a hand.'

The light in the boy's eyes had begin to shine again.

'He did?' Will asked, his lips just framing the words, and Halt nodded.

'He did. He left the safety of the battle line and leapt forward, armed only with a spear. He stood over his injured comrade and protected him from the Wargals. He killed one with the spear, then another smashed the head of the spear, leaving Daniel with only a spear shaft. So he used it like a quarterstaff and knocked down two others — left, right! Just like that!'

He flicked his hand to left and right to demonstrate. Will's eyes were intent on him now, seeing the battle as the Ranger described it.

'He was wounded then, as the spear shaft broke under another attack. It would have been enough to kill most men. But he simply took the sword from one of the Wargals he'd killed and struck down three more, all the time bleeding from a massive wound in his side.'

'Three of them?' Will asked.

'Three. He had the speed of a leopard. And remember, as a spearman, he had never really trained with the sword.'

He paused, remembering that day so long ago.

'You know, of course, that there is almost nothing that Wargals fear? They're called the Unminded Ones and once they begin a battle, they almost always finish it.

'*Almost* always. This was one of the few times I saw Wargals afraid. As your father struck out to either side, still standing over his wounded comrade, they began to back away. Slowly at first. Then they ran. They simply turned and ran.

'I have never seen any other man, no knight, no mighty warrior, who could send Wargals running in fear. Your father did. He may have been a sergeant, Will, but he was the mightiest warrior I ever had the privilege to watch. Then, as the Wargals retreated, he sank down on one knee beside the man he'd been protecting, still trying to shield him, even though he knew he was dying himself.

'He had taken half a dozen wounds. But it was probably the first that killed him.'

'And was his friend saved?' Will asked in a small voice.

Halt looked a little puzzled. 'His friend?' he asked.

'The man he protected,' Will explained. 'Did he survive?'

Somehow, he thought it would have been a tragedy if his father's valiant attempt had been unsuccessful.

'They weren't friends,' said Halt. 'Up until that moment, he had never laid eyes on the other man.' He paused, then added, 'Nor I on him.'

The significance of those last four words sank deep into Will's consciousness.

'*You?*' he whispered. 'You were the man he saved?'

Halt nodded. 'As I said, I only knew him for a few minutes. But he did more for me than any other man, before or since. As he was dying, he told me of his wife, and how she was back at their farm alone, with a baby due any day. He begged me to see that she was looked after.'

Will looked at the grim, bearded face he had grown to know so well. There was a deep sadness in Halt's eyes as he remembered that day.

'I was too late to save your mother. It was a difficult birth and she died shortly after you were born. But I brought you back here and Baron Arald agreed that you should be brought up in the Ward — until you were old enough to become my apprentice.'

'But all those years, you never . . .' Will stopped, lost for words. Halt smiled grimly at him.

'I never let on that I had placed you in the Ward? No. Think about it, Will. People are . . . strange about Rangers. How would they have reacted to you as you grew up? Wondering what sort of strange creature you were? We decided it would be better if nobody knew of my interest in you.'

Will nodded. Halt was right, of course. Life as a ward had been difficult enough. It would have been far more so if people had known he was somehow connected to Halt.

'So you took me as your apprentice because of my father?' said Will. But this time Halt shook his head.

'No. I made sure you were looked after because of your father. I chose you because you showed you had the abilities and the skills that were needed. And you also seem to have inherited some of your father's courage.'

There was a long, long silence between them as Will absorbed the story of his father's amazing battle. Somehow, the truth was more stirring, more inspiring than any fantasy he could have made up over the years to sustain himself. Eventually, Halt stood up to go and he smiled gratefully up at the grizzled figure, now silhouetted against the sky as the last light of day died.

'I think my father would be glad I chose the way I did,' he said, slipping the bronze oak leaf on its chain over his head. Halt merely nodded once, then turned away and went inside the cottage, leaving his apprentice to his own thoughts.

Will sat quietly for some minutes. Almost unthinkingly, his hand went to touch the bronze oakleaf symbol hanging at his throat. Faintly, the evening breeze carried the sounds of the Battleschool drill yard to him, and the nonstop hammering and clanking from the armoury that had been going on, night and day, for the past week. They were the sounds of Castle Redmont preparing for the coming war.

Yet strangely, for the first time in his life, he felt at peace.

BOOK 2

This one is for Katy

Prologue

Halt and Will had been trailing the Wargals for three days. The four heavy-bodied, brutish creatures, foot soldiers of the rebel warlord Morgarath, had been sighted passing through Redmont Fief, heading north. Once word reached the Ranger, he had set out to intercept them, accompanied by his young apprentice.

'Where could they have come from, Halt?' Will asked during one of their short rest stops. 'Surely we've got Three Step Pass well and truly bottled up by now?'

Three Step Pass provided the only real access between the Kingdom of Araluen and the Mountains of Rain and Night, where Morgarath had his headquarters. Now that the Kingdom was preparing for the coming war with Morgarath, a company of infantry and archers had been sent to reinforce the small permanent garrison at the narrow pass until the main army could assemble.

'That's the only place where they can come in sizeable

numbers,' Halt agreed. 'But a small party like this could slip into the Kingdom by way of the barrier cliffs.'

Morgarath's domain was an inhospitable mountain plateau that towered high above the southern reaches of the Kingdom. From Three Step Pass in the east, a line of sheer, precipitous cliffs ran roughly due west, forming the border between the plateau and Araluen. As the cliffs swung south-west, they plunged into another obstacle called the Fissure — a huge split in the earth that ran out to the sea, and separated Morgarath's lands from the kingdom of the Celts.

It was these natural fortifications that had kept Araluen, and neighbouring Celtica, safe from Morgarath's armies for the past sixteen years. Conversely, they also provided the rebel warlord with protection from Araluen's forces.

'I thought those cliffs were impassable?' Will said.

Halt allowed himself a grim smile. 'Nowhere is ever really impassable. Particularly if you have no respect for how many lives you lose trying to prove the fact. My guess is that they used ropes and grapnels and waited for a moonless night and bad weather. That way, they could slip past the border patrols.'

He stood, signifying that their rest stop was at an end. Will rose with him and they moved towards their horses. Halt gave a small grunt as he swung into the saddle. The wound he had suffered in the battle with the two Kalkara still troubled him a little.

'My main concern isn't where they came from,' he continued. 'It's where they're heading, and what they have in mind.'

The words were barely spoken when they heard a shout from somewhere ahead of them, followed by a commotion of grunting and, finally, the clash of weapons.

'And we may be about to find out!' Halt finished.

He urged Abelard into a gallop, controlling the horse with his knees as his hands effortlessly selected an arrow and nocked it to the string of his massive longbow. Will scrambled into Tug's saddle and galloped after him. He couldn't match Halt's hands-free riding skill. He needed his right hand for the reins as he held his own bow ready in his left hand.

They were riding through sparse woodland, leaving it to the sure-footed Ranger horses to pick the best route. Suddenly, they burst clear of the trees into a wide meadow. Abelard, under his rider's urging, slid to a stop, Tug following suit beside him. Dropping the reins to Tug's neck, Will's right hand instinctively reached for an arrow from his quiver and nocked it ready.

A large fig tree grew in the middle of the cleared ground. At the base of it there was a small camp. A wisp of smoke still curled from the fireplace and a pack and blanket roll lay beside it. The four Wargals they had been tracking surrounded a single man, who had his back to the tree. For the moment his long sword held them at bay, but the Wargals were making small feinting movements towards him, trying to find an advantage. They were armed with short swords and axes and one carried a heavy iron spear.

Will drew in a sharp breath at the sight of the creatures. After following their trail for so long, it was a shock to come upon them so suddenly in plain sight. Bear-like in build, they had long muzzles and massive, yellow canine fangs, exposed now as they snarled at their prey. They were covered in shaggy fur and wore black leather armour. The man was dressed similarly and his voice cracked in fear as he repelled their tentative attacks.

'Stand back! I'm on a mission for Lord Morgarath. Stand back, I order you! I order you in Lord Morgarath's name!'

Halt nudged Abelard around, allowing him room to draw the arrow he had ready on the string.

'Drop your weapons! All of you!' he shouted. Five pairs of eyes swung towards him as the four Wargals and their prey turned in surprise. The Wargal with the spear recovered first. Realising that the swordsman was distracted, he darted forward and ran the spear into his body. A second later, Halt's arrow buried itself in the Wargal's heart and he fell dead beside his stricken prey. As the swordsman sank to his knees, the other Wargals charged at the two Rangers.

Shambling and bear-like as they might be, they covered ground with incredible speed.

Halt's second shot dropped the left-hand Wargal. Will fired at the one on the right and realised instantly that he had misjudged the brute's speed. The arrow hissed through the space where the Wargal had been a second before. His hand flew to his quiver for another arrow and he heard a hoarse grunt of pain as Halt's third shot buried itself in the chest of the middle creature. Then Will loosed his second arrow at the surviving Wargal, now terrifyingly close.

Panicked by those savage eyes and yellow fangs, he snatched as he released and knew that his arrow would fly wide and the Wargal was almost upon him.

As the Wargal snarled in triumph, Tug came to his

master's aid. The little horse reared and lashed out with his front hooves at the horrific creature in front of him. Unexpectedly, he also danced forward a few steps, towards the threat, rather than retreating. Will, caught by surprise, clung to the pommel of the saddle.

The Wargal was equally surprised. Like all its kind, it had a deep-seated instinctive fear of horses — a fear born at the Battle of Hackham Heath sixteen years ago, where Morgarath's first Wargal army had been decimated by Araluan cavalry. It hesitated now for a fatal second, stepping back before those flashing hooves.

Halt's fourth arrow took it in the throat. At such short range, the arrow tore clean through. With a final grunting shriek, the Wargal fell dead on the grass.

White-faced, Will slid to the ground, his knees nearly giving way beneath him. He clung to Tug's side to stay upright. Halt swung down quickly and moved to the boy's side. His arm went round him.

'It's all right, Will.' His deep voice cut through the fear that filled Will's mind. 'It's over now.'

But Will shook his head, horrified by the rapid train of events.

'Halt, I missed . . . twice! I panicked and I missed!' He felt a deep sense of shame that he had let his teacher down so badly. Halt's arm tightened around him and he looked up at the bearded face and the dark, deep-set eyes.

'There's a big difference between shooting at a target and shooting at a charging Wargal. A target isn't usually trying to kill you.' Halt added the last few words in a more gentle tone. He could see that Will was in shock. And no wonder, he thought grimly.

'But . . . I missed . . .'

'And you've learned from it. Next time you won't miss. Now you know it's better to fire one good shot than two hurried ones,' Halt said firmly. Then he took Will's arm and turned him towards the camp site under the fig tree. 'Let's see what we have here,' he said, putting an end to the subject.

The black-clad man and the Wargal lay dead beside each other. Halt knelt beside the man and turned him over, whistling softly in surprise.

'It's Dirk Reacher,' he said, half to himself. 'He's the last person I would have expected to see here.'

'You know him?' Will asked. His insatiable curiosity was already helping him to put the horror of the previous few minutes to one side, as Halt had known it would.

'I chased him out of the Kingdom five or six years ago,' the Ranger told him. 'He was a coward and a murderer. He deserted from the army and found a place with Morgarath.' He paused. 'Morgarath seems to specialise in recruiting people like him. But what was he doing here . . .?'

'He said he was on a mission for Morgarath,' Will suggested but Halt shook his head.

'Unlikely. The Wargals were chasing him and only Morgarath could have ordered them to do that, which he'd hardly do if Reacher really was working for him. My guess is that he was deserting again. He'd run out on Morgarath and the Wargals were sent after him.'

'Why?' Will asked. 'Why desert?'

Halt shrugged. 'There's a war coming. People like Dirk try to avoid that sort of unpleasantness.'

He reached for the pack that lay by the camp fire and began to rummage through it.

'Are you looking for anything in particular?' Will asked. Halt frowned as he grew tired of looking through the pack and dumped its contents onto the ground instead.

'Well, it strikes me that if he were deserting Morgarath and coming back to Araluen, he'd have to bring something to bargain for his freedom. So . . .' His voice died away as he reached for a carefully folded parchment among the spare clothes and eating utensils. He scanned it quickly. One eyebrow rose slightly. After almost a year with the grizzled Ranger, Will knew that was the equivalent of a shout of astonishment. He also knew that if he interrupted Halt before he had finished reading, his mentor would simply ignore him. He waited until Halt folded the parchment, stood slowly and looked at his apprentice, seeing the question in the boy's eyes.

'Is it important?' Will asked.

'Oh, you could say so,' Halt told him. 'We appear to have stumbled on Morgarath's battle plans for the coming war. I think we'd better get them back to Redmont.'

He whistled softly and Abelard and Tug trotted to where their masters waited.

From the trees several hundred metres away, carefully downwind so that the Ranger horses would catch no scent of an intruder, unfriendly eyes were upon them. Their owner watched as the two Rangers rode away from the scene of the small battle. Then he turned south, towards the cliffs.

It was time to report to Morgarath that his plan had been successful.

One

It was close to midnight when the single rider reined in his horse outside the small cottage set in the trees below Castle Redmont. The laden pack pony trailing behind the saddle horse ambled to a halt as well. The rider, a tall man who moved with the easy grace of youth, swung down from the saddle and stepped up onto the narrow verandah, stooping to avoid the low-lying eaves. From the lean-to stable at the side of the house came the sound of a gentle nickering and his own horse's head rose as he answered the greeting.

The rider had raised his fist to knock at the door when he saw a light come on behind the curtained windows. He hesitated. The light moved across the room and, a second or so later, the door opened before him.

'Gilan,' Halt said, without any note of surprise in his voice. 'What are you doing here?'

The young Ranger laughed incredulously as he faced his former teacher.

'How do you do it, Halt?' he asked. 'How could you possibly know it was me arriving in the middle of the night, before you'd even opened the door?'

Halt shrugged, gesturing for Gilan to enter the house. He closed the door behind him and moved to the neat little kitchen, opening the damping vent on the stove and sending new life flaring into the wood coals inside. He tossed a handful of kindling into the stove and set a copper kettle on the hot plate over the fire chamber, shaking it first to make sure there was plenty of water in it.

'I heard your horse some minutes ago,' he said. 'Then, when I heard Abelard call a greeting, I knew it had to be a Ranger horse.' He shrugged again. Simple when you explained it, the gesture said. Gilan laughed again in reply.

'Well, that narrowed it down to fifty people, didn't it?' he said. Halt cocked his head to one side with a pitying look.

'Gilan, I must have heard you stumbling up that front step a thousand times when you were studying with me,' he said. 'Give me credit for recognising that sound once more.'

The younger Ranger spread his hands in a gesture of defeat. He unclasped his cloak and hung it over the back of a chair, moving a little closer to the stove. It was a chilly night and he watched Halt measuring coffee into a pot with some anticipation. The door to the rear room of the house opened and Will entered the small living room, his clothes pulled on hastily over his nightshirt, his hair still tousled from sleep.

'Evening, Gilan,' he said casually. 'What brings you here?'

Gilan looked from one to the other in something like despair. 'Isn't anybody surprised when I turn up in the middle of the night?' he asked, of no one in particular. Halt, busy by the stove, turned away to hide a grin. A few minutes earlier, he'd heard Will moving hurriedly to the window as the horse drew closer to the cottage. Obviously, his apprentice had overheard Halt's exchange with Gilan and was doing his best to emulate his own casual approach to the unexpected arrival. However, knowing Will as he did, Halt was sure that the boy was burning with curiosity over the reason for Gilan's sudden appearance. He decided he'd call his bluff.

'It's late, Will,' he said. 'You may as well go back to bed. We have a busy day tomorrow.'

Instantly, Will's nonchalant expression was replaced by a stricken look. The suggestion from his master was tantamount to an order. All thought of appearing casual departed instantly.

'Oh, please, Halt!' the boy exclaimed. 'I want to know what's going on!'

Halt and Gilan exchanged a quick grin. Will was actually hopping from one foot to another as he waited for Halt to rescind the suggestion that he should go to bed. The grizzled Ranger kept a straight face as he set three steaming mugs of coffee on the kitchen table.

'Just as well I made three cups then, isn't it?' he said and Will realised that he'd been having his leg pulled. He shrugged, grinning, and sat down with his two seniors.

'Very well, Gilan, before my apprentice explodes with curiosity, what is the reason for this unexpected visit?'

'Well, it has to do with those battle plans you discovered

last week. Now we know what Morgarath has in mind, the King wants the army ready on the Plains of Uthal before the dark of the next moon. That's when Morgarath plans to break out through Three Step Pass.'

The captured document had told them a great deal. Morgarath's plan called for five hundred Skandian mercenaries to make their way through the swamps of the fenlands and attack the Araluan garrison at Three Step Pass. With the Pass undefended, Morgarath's main army of Wargals would be able to break out and deploy into battle order on the Plains.

'So Duncan plans to beat him to the punch,' Halt said, nodding slowly. 'Good thinking. That way we control the battlefield.'

Will nodded in his turn and said in an equally grave voice, 'And we'll keep Morgarath's army bottled up in the Pass.'

Gilan turned slightly to hide a grin. He wondered if he had tried to copy Halt's mannerisms when he was an apprentice, and decided that he probably had.

'On the contrary,' he said, 'once the army's in place, Duncan plans to withdraw, then fall back to prepared positions and let Morgarath out onto the Plains.'

'Let him out?' Will's voice went up in pitch with surprise. 'Is the King crazy? Why would . . .'

He realised that both Rangers were looking at him, Halt with one eyebrow raised and Gilan with a quizzical smile playing at the corners of his mouth.

'I mean . . .' He hesitated, not sure if questioning the King's sanity might constitute treason. 'No offence or anything like that. It's just —'

'Oh, I'm sure the King wouldn't be offended to hear that a lowly apprentice Ranger thought he was crazy,' said Halt. 'Kings usually love to hear that sort of thing.'

'But Halt . . . to let him out, after all these years? It seems . . .' He was about to say 'crazy' again but thought better of it. He thought suddenly of his recent encounter with the Wargals. The idea of thousands of those vile beasts streaming unopposed out of the Pass made his blood run cold.

It was Halt who answered first. 'That's just the point, Will — *after all these years.* We've spent sixteen years looking over our shoulders at Morgarath, wondering what he's up to. In that time, we've had our forces tied up patrolling the base of the cliffs and keeping watch over Three Step. And he's been free to strike at us any time he likes. The Kalkara were the latest example, as you know only too well.'

Gilan glanced admiringly at his former teacher. Halt had instantly seen the reasoning behind the King's plan. Not for the first time, he understood why Halt was one of the King's most respected advisers.

'Halt's right, Will,' he said. 'And there's another reason. After sixteen years of relative peace, people are growing complacent. Not the Rangers, of course, but the village people who provide men at arms for our army, and even some of the barons and battlemasters in remote fiefs to the north.'

'You've seen for yourself how reluctant some people are to leave their farms and go to war,' Halt put in. Will nodded. He and Halt had spent the past week travelling to outlying villages in Redmont Fief to raise the levies of men who would make up the bulk of the army. On more than one occasion, they had been met with outright hostility — hostility that melted away as Halt exerted the full force of his personality and reputation.

'As far as King Duncan is concerned, now is the time to settle this,' Gilan continued. 'We're as strong as we'll ever be and any delay will only weaken us. This is the best opportunity we'll have to get rid of Morgarath once and for all.'

'All of which still begs my original question,' Halt said. 'What brings you here in the middle of the night?'

'Orders from Crowley,' Gilan said crisply. He placed a written despatch on the table and Halt, after an enquiring look at Gilan, unrolled it and read it. Crowley was the Commandant of the Rangers, Will knew, the most senior of all the fifty Rangers in the Corps. Halt read, then rolled the orders closed again.

'So you're taking despatches to King Swyddned of the Celts,' he said. 'I assume you're invoking the mutual defence treaty that Duncan signed with him some years ago?'

Gilan nodded, sipping appreciatively at the fragrant coffee. 'The King feels we're going to need all the troops we can muster.'

Halt nodded thoughtfully. 'I can't fault his thinking there,' he said softly. 'But . . .?' He spread his hands in a questioning gesture. If Gilan were taking despatches to Celtica, the sooner he got on with it the better, the gesture seemed to say.

'Well,' said Gilan, 'it's an official embassy to *Celtica*.' He laid a little stress on the last word and suddenly Halt nodded his understanding.

'Of course,' he said. 'The old Celtic tradition.'

'Superstition, more like it,' Gilan answered, shaking his head. 'It's a ridiculous waste of time as far as I'm concerned.'

'Of course it is,' Halt replied. 'But the Celts insist on it so what can you do?'

Will looked from Halt to Gilan and back again. The two Rangers seemed to understand what they were talking about. To Will, they might as well have been speaking Espanard.

'It's all very well in normal times,' Gilan said. 'But with all these preparations for war, we're stretched thin in every area. We simply don't have the people to spare. So Crowley thought . . .'

'I think I'm ahead of you,' said Halt and, finally, Will could bear it no longer.

'Well, I'm way behind you!' he burst out. 'What on earth are you two talking about? You are speaking Araluan, aren't you, and not some strange foreign tongue that just sounds like it, but makes no sense at all?'

Two

Halt turned slowly to face his impulsive young apprentice, and raised his eyebrows at the outburst. Will, subsiding, muttered, 'Sorry, Halt,' and the older Ranger nodded.

'I should think so. It's more than obvious that Gilan is asking if I'll release you to accompany him to Celtica.'

Gilan nodded confirmation of the fact and Will frowned, puzzled by the sudden turn of events. 'Me?' he said incredulously. 'Why me? What can I do in Celtica?'

The moment the words had left his mouth, he regretted them. He should have learnt by now never to give Halt that sort of opening. Halt pursed his lips as he considered the question.

'Not much, probably. The real question is, can you be spared from duty here? And the answer to that is "definitely".'

'Then why . . .' Will gave up. They would either explain or they wouldn't. And no amount of asking would make Halt deliver that explanation a second sooner than he chose to. In fact, he was beginning to think that the more questions he asked, the more Halt actually enjoyed keeping him dangling. It was Gilan who took pity on him, perhaps remembering how close-mouthed Halt could be when he chose.

'I need you to make up the numbers, Will,' he said. 'Traditionally, the Celts insist that an official embassy be made up of three people. And to be honest, Halt's right. You're one who can be spared from the main effort here in Araluen.' He grinned a little ruefully. 'If it makes you feel any better, I've been given the mission because I'm the most junior Ranger in the Corps.'

'But why three people?' Will asked, seeing that Gilan at least seemed disposed to answer questions. 'Can't one deliver the message?'

Gilan sighed. 'As we were saying, it's a superstition among the Celts. It goes back to the old days of the Celtic Council, when the Celts, the Scotti and the Hibernians were one alliance. They were ruled then by a triumvirate.'

'The point is,' Halt interrupted, 'of course Gilan can take the message to them. But if he's a sole messenger, they'll keep him waiting and fob him off for days, or even weeks, while they dither over form and protocol. And we don't have that sort of time to waste. There's an old Celtic saying that covers it: *One man may be deceit. Two can be conspiracy. Three is the number I trust.*'

'So you're sending me because you can do without me?' Will said, somewhat insulted by the thought. Halt decided that it was time to massage his young ego a little — but only a little.

'Well, we can, as a matter of fact. But you can't send just anyone on these embassies. The three members have to have some sort of official status or position in the world. They can't be simple men at arms, for example.'

'And you, Will,' Gilan added, 'are a member of the Ranger Corps. That will carry a certain amount of weight with the Celts.'

'I'm only an apprentice,' Will said, and was surprised when both men shook their heads in disagreement.

'You wear the Oakleaf,' Halt told him firmly. 'Bronze or silver, it doesn't matter. You're one of us.'

Will brightened visibly at his teacher's statement. 'Well,' he said, 'when you put it like that, I'd be delighted to join you, Gilan.'

Halt regarded him dryly. It was obviously time for the ego-stroking to end, he thought. Deliberately, he turned to Gilan.

'So,' he said, 'can you think of anyone else who's totally unnecessary to be the third member?'

Gilan shrugged, smiling as he saw Will subside. 'That's the other reason Crowley sent me here,' he said. 'Since Redmont is one of the larger fiefs, he thought you might be able to spare someone else from here. Any suggestions?'

Halt rubbed his chin thoughtfully, an idea forming. 'I think we might have just the person you need,' he said. He turned to Will. 'Perhaps you'd better get some sleep. I'll give Gilan a hand with the horses and then we'll go up to the castle.'

Will nodded. Now that Halt mentioned sleep, he felt an irresistible urge to yawn. He rose and headed for his small room.

'See you in the morning, Gilan.'

'Bright and early,' Gilan smiled and Will rolled his eyes in mock horror.

'I knew you'd say that,' he replied.

Halt and Gilan strolled through the fields towards Castle Redmont in companionable silence. Gilan, attuned to his old teacher's ways, sensed that Halt had something he wanted to discuss, and before too long, the older Ranger broke the silence.

'This embassy to Celtica could be just what Will needs,' he said. 'I'm a little worried about him.'

Gilan frowned. He liked the irrepressible young apprentice. 'What's the problem?' he asked.

'He had a bad time of it when we ran into those Wargals last week,' Halt said. 'He thinks he's lost his nerve.'

'And has he?'

Halt shook his head decisively. 'Of course not. He's got more courage than most grown men. But when the Wargals charged us, he rushed his shot and missed.'

Gilan shrugged. 'No shame in that, is there? After all, he's not yet sixteen. He didn't run, I take it?'

'No. Not at all. He stood his ground. Even got another shot away. Then Tug backed the Wargal off so I could finish it. He's a good horse, that one.'

'He has a good master,' Gilan said and Halt nodded.

'That's true. Still, I think a few weeks away from all of these war preparations will be good for the boy. It might get his mind off his troubles if he spends some time with you and Horace.'

'Horace?' Gilan asked.

'He's the third member I'm suggesting. One of the Battleschool apprentices and a friend of Will's.' Halt thought for a few moments then nodded to himself. 'Yes. A few weeks with people closer to his own age will do him good. After all, folk do say I can be a little grim from time to time.'

'You, Halt? Grim? Who could say such a thing?' Gilan said. Halt glanced at him suspiciously. Gilan was, all too obviously, just managing to keep a straight face.

'You know, Gilan,' he said, 'sarcasm isn't the lowest form of wit. It's not even wit at all.'

Even though it was after midnight, the lights were still burning in Baron Arald's office when Halt and Gilan reached the castle. The Baron and Sir Rodney, Redmont's Battlemaster, had a lot of planning to do, preparing for the march to the Plains of Uthal, where they would join the rest of the Kingdom's army. When Halt explained Gilan's need, Sir Rodney was quick to see where the Ranger's thinking was headed.

'Horace?' he said to Halt. The small, bearded Ranger nodded almost imperceptibly.

'Yes, it's not a bad idea at all,' the Battlemaster continued, pacing the room as he thought it over. 'He has the sort of status you need for the task — he's a Battleschool member, even if he is only a trainee. We can spare him from the force leaving here at the end of the week and . . .' At this he paused and looked meaningfully at Gilan. 'You might even find he's a useful person to have along.'

The younger Ranger looked at him curiously and Sir Rodney elaborated: 'He's one of my best trainees – a real natural with a sword. He's already better than most members of the Battleschool. But he does tend to be a bit formal and inflexible in his approach to life. Perhaps an assignment with two undisciplined Rangers might teach him to loosen up a little.'

He smiled briefly to show that he meant no offence by the joke, then glanced at the sword Gilan wore at his hip. It was an unusual weapon for a Ranger. 'You're the one who studied with MacNeil, is that right?'

Gilan nodded. 'The Swordmaster. Yes, that was me.'

'Hmmm,' muttered Sir Rodney, regarding the tall young Ranger with new interest. 'Well, you might see your way clear to giving Horace a few pointers while you're on the road. I'd take it as a favour and you'll find he's a quick learner.'

'I'd be glad to,' Gilan replied. He thought that he'd like to see this apprentice warrior. He knew from his time as Halt's apprentice that Sir Rodney wasn't given to over-stating praise for any of the students in the Battleschool.

'Well, that's settled then,' Baron Arald said, anxious to get back to planning the thousand and one details of the march to Uthal. 'What time will you be leaving, Gilan?'

'As soon after sun-up as I can, sir,' Gilan replied.

'I'll have Horace report to you before first light,' Rodney told him. Gilan nodded, sensing that the meeting was over. The Baron's next words confirmed it.

'Now if you two will excuse us, we'll get back to the relatively simple business of planning a war,' he said.

Three

The sky was heavy with sullen rain clouds. Somewhere the sun may have been rising, but here there was no sign of it, just a dull, grey light that filtered through the overcast and gradually, reluctantly, filled the sky.

As the little party crested the last ridge, leaving the massive shape of Castle Redmont behind them, the new day finally gave in to the clouds and it began to rain — a cold spring rain. It was light and misting, but persistent. At first, it ran off the riders' treated woollen cloaks. But, eventually, it began to soak into the fibres. After twenty minutes or so, all three were hunched in their saddles, trying to retain as much body warmth as they could.

Gilan turned to his two companions as they plodded along, eyes down, hunched over their horses' necks. He smiled to himself, then addressed Horace, who was keeping a position slightly to the rear, alongside the pack pony Gilan was leading.

'Well then, Horace,' he said, 'are we giving you enough adventure for the moment?'

Horace wiped the misting rain from his face, and grimaced ruefully.

'Less than I'd expected, sir,' he replied. 'But it's still better than close order drill.'

Gilan nodded and grinned at him.

'I imagine it is at that,' he said. Then he added kindly: 'There's no need to ride back there, you know. We Rangers don't stand on ceremony too much. Come and join us.'

He nudged Blaze with his knee and the bay horse stepped out to open a gap. Horace eagerly urged his horse forward, to ride level with the two Rangers.

'Thank you, sir,' he said gratefully. Gilan cocked an eyebrow at Will.

'Polite, isn't he?' he mused. 'Obviously manners are well taught in the Battleschool these days. Nice to be called "sir" all the time.'

Will grinned at the kindly meant jibe. Then the smile faded from his face as Gilan continued thoughtfully.

'Not a bad idea to have a bit of respect shown. Perhaps you could call me sir as well,' he said, turning his face away to study the treeline to one side, so that Will couldn't see the faint trace of a grin that insisted on breaking through.

Aghast, Will choked over his answer. He couldn't believe his ears.

'Sir?' he said finally. 'You really want me to call you sir, Gilan?' Then, as Gilan frowned slightly at him, he amended hurriedly and in great confusion: 'I mean, sir! You want me to call you sir . . . sir?'

Gilan shook his head. 'No. I don't think "sir-sir" is suitable. Nor "Sir Gilan". I think just the one sir would do nicely, don't you?'

Will couldn't think of a polite way of phrasing what was in his mind, and gestured helplessly with his hands. Gilan continued.

'After all, it'll do nicely to keep us all remembering who's in charge of this party, won't it?'

Finally, Will found his voice. 'Well, I suppose it will, Gil . . . I mean, sir.' He shook his head, surprised at this sudden demand for formality from his friend. He rode in silence for a few minutes, then heard an explosive sneezing sound from beside him as Horace tried, unsuccessfully, to smother his giggling. Will glared at him, then turned suspiciously to Gilan.

The young Ranger was grinning all over his face as he eyed the apprentice. He shook his head in mock sorrow.

'Joking, Will. Joking.'

Will realised his leg was being pulled again, and this time with Horace's full knowledge.

'I kne-ew,' he replied huffily dragging the word out into two syllables to show his disdain. Horace laughed out loud. This time, Gilan joined in.

They travelled south all day, finally making camp in the first line of foothills on the road to Celtica. Around midafternoon, the rain had slowly begun to peter out, but the ground around them was still sodden.

They searched under the thickest-foliaged trees for dry, dead wood, and gradually collected enough for a small camp fire. Gilan joined in with the two apprentices, sharing the work among the three of them, and they ate their meal in an atmosphere of friendship and shared experience.

Horace, however, was still a little in awe of the tall young Ranger. Will eventually realised that, by teasing him, Gilan was doing his best to set Horace at ease, making sure that he didn't feel left out. Will found himself warming to Halt's former apprentice even more than before. He reflected thoughtfully that he still had a lot to learn about managing people.

He knew that he faced at least another four years' training before he finished his apprenticeship. Then, he supposed, he'd be expected to carry out clandestine missions, gather intelligence about the Kingdom's enemies and perhaps lead elements of the army, just as Halt did. The thought that one day he would have to depend on his own wits and skill was a daunting one. Will felt secure in the company of experienced Rangers like Halt or Gilan. Their knowledge and ability invested them with a reassuring aura of invincibility and he wondered if he would ever be able to take his place alongside them. Right now, he told himself glumly, he doubted it.

He sighed. Sometimes, it seemed that life was determined to be confusing. Less than a year ago, he had been a nameless, unknown orphan in Castle Redmont's Ward. Since then he had begun to learn the skills of a Ranger, and basked in the admiration and praise of everyone at Redmont Fief when he had helped the Baron, Sir Rodney and Halt defeat the terrifying beasts known as the Kalkara.

He glanced across at Horace, the childhood enemy who had become his friend, and wondered if he felt the same bewildering conflict of emotions. The memory of their days in the Ward together reminded him of his other friends — George, Jenny and Alyss, now apprenticed to their own Craftmasters. He wished he'd had time to say goodbye to them before leaving for Celtica. Particularly Alyss. He shifted uncomfortably as he thought of her. Alyss had kissed him after that night at the inn and he still remembered the soft touch of her lips.

Yes, he thought, particularly Alyss.

Across the camp fire, Gilan observed Will through half-closed eyes. It wasn't easy being Halt's apprentice, he knew. Halt was a near-legendary figure and that laid a heavy burden on anyone apprenticed to him. There was a lot to live up to. He decided that Will needed a little distraction.

'Right!' he said, springing lithely to his feet. 'Lessons!'

Will and Horace looked at each other.

'Lessons?' said Will, in a pleading tone of voice. After a day in the saddle, he was hoping more for his bedroll.

'That's right,' Gilan said cheerfully. 'Even though we're on a mission, it's up to me to keep up the instruction for you two.'

Now it was Horace's turn to be puzzled. 'For me?' he asked. 'Why should I be taught any Ranger skills?'

Gilan picked up his sword and scabbard from where they lay beside his saddle. He withdrew the slender, shining blade from its plain leather receptacle. There was a faint hiss as it came free and the blade seemed to dance in the shifting firelight.

'Not Ranger skills, my boy. Combat skills. Heaven knows, we'll need them as sharp as possible before too long. There's a war coming, you know.' He regarded the heavy-set boy before him with a critical eye. 'Now, let's see what you know about that toothpick you're wearing.'

'Oh, right!' said Horace, sounding a little more pleased about this turn of events. He never minded a little sword practice and he knew it wasn't a Ranger skill. He drew his own sword confidently and stood before Gilan, point politely lowered to the ground. Gilan stuck his own sword point-first into the soft earth, and held out his hand for Horace's.

'May I see that, please?' he asked. Horace nodded and handed it to Gilan hilt-first.

Gilan hefted it, tossed it lightly, then swung it experimentally a few times.

'See this, Will? This is what you look for in a sword.'

Will looked at the sword, unimpressed. It looked plain to him. The blade was simple and straight. The hilt was leather wrapped around the steel tang and the crosspiece was a chunky piece of brass. He shrugged.

'It doesn't look special,' he said apologetically, not wanting to hurt Horace's feelings.

'It's not how they look that counts,' said Gilan. 'It's how they feel. This one, for example. It's well balanced so you can swing it all day without getting overtired, and the blade is light but strong. I've seen blades twice this thick snapped in half by a good blow from a cudgel. Fancy ones, too,' he added, with a smile, 'with engravings and inlays and jewels.'

'Sir Rodney says jewels in the hilt are just unnecessary weight,' said Horace. Gilan nodded agreement.

'What's more, they tend to encourage people to attack you and rob you,' he said. Then, all business again, he returned Horace's sword and took up his own.

'Very well, Horace, we've seen that the sword is good quality. Let's see about its owner.'

Horace hesitated, not sure what Gilan intended.

'Sir?' he said awkwardly. Gilan gestured to himself with his left hand.

'Attack me,' he said cheerfully. 'Have a swing. Take a whack. Lop my head off.'

Still Horace stood uncertainly. Gilan's sword wasn't in the guard position. He held it negligently in his right hand, the point downwards. Horace made a helpless gesture.

'Come on, Horace,' Gilan said. 'Let's not wait all night. Let's see what you can do.'

Horace put his own sword point-first into the earth.

'But you see, sir, I'm a trained warrior,' he said. Gilan thought about this and nodded.

'True,' he said. 'But you've been training for less than a year. I shouldn't think you'll chop too much off me.'

Horace looked to Will for support. Will could only shrug. He assumed that Gilan knew what he was doing. But he hadn't known him long, and, he'd never seen him so much as draw his sword, let alone practise with it. Gilan shook his head in mock despair.

'Come on, Horace,' he said. 'I do have a vague idea what this is all about.'

Reluctantly, Horace swung a half-hearted blow at Gilan. Obviously, he was worried that, if he should penetrate the Ranger's guard, he was not sufficiently experienced to pull the blow and avoid injuring him. Gilan didn't even raise his sword to protect himself. Instead, he swayed easily to one side and Horace's blade passed harmlessly clear of him.

'Come on!' he said. 'Do it as if you mean it!'

Horace took a deep breath and swung a full-blooded roundhouse stroke at Gilan.

It was like poetry, Will thought. Like dancing. Like the movement of running water over smooth rocks. Gilan's sword, seemingly propelled only by his fingers and wrist, swung in a flashing arc to intercept Horace's blow. There was a ring of steel and Horace stopped, surprised. The parry had jarred his hand through to the elbow. Gilan raised his eyebrows at him.

'That's better,' he said. 'Try again.'

And Horace did. Backhands, overhead cuts, round arm swings.

Each time, Gilan's sword flicked into position to block the stroke with a resounding clash. As they continued, Horace swung harder and faster. Sweat broke out on his forehead and his shirt was soaked. Now he had no thought of trying not to hurt Gilan. He cut and slashed freely, trying to break through that impenetrable defence.

Finally, as Horace's breath was coming in ragged gasps, Gilan changed from the blocking movement that had been so effective against Horace's strongest blows. His sword clashed against Horace's, then whipped around in a small, circular motion so that his blade was on top. Then, with a slithering clash, he ran his blade down Horace's, forcing the apprentice's sword point down to the ground. As the point touched the damp earth, Gilan swiftly put one booted foot on it to hold it there.

'Right, that'll do,' he said calmly. Yet his eyes were riveted on Horace's, making sure the boy knew that the practice session was over. Sometimes, Gilan knew, in the heat of the moment, the losing swordsman could try for just one more cut — at a time when his opponent had assumed the fight was over.

And then, all too often, it was.

He saw now that Horace was aware. He stepped back lightly from him, moving quickly out of the reach of the sword.

'Not bad,' said Gilan approvingly. Horace, mortified, let his sword drop to the turf.

'Not bad?' he exclaimed. 'It was terrible! I never once looked like . . .' He hesitated. Somehow, it didn't seem polite to admit that for the last three or four minutes, he'd been trying to hack Gilan's head from his shoulders. He finally managed to compromise by saying: 'I never once managed to break through your guard.'

'Well,' Gilan said modestly, 'I have done this sort of thing before, you know.'

'Yes,' panted Horace. 'But you're a Ranger. Everyone knows Rangers don't use swords.'

'Apparently, this one does,' said Will, grinning. Horace, to his credit, smiled wearily in return.

'You can say that again.' He turned respectfully to Gilan. 'May I ask where you learned your swordsmanship, sir? I've never seen anything like it.'

Gilan shook his head in mock reproof. 'There you go again with the "sir",' he said. Then, in answer: 'My

Swordmaster was an old man. A northerner named MacNeil.'

'MacNeil!' Horace whispered in awe. 'You don't mean *the* MacNeil? MacNeil of Bannock?'

Gilan nodded. 'He's the one,' he replied. 'You've heard of him then?'

Horace nodded reverently. 'Who hasn't heard of MacNeil?'

And at that stage, Will, tired of not knowing what was going on, decided to speak up.

'Well, I haven't, for one,' he said. 'But I'll make tea if anyone chooses to tell me about him.'

Four

'So tell me about this Neil person,' said Will, as the three of them settled comfortably by the fire, steaming mugs of herb tea warming their cupped hands.

'MacNeil,' Horace corrected him. 'He's a legend.'

'Oh, he's real enough,' said Gilan. 'I should know. I practised under him for five years. I started when I was eleven, then, at fourteen, I was apprenticed to Halt. But he always gave me leave of absence to continue my work with the Swordmaster.'

'But why did you continue to learn the sword after you started training as a Ranger?' Horace asked.

Gilan shrugged. 'Maybe people thought it was a shame to waste all that early training. I certainly wanted to continue, and my father is Sir David of Caraway Fief, so I suppose I was given some leeway in the matter.'

Horace sat up a little straighter at the mention of the name.

'Battlemaster David?' he said, obviously more than a little impressed. 'The new supreme commander?'

Gilan nodded, smiling at the boy's enthusiasm. 'The same,' he agreed. Then, seeing that Will was still in the dark, he explained further: 'My father has been appointed supreme commander of the King's armies, since Lord Northolt was murdered. He commanded the cavalry at the Battle of Hackham Heath.'

Will's eyes widened. 'When Morgarath was defeated and driven into the mountains?'

Both Horace and Gilan nodded. Horace continued the explanation enthusiastically.

'Sir Rodney says his co-ordination of the cavalry with flanking archers in the final stage of the battle is a classic of its kind. He still teaches it as an example of perfect tactics. No wonder your father was chosen to replace Lord Northolt.'

Will realised that the conversation had moved away from its original gambit.

'So what did your father have to do with this MacNeil character?' he asked, returning to the subject.

'Well,' said Gilan, 'my father was a former pupil as well. It was only natural that MacNeil should gravitate to his Battleschool, wasn't it?'

'I suppose so,' Will agreed.

'And it was only natural that I should come under his tutelage as soon as I could swing a sword. After all, I was the Battlemaster's son.'

'So how was it that you became a Ranger?' Horace asked. 'Weren't you accepted as a knight?'

Both Rangers looked at him quizzically, somewhat

amused by his assumption that a person only became a Ranger after failing to become a knight or a warrior. In truth, it was only a short time since Will had felt the same way, but now he conveniently overlooked the fact. Horace became aware of the extended lull in the conversation, then of the looks they were giving him. All of a sudden, he realised his gaffe, and tried to recover.

'I mean . . . you know. Well, most of us want to be knights, don't we?'

Will and Gilan exchanged glances. Gilan raised an eyebrow. Horace blundered on.

'I mean . . . no offence or anything . . . but everyone I know wants to be a warrior.' His embarrassment lessened as he pointed a forefinger at Will. 'You did yourself, Will! I remember when we were kids, you used to always say you were going to Battleschool and you'd be a famous knight!'

Now it was Will's turn to feel uncomfortable. 'And you always sneered at me, didn't you, and said I'd be too small?' he said.

'Well, you were!' said Horace, with some heat.

'Is that right?' Will replied, angrily. 'Well, does it occur to you that maybe Halt had already spoken to Sir Rodney and said he wanted me as an apprentice? And that's the reason why I wasn't selected for Battleschool? Has that ever occurred to you?'

Gilan interrupted at this point, gently stopping the argument before it got any further out of hand.

'I think that's enough of childhood squabbles,' he said firmly. Both boys, each ready with another verbal barb, subsided a little awkwardly.

'Oh . . . yes. Right,' mumbled Will. 'Sorry.'

Horace nodded several times, embarrassed at the petty scene that had just occurred. 'Me too,' he said. Then, curiosity piqued, he added: 'Is that how it happened, Will? Did Halt tell Sir Rodney not to pick you because he wanted you for a Ranger?'

Will dropped his gaze and picked at a loose thread on his shirt.

'Well . . . not exactly,' he said, then admitted, 'And you're right. I always did want to be a knight when I was a kid.' Then, turning quickly to Gilan, he added, 'But I wouldn't change now, not for anything!'

Gilan smiled at the two of them. 'I was the opposite,' he said. 'Remember, I grew up in the Battleschool. I may have started my training with MacNeil when I was eleven, but I began my basic training at around nine.'

'That must have been wonderful,' Horace said with a sigh. Surprisingly, Gilan shook his head.

'Not to me. You know what they say about distant pastures always looking greener?'

Both boys looked puzzled by this.

'It means you always want what you haven't got,' he said, and they both nodded their understanding. 'Well, that's the way I was. By the time I was twelve, I was sick to death of the discipline and drills and parades.' He glanced sidelong at Horace. 'There's a bit of that goes on in Battleschool, you know.'

The heavy-set boy sighed. 'You're telling me,' he agreed. 'Still, the horsemanship and practice combats are fun.'

'Maybe,' said Gilan. 'But I was more interested in the life the Rangers led. After Hackham Heath, my father and Halt had become good friends and Halt used to come visiting. I'd see him come and go. So mysterious. So adventurous. I started to think what it might be like to come and go as you please. To live in the forests. People know so little about Rangers, it seemed like the most exciting thing in the world to me.'

Horace looked doubtful. 'I've always been a little scared of Halt,' he said. 'I used to think he was some kind of sorcerer.'

Will snorted in disbelief. 'Halt? A sorcerer?' he said. 'He's nothing of the kind!'

Horace looked at him, pained once again. 'But you used to think the same thing!' he said.

'Well . . . I suppose so. But I was only a kid then.'

'So was I!' replied Horace, with devastating logic.

Gilan grinned at the two of them. They were both still boys. Halt had been right, he thought. It was good for Will to be spending some time in company with someone his own age.

Will turned to the older Ranger. 'So did you ask Halt to take you as an apprentice?' he asked, then, before receiving any answer, continued, 'What did he say to that?'

Gilan shook his head. 'I didn't ask him anything. I followed him one day when he left our castle and headed into the forest.'

'You followed him? A Ranger? You followed a Ranger into the forest?' said Horace. He didn't know whether to be impressed by Gilan's courage or appalled at his fool-hardiness. Will sprang to Gilan's defence.

'Gil's one of the best unseen movers in the Ranger Corps,' he said quickly. 'The best, probably.'

'I wasn't then,' said Gilan ruefully. 'Mind you, I

thought I knew a bit about moving without being seen. I found out how little I actually did know when I tried to sneak up on Halt as he stopped for a noon meal. First thing I knew was his hand grabbed me by the scruff of the neck and threw me in a stream.'

He smiled at the memory of it.

'I suppose he sent you home in disgrace then?' asked Horace, but Gilan shook his head again, a distant smile still on his face as he remembered that day.

'On the contrary, he kept me with him for a week. Said I wasn't too bad at sneaking around the forest and I might have some talent as an unseen mover. He started to teach me about being a Ranger — and by the end of the week, I was his apprentice.'

'How did your father take it when you told him?' Will asked. 'Surely he wanted you to be a knight like him? I guess he was disappointed.'

'Not at all,' said Gilan. 'The strange thing was, Halt had told him that I'd probably be following him into the forest. My father had already agreed that I could serve as Halt's apprentice, before I even knew I wanted to.'

Horace frowned. 'How could Halt have known that?'

Gilan shrugged and looked at Will meaningfully.

'Halt has a way of knowing things, doesn't he, Will?' he asked, grinning. Will remembered that dark night in the Baron's office, and the hand that had shot out of the darkness to seize his wrist. Halt had been waiting for him that night. Just as he'd obviously waited for Gilan to follow him.

He looked deep into the low embers of the fire before he answered.

'Maybe, in his own way, he is a kind of a sorcerer,' he said.

The three companions sat in comfortable silence for a few minutes, thinking about what had been discussed. Then Gilan stretched and yawned.

'Well, I'm for sleep,' he said. 'We're on a war footing these days so we'll set watches. Will, you're first, then Horace, then me. 'Night, you two.'

And so saying, he rolled himself into his grey-green cloak and was soon breathing deeply and evenly.

Five

They were on the road again before the sun was barely clear of the horizon. The clouds had cleared now, blown away by a fresh southerly wind, and the air was crisp and cold as their trail started to wind higher into the rocky foothills leading to the border with Celtica.

The trees grew more stunted and gnarled. The grass was coarse and the thick forest was replaced by short, windblown scrub.

This was a part of the land where the winds blew constantly, and the land itself reflected its constant scouring action. The few houses they saw in the distance were huddled into the side of hills, built of stone walls and rough thatch roofs. It was a cold, hard part of the Kingdom and, as Gilan told them, it would become harder as they entered Celtica itself.

That evening, as they relaxed around the camp fire, Gilan continued with Horace's instruction in swordsmanship.

'Timing is the essence of the whole thing,' he said to the sweating apprentice. 'See how you're parrying with your arm locked and rigid?'

Horace looked at his right arm. Sure enough, it was locked, stiff as a board. He looked pained.

'But I have to be ready to stop your stroke,' he explained.

Gilan nodded patiently, then demonstrated with his own sword. 'Look . . . see how I'm doing it? As your stroke is coming, my hand and arm are relaxed. Then, just before your sword reaches the spot where I want to stop it, I make a small counterswing, see?'

He did so, using his hand and wrist to swing the blade of his sword in a small arc. 'My grip tightens at the last moment, and the greater part of the energy of your swing is absorbed by the movement of my own blade.'

Horace nodded doubtfully. It seemed so easy for Gilan.

'But . . . what if I mistime it?'

Gilan smiled widely. 'Well, in that case, I'll probably just lop your head off your shoulders.' He paused. Horace obviously wasn't too pleased with that answer. 'The idea is *not* to mistime it,' Gilan added gently.

'But . . .' the boy began.

'And the way to develop your timing is?' Gilan interrupted. Horace nodded wearily.

'I know. I know. Practice.'

Gilan beamed at him again. 'That's right. So, ready? One and two and three and four, that's better, and three and four . . . No! No! Just a small movement of the wrist . . . and one and two . . .'

The ring of their blades echoed through the camp site.

Will watched with some interest, heightened by the fact that he wasn't the one who was working up a sweat.

After a few days of this, Gilan noticed that Will seemed a little too relaxed. He was sitting running a stone down the edge of his sword after a practice session with Horace when he glanced quizzically at the apprentice Ranger.

'Has Halt shown you the double knife sword defence yet?' he asked suddenly. Will looked up in surprise.

'The double knife . . . what?' he asked uncertainly. Gilan sighed deeply.

'Sword defence. Damn! I should have realised that there'd be more for me to do. Serves me right for taking two apprentices along with me.' He stood up with an exaggerated sigh, and motioned for Will to follow him. Puzzled, the boy did.

Gilan led the way to the clear ground where he and Horace had been practising their swordsmanship. Horace was still there, making shadow lunges and cuts at an imaginary foe as he counted time to himself under his breath. Sweat ran freely down his face and his shirt was dark with it.

'Right, Horace,' called Gilan. 'Take a break for a few minutes.'

Gratefully, Horace complied. He lowered the sword, and sank onto the trunk of a fallen tree.

'I think I'm getting the feel of it,' he said. Gilan nodded approvingly.

'Good for you. Another three or four years and you might just have it mastered.' He spoke cheerfully, but Horace's face dropped as the prospect of long years of weary practice stretched out in front of him.

'Look on the bright side, Horace,' Gilan said. 'By that time, there'd be less than a handful of swordsmen in the Kingdom who could best you in a duel.'

Horace's face brightened somewhat, then sagged again as Gilan added: 'The only trick is, knowing who those handful are. Be most uncomfortable if you accidentally challenged one of them and then found out, wouldn't it?'

He didn't wait for an answer, but turned to the smaller boy.

'Now, Will,' he said. 'Let's see those knives of yours.'

'Both of them?' Will hesitated and Gilan rolled his eyes to heaven. The expression was remarkably like the one that Halt used when Will asked one question too many.

'Sorry,' Will mumbled, unsheathing his two knives and holding them out to Gilan. The older Ranger didn't take them. He quickly inspected their edges and checked to see that the fine layer of rust proofing oil was on them. He nodded, satisfied, when he saw everything was as it should be.

'Right,' he said. 'Saxe knife goes in your right hand, because that's the one you use to block a sword cut . . .'

Will frowned. 'Why would I need to block a sword cut?'

Gilan leaned forward and rapped him none too gently on the top of his head with his knuckles.

'Well, perhaps to stop it splitting your skull might be a good reason,' he suggested.

'But Halt says Rangers don't fight at close quarters,' Will protested. Gilan nodded agreement.

'It's certainly not our role. But, if the occasion arises when we have to, it's a good idea to know how to go about it.'

As they'd been talking, Horace had risen from his spot on the log and moved closer to watch them. He interrupted, a trifle scornfully.

'You don't think a little knife like that is going to stop a proper sword, do you?' he asked. Gilan raised one eyebrow at him.

'Take a closer look at that "little knife" before you sound so certain,' he invited. Horace held out his hand for the knife. Will quickly reversed it and placed its hilt into Horace's hand.

Will had to agree with Horace. The saxe knife was a large knife. Almost a short sword, in fact. But compared to a real sword, like Horace's or Gilan's, it seemed woefully inadequate.

Horace swung the knife experimentally, testing its balance.

'It's heavy,' he said finally.

'And hard. Very, very hard,' Gilan told him. 'Ranger knives are made by craftsmen who've perfected the art of hardening steel to an amazing degree. You'd blunt your sword edge against that, and barely leave a nick on it.'

Horace pursed his lips. 'Even so, you've been teaching me the idea of movement and leverage all week. There's a lot less leverage in a short blade like this.'

'That's true,' Gilan agreed. 'So we have to find another source of leverage, don't we? And that's the shorter knife. The throwing knife.'

'I don't get it,' said Horace, the frown deepening between his eyebrows. Will didn't either, but he was glad the other boy had admitted his ignorance first. He adopted a knowing look as he waited for Gilan to explain. He should have known better. The Ranger's sharp eyes missed very little.

'Well, perhaps Will could explain it for you?' Gilan said pleasantly.

He cocked his head at Will expectantly. Will hesitated.

'Well . . . it's the . . . ah . . . um . . . the two knife defence,' he stammered. There was a long pause as Gilan said nothing, so Will added, just a little doubtfully: 'Isn't it?'

'Of course it is!' Gilan replied. 'Now would you care to demonstrate?' He didn't even wait for Will's reply, but went on with barely a pause: 'I thought not. So, please, allow me.'

He took Will's saxe knife and withdrew his own throwing knife from its sheath. Then he gestured to Horace's sword with the smaller knife.

'Right then,' he said, all business. 'Pick up your sticker.'

Horace did so, doubtfully. Gilan gestured him out to the centre of the practice area, then took a ready stance. Horace did the same, sword point up.

'Now,' said Gilan, 'try an overhand cut at me.'

'But . . .' Horace gestured unhappily to the two smaller weapons in Gilan's grasp. Gilan rolled his eyes in exasperation.

'When will you two learn?' he asked. 'I do know what I'm doing. Now get on with it!'

He actually shouted the last words at Horace. The big apprentice, galvanised into action, and conditioned to instant obedience to shouted commands by his months spent on the drill field, swung his sword in a murderous overhand cut at Gilan's head.

There was a ringing clash of steel and the blade stopped dead in the air. Gilan had crossed the two Ranger knives in front of it, the throwing knife supporting the saxe knife blade, and blocked the cut easily. Horace stepped back, a little surprised.

'See?' said Gilan. 'The smaller knife provides the support, or the extra leverage, for the bigger weapon.' He addressed these remarks mainly to Will, who looked on with great interest. Then he spoke to Horace again. 'Right. Underhand cut please.'

Horace swung underhand. Again, Gilan locked the two blades and blocked the stroke. He glanced at Will, who nodded his understanding.

'Now, side cut,' Gilan ordered. Again, Horace swung. Again, the sword was stopped cold.

'Getting the idea?' Gilan asked Will.

'Yes. What about a straight thrust?' he asked. Gilan nodded approvingly.

'Good question. That's a little different.' He turned back to Horace. 'Incidentally, if you're ever facing a man using two knives, thrusting is your safest and most effective form of attack. Now, thrust please.'

Horace lunged with the point of his sword, his right foot leading the way in a high-stepping stamp to deliver extra momentum to the stroke. This time, Gilan used only the saxe knife to deflect the blade, sending it gliding past his body with a slither of steel.

'We can't stop this one,' he instructed Will. 'So we simply deflect it. On the positive side, there's less force behind a thrust, so we can use just the saxe knife.'

Horace, meeting no real resistance to the thrust, had

stumbled forward as the blade was deflected. Instantly, Gilan's left hand was gripping a handful of his shirt and had pulled him closer, until their shoulders were almost touching. It happened so quickly and casually that Horace's eyes widened in surprise.

'And this is where a short blade comes in very handy indeed,' Gilan pointed out. He mimed an underarm thrust with the saxe knife into Horace's exposed side. The boy's eyes widened even further as he realised the full implications of what he had just been shown. His discomfort increased as Gilan continued his demonstration.

'And of course, if you don't want to kill him, or if he's wearing a mail shirt, you can always use the saxe blade to cripple him.'

He mimed a short swing to the back of Horace's knee, bringing the heavy, razor-sharp blade to a halt a few centimetres from his leg.

Horace gulped. But the lesson still wasn't over.

'Or remember,' Gilan added cheerfully, 'this left hand, holding his collar, also has a rather nasty, rather sharp stabbing blade attached to it.' He waggled the short, broad-bladed throwing knife to bring their attention to it.

'A quick thrust up under the jaw and it's goodnight swordsman, isn't it?'

Will shook his head in admiration.

'That's amazing, Gilan!' he breathed. 'I've never seen anything like it.'

Gilan released his grip on Horace's shirt and the boy stepped back quickly, before any more demonstrations of his vulnerability might be made.

'We don't make a lot of noise about it,' the Ranger admitted. 'It's preferable to run into a swordsman who doesn't know the dangers involved in the double knife defence.' He glanced apologetically at Horace. 'Naturally, it's taught in the Kingdom's Battleschools,' he added. 'But it's a second year subject. Sir Rodney would have shown you next year.'

Will stepped forward into the practice ground. 'Can I try it?' he asked eagerly, unsheathing his throwing knife.

'Of course,' said Gilan. 'You two may as well practise together in the evenings from now on. But not with real weapons. Cut some practice sticks to use.'

Horace nodded at the wisdom of this. 'That's right, Will,' he said. 'After all, you're just starting to learn this and I wouldn't want to hurt you.' He thought about it, then added with a grin, 'Well, not too badly, anyway.'

The grin faded as Gilan corrected him. 'That's one reason, of course,' said the Ranger. 'But we also don't have the time for you to be re-sharpening your sword every night.'

He glanced meaningfully down at Horace's blade. The apprentice followed his gaze and let out a low moan. There were two deep nicks in the edge of his blade, obviously from the overhand and underhand cuts that Gilan had blocked. One glance told Horace that he'd spend at least an hour honing and sharpening to get rid of them. He looked questioningly at the saxe knife, hoping to see the same result there. Gilan shook his head cheerfully and brought the heavy blade up for inspection.

'Not a mark,' he said, grinning. 'Remember, I told you that Ranger knives are specially made.'

Ruefully, Horace rummaged in his pack for his sharpening steel and, sitting down on the hard-packed sand, began to draw it along the edge of his sword.

'Gilan,' Will said. 'I've been thinking . . .'

Gilan raised his eyebrows to heaven in mock despair. Again, the expression reminded Will forcefully of Halt. 'Always a problem,' said the Ranger. 'And what did you think?'

'Well,' began Will slowly, 'this double knife business is all well and good. But wouldn't it be better just to shoot the swordsman before he got to close quarters?'

'Yes, Will. It certainly would,' Gilan agreed patiently. 'But what if you were about to do that and your bowstring broke?'

'I could run and hide,' he suggested, but Gilan pressed him.

'What if there were nowhere to run? You're trapped against a sheer cliff. Nowhere to go. Your bowstring just broke and an angry swordsman is coming at you. What then?'

Will shook his head. 'I suppose then I'd have to fight,' he admitted reluctantly.

'Exactly,' Gilan agreed. 'We avoid close combat wherever possible. But if the time comes when there's no other choice, it's a good idea to be prepared, isn't it?'

'I guess,' Will said. Then Horace chimed in with a question.

'What about an axeman?' he said. Gilan looked at him, nonplussed for a moment.

'An axeman?' he asked.

'Yes,' said Horace, warming to his theme. 'What about

if you're facing an enemy with a battleaxe? Do your knives work then?'

Gilan hesitated. 'I wouldn't advise anyone to face a battleaxe with just two knives,' he said carefully.

'So what should I do?' Will joined in. Gilan glared from one boy to the other. He had the feeling he was being set up.

'Shoot him,' he said shortly. Will shook his head, grinning.

'Can't,' he said. 'My bowstring's broken.'

'Then run and hide,' said Gilan, between gritted teeth.

'But there's a cliff,' Horace pointed out. 'A sheer drop behind him and an angry axeman coming at him.'

'What do I do?' prompted Will.

Gilan took a deep breath and looked them both in the eye, one after the other.

'Jump off the cliff. It'll be less messy that way.'

Six

'Where the devil is everyone?'

Gilan brought Blaze to a halt and looked around the deserted border post. There was a small guardhouse by the side of the road, barely large enough to keep two or three men sheltered from the wind. Further back was a slightly larger garrison house. Normally, at a small, remote border post like this, there would be a garrison totalling half a dozen men, who would live in the garrison house and take shifts at the guardhouse by the road.

Like the majority of buildings in Celtica, both structures were built in the grey sintered stone of the region, flat river stones that had been split lengthwise, with roof tiles of the same material. Wood was scarce in Celtica. Even fires for heating used coal or peat wherever possible. Whatever timber was available was needed for shoring up the tunnels and galleries of Celtica's iron and coal mines.

Will looked around him uneasily, peering into the scrubby heather that covered the windswept hills as if expecting a sudden horde of Celts to rise up from it. There was something unnerving about the near silence of the spot — there was no sound but the quiet sighing of the wind through the hills and heather.

'Perhaps they're between shifts?' he suggested his voice seeming unnaturally loud.

Gilan shook his head. 'It's a border post. It should be garrisoned at all times.'

He swung down from the saddle, making a motion for Will and Horace to stay mounted. Tug, sensing Will's uneasiness, sidestepped nervously in the road. Will calmed him with a gentle pat on the neck. The little horse's ears went up at his master's touch and he shook his head, as if to deny that he was in any way edgy.

'Could they have been attacked and driven off?' Horace asked. His mindset always worked towards fighting, which Will supposed was only natural in a Battleschool apprentice.

Gilan shrugged as he pushed open the door of the guardhouse and peered inside.

'Maybe,' he said, looking round the interior. 'But there doesn't seem to be any sign of fighting.'

He leaned against the doorway, frowning. The guard-house was a single-roomed building, with minimal furnishing of a few benches and a table. There was nothing here to give him any clue as to where the occupants had gone.

'It's only a minor post,' he said thoughtfully. 'Perhaps the Celts have simply stopped manning it. After all, there's been a truce between Araluen and Celtica for over thirty years now.' He pushed himself away from the doorway and jerked a thumb towards the garrison house.

'Maybe we'll find something down there,' he said.

The two boys dismounted. Horace tethered his horse and the pack pony to the counterweighted bar that could swing down to close the road. Will simply let Tug's reins fall to the ground. The Ranger horse was trained not to stray. He took his bow from the leather bow scabbard behind the saddle and slung it across his shoulders. Naturally, it was already strung. Rangers always travelled with their bows ready for use. Horace, noticing the gesture, loosened his sword slightly in its scabbard and they set off after Gilan for the garrison house.

The small stone building was neat, clean and deserted. But here at least there were signs that the occupants had left in a hurry. There were a few plates on a table, bearing the dried-out remains of food, and several closet doors hung open. Items of clothing were scattered on the floor in the dormitory, as if their owners had hurriedly crammed a few belongings into packs before leaving. Several of the bunks were missing blankets.

Gilan ran a forefinger along the edge of the dining room table, leaving a wavy line in the layer of dust that had gathered there. He inspected the tip of his finger and pursed his lips.

'They didn't leave recently,' he said.

Horace, who had been peering into the small supply room under the stairs, started at the sound of the Ranger's voice, bumping his head on the low door sill.

'How can you tell?' he asked, more to cover his own

embarrassment than out of real curiosity. Gilan swept an arm around the room.

'Celts are neat people. This dust must have settled since they left. At a guess, I'd say the place has been empty for at least a month.'

'Maybe it's like you said,' Will suggested, coming down the steps from the command room. 'Maybe they decided they didn't need to keep this post manned any more.'

Gilan nodded several times. But his expression showed he wasn't convinced.

'That wouldn't explain why they left in a hurry,' he said. He swept his arm around the room. 'Look at all of this — the food on the table, the open closets, the clothes scattered on the floor. When people close down a post like this, they clean up and take their belongings with them. Particularly Celts. As I said, they're very orderly.'

He led the way outside again and swept his gaze around the deserted landscape, as if hoping to find some clue to the puzzle there. But there was nothing visible except their own horses, idly cropping the short grass that grew by the guardhouse.

'The map shows the nearest village is Pordellath,' he said. 'It's a little out of our way but perhaps we can find out what's been going on here.'

Pordellath was only five kilometres away. Because of the steep nature of the land, the path wound and zigzagged up the hillsides. Consequently, they had almost reached the little village before it came in sight. It was late in the day and both Will and Horace were feeling the pangs of hunger. They hadn't stopped for their normal noon meal, initially because they'd been in a hurry to reach the border post, then because they had pressed on to Pordellath. There would be an inn in the village and both boys were thinking fondly of a hot meal and cool drinks. As a result of this preoccupation, they were surprised when Gilan reined in as the village came into sight around the shoulder of a hill, barely two hundred metres away.

'What the hell is going on here?' he asked. 'Look at that!'

Will and Horace looked. For the life of him, Will couldn't see what might be bothering the young Ranger.

'I don't see anything,' he admitted. Gilan turned to him.

'Exactly!' he agreed. 'Nothing! No smoke from the chimneys. No people in the streets. It looks as empty as the border post!'

He nudged Blaze with his knees and the bay horse broke into a canter on the stony road. Will followed, with Horace's horse a little slower to respond. Strung out in a line, they clattered into the village, finally drawing rein in the small market square.

There wasn't much to Pordellath. Just the short main street by which they'd entered, lined with houses and shops on either side, and widening into the small square at the end. It was dominated by the largest structure which was, in Celtic fashion, the Riadhah's dwelling. The Riadhah was the hereditary village head man — a combined clan chief, mayor and sheriff. His authority was absolute and he ruled unchallenged over the villagers.

When there were any villagers for him to rule. Today there was no Riadhah. There were no villagers. Only the faint, dying echoes of the horses' hooves on the cobbled surface of the square.

'Hello!' Gilan shouted, and his voice echoed down the narrow main street, bouncing off the stone buildings, then reaching out to the surrounding hills.

'Oh – oh – oh . . .' it went, gradually tailing away into silence. The horses shifted nervously again. Will was reluctant to seem to correct the Ranger, but he was uneasy at the way he was advertising their presence here.

'Maybe you shouldn't do that?' he suggested. Gilan glanced at him, a trace of his normal good humour returning as he sensed the reason for Will's discomfort.

'Why's that?' he asked.

'Well,' Will said, glancing nervously around the deserted market square, 'if somebody has taken away the people here, maybe we don't want them to know that we've arrived.'

Gilan shrugged. 'I think it's a little late for that,' he said. 'We came galloping in here like the King's cavalry, and we've been travelling the road completely in the open. If anybody was looking out for us, they would have already seen us.'

'I suppose so,' said Will doubtfully.

Horace, meanwhile, had edged his horse up close to one of the houses and was leaning down from the saddle to peer in under the low windows, trying to see inside. Gilan noticed the movement.

'Let's take a look around,' he said, and dismounted.

Horace wasn't terribly eager to follow his example.

'What if this is some kind of plague or something?' he said.

'A plague?' asked Gilan.

Horace swallowed nervously. 'Yes. I mean, I've heard of this sort of thing happening years and years ago; whole towns would be wiped out by a plague that would sweep in and just . . . sort of . . . kill people where they stood.' As he said it, he was edging his horse away from the building, and out to the centre of the square. Will inadvertently began to follow suit. The moment Horace had raised the idea, he'd had pictures of the three of them lying dead in the square, faces blackened, tongues protruding, eyes bulging from their final agonies.

'So this plague could just come out of thin air?' Gilan asked calmly. Horace nodded several times.

'Nobody really knows how they spread,' he said. 'I've heard that it's the night air that carries plague. Or the west wind, sometimes. But however it travels, it strikes so fast there's no escape. It simply kills you where you stand.'

'Every man, woman and child in its path?' Gilan prompted. Again, Horace's head nodded frantically.

'Everyone. Kills 'em stone dead!'

Will was beginning to feel a lumpy dryness in the back of his throat, even as the other two were speaking. He tried to swallow and his throat felt raspy. He had a moment of panic as he wondered if this wasn't the first sign of the onset of the plague. His breath was coming faster and he almost missed Gilan's next question.

'And then it just . . . dissolves the dead bodies away into thin air?' he asked mildly.

'That's right!' Horace began, then realised what the Ranger had said. He hesitated, looked around the deserted village and saw no signs of people struck dead where they stood. Will's throat, coincidentally, suddenly lost that lumpy, raspish feeling.

'Oh,' said Horace, as he realised the flaw in his theory. 'Well, maybe it's a new strain of plague. Maybe it does sort of dissolve the bodies.'

Gilan looked at him sceptically, his head to one side.

'Or maybe there were one or two people who were immune, and they buried all the bodies?' Horace suggested.

'And where are those people now?' Gilan asked. Horace shrugged.

'Maybe they were so sad that they couldn't bear to live here anymore,' he said, trying to keep the theory alive a little longer.

Gilan shook his head. 'Horace, whatever it was that drove the people away from here, it wasn't the plague.' He glanced at the rapidly darkening sky. 'It's getting late. We'll take a look around, then find a place to stay the night.'

'Here?' said Will, his voice cracking with nerves. 'In the village?'

Gilan nodded. 'Unless you want to camp out in the hills,' he suggested. 'There's precious little shelter and it usually rains at night in these parts. Personally, I'd rather spend the night under a roof — even a deserted one.'

'But . . .' Will began and then could find no rational way to continue.

'I'm sure your horse would rather spend the evening under cover than out in the rain too,' Gilan added gently, and that tipped the balance with Will. His basic instinct was to look after Tug, and it was hardly fair to condemn the pony to a wet, uncomfortable night in the hills just because his owner was afraid of a few empty houses. He nodded and swung down from the saddle.

Seven

There were no answers to be found in Pordellath. The three companions went through the village and found the same signs of sudden departure that they had seen at the border post. There was evidence of some hasty packing, but in the majority of houses, most of the occupants' possessions were still in place. Everything spoke of a population that had departed in a hurry, taking what they could carry on their backs and little more. Tools, utensils, clothes, furniture and other personal goods had been left behind. But they could find no clue as to where the people of Pordellath had gone. Or why they had departed.

As it began to grow dark, Gilan finally called an end to their search. They returned to the Riadhah's house, where they unsaddled the horses and rubbed them down in the shelter of the small porch at the front of the building.

They spent an uneasy night in the house. At least, Will did and he assumed Horace was as uncomfortable as he was. Gilan, for his part, seemed relatively unperturbed, rolling himself into his cloak and falling instantly asleep when Will relieved him after the first watch. But Gilan's manner was more subdued than normal and Will guessed that the Ranger was more concerned by this baffling turn of events than he was letting on.

As he stood his watch, Will was amazed at how much noise a house could make. Doors creaked, floors groaned, the ceiling seemed to sigh with every breath of wind outside. And the village itself seemed full of loose items that would bang and clatter as well, bringing Will to a nervous, wide-eyed attention as he sat by the unglazed window in the front room of the house, the wooden shutters hooked back to keep them secure.

The moon seemed keen to join in on the subterfuge as well, soaring high above the village and casting deep pools of shadow between the houses of the village. Shadows that seemed to move slightly when you caught sight of them out of the corner of your eye, then stopped as soon as you stared directly at them.

More movement came as clouds flew across the face of the moon, alternately causing the main square to be illuminated, then plunged into sudden darkness.

Just after midnight, as Gilan had predicted, a steady rain set in and the other noises were joined by the gurgle of running water and the plash-plash-plash of drops falling off eaves and into puddles below.

Will woke Horace to take over the watch at around two in the morning. He piled up a stack of cushions and bed-covers on the floor of the main room, wrapped his cloak around him and lay down.

Then he lay awake for another hour and a half, listening to the creaks, the groans, the gurgles and the splashes, wondering whether Horace had dropped off to sleep and whether, even now, some unseen horror was creeping up on the house, bloodthirsty and unstoppable.

He was still worrying about it when he finally fell asleep.

They were on the road early the following morning. The rain had stopped just before dawn and Gilan was keen to press on to Gwyntaleth, the first large town on their route, and find some answers to the puzzles that they had found so far in Celtica. They had a quick, cold breakfast, washed down with icy water from the village well, then saddled up and rode out.

They wound down the stony path from the village, taking their time on the uneven surface. But when they hit the main road once more, they urged their horses into a canter. They held the canter for twenty minutes, then rested the horses by riding at a walk for the next twenty. They maintained that alternating, steady pattern through the morning.

They ate a quick meal in the middle of the day, then rode on. This was the principal mining area of Celtica and they passed at least a dozen coal or iron mines: large black holes cut into the sides of hills and mountains, surrounded by timber shoring and stone buildings. Nowhere, however, did they see any sign of life. It was as if the inhabitants of Celtica had simply vanished from the face of the earth.

'They may have deserted their border post, and even their villages,' Gilan muttered once, almost to himself. 'But I've never yet met a Celt who would desert a mine while there was an ounce of metal still to be torn from it.'

Eventually, in midafternoon, they came over a crest and there, in a valley dropping away from them, were the neat rows of stone roofs that formed Gwyntaleth township. A small spire in the centre of the town marked a temple — the Celts had their own unique religion, which had to do with the gods of fire and iron. A larger tower formed the main defensive position for the town.

They were too far away to make out whether there might be any movement of people in the streets. But, as before, there was no sign of smoke from the chimneys and, even more significantly, according to Gilan, no noise.

'Noise?' Horace asked. 'What kind of noise?'

'Banging, hammering, clanking,' Gilan answered him briefly. 'Remember, the Celts don't just mine iron ore. They work the iron as well. With the breeze blowing from the south-west as it is, we should be able to hear the forges at work, even from this distance.'

'Well, let's go see then,' Will said, and began to urge Tug forward. Gilan, however, put up a hand to restrain him.

'I think perhaps I might go on ahead alone,' he said slowly, his eyes never leaving the town in the valley below them. Will looked at him, puzzled.

'Alone?' he asked and Gilan nodded.

'You noted yesterday that we were making ourselves pretty obvious when we rode into Pordellath. Perhaps it's time we became a little more circumspect. Something is going on and I'd like to know what it is.'

Will had to agree that it made good sense for Gilan to go on alone. After all, he was possibly the best unseen mover in the Ranger Corps, and Rangers were the best unseen movers in the Kingdom.

Gilan motioned for them to fall back from the crest they were standing on, and down the other side to a spot where a small gully formed a sheltered camp site, out of the wind.

'Set up a camp here,' he told them. 'No fires. We'll have to stay with cold rations until we know what's going on. I should be back some time after dark.'

And with that, he wheeled Blaze and trotted him back over the crest and down the road towards Gwyntaleth.

Will and Horace took half an hour or so to set up the camp site. There was little to do. They attached their tarpaulin to some scrubby bushes growing out of the stone wall of the gully, weighing down the other end with rocks. At least there were plenty of them. This gave them a triangular shelter in case the rain set in again. Then they prepared a fireplace in front of the shelter. Gilan had said no fires, but if he arrived back in the middle of the night and changed those orders, they might as well be ready.

It took a considerably longer time to stack a supply of firewood. The only real source was the scrubby heather that covered the hillsides. The roots and branches of the bush were tough but highly flammable. The two boys hacked out a reasonable supply, Horace using the small hatchet he carried in his pack and Will his saxe knife. Eventually, with all their housekeeping taken care of, they sat on either side of the empty fireplace, their backs leaning against rocks. Will spent a few minutes running his sharpening stone over the saxe knife, restoring its razor-sharp edge.

'I really prefer camping in forest areas,' Horace said, shifting his back for the tenth time against the unyielding rock behind him.

Will grunted in reply. But Horace was bored and kept on talking, more for the sake of having something to do than because he really wanted to.

'After all, in a forest, you have lots of firewood, ready to hand. It just falls out of the trees for you.'

'Not while you wait,' Will disagreed. He, too, was talking more for the sake of it than anything else.

'No. Not while you wait. Usually it's already happened before you arrive,' Horace said. 'Plus in a forest, you've usually got pine needles or leaves on the ground. And that makes for a softer sleeping place. And there are logs and trees to sit on and lean against. And they have a lot fewer sharp edges than rock.'

Again, he wriggled his back to a temporarily more comfortable spot. He glanced up at Will, rather hoping that the apprentice Ranger might disagree with him. Then they could argue to pass the time. Will however, merely grunted again. He inspected the edge of his saxe knife, slid the knife back into its scabbard and lay back. Uncomfortable, he sat up again, undid the knife belt and draped it over his pack, along with his bow and quiver. Then he lay back, his head on a flat piece of stone. He closed his eyes. The sleepless night he had spent had left him drained and flat.

Horace sighed to himself, then took out his sword and began honing its edge — quite unnecessarily, as it was already razor-sharp. But it was something to do. He rasped away, glancing occasionally at Will to see if his friend was asleep. For a moment, he thought he was, but then the smaller boy suddenly squirmed around, sat up and reached for his cloak. Bundling it up, he put it on the flat stone he was using as a head rest, then lay back again.

'You're right about forests,' he said crankily. 'Much more comfortable places to camp.'

Horace said nothing. He decided his sword was sharp enough and slid it back into its oiled leather scabbard, leaning the sheathed weapon against the rock face beside him.

He watched Will again, as he tried to find a comfortable spot. No matter how he twisted and squirmed, there was always a pebble or a piece of rock poking into his back or side. Five or ten minutes passed, then Horace finally said:

'Want to practise? It'll pass the time.'

Will opened his eyes and considered the idea. Reluctantly, he admitted to himself that he was never going to get to sleep on this hard, stony ground.

'Why not?' He rummaged in his pack for his practice weapons, then joined Horace on the far side of the tent, where he was scraping a practice circle in the sandy gully floor. The two boys took up their positions, then, at a nod from Horace, they began.

Will was improving but Horace was definitely the master at this exercise. Will couldn't help admiring the speed and balance he showed as he wielded the wooden sword in a dazzling series of backhands, forehands, side cuts and overheads. Furthermore, when he knew he had beaten Will's defensive posture, he would, at the last moment, hold back from whacking him. Instead, he would lightly touch the spot where his blow would have fallen, to demonstrate the point.

He didn't do it with any sense of superiority, either. Weapons practice, even with wooden weapons, was a serious part of Horace's life nowadays. It wasn't something to crow about when you were better than your opponent. Horace had learned only too well in dozens of practice bouts at the Battleschool that it never paid to underestimate an opponent.

Instead, he used his superior ability to help Will, showing him how to anticipate strokes, teaching him the basic combinations that all swordsmen used and the best way to defeat them.

As Will ruefully acknowledged, knowing how to do it was one thing. Actually doing it was an entirely different matter. He realised how much his former enemy had matured and wondered if the same changes were evident in himself. He didn't think so. He didn't feel any different. And whenever he saw himself in a mirror he didn't seem to look any different either.

'Your left hand is dropping too far,' Horace pointed out as they paused between bouts.

'I know,' Will said. 'I'm expecting a side cut and I want to be ready for it.'

Horace shook his head. 'That's all very well, but if you drop it too far, it's easy for me to feint a side cut then swing up into an overhand. See?'

He showed Will the action he was describing, beginning the sword in a wide sideways sweep then, with a powerful wrist movement, taking it up into a high swinging downward stroke. He stopped the wooden blade a few centimetres from Will's head and the Ranger apprentice saw that his counterstroke would have been far too late.

'Sometimes I think I'll never learn these things,' he said.

Horace patted him encouragingly on the shoulder. 'Are you kidding?' he asked. 'You're improving every day. And besides, I could never shoot or use those throwing knives the way you do.'

Even while they had been on the road, Gilan had insisted that Will practise his Ranger skills as often as was practical. Horace had been impressed, to say the least, when he had seen how adept the smaller boy had become. Several times, he had shuddered when he thought what might happen if he had to face an archer such as Will. His accuracy with the bow was uncanny, as far as Horace was concerned. He knew that Will could place arrows into every gap in his armour if he chose. Even into the narrow vizor slit of a full-face jousting helmet.

What he didn't appreciate was that Will's accuracy was nothing more than average as far as Ranger standards were concerned.

'Let's try it again,' Will suggested wearily. But another voice interrupted them.

'Let's not, little boys. Let's put down our nasty sharp sticks and stand very still, shall us?'

The two apprentices whirled around at the words. There, at the mouth of the small U-shaped gully where they had built their camp, stood two ragged-looking figures. Both were heavily bearded and unkempt and both were dressed in a strange mixture of clothing — some of it tattered and threadbare, while some items were new and obviously very costly. The taller of the two wore a richly brocaded satin vest, but it was thick with dirt. The other sported a scarlet hat with a bedraggled feather in it. He also carried an iron-spiked wooden club, holding it in a hand that was swathed in a dirty bandage. His companion had a long sword, jagged and nicked along the edges. He flourished it now at the two boys.

'Come on now, you boys. Sharp sticks're danger-orius for the likes of you,' he said, and let go a hoarse, guttural laugh.

Will's hand dropped automatically to reach for the saxe knife, encountering nothing. With a sinking feeling, he realised that his knife belt, bow and quiver were all neatly piled on the far side of the fireplace, where he had been sitting. The two intruders would stop him before he could reach them. He cursed himself for his carelessness. Halt would be furious, he thought. Then, looking at the sword and club, he realised that Halt's annoyance might be the least of his worries.

Eight

Will felt Horace's hand on his shoulder as the bigger boy began to pull him back from the two bandits.

'Back away, Will,' Horace said quietly.

The man with the club laughed. 'Yes, Will, you back away. You stay away from that nasty little bow I see over there. We don't hold no truck with bows, do us, Carney?'

Carney grinned at his companion. 'That we don't, Bart, that we don't.' He looked back at the two boys and frowned angrily. 'Didn't we tell you to drop those sticks?' he demanded, his voice rising in pitch and very, very ugly in tone. Together, the two men began to advance across the clearing.

Horace's grip now tightened and he jerked Will to one side, sending him sprawling. As he fell, he saw Horace turn to the rocks behind him and grab up his sword. He flicked it once and the scabbard sailed clear of the blade. That easy action alone should have warned Bart and Carney that they were facing someone who knew more than a little about handling weapons. But neither of them was overly bright. They simply saw a boy of about sixteen. A big boy, perhaps, but still a boy. A child, really, with a grown-up weapon in his hand.

'Oh dear,' said Carney. 'Have we got our daddy's sword with us?'

Horace eyed him, suddenly very calm. 'I'll give you one chance,' he said, 'to turn around and leave now.'

Bart and Carney exchanged mock terrified looks.

'Oh dear, Bart,' said Carney. 'It's our one chance. What'll us do?'

'Oh dear,' said Bart. 'Let's run away.'

They began to advance on Horace and he watched them coming. He had the practice stick in his left hand now and the sword in his right. He tensed, balanced on the balls of his feet as they advanced on him, Carney with the rusty, ragged-edged sword snaking in front of him and Bart with the spiked cudgel laid back on his shoulder, ready for use.

Will scrambled to his feet and began to move towards his weapons. Seeing the action, Carney, moved to cut him off. He hadn't gone a pace when Horace attacked.

He darted forward and his sword flashed in an overhead cut at Carney. Startled by the sheer speed of the apprentice warrior's move, Carney barely had time to bring his own blade up in a clumsy parry. Thrown off balance and totally unprepared for the surprising force and authority behind the stroke, he stumbled backwards and sprawled in the dust.

In the same instant, Bart, seeing his companion in trouble, stepped forward and swung the heavy club in a vicious arc at Horace's unprotected left side. His expectation was for Horace to try to leap back to avoid the blow. Instead, the apprentice warrior stepped forward. The practice stick in his left hand flicked up and outwards, catching the heavy cudgel in its downward arc and deflecting it away from its intended line. The club's spiked head thudded dully into the stony ground and Bart let go a deep 'whoof' of surprise, the impact jarring his arm from shoulder to wrist.

But Horace wasn't finished yet. He continued the forward lunge, and now he and Bart stood shoulder to shoulder. It was too close for Horace to use the blade of his sword. Instead, he swung his right fist, hammering the heavy brass pommel of his sword hilt into the side of Bart's head.

The bandit's eyes glazed and he collapsed to his knees, semi-conscious, head swaying slowly from side to side.

Carney, back-pedalling furiously through the sand, had regained his feet. Now he stood watching Horace, puzzled and angry. Unable to grasp the fact that he and his companion had been bested by a mere boy. Luck, he thought. Sheer, dumb luck!

His lips formed into a snarl and he gripped the sword tightly, advancing once more on the boy, mouthing threats and curses as he went. Horace stood his ground, waiting. Something in the boy's calm gaze made Carney hesitate. He should have gone with his first instincts and given the fight away then and there. But anger overcame him and he started forward again.

By now, he was paying no attention to Will. The Ranger's apprentice darted around the camp site, grabbing his bow and quiver and hastily stepping his right foot through the recurve to brace the bow against his left while he slid the string up into its notch.

Quickly, he selected an arrow and nocked it to the string. He was about to draw back when a calm voice behind him said:

'Don't shoot him. I'd rather like to see this.'

Startled, he turned to find Gilan behind him, almost invisible in the folds of his Ranger cloak, leaning nonchalantly on his longbow.

'Gilan!' he began, but the Ranger made a sound for silence.

'Just let him go,' he said softly. 'He'll be fine as long as we don't distract him.'

'But . . .' Will began desperately, looking to where his friend was facing a full-grown, very angry man. Sensing his concern, Gilan hurried to reassure him.

'Horace will handle him,' he said. 'He really is very good, you know. A natural, if ever I saw one. That bit with the practice stick and the hilt strike was sheer poetry. Lovely improvisation!'

Shaking his head in wonder, Will turned back to the fight. Now Carney attacked, hacking and lunging and cutting with a blind fury and terrifying power. Horace gradually gave way before him, his own sword moving in small, semi-circular actions that blocked every cut and hack and thrust and jarred Carney's wrist and elbow with the strength and impenetrability of his defence. All the while, Gilan was whispering an approving commentary beside Will.

'Good boy!' he said. 'See how he's letting the other

fellow start proceedings? Gives him an idea of how skilful he might be. Or otherwise. My God, he's got the timing of that defensive swing just about perfect! Look at that! And that! Terrific!'

Now Horace had apparently decided not to back away any further. Continuing to parry Carney's every stroke with obvious ease, he stood his ground, letting the bandit expend his strength like the sea breaking on a rock. And as he stood, Carney's strokes became slower and more ragged. His arm was beginning to ache with the effort of wielding the long, heavy sword. He was really more accustomed to using a knife to the back of most of his opponents and he hadn't looked for this engagement to go past one or two crushing, hacking strokes to break down the boy's guard before killing him. But his most devastating blows had been flicked aside with apparent contempt.

He swung again, losing his balance in the follow-through. Horace's blade caught his, spun it in a circle, holding it with his own, then let it rasp down its length until their crosspieces locked.

They stood there, eye to eye, Carney's chest heaving, Horace absolutely calm and totally in control. The first worm of fear appeared in Carney's stomach as he realised that, boy or not, he was hopelessly outmatched in this contest.

And at that point, Horace went on the attack.

He drove his shoulder into Carney's chest, unlocking their blades and sending the bandit staggering back. Then, calmly, Horace advanced, swinging his sword in confusing, terrifying combinations. Side, overhead, thrust. Side, side, backhand, overhead. Thrust. Thrust. Thrust. Forehand.

Backhand. One combination flowed smoothly into the next and Carney scrambled desperately, trying to bring his own blade between himself and the implacable sword that seemed to have a life and an inexhaustible energy all its own. He felt his wrist and arm tiring, while Horace's strokes grew stronger and firmer until finally, with a dull and final CLANG, Horace simply beat the sword from his numbed grasp.

Carney sank to his knees, sweat pouring off him and running into his eyes, chest heaving with exertion, waiting for the final stroke that would end it all.

'Don't kill him, Horace!' called Gilan. 'I'd like to ask him some questions.'

Horace looked up, surprised to see the tall Ranger standing there. He shrugged. He wasn't really the type to kill an opponent in cold blood anyway. He flicked Carney's sword to one side, way out of reach. Then, setting one boot against the defeated bandit's shoulder, he shoved him over in the dust on his side.

Carney lay there, sobbing, unable to move. Terrified. Worn out. Physically and mentally defeated.

'Where did you come from?' Horace asked Gilan indignantly. 'And why didn't you give me a hand?'

Gilan grinned at him. 'You didn't seem to need one, from what I could see,' he replied. Then he gestured behind Horace to where Bart was slowly rising from his kneeling position, shaking his head as the effect of the hilt strike began to wear off.

'I think your other friend needs a little attention,' he suggested. Horace turned and casually raised his sword, swinging it to clang, flat-bladed, against Bart's skull.

Another small moan and Bart went face down in the sand.

'I really think you might have said something,' he said.

'I would have if you were in trouble,' Gilan said. Then he moved across the clearing to stand over Carney. He seized the bandit by the arm and dragged him upright, frogmarching him across the clearing to throw him, none too gently, against the rock face at the far side. As Carney began to sag forward, there was a hiss of steel on leather and Gilan's saxe knife appeared at his throat, keeping him upright.

'It seems these two caught you napping?' Gilan asked Will. The boy nodded, shamefaced. Then, as the full import of the comment sank in, he asked:

'Just how long have you been here?'

'Since they arrived,' Gilan said. 'I hadn't gone far when I saw them skulking through the rocks. So I left Blaze and doubled back here, trailing them. Obviously they were up to no good.'

'Why didn't you say something then?' Will asked incredulously.

For a moment, Gilan's eyes hardened. 'Because you two needed a lesson. You're in dangerous territory, the population seems to have mysteriously disappeared and you stand around practising sword craft for all the world to see and hear.'

'But,' Will stammered, 'I thought we were supposed to practise?'

'Not when there's no one else to keep an eye on things,' Gilan pointed out reasonably. 'Once you start practising like that, your attention is completely distracted. These two made enough noise to alert a deaf old granny. Tug even gave you a warning call twice and you missed it.'

Will was totally crestfallen. 'I did?' he said and Gilan nodded. For a moment, his gaze held Will's, until he was sure the lesson had been driven home and the point taken. Then he nodded slightly, signifying that the matter was closed. Will nodded in return. It wouldn't happen again.

'Now,' said Gilan, 'let's find out what these two beauties know about the price of coal.'

He turned back to Carney, who was now going quite cross-eyed as he tried to watch the gleaming saxe knife pressed against his throat.

'How long have you been in Celtica?' Gilan asked him. Carney looked up at him, then back to the heavy knife.

'Tuh-tuh-tuh-ten or eleven days, my lord,' he stammered eventually.

Gilan made a pained face. 'Don't call me "my lord",' he said, adding as an aside to the two boys, 'These people always try to flatter you when they realise they're in trouble. Now . . .' He returned his gaze to Carney. 'What brought you here?'

Carney hesitated, his eyes sliding away from Gilan's direct gaze so that the Ranger knew he was going to lie even before the bandit spoke.

'Just . . . wanted to see the sights, my . . . sir,' he amended, remembering at the last moment Gilan's instruction not to call him 'my lord'. Gilan sighed and shook his head with exasperation.

'Look, I'd just as soon lop your head off here and now. I really doubt that you have anything useful to tell me.

But I'll give you one last chance. Now let's have THE TRUTH!'

He shouted the last two words angrily, his face suddenly only a few centimetres away from Carney's. The sudden transition from the languid, joking manner he had been using came as a shock to the bandit. Just for a few seconds, Gilan let his good-natured shield slip and Carney saw through to the white hot anger that was just below the surface. In that instant, he was afraid. Like most people, he was nervous of Rangers. Rangers were not people to make angry. And this one seemed to be very, very angry.

'We heard there were good pickings down here!' he answered immediately.

'Good pickings?' Gilan asked and Carney nodded dutifully, the flood gates of conversation now well and truly open.

'All the towns and cities deserted, like. Nobody there to guard them, and all their valuables left lying around for us'n to take as we chose. We didn't harm nobody though,' he concluded, a little defensively.

'Oh no. You didn't harm them. You just crept in while they were gone and stole everything of value that they owned,' Gilan told him. 'I should think they'd be almost grateful for your contribution!'

'It was Bart's idea, not mine,' Carney tried and Gilan shook his head sadly.

'Gilan?' Will said tentatively, and the Ranger turned to look at him. 'How would they have heard that the towns were deserted? We didn't hear a thing.'

'Thieves' grapevine,' Gilan told the two boys. 'It's like the way vultures gather whenever an animal is in trouble.

The intelligence network between thieves and robbers and brigands is incredibly fast. Once a place is in trouble, word spreads like wildfire and they come down on it in their scores. I should imagine there are plenty more of them through these hills.'

He turned back to Carney as he said it, prodding the saxe knife a little deeper into the flesh of his neck, just holding it back so that it didn't draw blood.

'Aren't there?' he asked. Carney went to nod, realised what might happen if his neck moved, gulped instead and whispered:

'Yes, sir.'

'And I should imagine you've got a cave somewhere, or a deserted mine tunnel, where you've stowed the loot you've stolen so far?'

He eased the pressure on the knife and this time Carney was able to manage a nod. His fingers fluttered towards the belt pouch that he wore at his waist, then stopped as he realised what he was doing. But Gilan had caught the gesture. With his free hand, he ripped open the pouch and fumbled inside it, finally withdrawing a grubby sheet of paper, folded in quarters. He passed it to Will.

'Take a look,' he said briefly and Will unfolded the paper, revealing a clumsily drawn map with reference points, directions and distances all indicated.

'They've buried their loot, by the look of this,' he said and Gilan nodded, smiling thinly.

'Good. Then without their map, they won't be able to find it again,' he said, and Carney's eyes shot wide open in protest.

'But that's ours . . .' he began, stopping as he saw the dangerous glint in Gilan's eyes.

'It was stolen,' the Ranger said, in a very low voice. 'You crept in like jackals and stole it from people who are obviously in deep trouble. It's not yours. It's theirs. Or their family's, if they're still alive.'

'They're still alive,' said a new voice from behind them. 'They've run from Morgarath — those he hasn't already captured.'

Nine

If she hadn't spoken, they would have taken her for a boy. It was the soft voice that gave her away. She stood at the edge of the camp site, a slender figure with blonde hair cut short — to a boy's length — dressed in a ragged tunic, breeches and soft leather boots, bound up to the knee. A stained and torn sheepskin vest seemed to be her only protection against the cold mountain nights for she wore no cloak and carried no blankets. Just a small bandanna tied into a bundle which, presumably, contained all her belongings.

'Where the devil did you spring from?' Gilan asked, turning to face her. He sheathed his saxe knife as he did so and allowed Carney to fall gratefully to his knees, exhausted.

The girl, who Will could now see was around his own age and, underneath a liberal coating of dirt, remarkably pretty, gestured vaguely.

'Oh . . .' She paused uncertainly, trying to gather her

thoughts, and Will realised she was close to the point of exhaustion. 'I've been hiding out in the hills for several weeks now,' she said finally. Will had to admit she looked as if she had been.

'Do you have a name?' asked Gilan, not unkindly. He too could see the girl was worn out.

She hesitated. She appeared uncertain as to whether to give them her name or not.

'Evanlyn Wheeler, from Greenfield Fief,' she said. Greenfield was a small coastal fief in Araluen. 'We were here visiting friends . . .' She stopped and looked away from Gilan. She seemed to be thinking for a second, before she amended the statement. 'Rather, my mistress was visiting friends, when the Wargals attacked.'

'Wargals!' Will said, the word jerked from him, and she turned a level pair of brilliant green eyes upon him. As he looked into them, he realised she was more than pretty. Much, much more. She was beautiful. The strawberry blonde hair and green eyes were complimented by a small, straight nose and a full mouth that Will thought would look quite delightful if she were smiling. But right now, a smile was a long way from the girl's thoughts. She gave a sad little lift of her shoulders as she answered him.

'Where did you think all the people have gone?' she asked him. 'Wargals have been attacking towns and villages throughout this part of Celtica for weeks now. The Celts couldn't stand against them. They were driven out of their homes. Most of them escaped to the South-West Peninsula. But some were captured. I don't know what's happened to them.'

Gilan and the two boys exchanged looks. Deep down, they'd all been expecting to hear something of the kind. Now, it was out in the open.

'I thought I saw Morgarath's hand behind all this,' Gilan said softly and the girl nodded, tears forming in her eyes. One of them slid down her cheek, tracking its way through the grime there. She put a hand to her eyes, and her shoulders began to shake. Quickly, Gilan stepped forward and caught her just before she fell. He lowered her gently to the ground, leaning her against one of the rocks that the boys had positioned around the fireplace. His voice was gentle and compassionate now.

'It's all right,' he said to her. 'You're safe now. Just rest here and we'll get you something hot to eat and drink.' He glanced quickly at Horace. 'Get a fire going, please, Horace. Just a small one. We're fairly sheltered here and I think we can risk it. And Will,' he added, raising his voice so that it carried clearly, 'if that bandit makes another move to get away, would you mind shooting him through the leg?'

Carney, who had taken the opportunity created by Evanlyn's surprising appearance to begin crawling quietly away towards the surrounding rocks, now froze where he was. Gilan threw an angry glare at him, then revised his orders.

'On second thoughts, you do the fire, Will. Horace, tie those two up.'

The two boys moved quickly to the tasks he had set them. Satisfied that everything was in hand, Gilan now removed his own cloak and wrapped it around the girl. She had covered her face with both hands and her shoulders were still shaking, although she made no noise. He put his arms around her and murmured gently, reassuring her once more that she was safe.

Gradually, her silent, racking sobs diminished and her breathing became more regular. Will, engaged in heating a pot of water for a hot drink, looked at her in some surprise as he realised that she'd fallen asleep. Gilan motioned for silence and said quietly:

'She's obviously been under a great strain. It's best to let her sleep. You might prepare one of those excellent stews that Halt taught you to make. '

In his pack, Will carried a selection of dried ingredients that, when blended together in boiling water and simmered, resulted in delicious stews. They could be augmented by any fresh meat and vegetables that the travellers picked up along the way but, even without them, they made a far tastier meal than the cold rations the three had been eating that day.

He set a large bowl of water over the fire and soon had a delicious beef stew simmering and filling the cold evening air with its scent. At the same time, he produced their dwindling supply of coffee and set the enamel pot full of water in the hot embers to the side of the main fire. As the water bubbled and hissed to boiling point, he lifted the lid of the pot with a forked stick and tossed in a handful of grounds. Soon the aromatic scent of fresh coffee mingled with the stew and their mouths began to water. Around the same time, the savoury smells must have penetrated Evanlyn's consciousness. Her nose twitched delicately, then those startling green eyes flicked open. For a second or two, there was alarm in them as she tried to remember where she was. Then she caught sight of Gilan's reassuring face and she relaxed a little.

'Something smells awfully good,' she said and he grinned at her.

'Perhaps you could try a bowlful and then tell us what's been going on in these parts.' He made a sign to Will to fill an enamel bowl with the stew. It was Will's own bowl, as they didn't have any spare eating utensils. His stomach growled as he realised he'd have to wait until Evanlyn had finished before he could eat. Horace and Gilan, of course, simply helped themselves.

Evanlyn began wolfing down the savoury stew with an enthusiasm that showed she hadn't eaten in days. Gilan and Horace also set to quite happily. A whining voice came from the far rock wall, where Horace had tied the two bandits, sitting them back to back.

'Can we have something to eat, sir?' asked Carney. Gilan barely paused between mouthfuls and threw a disdainful glance at them.

'Of course not,' he said, and went back to enjoying his dinner.

Evanlyn seemed to realise that, aside from the bandits, only Will wasn't eating. She glanced down at the plate and spoon she was holding, looked at the identical implements being used by Gilan and Horace, and seemed to realise what had happened.

'Oh,' she said, looking apologetically at Will, 'would you like to . . .?' She offered the enamel plate to him. Will was tempted to share it with her, but realised that she must be nearly starving. In spite of her offer, he could see that she was hoping he'd refuse. He decided that there was a difference between being hungry, which he was, and starving, which she was, and shook his head, smiling at her.

'You go ahead,' he said. 'I'll eat when you've finished.'

He was a little disappointed when she didn't insist, but went back to wolfing down great spoonfuls of the stew, pausing occasionally for a deep draught of hot, freshly brewed coffee. As she ate, it seemed that a little colour returned to her cheeks. She cleaned the plate and looked wistfully at the stewpot still hanging over the fire. Will took the hint and ladled out another healthy dollop of stew and she set to once again, hardly pausing to breathe. This time, when the plate was empty, she smiled shyly and handed it back to him.

'Thanks,' she said simply and he ducked his head awkwardly.

'S'all right,' he mumbled, filling the plate again for himself. 'I suppose you were pretty hungry.'

'I was,' she agreed. 'I don't think I've eaten properly in a week.'

Gilan hitched himself into a more comfortable position by the small fire they kept burning. 'Why not?' he asked. 'I would have thought there was plenty of food left in the houses? You could have taken some of that?'

She shook her head, her eyes showing the fear that had gripped her for the previous few weeks. 'I didn't want to risk it,' she said. 'I didn't know if there'd be more of Morgarath's patrols around, so I didn't dare go into any of the towns. I found a few vegetables and the odd piece of cheese in some of the farmhouses, but precious little else.'

'I think it's time you told us what you know about events here,' Gilan told her and she nodded agreement.

'Not that I know too much. As I said, I was here with
... my mistress, visiting ... friends.' Again, there was just
the slightest hesitation in her words. Gilan frowned
slightly, noticing it.

'Your mistress is a noble lady, I take it? A knight's wife,
or perhaps a lord's wife?'

Evanlyn nodded. 'She is daughter to ... Lord and
Lady Caramorn of Greenfield Fief,' she said quickly. But
again there was that fleeting hesitation. Gilan pursed his
lips thoughtfully.

'I've heard the name,' he said. 'Can't say I know them.'

'Anyway, she was here visiting a lady of King Swyddned's
court — an old friend — when Morgarath's force attacked.'

Gilan frowned once more. 'How did they accomplish
that?' he wanted to know. 'The cliffs and the Fissure are
impassable. You couldn't get an army down the cliffs, let
alone across the Fissure.'

The cliffs rose from the far side of the Fissure to form
the boundary between Celtica and the Mountains of Rain
and Night. They were sheer granite, several hundred
metres in height. There were no passes, no way up or
down — certainly not for large numbers of troops.

'Halt says no place is ever really impassable,' Will put
in. 'Particularly if you don't mind losing lives in the
attempt.'

'We ran into a small party of Celts escaping to the
south,' the girl said. 'They told us how the Wargals
managed it. They used ropes and scaling ladders and came
down the cliffs by night, in small numbers. They found a
few narrow ledges, then used the scaling ladders to cross
the Fissure.

'They picked the most remote spot they could find, so they went undetected. During the day, those already across the Fissure hid among the rocks and valleys until they had the entire force assembled. They wouldn't have needed many. King Swyddned didn't keep a large standing army.'

Gilan made a disapproving sound and caught Will's eye.

'He should have. The treaty obliged him to. But remember what we said about people growing complacent? Celts would rather dig in their ground than defend it.' He gestured for the girl to continue.

'The Wargals overran the countryside, concentrating on the mines in particular. For some reason, they wanted the miners alive. They killed anyone else.

Gilan rubbed his chin thoughtfully. 'Pordellath and Gwyntaleth are both totally deserted,' he said. ' Any idea where the people might have gone?'

'A lot of the people in the towns got away in time,' she told him. 'They'll have headed south. The Wargals seem to be driving them that way.'

'Makes sense, I suppose,' Gilan commented. 'Keeping them bottled up in the south would prevent word getting out to Araluen.'

'That's what the captain of our escort said,' Evanlyn agreed. 'King Swyddned and most of his surviving army retreated to the south-west coast to form a defensive line. Any Celts who managed to get away from the Wargals have joined him there.'

'And what about you?' Gilan wanted to know.

'We were trying to escape back to the border when we were cut off by a war party,' she told them. 'Our men held them off while my lady and I escaped. We were almost clear but her horse stumbled and they caught her. I wanted to go back for her but she screamed at me to get away. I couldn't . . . I wanted to help her but . . . I just . . .'

Tears began to cascade down her cheeks once more. She didn't seem to notice, making no attempt to wipe them away, just staring silently into the fire as the horror of it all came back to her. When she spoke once more, her voice was almost inaudible.

'I got clear and I turned back to watch. They were . . . they were . . . I could see them . . .' Her voice died away. Gilan reached forward and took her hand.

'Don't think about it,' he said gently and she looked up at him, gratitude in her eyes. 'I take it that after . . . that . . . you got away into the hills?'

She nodded several times, her thoughts still vivid with the terrible scenes she had witnessed. Will and Horace sat in silence. Will glanced at his friend and a look of understanding passed between them. Evanlyn had been lucky to escape.

'I've been hiding ever since,' she said quietly. 'My horse went lame about ten days back and I turned him loose. Since then, I've kept moving back towards the north by night and hiding by day.' She indicated Bart and Carney, sitting trussed like two captive chickens on the far side of the clearing. 'I saw those two a few times, and others like them. I didn't make myself known to them. I didn't think I could trust them.'

Carney assumed a hurt look. Bart was still too dizzy from the crack Horace had given him with the flat of his sword to be taking any interest in proceedings.

'Then I saw you three earlier today from across a valley and I recognised you as King's Rangers — well, two of you, anyway,' she amended. 'All I could think was "Thank God".'

Gilan looked up at her at that, a small frown of concentration creasing his forehead. She didn't notice the reaction as she went on.

'It took me most of the day to reach you. It wasn't far as the crow flies, but there was no way across the valley that separated us. I had to go the long way around. Then down and up again. I was terrified that you'd be gone by the time I got here. But luckily, you weren't,' she added, unnecessarily.

Will was leaning forward, elbow on his knee and hand propped under his chin, trying to piece together all she'd told them.

'Why would Morgarath want miners?' he asked of nobody in particular. 'He doesn't have mines, so it doesn't make sense.'

'Maybe he's found some?' Horace suggested. Maybe he's found gold up there in the Mountains of Rain and Night and he needs slaves to dig it out.'

Gilan gnawed thoughtfully at a thumbnail as he considered what Horace had said. 'That could be,' he said at last. 'He's going to need gold to pay off the Skandians. Maybe he's mining his own.'

Evanlyn had sat up a little straighter at the mention of the sea wolves.

'Skandians?' she asked. 'Are they in league with Morgarath now?'

Gilan nodded. 'They've got something cooking,' he

told her. 'The entire Kingdom's on alert. We were bringing despatches to King Swyddned from Duncan.'

'You'll have to go south-west to find him,' Evanlyn replied. Will noticed that she had started a little at the mention of King Duncan's name. 'But I doubt he'll leave his defensive positions there.'

Gilan was already shaking his head. 'I think this is more important than taking despatches to Swyddned. After all, the main thrust of them was to tell him that Morgarath was on the move. I guess he knows that by now.'

He stood up, stretching and yawning. It was already full dark.

'I suggest we get a good night's sleep,' he said, 'and start back north in the morning. I'll take first watch, so you can keep my cloak, Evanlyn. I'll take Will's when he relieves me.'

'Thank you,' Evanlyn said simply and all three of them knew she was talking about more than just the use of the cloak. Will and Horace moved to douse the fire as Gilan took his longbow and moved to a rock outcrop that gave him a good view of the track leading to and from their camp site.

As Will was helping Evanlyn arrange a sleeping spot, he heard Carney's whining voice once more.

'Sir, please, could you loosen these ropes a little for the night? They're awful tight, like.'

And he heard Gilan's uncaring, 'Of course not,' as he climbed up onto the rocks to take the first watch.

Ten

The following morning, of course, they were faced with the problem of what to do with Bart and Carney.

The two bandits had spent a supremely uncomfortable night, tied back to back and forced to sit upright on the stony ground. As each watch changed, Gilan had loosened their bonds for a few minutes to give their cramped muscles a brief respite. He even eventually relented and allowed them a small amount of the party's food and water. But it was still a very unpleasant experience for them, made even more so because they had no idea what he planned to do with them in the morning.

And, truth be told, neither did Gilan. He had no wish to take them along as prisoners. As it was, they had only four horses, counting the pack horse that had been carrying their camping supplies and would now have to carry Evanlyn as well. He felt that the news of Morgarath's puzzling foray into Celtica should be taken back to King

Duncan as soon as possible, and dragging two prisoners along on foot would slow them down immeasurably. In addition, he was already considering the idea that he might push on ahead at top speed, allowing the other three to follow at their own pace. He knew the clumsy pack pony would never keep up with Blaze's mile-eating lope.

So, faced with these two problems, he frowned to himself as he ate breakfast, allowing himself the luxury of a second cup of coffee from their dwindling supply. After all, he thought, if he did go on ahead, it was the last coffee he'd see for some days. After a while he glanced up, caught Will's eye and beckoned him over.

'I'm thinking of pushing on ahead,' he said quietly. Instantly he saw the look of alarm in Will's eyes.

'You mean alone?' Will asked and Gilan nodded.

'This is vital news, Will, and I need to get it to King Duncan as soon as possible. Aside from anything else, it means that there'll be no reinforcements coming from Celtica. He needs to know that.'

'But . . .' Will hesitated. He looked around the little camp site as if searching for some argument against Gilan's idea. The tall Ranger was a comforting presence. Like Halt, he always seemed to know the right thing to do. Now, the thought that he was planning to leave them created a sense of near-panic in Will's mind. Gilan recognised the self-doubt that was racking the boy. He stood and placed a hand on his shoulder.

'Let's walk a little,' he said and they began to pace away from the camp site. Blaze and Tug glanced up curiously as they passed then, realising they weren't required, went back to cropping the sparse vegetation.

'I know you're worried about what happened with those four Wargals,' Gilan said. Will stopped walking and looked up at him.

'Halt told you?' he said. There was a note of doubt in his voice. He wondered what Halt had said about his behaviour. Gilan nodded gravely.

'Of course he told me. Will, you have nothing to be ashamed of, believe me.'

'But, Gil, I panicked. I forgot all my training and I . . .'

Gilan held up a hand to stop the torrent of self-recrimination that he sensed was about to pour out.

'Halt says you stood your ground,' he said firmly. Will shuffled his feet.

'Well . . . I suppose so. But . . .'

'You were scared but you didn't run. Will, that's not cowardice. That's courage. That's the highest form of courage. Weren't you scared when you killed the Kalkara?'

'Of course,' Will said. 'But that was different. It was forty metres away and attacking Sir Rodney.'

'Whereas,' Gilan finished for him, 'the Wargal was ten metres away and coming straight at you. Big difference.'

Will wasn't convinced. 'It was Tug who saved me,' he said. Gilan allowed himself a grin.

'Maybe he thought you were worth saving. He's a smart horse. And while Halt and I aren't nearly as smart as Tug, we think you've got what it takes, too.'

'Well, I've been beginning to doubt it,' Will said. But for the first time in some weeks, he felt his confidence lift a little.

'Then don't!' Gilan said forcefully. 'Self doubt is a disease. And if it gets out of control, it becomes self fulfilling. You have to learn from what happened with those Wargals. Use the experience to make you stronger.'

Will thought about Gilan's words for a few seconds. Then he took a deep breath and squared his shoulders.

'All right,' he said. 'What do you want me to do?'

Gilan studied him for a moment. There was a new-found determination in the boy's stance.

'I'm going to leave you in command,' he said. 'There's no point now continuing on with the mission, so follow on behind me to Araluen as quickly as you can.'

'To Redmont?' Will asked and Gilan shook his head.

'By now, the army will be on the move to the Plains of Uthal. That's where I'm heading and that's where Halt will be. We'll go over the map before I leave and plan the best route for you.'

'What about the girl?' Will asked. 'Should I bring her along or leave her somewhere safe once we're back in Araluen?'

Gilan considered the point for a moment. 'Bring her. The King and his advisers may want to question her some more. She'll be in the middle of the Araluan army, so she'll be as safe as anywhere else.'

He hesitated, then decided to share his suspicions with Will. 'There's something else about her, Will,' he began.

'You think her story isn't quite right?' Will interrupted. 'She keeps hesitating and stopping, as if she's afraid to tell us something.' Another thought struck him and he lowered his voice instinctively, even though the camp site was well out of earshot. 'You don't think she's a spy, do you?'

Gilan shook his head. 'Nothing so dramatic. But remember when she said she saw us and thought, "Thank

God they're Rangers"? Ordinary people don't think that way about us. Only the nobles are comfortable around Rangers.'

Will frowned. 'So you think . . .' He hesitated. He wasn't sure what Gilan thought.

'I think she may be the lady and she's assumed her maid's identity.'

'So on the one hand, she sees Rangers and is glad, then she doesn't trust us enough to tell us the truth? It doesn't make sense, Gil!' Will said. Gilan shrugged.

'It may not be that she doesn't trust us. She may have other reasons for not saying who she really is. I don't think it's a problem for you. I just think you should be aware of it.'

They turned and began to walk back to the camp

'I don't like to leave you in the lurch,' Gilan said. 'But you're not exactly unarmed. You've got your bow and your knives, and of course, there's Horace.'

Will glanced across to where the muscular apprentice was sharing a joke with Evanlyn. As she threw back her head and laughed, he felt a small pang of jealousy. Then he realised that he should be glad to have Horace along with him.

'He's not bad with that sword of his, is he?' he said.

Gilan shook his head in admiration. 'I'd never tell him, because it doesn't do a swordsman any good to have an inflated opinion of himself, but he's a lot better than not bad.' He looked down at Will. 'That's not to say you should go looking for trouble. There may still be Wargals between here and the border, so travel by night and hide up in the rocks by day.'

'Gil,' Will said, as an awkward thought struck him. 'What are we going to do about those two?' He jerked a thumb towards the two bandits, still tied back to back, still trying to doze off and still jerking each other awake as they did so.

'That's the question, isn't it?' said the Ranger. 'I suppose I could hang them. I do have the authority. After all, they did try to interfere with officers on the King's business. And they're looting in time of war. They're both capital offences.'

He cast his gaze around the rocky hills surrounding them. 'The question is whether I can actually do that here,' he murmured.

'You mean,' said Will, not liking the way his friend was thinking, 'you may not have the authority to hang them now that we're not in the Kingdom itself?'

Gilan grinned at him. 'I hadn't considered that. I was actually thinking that it'd be a bit difficult when there isn't a tree over a metre high within a hundred kilometres.'

Will heaved a small inner sigh of relief as he realised Gilan hadn't been serious. Then the Ranger's grin faded and he said warningly:

'The one thing I do know is that we don't want them coming after you three again. So make no mention of my plans until we've got rid of them, all right?'

In the end, the solution was a simple one. First, Gilan had Horace break the blade of Carney's sword by levering it sharply between two rocks. Then he hurled Bart's cudgel into the ravine by the road's edge. They heard it clattering and bouncing off the rocky slope for several seconds.

Once that was done, Gilan forced the two men to strip to their underwear.

'You needn't watch this,' he told Evanlyn. 'It won't be a pretty sight.'

Smiling to herself, the girl retreated inside the tent while the two men stripped down to their ragged underpants. They were shivering now in the cold mountain air.

'And your boots,' Gilan ordered and the two men sat awkwardly on the stony ground and removed their boots. Gilan nudged the piles of clothing with one toe.

'Now bundle 'em up and tie them in a ball with your belts,' he ordered and watched as Bart and Carney complied. When all was ready, he called Horace over and jerked a thumb at the two bundles of clothes and boots.

'Send 'em after the cudgel, Horace,' he ordered. Horace grinned as he began to understand. Bart and Carney understood too and started a chorus of protest. It stopped as Gilan swung an icy stare upon them.

'You're getting off lightly,' he told them in a cold voice. 'As I mentioned to Will earlier, I could hang you if I chose to.'

Bart and Carney instantly went quiet, then Gilan gestured for Horace to tie them up again. Meekly, they submitted, and in a few minutes they were back to back again, shivering in the keen wind that circled and dipped around the hills. Gilan considered them for a moment or two.

'Throw a blanket over them,' he said reluctantly. 'A horse blanket.'

Will obliged, grinning. He took care not to use Tug's blanket, but used the one belonging to the sturdy pack pony.

Gilan began to saddle Blaze, speaking to the others over his shoulder. 'I'm going to scout around Gwyntaleth. There may be someone there who can shed a little more light on what Morgarath is up to.' He looked meaningfully at Will and the apprentice realised that Gilan was saying this to throw the two bandits off. He gave a slight nod.

'I should be back about sunset,' Gilan continued loudly. 'Try to have something hot waiting for me then.'

He swung up into the saddle and beckoned Will closer. Leaning down, he whispered:

'Leave those two tied up and head off at sunset. They'll eventually get themselves loose but then they'll have to retrieve their boots and clothes. They won't go anywhere in these mountains without them. It will give you a day's start over them and that should take you clear.'

Will nodded. 'I understand. Ride safely, Gilan.' The Ranger nodded. He seemed to hesitate for a moment, then came to a decision.

'Will,' he said quietly. 'We're in uncertain times and none of us know what might be around the corner. It might be a good idea if you told Horace Tug's code word.'

Will frowned. The code word was a jealously guarded secret and he was reluctant to let anyone know it, even a trusted comrade like Horace. Seeing his hesitation, Gilan continued.

'You never know what might happen. You could be injured or incapacitated and, without the code word, Horace won't be able to make Tug obey him. It's just a precaution,' he added. Will saw the sense in the idea and nodded.

'I'll tell him tonight,' he said. 'Take care, Gilan.'

The tall Ranger leaned down and gripped his hand tightly.

'One other thing. You're in command here, and the others will take the lead from you. Don't give them any sign that you're not sure of yourself. Believe in yourself and they'll believe in you too.'

He nudged Blaze with his knee and the bay swung round towards the road. Gilan raised a hand in farewell to Horace and Evanlyn and cantered away. The dust of his passage was quickly dispersed by the keening wind.

And then Will felt very small. And very alone.

Eleven

They rode as hard as they could that night, held back somewhat by the docile pace that was all the pack pony could manage.

The rain came back during the night to make them more miserable. But then, an hour before dawn, it cleared, so that the first streaks of light in the east painted the sky a dull pearl colour. With the gathering light, Will began to look for a place to make camp.

Horace noticed him looking around. 'Why don't we keep going for a couple more hours?' he suggested. 'The horses aren't really tired yet.'

Will hesitated. They'd seen no sign of anyone else during the night, and certainly no evidence of any Wargals in the area. But he didn't like to go against Gilan's advice. In the past, he'd found that advice given by senior Rangers usually turned out to be worth following. Finally, the decision was made for him when they rounded a bend in the road and saw a thicket of shrubs set back about thirty metres from the road. The bushes, while not more than three metres high at their tallest point, offered a thick screen, providing shelter from both the wind and any unfriendly eyes that might chance to come along.

'We'll camp here,' Will said, indicating the bushes. 'That's the first decent-looking camp site we've passed in hours. Who knows when we'll see another?'

Horace shrugged. He was quite content to let Will make the decisions. He had only been making a suggestion, not trying to usurp the Ranger apprentice's authority in any way. Horace was essentially a simple soul. He reacted well to commands and to other people making decisions. Ride now. Stop here. Fight there. As long as he trusted the person making the decisions, he was happy to abide by them.

And he trusted Will's judgement. He had a hazy idea that Ranger training somehow made people more decisive and intelligent. And of course, in that he was right, to a large degree.

As they dismounted and led their horses through the thick bushes into a clearing beyond, Will gave a small sigh of relief. He was stiffer than he'd realised after a full night in the saddle with only a few brief rests. Several good hours' sleep seemed like a capital idea right now. He helped Evanlyn down from the pack pony — riding on the pack saddle as she had to, it was a little awkward for her to dismount. Then he began unstrapping their packs of food supplies and the rolled canvas length that they used as a weather shelter.

Evanlyn, with barely a word to him, stretched, then walked a few paces away to sit down on a flat rock.

Will, his forehead creased in a frown, tossed one of the food packs onto the sand at her feet.

'You can start getting a meal ready,' he said, more abruptly than he'd really intended. He was annoyed that the girl would sit down and make herself comfortable, leaving the work to him and Horace. She glanced down at the pack and flushed angrily.

'I'm not particularly hungry,' she told him. Horace started forward from where he was unsaddling his horse.

'I'll do it,' he said, keen to avoid any conflict between the other two. But Will held up a hand to stop him.

'No,' he said. 'I'd like you to rig the shelter. Evanlyn can get the food out.'

His eyes locked with hers. They were both angry but she realised she was in the wrong. She shrugged faintly and reached for the pack. 'If it means so much to you,' she muttered, then asked: 'Is it all right if Horace makes the fire for me? He can do it a lot quicker than I.'

Will considered the idea, screwing up his face thoughtfully. He was reluctant to light a fire while they were still in Celtica. It hardly seemed logical to travel by night to avoid being seen, then light a fire whose smoke might be visible in daylight. Besides, there was another consideration that Gilan had pointed out to him the previous day.

'No fire,' he said decisively and Evanlyn tossed the food pack down sulkily.

'Not cold food again!' she snapped. Will regarded her evenly.

'Not so long ago, you would have happily eaten anything — hot or cold — as long as it was food,' he reminded her and she dropped her eyes from his. 'Look,' he added, in a more reasoning tone, 'Gilan knows more about these things than any of us and he told us to make sure we aren't spotted. All right?'

She muttered something. Horace was watching the two of them, his honest face troubled by the conflict between them. He offered a compromise.

'I could just make a small fire for cooking,' he suggested. 'If we built it in under these bushes, the smoke should be pretty hard to see by the time it filters through.'

'It's not just that,' Will explained, slinging their water bags over one shoulder and taking his bow from the saddle scabbard. 'Gil says the Wargals have an amazingly keen sense of smell. If we did light a fire, the smell of the smoke would hang around for hours after we'd put it out.'

Horace nodded, conceding the point. Before anyone could raise any more objections, Will headed towards the jumble of rocks behind the camp site.

'I'm going to scout around,' he announced. 'I'll see if there's any water in the area. And I'll just make sure we're alone.'

Ignoring the girl's 'As if we're not,' which was muttered just loud enough for him to hear it, he began to scramble up the rocks. He made a careful circuit of the area, staying low and out of sight, moving from cover to scant cover as carefully as he could. *Whenever you're scouting,* Halt had once said to him, *move as if there's somebody there to see you. Never assume that you're on your own.*

He found no sign of Wargals or of Celts. But he did come across a small, clear stream that sluiced cold water over a bed of rocks. It was running fast enough to look safe for drinking, so he tested it and, satisfied that it wasn't polluted, filled their water bags to the brim. The cold fresh water tasted particularly good after the leathery-tasting supply from the bags. Once water had been in a water bag for more than a few hours, it began to taste more like the bag and less like water.

Back at the camp site, Horace and Evanlyn were waiting for his return. Evanlyn had set out a plate of dried meat and the hard biscuit they had been eating in place of bread for some time now. He was grateful that she'd also put a small amount of pickle on the meat. Any addition to the tasteless meal was welcome. He noticed as they were eating that there was none on her plate.

'Don't you like pickles?' he asked, through a mouthful of meat and biscuit. She shook her head, not meeting his eyes.

'Not really,' she replied.

But Horace wasn't prepared to let it rest at that. 'She gave you the last of them,' he told Will.

For a moment, Will hesitated, embarrassed. He'd just mopped up the last small mouthful of the tangy yellow pickles on a corner of biscuit, and popped it into his mouth. There was no way now he could offer to share it.

'Oh,' he mumbled, realising this was her way of making the peace between them. 'Um . . . well, thanks, Evanlyn.'

She tossed her head. With her close cropped hair, the effect was a little wasted and the thought struck him that she was probably used to making that gesture with long blonde locks that would accentuate the movement.

'I told you,' she said. 'I don't like pickles.' But now there was a hint of a grin in her voice, and the earlier bad humour was gone. He looked up at her and grinned in reply.

'I'll take the first watch,' he said. It seemed as good a way as any of letting her know he didn't hold a grudge.

'If you take the second watch as well, you can have my pickles too,' offered Horace, and they all laughed. The atmosphere in the little camp site lightened considerably as Horace and Evanlyn busied themselves shaking out blankets and cloaks and gathering some of the leafier branches from the bushes around them to shape into beds.

For his part, Will took one of the water bottles and his cloak and climbed up onto one of the larger rocks surrounding their camp. He settled himself as comfortably as possible, with a clear view of the rocky hills behind them in one direction, and over the bushes that screened them from the road in the other. Mindful as ever of Halt's teaching, he settled himself among a jumble of rocks that formed a more or less natural nest, allowing him to peer between them on either side, without raising his head above the horizon level. He wriggled himself around for a few minutes, wishing there were not so many sharp stones to dig into him. Then he shrugged, deciding that at least they'd stop him from dozing off during his watch.

He donned his cloak and raised the hood. As he sat there, unmoving among the grey rocks, he seemed to blend into the background until he was almost invisible.

➤

It was the sound that first alerted him. It came and went vaguely with the breeze. As the breeze grew stronger, so did the sound. Then, as the breeze faded, he could no longer hear anything, so that at first he thought he was imagining things.

Then it came again. A deep, rhythmic sound. Voices, perhaps, but not like any he'd heard. It could have been singing, he thought, then, as the breeze blew a little harder, he heard it again. Not singing. There was no melody to it. Just a rhythm. A constant, unvarying rhythm.

Again the breeze died and the sound with it. Will felt the hairs on the back of his neck rising. There was something unhealthy about that sound. Something dangerous. He sensed it in every fibre of his body.

There it was again! And this time, he had it. Chanting. Deep voices chanting in unison. A tuneless chanting that had an unmistakable menace to it.

The breeze was from the south-west, so the sound was coming from the road where they had already travelled. He raised himself slowly and carefully, peering under one hand in the direction of the breeze. From this point he could make out various curves and bends in the road, although some of it disappeared behind the rocks and hills. He estimated that he could see sections of the road for perhaps a kilometre and there was no sign of movement.

Quickly, he scrambled down from the rocks and hurried to wake the others.

The chanting was closer now. It no longer died away as the breeze came and went. It was growing louder and more defined. Will, Horace and Evanlyn crouched among the bushes, listening as the voices came closer.

'Maybe you two should move back a little,' Will

suggested. He knew that, wrapped in his Ranger cloak, with his face concealed deep within the cowl, he would be virtually invisible. He wasn't so sure about the others. Without any reluctance, they squirmed back, deeper into the cover of the thick shrubs. Horace's reaction was a mixture of curiosity and nervousness. Evanlyn, Will noted, was pale with fear.

Just in case the chanters had scouts deployed, Will had quickly struck their camp, obliterating any traces that they may have left. He'd led the horses a hundred metres back into the rocks and tethered them there, leaving the camping equipment with them. Then, with Horace and Evanlyn, he had sought the cover of the thick scrub, hiding deep within the bushes but leaving himself a relatively clear view of the road.

'Who are they?' Horace breathed as the chanting grew louder still. Will estimated that it was coming from somewhere around the nearest bend in the road, a mere hundred metres away.

'Don't you know?' Evanlyn replied, her voice strained with terror. 'They're Wargals.'

Twelve

ill and Horace both turned quickly to look at her.

'Wargals? How do you know?' Will asked.

'I've heard them before,' she said in a small voice, biting her lip. 'They make that chanting sound as they march.'

Will frowned. The four Wargals he and Halt had tracked had made no chanting sound. But then he realised that they had been tracking their own quarry at the time. Out of the corner of his eye, Will saw a movement at the bend in the road.

'Get down!' he hissed urgently. 'Keep your faces down!' And both Horace and Evanlyn dropped their faces into the sand. He reached up and pulled the shadowing depths of his cowl further over his own face, then held a forearm draped in the folds of his cloak to obscure everything but his eyes.

The chant, he saw now, was a form of cadence, designed to keep the Wargals moving at the same pace — in the same way a sergeant might call the step for a troop of infantry. He counted perhaps thirty in the group. Big, heavy-set figures, dressed in dark metal-studded jackets and breeches of some heavy material. They ran at a steady jog, chanting the guttural, wordless rhythm — which, he realised now, was nothing more than a series of grunts.

They were all armed, with an assortment of short spears, maces and battleaxes, which they carried ready for use.

As yet, he couldn't make out their features. They ran with a shambling movement in two files. Then he realised that they were escorting another group between the two files: prisoners.

Now the group was closer, he realised that the prisoners — about a dozen of them — were staggering along, trying desperately to keep pace with the chanting Wargals. He recognised them as Celts — miners, judging by the leather aprons and skull caps they wore. They were exhausted and as he watched, he could see the Wargals using short whips to urge them along.

The chanting grew louder.

'What's happening?' Horace whispered and Will could have cheerfully choked him.

'Shut up!' he shot back. 'Not another word!'

Now the Wargals were closer and he could make out their faces. He felt the hairs on the back of his neck begin to rise as he saw the thick, heavy jowls and noses that had lengthened and thickened almost to the size of muzzles. The eyes were small and savage and seemed to glow with a red hatred as they lashed their whips at the Celts. Once, as one of them snarled at a stumbling prisoner, Will caught a quick glimpse of yellow fangs. He was tempted to shrink down further. But he knew any movement now would risk discovery. He had to trust to the shelter of his cloak. He wanted to close his eyes to those animal-like faces, but somehow, he couldn't. He stared in fascinated horror as the terrible Wargals, creatures from a nightmare, chanting incessantly, jogged past the spot where he lay.

The Celt miner couldn't have lost his footing at a worse place.

Lashed by one of the Wargals, he stumbled, staggered, then crashed over in the road, bringing down the prisoners on either side of him. Will could see now that they were roped together with a thick rawhide leash.

As the column came to a confused stop, the chanting broke up into a series of snarls and growls from the Wargals. The two prisoners who had been brought down struggled to their feet, under a rain of lashes from their captors. The miner who had caused the fall lay still, in spite of the vicious whipping from one of the Wargals.

Finally another joined the first, and began beating at the still figure with the butt of his heavy, steel-shod spear. There was no reaction from the miner. Watching in horror, Will realised that the man was dead. Eventually, that same realisation came to the Wargals. At an incomprehensible command from one who must have been in charge, the two stopped beating the dead man and cut the bonds that attached him to the central leash. Then they picked up the limp body and threw it clear, hurling it towards the thicket where Will and the others sheltered.

The body crashed into the bushes closest to the road and Will heard Evanlyn utter a small cry of fear. Face down, not knowing what was happening, the sudden crashing in the bushes had obviously been too much for her to bear. She bit the noise off almost as soon as it started, but she was just a little too late.

The leader of the Wargals seemed to have heard something. He turned now and stared hard at the spot where the body lay, wondering if the noise had come from the miner. Obviously, he was suspicious that the dead man might be merely foxing, in an effort to escape. He pointed and shouted an order and the Wargal with the spear stepped forward and ran it casually through the dead body.

Still the commander's suspicions weren't satisfied. For a long moment, he stared into the bushes, looking straight at the spot where Will lay, wrapped in the protective camouflage of his Ranger cloak. The apprentice found himself staring deep into the angry red eyes of the savage thing out on the road. He wanted to drop his eyes away from that gaze, convinced that the creature could see him. But all of Halt's training over the past year told him that any movement now would be fatal, and he knew that dropping his eyes could lead to a tiny, involuntary movement of his head. The true value of the camouflaged cloaks lay not in magic as so many people believed, but in the wearer's ability to remain unmoving under close scrutiny.

Forcing himself to believe, Will remained motionless, staring at the Wargal. His mouth was dry. His heart pounded at what seemed like twice its normal rate. He could hear the heavy, rasping breathing of the bear-like figure, see the nostrils twitching slightly as it sampled the light breeze, testing for unknown scents.

Finally, the Wargal turned away. Then, in an instant, it whipped back again to stare once more. Fortunately, Will's training had covered that particular trick as well. He made no movement. This time, the Wargal grunted, then called an order to the group.

Chanting once more, they moved out, leaving the dead miner on the roadside.

As the sound receded and they disappeared round the next bend in the road, Will felt Horace moving behind him.

'Stay still!' he whispered fiercely. It was possible that the Wargals had a sweeper following — a silent-moving rear scout who might catch unwary fugitives who thought the danger was past.

He forced himself to count to one hundred before he allowed the others to move, crawling clear of the bushes and stretching their stiff and aching limbs.

Signalling to Horace to take Evanlyn back to the camp site, Will stepped cautiously into the road to check the Celt. As he had suspected, the man was dead. He had obviously been beaten many times over the past few days. His face was bruised and cut by the whips and fists of the Wargals.

There was nothing he could do for the man so he left him where he lay and went to rejoin the others.

Evanlyn was sitting crying. As he approached, she looked up at him, her face streaked with tears and her shoulders heaving with the great sobs that shook her. Horace stood by, a helpless expression on his face, making useless little movements with his hands.

'I'm sorry,' Evanlyn finally managed to gasp. 'It's just

that . . . chanting . . . those voices . . . I could remember everything when they . . .'

'It's all right,' Will told her quietly. 'My God, they're horrible creatures!' he added, shaking his head at Horace. The warrior apprentice swallowed once or twice. He hadn't seen the Wargals. He'd lain there throughout the entire encounter with his face pressed hard into the sandy ground. In a way, thought Will, that must have been just as terrifying.

'What are they like?' Horace asked in a small voice. Will shook his head again. It was almost impossible to describe.

'Like beasts,' he said. 'Like bears . . . or a cross between a bear and a dog. But they walk upright like men.'

Evanlyn gave another shuddering cry. 'They're vile!' she said bitterly. 'Vile, horrible creatures. Oh God, I hope I never see them again!'

Will moved to her and patted her shoulder awkwardly.

'They're gone now,' he said quietly, as if soothing a small child. 'They're gone and they can't hurt you.'

She made an enormous effort and gathered her courage. She looked up at him, a frightened smile on her face. She reached up and took his hand in her own, taking comfort from the mere contact.

He let her hold his hand for a while. He wondered how he was going to tell them what he had decided to do.

Thirteen

'Follow them? Are you out of your mind?'

Horace stared at the small, determined figure, unable to believe what he was hearing. Will didn't say anything, so Horace tried again.

'Will, we've just spent half an hour hiding behind a bush hoping those things wouldn't see us. Now you want to follow them and give them another chance?'

Will glanced around to make sure that Evanlyn was still out of earshot. He didn't want to alarm the girl unnecessarily.

'Keep your voice down,' he warned Horace, and his friend spoke more softly, but no less vehemently.

'Why?' he asked. 'What can we possibly gain by following them?'

Will shifted uneasily from one foot to the other. Frankly, the idea of following the Wargals was already frightening him. He could feel his pulse rate was running higher than normal. They were terrifying creatures, and obviously totally devoid of any feelings of mercy or pity, as the fate of the prisoner had shown. Still, he could see that this was an opportunity that shouldn't be wasted.

'Look,' he said quietly. 'Halt always told me that knowing why your enemy is doing something is just as important as knowing what he's doing. Sometimes more important, in fact.'

Horace shook his head stubbornly. 'I don't get it,' he said. To him this idea of Will's was a crazy, irresponsible and terrifyingly dangerous impulse.

To be truthful, Will wasn't absolutely sure that he was right either. But Gilan's parting words about not showing uncertainty rang in his ears and his instincts, honed by Halt's training, told him this was an opportunity he shouldn't miss.

'We know that the Wargals are capturing Celtic miners and carrying them off,' he said. 'And we know Morgarath doesn't do anything without a reason. This might be a chance to find out what he's up to.'

Horace shrugged. 'He wants slaves,' he said and Will shook his head quickly.

'But why? And why only miners? Evanlyn said they were only interested in the miners. Why? Can't you see?' he appealed to the bigger boy. 'This could be important. Halt says that wars often turn on the smallest piece of information.'

Horace pursed his lips, thinking over what Will had said. Finally, he nodded slowly.

'Okay,' he agreed. 'I guess you may be right.' Horace wasn't a fast thinker, or an original one. But he was methodical and, in his own way, logical. Will had instinctively seen the necessity for following the Wargals.

Horace had to work his way through it. Now that he had, he could see Will wasn't acting on some wild adventurous impulse. He trusted the Ranger apprentice's line of reasoning. 'Well, if we're going to follow them, we'd better get moving,' he added and Will looked at him in surprise, shaking his head.

'We?' he said. 'Who said anything about "we"? I plan to follow them alone. Your job is to get Evanlyn back safely.'

'Says who?' asked the bigger boy, with some belliger- ence. 'My job, as it was explained to me by Gilan, was to stay with you and keep you out of trouble.'

'Well, I'm changing your orders,' Will told him. But this time Horace laughed.

'So who died and left you the boss?' he scoffed. 'You can't change my orders. Gilan gave me those orders and he outranks you.'

'And what about the girl?' Will challenged him. For a moment, Horace was stuck for an answer.

'We'll give her food and supplies and the pack horse,' he said. 'She can make her own way back.'

'That's very gallant of you,' Will said sarcastically. Horace merely shook his head again, refusing to be baited into an argument on that score.

'You're the one who said this is so darned important,' he replied. 'Well, I'm afraid I think you're right. So Evanlyn will simply have to take her chances, just like us. We're close to the border now anyway and one more night's riding will see her out of Celtica.'

In truth, Horace didn't like the thought of leaving Evanlyn to her own devices. He'd grown genuinely fond of the girl. She was bright and amusing and good company.

But his time in Battleschool had given him a strong sense of duty, and personal feelings came second.

Will tried one more time. 'I can move a lot faster without you,' he pointed out but Horace cut him off immediately.

'So what? We won't need speed if we're following the Wargals. We've got horses. We'll have no trouble keeping up with them, particularly as they have to drag those prisoners along.' He found he was rather enjoying the experience of arguing with Will and coming up with winning points. Maybe, he decided, spending time with Rangers had done him more good than he'd realised.

'Besides, what if we find out something really important? And what if you want to keep following them and we still have to get a message back to the Baron? If there are two of us, we can split up. I can take a message back while you keep following the Wargals.'

Will considered the idea. Horace had a point, he had to concede. It would make sense to have someone else along with him, now that he thought about it.

'All right,' he said finally. 'But we're going to have to tell Evanlyn.'

'Tell me what?' the girl asked. Unnoticed by either of them, she'd approached to within a few metres of where they had been standing, arguing in lowered voices. The two boys now looked guiltily at each other.

'Uh . . . Will had this idea, you see . . .' Horace began, then stopped, looking at Will to see if his friend was going to continue. But, as it turned out, there was no need.

'You're planning to follow the Wargals,' the girl said flatly and the two apprentices exchanged looks, before Will answered.

'You were listening?' he accused her. She shook her head.

'No. It's the obvious thing to do, isn't it? This is our chance to find out what they're up to and why they're kidnapping the miners.'

For the second time in a few minutes, Will found himself picking up on the use of the plural. 'Our chance?' he asked her. 'What exactly do you mean by "our" chance?'

Evanlyn shrugged. 'Obviously, if you two are following them, I'm coming along with you. You're not leaving me out here on my own in the middle of nowhere.'

'But . . .' Horace began and she turned to look calmly at him. 'These are Wargals,' he said.

'I had gathered that.'

Horace cast a hopeless glance at Will. The apprentice Ranger shrugged, so Horace tried again. 'It'll be dangerous. And you . . .'

He hesitated. He didn't want to remind her of her fear of the Wargals, and the reasons for it. Evanlyn realised his predicament and she smiled wanly at him.

'Look, I'm scared of those things,' she said. 'But I assume you're planning to follow them, not join up with them.'

'That was the general idea,' Will said and she turned her level gaze on him.

'Well, with the noise they make, we shouldn't have to get too close to them,' she told him. 'And besides, this might be a chance to spoil whatever plans they have. I think I'd enjoy that.'

Will regarded her with a new respect. She had every reason to fear the Wargals, more than he or Horace. Yet she was willing to put that fear aside in order to strike a blow against Morgarath.

'You're sure?' he said finally and she shook her head.

'No. I'm not sure at all. I feel decidedly queasy at the prospect of getting within earshot of those things again. But equally, I don't like the idea of being abandoned here on my own.'

'We weren't abandoning you . . .' Horace began and she turned back to him.

'Then what would you call it?' she asked him, smiling faintly to take the sting out of her words. He hesitated.

'Abandoning you, I guess,' he admitted.

'Exactly,' she said. 'So, given the choice of running into another group of Wargals, or more bandits, or following some Wargals with you two, I'll choose the latter.'

'We're only a day from the border,' Will pointed out to her. 'Once you're across that, you'll be relatively safe.'

But she shook her head decisively.

'I feel more secure with you two,' she said. 'Besides, it might be handy for you to have someone else along. It'll be one more person to keep watch at night. That means you'll get more sleep.'

'That's the first sensible reason I've heard for her coming along so far,' said Horace. Like Will, he realised that she'd made her mind up. And both boys somehow knew that when Evanlyn did that, there was no way on earth they were going to make her change it. She grinned at him.

'Well,' she said, 'are we going to stand here all day nattering? Those Wargals aren't getting any closer while we're doing it.'

And, turning on her heel, she led the way to where the horses were tethered.

Fourteen

ollowing the Wargals was easier than they expected. The creatures were single minded, concentrating only on the task in hand, which was to take the Celt miners to their end destination. They feared no attack in these parts, having already driven the occupants out, so they posted no forward scouts or sweepers. Their constant chanting, ominous as it might sound at first, also served to mask any sounds that might have been made by their pursuers.

At night, they simply camped wherever they might find themselves to be. The miners remained chained together and sentries were posted to keep watch over them while the rest of the group slept.

By the beginning of the second day, Will began to have an idea of the direction the Wargals were heading. He had been riding some thirty metres in the lead, relying on Tug to sense any danger ahead. Now he dropped back a little, waiting for Horace and Evanlyn to come level with him.

'We seem to be heading for the Fissure,' he said, more than a little puzzled.

Already, in the distance, they could make out the high, brooding cliffs that towered over the massive split in the earth. Celtica itself was a mountainous country, but Morgarath's domain reared hundreds of metres above it.

'I wouldn't care to come down those cliffs on ropes and scaling ladders,' Horace said, nodding towards them.

'Even if you did, you'd have to find a level space on the other side to cross from,' Will agreed. 'And apparently, there are precious few of them. For the most part, the cliffs go right down to the bottom.'

Evanlyn looked from one to the other. 'Yet Morgarath has done it once,' she said. 'Maybe he's planning to attack Araluen the same way.'

Horace brought his horse to a halt, considering what she'd said. Will and Evanlyn stopped beside him. He chewed his lip for a few seconds as he thought back over the lessons that Sir Rodney's instructors had dinned into him. Then he shook his head.

'It's a different situation,' he said finally. 'The attack on Celtica was more of a raid than an invasion. He wouldn't have needed more than five hundred men for that and they could travel light. To attack Araluen, he'll need an army — and he wouldn't get an army down those cliffs and across with a few ladders and rope bridges.'

Will regarded him with interest. This was a side of Horace that was new to him. Apparently, Horace's learning curve in the past seven or eight months had gone beyond his mere skill with the sword.

'But surely, if he had enough time . . .?' he began but

Horace shook his head again, more decisively this time.

'Men, yes, or Wargals in this case. Given enough time, you could get them down and across. It would take months but you could manage it. Although the longer it took, the more chance word would get out about what you were doing. 'But an army needs equipment — heavy weapons, supply wagons, provisions, tents, spare weapons and blacksmith's equipment to repair them. Horses and oxen to pull the wagons. You'd never get all that down cliffs like those. And even if you did, how would you get it across? It's just not feasible. Sir Karel used to say that . . .'

He realised the others were regarding him with a certain amount of respect and he flushed. 'Didn't mean to go on and on,' he mumbled, and urged his horse forward again.

But as Will followed, he was shaking his head, impressed by his friend's grasp of the subject. 'Not at all,' he said. 'You're making good sense.'

'Which still leaves us the question, what is he up to?' Evanlyn said.

Will shrugged. 'I suppose we'll find out soon enough,' he said, and urged Tug forward to take up the point position once more.

They found out the following evening.

As before, the first hint as to what was taking place came by sound: the ring and thud of hammers striking stone or wood. Then they heard a thinner sound as they drew closer. A constant but irregular cracking sound. Will signalled for the others to stop and, dismounting, he proceeded carefully along the road to the final bend.

Shrouded in his cloak, and moving carefully from one patch of cover to the next, he moved off the road and cut across country to find a vantage point from which to view the next stretch of road. Almost immediately, he saw the top of the massive wooden structure that was being constructed: four wooden towers, linked by heavy rope cables and a timber framework. His heart sinking, he already knew what he was looking at. But he moved closer to make sure.

It was as he feared. An immense wooden bridge was in the final stages of construction. On the far side of the Fissure, Morgarath had discovered one of the few places where a narrow ledge ran, almost level with the Celtic side. The natural ledge had been dug out and widened until there was a sizeable piece of level ground there. The four towers stood, two either side of the Fissure, linked by massive rope cables. Supported by them, a wooden roadway was half completed — capable of taking six men abreast across the dizzying depths of the Fissure.

Figures recognisable as Celt prisoners swarmed over the structure, hammering and sawing. The cracking sound was made by the whips used by the Wargal overseers.

Beyond them, the sound of hammers on stone came from the mouth of a tunnel that opened onto the ledge some fifty metres south of the bridge. It was little more than a crack in the cliff face — only a little wider than a man's shoulders — but as he watched, the Celt prisoners were hard at work at its entrance, gouging at the hard rock, widening and enlarging the small opening.

Will glanced up at the dark cliffs towering on the other side. There was no sign of ropes or ladders leading down to the ledge. The Wargals and their prisoners must access it via the narrow crack in the rock, he reasoned.

The party they had been following was crossing the Fissure now. The final fifteen metres of roadway was yet to be constructed, and only a temporary timber footway was in place. It was barely wide enough for the Celts to cross, tethered in pairs as they were, but the miners of Celtica were used to awkward footing and dizzy drops and they crossed without incident.

He'd seen enough for the time being, he thought. It was time to get back. He wriggled his way backwards into the cover of the broken rocks. Then, bending almost double, he ran back to where the others were waiting.

When he reached them, he slumped down, leaning back against the rocks. The tension of the last two days was beginning to tell on him, along with the strain of being in command. He was a little surprised to realise that he was physically exhausted. He had no idea that mental tension could sap a person's strength so thoroughly.

'So what's going on? Did you see anything?' Horace said. Will looked up at him, wearily.

'A bridge,' he told him. 'They're building a huge bridge.'

Horace frowned, puzzled by it all. 'Why would Morgarath want a bridge?'

'It's a huge bridge, I said. Big enough to bring an army across. Here we've been discussing how Morgarath couldn't move an army and all its equipment down the cliffs and across the Fissure, and all the time, he's been building a bridge to do it.'

Evanlyn picked at a loose thread on her jacket. 'That's why he wanted the Celts,' she said. When both boys looked at her, she elaborated. 'They're expert builders and tunnellers. His Wargals wouldn't have the skill for an undertaking like this.'

'They're tunnelling too,' Will said. 'There's a narrow crack — sort of a cave mouth — in the far side that they're widening.'

'Where does it lead to?' Horace asked and Will shrugged.

'I don't know. It might be important to find out. After all, the plateau on the other side is still hundreds of feet above this point. But there must be some access between the two because there's no sign of ropes or ladders.'

Horace stood and began to pace back and forth as he considered this new information. His face was screwed up in thought.

'I don't get it,' he said finally.

'It's not that hard to "get", Horace,' Will told him, with some asperity. 'There's a barking great bridge being built over the Fissure — big enough for Morgarath and all his Wargals *and* their supply wagons *and* their blacksmiths *and* their oxen and Uncle Tom Cobbley and all to come waltzing over.'

Horace waited until Will had finished his tirade. Then he cocked his head to one side.

'Finished?' he said mildly and Will, realising that he'd been a little excessive, made a vaguely apologetic gesture for Horace to continue.

'What I don't get,' Horace said, enunciating very carefully, 'is why it was never mentioned in those plans you captured.'

Evanlyn looked up curiously. 'Plans?' she said. 'What plans?'

But Will, realising that Horace had made a vital point, gestured for her to wait for an explanation.

'You're right,' he said softly. 'The plans never mentioned a bridge across the Fissure.'

'And it's not as if it's a small undertaking. You'd think it would be in there somewhere.' Horace said. Will nodded agreement. Evanlyn, her curiosity thoroughly piqued by now, repeated her question.

'What are these plans you keep talking about?'

Horace took pity on her, realising how frustrating their conversation must be for her.

'Will and Halt — his Craftmaster — captured a copy of Morgarath's battle plans a couple of weeks ago. There was a lot of detail about how his forces are going to break out of the Mountains via Three Step Pass. There was even the date on which they were going to do it and how Skandian mercenaries were going to help them. Only there was no mention of this bridge.'

'Why not?' Evanlyn asked. But Will was beginning to see what Morgarath had in mind, and his horror was growing by the second.

'Unless,' he said, 'Morgarath *wanted* us to capture those plans.'

'That's crazy,' Horace said instantly. 'After all, one of his men died as a result.'

Will met his gaze evenly. 'Would that stop Morgarath? He doesn't care about other people's lives. Let's think it through. Halt has a saying: *When you can't see the reason for something, look for the possible result — and ask yourself who might benefit from it.*'

'So,' said Evanlyn, 'what's the result of your finding those plans?'

'King Duncan has moved the army to the Plains of Uthal to block Three Step Pass,' said Horace promptly. Evanlyn nodded and continued with the second part of the equation.

'And who might benefit from that?'

Will looked up at her. He could see she'd reached the same conclusion he had. Very slowly, he said:

'Morgarath. If those plans were false.'

Evanlyn nodded agreement. Horace was not quite so quick to see the point.

'False? What do you mean?'

'I mean,' said Will, 'Morgarath wanted us to find those plans. He wanted the Araluan army assembled at the Plains of Uthal — the whole army. Because Three Step Pass isn't where the real attack will come from. The real attack will come from here — a surprise attack from behind. And our army will be trapped and destroyed.'

Horace's eyes widened in horror. He could envisage the result of a massive attack from the rear. The Araluans would be caught between the Skandians and Wargals in front of them and another army of Wargals in their rear. It was a recipe for disaster — the kind of disaster every general feared.

'Then we've got to tell them,' he said. 'Right away.'

Will nodded. 'We've got to tell them. But there's one more thing I want to see. That tunnel they're digging. We don't know if it's finished, or half finished, or where it goes. I want to take a look at it tonight.'

But Horace was shaking his head before he even finished. 'Will, we've got to go *now*,' he said. 'We can't hang around here just to satisfy your curiosity.'

It was Evanlyn who solved the argument. 'You're right,

Horace,' she said. 'The King must know about this as soon as possible. But we have to be sure that we're not taking him another red herring. The tunnel Will's talking about could be weeks away from completion. Or it could lead to a dead end. This whole thing could be yet another ruse to convince the army to divert forces to protect their rear. We have to find out as much as possible. If that means waiting a few more hours, then I say we wait.'

Will glanced at the girl curiously. She certainly seemed to have more of an air of authority and decision than one would expect from a lady's maid. He decided that Gilan's theory was correct.

'It'll be dark in an hour, Horace. We'll go across tonight and take a closer look.'

Horace looked from one of his companions to the other. He wasn't happy. His instinct was to ride now, as fast as he could, and spread the word of this bridge. But he was outvoted. And he still believed Will's powers of deduction were better than his own. He was trained for action, not this sort of tortuous thinking. Reluctantly, he allowed himself to be convinced.

'All right,' he said. 'We'll look tonight. But tomorrow, we leave.'

Wrapped in his cloak and moving carefully, Will returned to his former vantage point. He studied the bridge carefully, thinking that Halt would expect him to be able to draw an accurate plan of the structure.

He hadn't been in position for more than ten minutes when a horn blast rang out.

He froze, terrified. For a moment, he thought it was an alarm and that an alert sentry had spotted him moving among the rocks. Then he heard more cracking of whips and the grunting cries of the Wargals and, as he raised his head, he saw that they were driving the Celts off the bridge and back towards the half-finished tunnel. The prisoners, as they went, downed their tools in stacks. Wargals began re-shackling them to a central leash.

Glancing up to the west, Will saw the last curve of the sun dropping behind the hills and he realised that the horn had simply been sounding the end of the working day. Now the prisoners were being returned to wherever it was that they were kept.

There was one brief altercation, a few metres from the tunnel mouth, as two of the Celt prisoners stopped to try to lift a prone figure that lay there. Angrily, the Wargal guards surged forward, beating the miners away with their whips and forcing them to leave the still figure where it lay.

Then, one after the other, they filed through the narrow entrance of the tunnel and disappeared.

The shadows of the huge bridge lengthened across the hillside. Will remained unmoving for another ten minutes, waiting to see if any Wargals re-emerged from the tunnel. But there was no sound, no sign of anyone returning. Only the still form lying by the tunnel mouth remained. In the rapidly worsening light, Will couldn't make it out clearly. It looked like the body of a miner. But he couldn't be sure.

Then the figure moved and he realised that, whoever it was, he was still alive.

Fifteen

reading carefully, Will and Horace made their way across the narrow plank path that bridged the last fifteen metres of the Fissure. Will, with his excellent head for heights, could have run lightly across it without a problem. But he went slowly out of regard for his bigger, less nimble, friend.

When they finally made it to the finished roadway, Horace heaved a sigh of relief. Now they took a moment to examine the structure. It was built with all the thorough-ness that Celts were famous for. As a nation, they'd developed the art of tunnelling and bridging over the centuries and this was a typical sturdy structure.

The smell of fresh sawn pine planking filled the cold night air and, overlaid on that, there was another sweetish, aromatic smell. They looked at each other, puzzled, for a moment. Then Horace recognised it.

'Tar,' he said and they looked around to see that the massive rope cables and support ropes were thick with the stuff. Will touched a hand on one and it came away sticky.

'I guess it prevents the ropes fraying and rotting,' he said carefully, noticing that the main cables were constructed of three heavy ropes twisted and plaited together, then thickly coated with the tar to protect them. Also, as the tar hardened, it would bind the three together more permanently.

Horace glanced around. 'No guards?' he commented. There was a disapproving note in his voice.

'They're either very confident or very careless,' Will agreed.

It was full night now and the moon was yet to rise. Will moved towards the eastern bank of the Fissure. Loosening his sword in its scabbard, Horace followed him.

The figure by the tunnel mouth lay as Will had last seen it. There had been no further sign of movement. The two boys approached him carefully now and knelt beside him — for now they could see that it was a Celt miner. His chest rose and fell — barely moving.

'He's still alive,' Will whispered.

'Only just,' Horace replied. He placed his forefinger to the Celt's neck to gauge the pulse there. At the touch, the man's eyes slowly opened and he gazed up at the two of them, uncomprehending.

'Who . . . you?' he managed to croak. Will unslung the water bottle from his shoulder and moistened the man's lips with a little of the liquid. The tongue moved greedily across the wetness and the man croaked again, trying to rise on one elbow.

'More.'

Gently, Will stopped him moving, and gave him a little more water.

'Rest easy, friend,' he said softly. 'We're not going to harm you.'

It was obvious that somebody had done him harm – and plenty of it. His face was matted with the dried blood that had welled from a dozen whip cuts. His leather jerkin was shredded and torn and his bare torso underneath showed signs of more whipping – recent and from long ago.

'Who are you?' Will asked softly.

'Glendyss,' the man sighed, seeming to wonder at the sound of his own name. Then he coughed, a racking, rattling cough that shook his chest. Will and Horace exchanged sad glances. Glendyss didn't have long, they both realised.

'When did you come here?' Will asked the man, gently allowing more water to trickle through the dried, cracked lips.

'Months . . .' Glendyss replied in a voice they could barely hear. 'Months and months I've been here . . . working on the tunnel.'

Again, the two boys looked at one another. Maybe the man's mind was wandering.

'Months?' Will pressed him. 'But the Wargal attacks only started a month ago, surely?'

But Glendyss was shaking his head. He tried to speak, coughed and subsided, gathering his fading strength. Then he spoke, so softly that Will and Horace had to lean close to hear him.

'They took us almost a year ago . . . from all over. Secretly . . . a man here, two men there . . . fifty of us in all. Most of the others . . . dead . . . by now. Me soon.' He stopped, gasping for breath again. The effort of speaking was almost too much for him. Will and Horace looked at each other, puzzling over this new information.

'How was it that nobody knew this was happening?' Horace asked his friend. 'I mean, fifty people go missing and nobody says anything?'

But Will shook his head. 'He said they took them from villages all over Celtica. So one or two men go missing — people might talk about it locally, but nobody could see the entire picture.'

'Still,' said Horace, 'why do it? And why are they so open about it now?'

Will shrugged. 'Maybe we'll get an idea on that if we take a look around,' he said.

They hesitated uncertainly, not sure what they could do for the crumpled, battered form beside them. As they waited, the moon rose, soaring over the hills and flooding the bridge and the bank with soft pale light. It touched on Glendyss's face and his eyes opened. Then he tried weakly to raise an arm to ward off the light. Gently, Will leaned forward to shield him.

'I'm dying,' said the miner, with a sudden clarity and a sense of peace. Will hesitated, then answered simply.

'Yes.' It would have been no kindness to lie to him, to try to cheer him along and protest that he would be all right. He was dying and they all knew it. Better to let him prepare, to let him face death with dignity and calm. The hand clutched feebly at Will's sleeve and he took it in his own, pressing it gently, letting the Celt feel the contact with another person.

'Boys,' he said weakly. 'Don't let me die out here . . . in the light.'

Again, Horace and Will exchanged glances.

'I want the peace of the Out of Light,' he continued softly, and Will suddenly understood.

'I guess Celts like the darkness. They spend most of their lives in tunnels and mines, after all. Maybe that's what he wants.'

Horace leaned forward. 'Glendyss?' he said. 'Do you want us to carry you into the tunnel?'

The miner's head had swivelled to Horace as the boy spoke. Now he nodded, faintly. Just enough for them to make out the action.

'Please,' he whispered. 'Take me to the Out of Light.'

Horace nodded to him, then slipped his arms under the Celt's shoulders and knees to lift him. Glendyss was only small and the weeks he had spent in captivity had obviously been a time of starvation for him. He was an easy burden for Horace to lift.

As the warrior apprentice stood straight with Glendyss cradled in his arms, Will motioned for him to wait. He sensed that once Glendyss was in the peace of the dark tunnel, he would let go the faint thread that held him to life. And there was one more question Will needed answered.

'Glendyss,' he said softly. 'How long do we have?'

The miner looked at him wearily, uncomprehending. Will tried again.

'How long before they finish the bridge?' he asked. This time, he could see a light of understanding in the Celt's eyes. Glendyss thought for a second or two.

'Five days,' he replied. 'Maybe four. More workers came today . . . so maybe four.'

Then his eyes closed, as if the effort had been too much. For a second, they thought he had died. But then his chest heaved with a massive shudder and he continued to breathe.

'Let's get him into the tunnel,' Will said.

They squeezed through the narrow opening. For the first ten metres, the walls of the tunnel were close enough to touch. Then they began to widen, as the results of the Celts' labour became evident. It was a dark confined place, lit only by the dim flames of torches set in brackets every ten to twelve metres. Some of these were guttering now, and provided only a fitful, uncertain light. Horace looked around uneasily. He didn't like heights and he definitely didn't like confined spaces.

'Here's the answer,' Will said. 'Morgarath needed those first fifty miners to do this work. Now that the tunnel is nearly finished, he needs more men to get the bridge built as quickly as possible.'

Horace nodded. 'You're right,' he agreed. 'The tunnelling would take months, but nobody would see it was going on. Once they started building the bridge, the risk of discovery would be much higher.'

In the wider reaches of the tunnel, they found a small sandy patch, almost a grotto, off to one side. They laid Glendyss in it. Will realised that this must have been what the two Celts had been trying to do for their countryman when the stop work horn had sounded.

He hesitated. 'I wonder what the Wargals will think when they find him here tomorrow?'

Horace merely shrugged. 'Maybe they'll think he crawled in here by himself,' he suggested. Will thought about it doubtfully. But then he looked at the peaceful expression on the dying miner's face in the gloomy light and he couldn't bring himself to take the man back outside once more.

'Just put him a little further in, as far out of sight as you can,' he said.

There was a small elbow of rock and Horace gently placed the miner behind it. He was now visible only if you looked carefully and Will decided that was good enough. Horace stepped back into the main tunnel. Will noticed that he was still glancing uneasily around.

'What do we do now?' Horace asked. Will came to a decision.

'You can wait here for me,' he said. 'I'm going to see where this leads.'

Horace didn't argue. The thought of going further into that dark, winding tunnel didn't appeal to him at all. He found a place to sit, close to one of the brighter torches.

'Just make sure you come back,' he said. 'I don't want to have to come looking for you.'

Sixteen

The tunnel, level at first, began to angle steeply upwards as Will went on, leaving Horace behind him. The walls and floor showed evidence of the Celts' picks and drills as they had torn and gouged at the rock to widen the path.

Will guessed that the original narrow tunnel had been nothing more than a natural fault in the rock — a mere crevice. But as he went on, he saw how much it had been widened, until there was room for four or five men to walk abreast. And still it climbed up into the heart of the mountains.

A circle of light showed the end of the tunnel. He estimated that he'd travelled maybe three hundred metres in total and the end was another forty away. The light that he could see seemed to be stronger than simple moonlight and, as he carefully emerged from the tunnel, he saw why.

Here, the hills separated, forming a large valley about two hundred metres across and half a kilometre long. To one side, the moonlight showed him massive wooden structures leading up to the higher reaches of the plateau. Staircases, he realised after a few moments' study. The floor of the valley was lit with camp fires and there were hundreds of figures moving in the flickering orange light. Will guessed that this would be the assembly area for Morgarath's army. At the moment, it was where the Wargals kept their Celt prisoners at night.

He paused, trying to form a picture of the overall situation. The plateau that formed the greater part of Morgarath's domain was still at least fifty metres above this point. But the staircases and the less formidable slope of the surrounding hills would provide relatively easy access down to this valley. The valley itself must be some thirty metres above the level where the bridge stood. The sloping tunnel would take troops down to the bridge from here. Once again, Halt's words echoed in his ear: *nowhere is really impassable.*

He moved to the left of the tunnel mouth and found cover in a jumble of rocks and boulders while he took stock of the situation. There was a rough stockade in the centre of the valley. Inside the wooden fencing, he could see a large number of small fires, each with a group of figures seated or sprawled around it. This was the prisoner's compound, he guessed.

Large fires outside the compound marked the places where the Wargals were camped. He could see the hulking, shambling forms clearly against the firelight as they moved around. Yet there was one fire close to him that seemed different. The figures seemed more upright, more humanoid in the way they stood and carried themselves.

Curiously, he worked his way closer to it, sliding through the night with barely a sound, moving quickly from one patch of cover to the next, until he was just at the outer ring of light thrown by the fire — a spot where he knew the darkness, by contrast, would seem more intense to those sitting around the fire.

There was a haunch of some kind of meat roasting slowly over the fire and the smell of it set his mouth watering. He'd been travelling for days on cold rations and the meat filled the air with a delicious fragrance. He felt his stomach begin to rumble and fear stabbed through him. It would be unthinkably bad luck to be betrayed by a rumbling stomach, he thought. The fear did the trick, killing his appetite. His digestion more or less under control, he edged his face around a boulder, low to the ground, to get a better look at the figures eating by the fire.

As he did so, one of them leaned forward to slice off a chunk of the meat, juggling the hot, greasy food in his hand as he took it. The movement let the firelight shine clearly on him and Will could see that these were not Wargals. From their rough sheepskin vests, woollen legging bound with tapes and heavy seal fur boots, he recognised them as Skandians.

Further study showed him their horned helmets, round wooden shields and battle axes piled to one side of the camp site. He wondered what they were doing here, so far from the ocean.

The man who had moved finished his meat and wiped his hands on his sheepskin vest. He belched, then settled himself in a more comfortable spot by the fire.

'Be domned glod when Olvak's men get 'ere,' he said in the thick, almost indecipherable accent of Skandia. Will knew that Skandians spoke the same tongue as the Kingdom. Hearing it now for the first time, though, he barely recognised it.

The other sea wolves growled their agreement. There were four of them round the fire. Will edged forward a little to hear them more clearly, then froze, horrified, as he saw the unmistakable shambling form of a Wargal moving directly towards him from the other side of the fire.

The Skandians heard him coming and looked up warily. With an immense feeling of relief, Will realised that the creature was not coming towards him but was approaching the Skandians' fire.

''Ullo,' said one of the Skandians in a low voice. ''Ere comes one of Morgarath's beauties.'

The Wargal had stopped on the far side of the fire. He grunted something unintelligible at the group of sea raiders. The one who had just spoken shrugged.

'Sorry, 'andsome. Didn't catch that,' he said. There was an obvious note of hostility in his voice. The Wargal seemed to sense it. He repeated his statement, growing angry now. Again, the circle of Skandian warriors shrugged at him.

The Wargal grunted again, growing angrier by the minute. He gestured at the meat hanging over the fire, then at himself. He shouted at the Skandians now, making eating gestures.

'Ugly brute wants our venison,' said one of the Skandians. There was a low growl of dissent from the group.

'Let 'im catch 'is own,' said the first man. The Wargal stepped inside the circle now. He had stopped shouting. He simply pointed to the meat, then turned his red, glaring eyes on the speaker. Somehow, the silence was more menacing than his shouting had been.

'Careful, Erak,' warned one of the Skandians, 'we're outnumbered here at the moment.'

Erak scowled at the Wargal for a second, then seemed to realise the wisdom of his friend's advice. He gestured angrily at the meat.

'Go on then. Take it,' he said curtly. The Wargal stepped forward and snatched the wooden spit from the fire, taking a huge bite at the meat and tearing a large chunk loose. Even from where he was lying, scarcely daring to breathe, Will could see the ugly light of triumph in the red, animal eyes. Then the Wargal turned abruptly and bounded out of the circle, forcing several of the Skandians to move hurriedly aside to avoid being trampled on. They heard its guttural laugh as it faded into the darkness.

'Damn things give me the heebies,' muttered Erak. 'Don't know why we have to have anything to do with them.'

''Cause Horth don't trust Morgarath,' one of the others told him. 'If we're not along, these damn bear-men will keep all the plunder for themselves and all we'll get is the hard fighting at the Plains of Uthal.'

'And hard marching too,' put in another. 'Wouldn't be any fun with Horth's men, either, working their way round Thorntree Forest to take the enemy in the rear. That's rough going, all right.'

Will frowned as he heard that. Obviously, Morgarath and Horth, who, Will assumed, was a Skandian war leader, were planning another treacherous surprise for the Kingdom's forces. He tried to picture a map of the countryside around the Plains of Uthal, but his memory was sketchy. He wished he'd paid more attention to the geography lessons Halt had taught him.

'Why is geography so important?' he remembered asking his teacher.

'Because maps are important if you want to know where your enemy is and where he's going,' had been the reply. Glumly, Will realised now how right he had been. Halt had shaken his head at him then, in that mock serious way he had. Suddenly, thinking of his wise and capable teacher, Will felt very lonely and more than a little out of his depth.

'Anyway,' Erak was saying, 'things'll be different when Olvak's men get 'ere. Although they seem to be taking their damned time about it.'

'Relax,' said the other speaker. 'It'll take a few days to get five 'undred men up them South Cliffs. Think 'ow long it took us.'

'Yeah,' said another. 'But we were blazing a trail. All they 'ave to do is follow it.'

'Well, they can't get 'ere too soon for me,' said Erak, rising and stretching. 'Well, I'm for sleep, lads, just as soon as I've done the necessaries.'

'Well, don't do 'em 'ere by the fire,' said one of the others irritably. 'Go up behind them rocks there.'

Horrified, Will realised that the Skandian had gestured towards the rocks where he was hiding. And now Erak, laughing at the other man, was turning and heading his way. It was definitely time to go. He scuttled backwards a few metres, then, crawling rapidly on his stomach, used all his training and natural skill to blend with the available cover.

He'd gone perhaps twenty metres when he heard a splashing sound from the spot where he'd been eaves-dropping. Then he heard a contented sigh and, looking back, saw the shaggy-haired form of Erak silhouetted against the glow of the hundred or so camp fires in the valley.

Realising that the Skandian was intent on what he was doing, Will slipped through the darkness and back into the tunnel. He went carefully for the first few metres, allowing his eyes to become accustomed to the dim light of the torches Then he began to run, his soft hide boots making barely a noise on the sandy floor.

Seventeen

He had found Horace waiting for him, his hand ready on his sword hilt, where he had left him in the tunnel.

'Did you find out anything?' the apprentice warrior whispered hoarsely. Will let go a pent-up breath, realising that he'd been holding it for some time now.

'Plenty,' he said. 'All of it bad.'

He held up a hand to forestall Horace's further questions.

'Let's get back across the bridge,' he said. 'I'll tell you then.' He glanced into the side tunnel where they had left the Celt miner.

'Have you heard anything more from Glendyss?' he asked. Horace shrugged sadly.

'He started moaning about an hour ago. Then he went quiet. I think he's dead. At least he died the way he wanted to,' he said, then he followed Will back through the dimly lit tunnel to the bridge.

They made their way across the planking again, to where Evanlyn waited with the horses, well back from the bridge and out of sight. When they were close, Will called her name softly, so as to avoid startling her. Horace had left his dagger with Evanlyn and Will thought an armed Evanlyn would not be a person to approach unexpectedly.

As he described the scene at the other end of the tunnel, he hastily scratched a map in the sand for them.

'Somehow, we're going to have to find a way to delay Morgarath's forces,' he said.

The other two looked at him curiously. Delay them? How could two apprentices and a girl delay five hundred Skandians and several thousand relentless Wargals?

'I thought you said we should get word to the King,' Evanlyn said.

'We don't have time any more,' Will said simply. 'Look.'

They leaned forward, as he smoothed over the diagram he had drawn in the sand and hastily sketched out a new one. He wasn't sure that it was totally accurate, but at least it included the most important features of the Kingdom, as well as the Southern Plateau, where Morgarath ruled.

'They said they have more Skandians coming up the cliffs on the south coast – to join with the Wargals we've already seen. They'll cross the Fissure here, where we are, and move north to attack the barons in the rear, while they wait for Morgarath to try to break out of Three Step Pass.'

'Yes,' said Horace. 'We know that. We guessed it as soon as we saw the bridge.'

Will looked up at him and Horace fell silent. He realised the Ranger apprentice had something else to say.

'But,' said Will, emphasising the word and pausing for a moment, 'I also heard them saying something about Horth and his men marching around Thorntree Forest. That's up here to the north of the Plains of Uthal.'

Evanlyn grasped the point immediately. 'Which would bring the Skandians north-west of the King's army. They'd be trapped between the Wargals and Skandians who have crossed the bridge and the other force from the north.'

'Exactly,' said Will, meeting her gaze. They could both appreciate how dangerous that situation would be for the assembled barons. Expecting a Skandian attack through the fenlands, to the east, they'd be taken by surprise from not one, but two different directions, caught between the arms of a pincer and crushed.

'Then we'd better warn the King, surely!' insisted Horace.

'Horace,' said Will patiently. 'It would take us four days to reach the Plains.'

'Even more reason to get going. We haven't a moment to waste!' said the young warrior.

'And then,' put in Evanlyn, seeing Will's point, 'it would take at least another four days for any sort of force to get back here and hold the bridge. Maybe more.'

'That's eight days all told,' said Will. 'Remember what that poor miner said? The bridge will be ready in four days. The Wargals and Skandians will have plenty of time to cross the Fissure, assemble in battle formation and attack the King's army.'

'But . . .' Horace began and Will interrupted him.

'Horace, even if we get warning to the King and the barons, they'll be badly outnumbered and they'll be caught between two forces — with no way to retreat. The swamps of the fenlands will be behind them. Now I know we have to get a warning to them. But we can also do something here to even the numbers.'

'Plus,' Evanlyn put in, and Horace turned to face her, 'if we can do something to stop the Wargals and Skandians crossing here, the King will have the advantage over this northern force of Skandians.'

Horace nodded. 'They won't be outnumbered, I guess,' he said.

Evanlyn nodded, but then added, 'That's part of it. But those Skandians will be expecting reinforcements to attack the King from the rear — reinforcements that will never arrive.'

Understanding dawned in Horace's eyes. He nodded slowly, several times. Then the frown returned. 'But what can we do to stop the Wargals here?' he asked.

Will and Evanlyn exchanged a glance. He could see they'd come to the same conclusion. They both spoke at the same time.

'Burn the bridge,' they said.

Eighteen

Blaze's head hung low as he trotted slowly into the outskirts of the King's camp on the Plains of Uthal. Gilan swayed wearily in the saddle. He had barely slept in the past three days, snatching only brief rests once every four hours.

Two guards stepped forward to query his progress and the young Ranger fumbled inside his shirt for the silver amulet in the form of an oak leaf — the Rangers' badge of office. At the sight of it, the guards stepped back hurriedly to clear the way. In times like these, nobody delayed a Ranger — not if he knew what was good for him.

Gilan rubbed his gritty eyes 'Where is the War Council tent?'

One of the guards pointed with his spear to a larger than normal tent, set up on a knoll overlooking the rest of the camp. There were more guards there, and a large number of people coming and going, as one would expect at the nerve centre of an army.

'There, sir. On that small rise.'

Gilan nodded. He'd come so far, so fast, finishing the four-day journey in just over three days. Now, these few hundred metres seemed like miles to him. He leaned forward and whispered in Blaze's ear.

'Not much farther, my friend. One more effort, please.'

The exhausted horse's ears twitched and his head came up a little. At Gilan's gentle urging, he managed to raise a slow trot and they passed through the camp.

Dust drifting on the breeze, the smell of woodsmoke, noise and confusion: the camp was like any army camp anywhere in the world. Orders being shouted. The clang and rattle of arms being repaired or sharpened. Laughter from tents, where men lay back relaxing with no duties to be performed — until their sergeants found them and discovered jobs for them to be doing. Gilan smiled tiredly at the thought. Sergeants seemed to be totally averse to seeing their men having an easy time of it.

Blaze came to a halt once more and Gilan realised, with a jerk, that he'd actually nodded off in the saddle. Before him, two more guards barred the way to the War Council compound. He looked at them blearily.

'King's Ranger,' he croaked, through a dry throat. 'Message for the Council.'

The guards hesitated. This dust-covered, half-asleep man, seated on a lathered, exhausted bay horse, might well be a Ranger. He was certainly dressed like a Ranger, as far as they could tell. Yet the guards knew most of the senior Rangers by sight, and they had never seen this young man before. And he showed no sign of identification.

What's more, they noticed, he carried a sword, which

was definitely not a Ranger's weapon, so they were reluctant to admit him to the carefully guarded War Council compound. Irritably, Gilan realised that he had neglected to leave the silver oakleaf device hanging outside his shirt. The effort of finding it again suddenly became intense. He fumbled blindly at his collar. Then a familiar, and very welcome, voice cut through his consciousness.

'Gilan! What's happened? Are you all right?'

That was the voice that had meant comfort and security to him throughout his five years as an apprentice. The voice of courage and capability and wisdom. The voice that knew exactly what action should be taken at any point in time.

'Halt,' he murmured, and realised that he was swaying, then falling from the saddle. Halt caught him before he hit the ground. He glared at the two sentries, who were standing by, not sure whether to help or not.

'Give me a hand!' he ordered and they leapt forward, dropping their spears with a clatter, to support the semi-conscious young Ranger.

'Let's get you somewhere to rest,' Halt said. 'You're all in.'

But Gilan summoned some last reserves of energy and, pushing clear of the soldiers, steadied himself on his own feet. 'Important news,' he said to Halt. 'Must see the Council. There's something bad going on in Celtica.'

Halt felt a cold hand of premonition clutch his heart. He cast his gaze around, looking back down the path where Gilan had come. Bad news from Celtica. And Gilan apparently alone.

'Where's Will?' he asked quickly. 'Is he all right?'

His heart lifted as Gilan nodded, a shadow of his normal grin showing through the bone-weariness.

'He's all right,' Gilan told the grizzled Ranger. 'I came on ahead.'

As they had been talking, they had begun to move towards the central pavilion. There were more guards on duty here but they moved out of the way at the sight of the senior Ranger. He was a familiar figure round the War Council. He put out a hand now to steady his former apprentice and they entered the cool shade of the Council pavilion.

A group of half a dozen men were clustered round a sand map — a large table with the main features of the Plains and Mountains modelled in sand. They turned now at the sound of the new arrivals and one of them hurried forward, concern written on his face.

'Gilan!' he cried. He was a tall man, and his greying hair showed him to be in his late fifties. But he still moved with the speed and grace of an athlete, or a warrior. Gilan gave that tired smile again.

'Morning, Father,' he said, for the tall grey-haired man was none other than Sir David, Battlemaster of Caraway Fief and field commander of the King's army. The Battle-master looked quickly to Halt and caught the quick nod of reassurance there. Gilan was all right, he realised, just exhausted. Then, his sense of duty caught up with his fatherly reaction.

'Greet your King properly,' he said softly, and Gilan looked up to the group of men, all their attention now focused on him.

He recognised Crowley, the Ranger Corps Commandant, and Baron Arald and two other senior Barons of the realm — Thorn of Drayden and Fergus of Caraway. But the figure in the centre took his attention. A tall blonde man in his late thirties, with a short beard and piercing green eyes. He was broad-shouldered and muscular, because Duncan was not a king who let other men do all his fighting for him. He had trained with sword and lance since he was a boy and he was regarded as one of the most capable knights in his own Kingdom.

Gilan attempted to sink to one knee. His joints screamed in protest and tried to lock up on him. The pressure of Halt's hand under his arm was all that stopped him falling once again.

'My lord . . .' he began apologetically, but Duncan had already stepped forward, seizing his hand to steady him. Gilan heard Halt's introduction.

'Ranger Gilan, my lord, attached to Meric Fief. With messages from Celtica.'

Suddenly, the King was galvanised with interest. 'Celtica?' he repeated, studying Gilan more closely. 'What's happening there?'

The other Council members had moved from the sand map to group around Gilan. Baron Arald spoke: 'Gilan was carrying your messages to King Swyddned, my lord,' he said. 'Invoking our mutual defence treaty and requesting that Swyddned send troops to join us —'

'They won't be coming,' Gilan interrupted. He realised he had to tell the King his news before he collapsed from exhaustion. 'Morgarath has them bottled up on the southwest peninsula.'

There was a stunned silence in the Council tent. Finally, it was Gilan's father who broke it. 'Morgarath?' he said, incredulously. 'How? How could he get any sort of army into Celtica?'

Gilan shook his head, suppressing a huge need to yawn. 'They sent small numbers down the cliffs, until they had enough troops to catch the Celts by surprise. As you know, Swyddned keeps only a small standing army . . .'

Baron Arald nodded, anger showing on his face. 'I warned Swyddned, my lord,' he put in. 'But those damned Celts have always been more interested in digging than protecting their own land.'

Duncan made a small, pacifying gesture with one hand. 'No time now for recriminations, Arald,' he said softly. 'What's done is done, I'm afraid.'

'I should imagine Morgarath has been watching them for years, waiting for their greed to overcome their good sense,' Baron Thorn said bitterly. The other men nodded quietly. Morgarath's ability to maintain a network of spies was all too well known to them.

'So Celtica has been defeated by Morgarath? Is this what you're telling us?' Duncan asked. This time, as Gilan shook his head, there were relieved glances around the tent.

'The Celts are holding out in the south-west, my lord. They're not defeated yet. But the strange business of it all is that Wargal raiding parties have been carrying off the Celt miners.'

'What?' This time it was Crowley who interrupted. 'What earthly use has Morgarath for miners?'

Gilan shrugged in reply. 'I've no idea, sir,' he told his

chief. 'But I thought I'd better get here with the news of it as soon as possible.'

'You saw this happening, then, Gilan?' Halt asked, frowning darkly as he puzzled over what the young Ranger had just told them.

'Not exactly,' Gilan admitted. 'We saw the empty mining towns and the deserted border posts. We were heading deeper into Celtica when we met a young girl who told us about the raids.'

'A young girl?' the King said. 'A Celt?'

'No, my lord. She was Araluan. A lady's maid whose mistress was visiting Swyddned's court. Unfortunately, they ran into a Wargal war party. Evanlyn was the only one to escape.'

'Evanlyn?' Duncan said, his voice the merest whisper. The others turned to him as he spoke. The King's face had turned a chalky white and his eyes were wide with horror.

'That was her name, my lord,' said Gilan, puzzled by the King's reaction. But Duncan wasn't listening. He had turned away and moved blindly to a canvas chair set by his small reading table. He dropped into the chair, his head sunk in his hands. The members of his War Council moved towards him, alarmed at his reaction.

'My lord,' said Sir David of Caraway. 'What is it?'

Duncan slowly raised his eyes to meet the Battle-master's.

'Evanlyn . . .' he said, his voice breaking with emotion. 'Evanlyn was my daughter's maid.'

Nineteen

here was no time to put the plan into action that night — dawn was less than an hour away. At one stage, Will had suggested that Horace and Evanlyn should leave him behind to burn the bridge, while they rode to take the news to Araluen. But Horace had refused.

'If we go now, we won't know if you've succeeded or not, so what do we tell the King? There might be a bridge or there might not be?' he said, in another example of the solid commonsense that had become part of his thinking. 'And besides, destroying a bridge this size might be a little more than you can manage alone — even a famous Ranger like yourself.'

He smiled as he said the last words, to let Will know he meant no insult. Will conceded the point. Secretly, he was glad they would be with him. He shared Horace's doubt that he might not be able to handle the task alone.

They slept fitfully until dawn, finally woken by the sounds of shouting and whips as the Wargals drove the miners back to their task of finishing the bridge. Throughout the day, they watched with alarm as the completed footway crept closer and closer to the side of the ravine where they lay hidden. With a sinking feeling, Will realised that the estimate given them by the dying miner was not to be relied upon. Perhaps the extra numbers of slaves were the reason, but it was obvious that the bridge would be all but completed by the end of the following day.

'We'll have to do it tonight.'

He breathed the words in Evanlyn's ear. The two of them lay prone on the rocks, overlooking the building site. Horace was a few metres away, dozing quietly in the cold morning sun. The girl shifted her position so that her mouth was closer to his ear and whispered back.

'I've been thinking, how will we get this fire started? There's barely enough wood around here for a decent camp fire.'

The same question had been taxing Will's brain throughout the night. Then the answer had come to him. He smiled quietly as he watched a group of Celt miners hammering pine boards onto the bridge framework to form the roadway.

'There's plenty of good firewood here,' he replied. 'If you know where to look for it.'

Evanlyn glanced at him, puzzled, then followed the line of his gaze. The frown on her forehead disappeared and she smiled slowly.

As dusk fell, the Wargals herded their weary, starving slaves back from the bridge and into the tunnel. Will noticed that by the end of the afternoon, the work of enlarging the tunnel seemed to have been completed. They waited an hour longer, until full darkness. During that time, there had been no sign of any activity from the tunnel. Now that they knew to look for it, they could see the loom of the firelight from the valley at the other end of the tunnel, reflecting on the low, scudding clouds.

'I hope it doesn't rain,' said Horace suddenly. 'That'd put paid to our idea all right.'

Will stopped in his tracks and looked up at him quickly. That unpleasant thought hadn't occurred to him. 'It isn't going to rain,' he said firmly, and hoped he was right. He continued on then, leading Tug gently to the unfinished end of the bridge. The little horse stopped there, ears pricked and nostrils twitching to the scents of the night air.

'Alert,' said Will softly to the horse, the command word that told him to give warning if he sensed approaching danger. Tug tossed his head once, signifying that he understood. Then Will led the way across the framework of the bridge to where the footway was completed, stepping lightly as he crossed the narrow beams above the dizzying drop. Horace and Evanlyn followed, more carefully. But this night, to Horace's relief, there was less distance to travel before they reached the firm and comforting surface of the completed bridge. He realised that Will was right. Another day would see the bridge completed.

Will unslung his bow and quiver and laid them on the planking. Then he drew his saxe knife from its scabbard and, dropping to his knees, began to prise up one of the nearest planks from the bridge walkway. The wood was soft pine, roughly sawn, and perfect firewood. Horace drew his dagger and began prising up the planks in the next row. As they loosened them, Evanlyn moved them to one side, stacking them in a pile. When she had six planks, each over a metre long, she gathered them up and ran lightly to the far side of the bridge, stacking them on the far bank of the fissure, close to where the massive, tarred cables were fastened to wooden pylons. By the time she returned, Will and Horace were well on the way to removing another six. These she took to the other cable. Will had explained his plan to them earlier in the day. To make sure there was no remaining structure on the far side, they would need to burn through both cables and pylons at that end, letting the bridge fall into the depths of the Fissure. The Wargals might be able to span the Fissure with a small, temporary rope affair, but nothing substantial enough to permit large numbers of troops to cross in a short time.

Once they had burnt the bridge, they would ride full speed to alert the King's army to the threat in the south. Any small numbers of Wargals who might cross the Fissure could then be easily dealt with by the Kingdom's troops.

The two boys continued levering the planks free and setting them to one side for Evanlyn. In her turn, she maintained her constant ferrying back and forth across the bridge, until the stacks by each pylon were piled high. In spite of the cold night, both boys were sweating freely with the effort. Finally, Evanlyn laid a hand on Will's shoulder as he prised up one board and began immediately on another.

'I think it's enough,' she said simply and he stopped, rocking back on his heels and wiping his forehead with the back of his left hand. She gestured towards the other end of the bridge, where there were at least twenty planks piled up on either side of the road. He eased the cramps out of his neck, rolling his head from side to side, then stood up.

'You're right,' he told her. 'That should be enough to get the rest of it burning.'

Gesturing for the others to follow, he picked up his bow and quiver and led the way to the far side of the bridge. He looked critically at the two piles of wood for a moment or two.

'We'll need kindling,' he said, glancing around to see if there were any small trees or bushes in the vicinity where they might find light wood to help them start their fire. Of course, there were none. Horace held out his hand for Will's saxe knife.

'Lend me that for a moment,' he asked and Will handed it to him. Horace tested the balance of the heavy knife for a moment. Then, taking one of the long planks, Horace stood it on end and, in a bewilderingly fast series of flashing strokes, sliced it into a dozen thin lengths.

'It's not quite sword practice,' he grinned at them. 'But it's close enough.'

As Will and Evanlyn began forming the thin pine strips into two small pyres, Horace took another plank and whittled more carefully, carving off thin curls from the pine to catch the first sparks from the flint and steel they would use to light the fire. Will glanced once to see what Evanlyn was doing. Satisfied that she knew what she was about, he turned back to his own task, accepting the shaved pine from Horace as the other boy passed it to him in handfuls and stacking it around the base of the kindling.

As Will moved across to Evanlyn's side to do the same with her fire, Horace split a few more planks in halves, then snapped the thinner lengths in two. Will looked up nervously at the noise.

'Keep it down,' he warned the apprentice warrior. 'Those Wargals aren't exactly deaf, you know, and the sound might carry through the tunnel.'

Horace shrugged. 'I'm finished now anyway,' he said.

Will paused and studied both pyres. Satisfied that they had the right combination of kindling and light wood to get them going, he motioned the others to cross back to the other side.

'You two get going,' he told them. 'I'll start the fires and follow you.'

Horace needed no second invitation. He didn't want to have to run across the bare beams of the bridge with the fire licking around the cables behind him. He wanted plenty of time to negotiate the gap. Evanlyn hesitated for a moment, then saw the sense in what Will had said.

They crossed carefully, trying not to look down into the agonising depths below the bridge as they negotiated the last ten metres. There was a wider gap now, of course, as they'd removed some of the boards that formed the road surface. Safe on the other side, they turned and waved to Will. They saw him, a crouched, indistinct figure in the shadows beside the right-hand bridge support. There was a bright flash as he struck his flint and steel together. Then another. And this time, a small yellow glow of light formed at the base of the piled wood as the pine shavings caught fire and the flame grew.

Will blew on it gently and watched the eager little yellow tongues spread out, licking at the rough pine, feeding on the flammable resin that filled the grain of the wood and growing larger and more voracious by the second. He saw the first of the thin stakes take fire, then the flames shot up, licking greedily around the rope balustrade of the bridge and beginning to reach for the heavy cable. The tar began sizzling. Drops melted and fell into the flames, flaring up with a bright blue flash each time.

Satisfied that the first fire was well under way, Will ran to the opposite side and went to work with his flint and steel once more. Again, the watchers saw the bright flashes, then the small, rapidly growing pool of yellow.

Will, now silhouetted clearly by the light of the two fires, stood erect and stepped back, watching to make sure that they were both properly alight. Already, the right-hand pylon and cable were beginning to smoke in the heat of the fire. Satisfied at last, Will gathered his bow and quiver and ran back across the bridge, barely slowing when he reached the narrow beams.

Reaching their side, he turned to look back at his handiwork. The right-hand cable was now blazing fiercely. A sudden gust of wind sent a shower of sparks high into the air above it. The left-hand fire didn't seem to be burning nearly as well. Perhaps it was a trick or an eddy of the wind that stopped the flames reaching the tar-soaked rope on that side. Perhaps the wood they had used was damp. But as they watched, the fire beneath the left-hand cable slowly died away to a red glow of embers.

Twenty

Gilan dropped his eyes from the tortured gaze of his King. Everyone in the tent could see the pain there as Duncan realised that his daughter had been killed by Morgarath's Wargals. Gilan looked around the other men, seeking some form of support from them. None of them, he saw, could bring themselves to meet their monarch's eyes.

Duncan rose from the chair and walked to the doorway of the tent, looking to the south-west as if he could somehow see his daughter across the distance.

'Cassandra left to visit Celtica eight weeks ago,' he said. 'She's a good friend of Princess Madelydd. When all this business with Morgarath started, I thought she'd be safe there. I saw no reason to bring her back.' He turned away from the door and his gaze held Gilan's. 'Tell me. Tell me everything you know . . .'

'My lord . . .' Gilan stopped, gathering his thoughts. He knew he had to tell the King as much as possible. But he also wanted to avoid causing him unnecessary pain. 'The girl saw us and came to us. She recognised Will and myself as Rangers. Apparently, she had managed to escape when the Wargals attacked their party. She said the others were . . .'

He hesitated. He couldn't go on.

'Continue,' Duncan said. His voice was firm. He was in control once more.

'She said the Wargals had killed them, my lord. All of them,' Gilan finished in a rush. Somehow, he felt it might be easier if he said it quickly. 'She didn't tell us details. She wasn't up to it. She was exhausted — mentally and physically.'

Duncan nodded. 'Poor girl. It must have been a terrible thing to witness. She's a good servant — more of a friend to Cassandra, in fact,' he added softly.

Gilan felt the need to keep talking to the King, to give the King whatever detail he could about the loss of his daughter. 'At first, we almost mistook her for a boy,' he said, remembering the moment when Evanlyn had walked into their camp. Duncan looked up, confusion on his face.

'A boy?' he said. 'With that mass of red hair?'

Gilan shrugged. 'She'd cut it short. Probably to conceal her appearance. The Celtic foothills are full of bandits and robbers at the moment, as well as Wargals.'

Something was wrong, he sensed. He was bone-weary, aching for sleep, and his brain wasn't functioning as it should. But the King had said something that wasn't right. Something that . . .

He shook his head, trying to clear it, and swayed on his feet, glad of Halt's ready arm to steady him. Seeing the movement, Duncan was instantly apologetic.

'Ranger Gilan,' he said, stepping forward and seizing his hand. 'Forgive me. You're exhausted and I've kept you here because of my own personal sorrow. Please, Halt, see that Gilan has food and rest.'

'Blaze . . .' Gilan started to say, remembering his dust-covered, weary horse outside the tent. Halt replied gently.

'It's all right. I'll look after Blaze.' He glanced at the King once more, nodding his head towards Gilan. 'With your majesty's permission?'

Duncan waved the two of them out.

'Yes, please, Halt. Look after your comrade. He's served us well.'

As the two Rangers left the tent, Duncan turned to his remaining advisers. 'Now, gentlemen, let's see if we can put some reason to this latest move by Morgarath.'

Baron Thorn cast a quick glance at the others, seeking and gaining their assent to act as spokesman. 'My lord,' he said awkwardly, 'perhaps we should give you some time to come to terms with this news . . .' The other councillors all mumbled their agreement to the idea but Duncan shook his head firmly.

'I'm the King,' he said simply. 'And for the King, private matters come last. Matters of the Kingdom come first.'

'It's gone out!' said Horace, in an agony of disappointment.

The three of them looked, desperately hoping that he was wrong, that their eyes were somehow deceiving them. But he was right. The fire under the left-hand pylon had died away to a small, glowing heap of embers.

By contrast, the other side was well and truly alight, with the fire running fiercely up the tarred rope side rails to the massive cable supporting the right side of the bridge. Indeed, as they watched, one of the three ropes forming the cable burned through and the right-hand side of the bridge creaked alarmingly.

'Maybe one side will be enough?' Evanlyn suggested hopefully, but Will shook his head in frustration, willing the second fire to flare up again.

'The right-hand pylon is damaged, but it's still useable,' he pointed out. 'If the left-hand side survives, they can still get across to this side. And if they can do that, they might be able to repair the whole thing before we can get warning to King Duncan.'

Resolutely, he hitched his bow over his shoulder and started across the bridge once more.

'Where are you going?' Horace asked him, eyeing the structure with distrust. The bridge had taken a definite lean to one side now that part of the right-hand cable had burned through. As he put the question, the structure trembled again, settling a little further towards the bottom of the abyss.

Will paused, balanced on the bare beam that stretched across the gap.

'I'll have to relight it,' he said. 'We've got to make sure there's nothing left on that side for them to salvage.'

And, so saying, he ran to the far side. Horace felt queasy watching him move so quickly across that massive drop, with nothing but a narrow beam beneath him. Then he and Evanlyn watched in a fever of impatience as Will crouched by the embers. He began fanning them, then leaned down and blew on them until a small tongue of flame flickered inside the pile of unburnt kindling.

'He's done it!' Evanlyn cried, then the triumph in her voice died as the flicker faded. Once again, Will leaned down and began to blow gently on the embers. Something else gave on the right-hand side cable and the bridge lurched, sinking further to that side.

'Come on! Come on!' Horace said over and over to himself, his hands clenching and unclenching as he watched his friend.

Then Tug gave a quiet whinny.

Both Horace and Evanlyn turned to look at the small horse. If it had been either of their own mounts, they wouldn't have reacted. But they knew Tug was trained to remain silent, unless . . .

Unless! Horace looked to where Will was crouched over the remains of the fire. Obviously, he hadn't heard Tug's warning. Evanlyn seized Horace's arm and pointed.

'Look!' she said and he followed her pointing finger to the mouth of the tunnel, where a glimmer of light was showing. Someone was coming! Tug pawed the ground and whinnied again, a little louder this time, but Will, close to the noise of the burning right-hand cable, didn't hear. Evanlyn came to a decision.

'Stay here!' she told Horace, and started out across the wooden beam framework. She inched her way carefully, her heart in her mouth as the weakened bridge structure lurched and swayed. Below her was blackness, and, at the very bottom, the silver glimmer of the river that ran wildly through the base of the Fissure. She swayed, recovered, then went on. The roadway was only eight metres away now. Now five. Now three.

The bridge swayed again and she hung there for an awful moment, arms spread to hold her balance, teetering over that horrific drop. Behind her, she heard Horace's warning cry. Taking a deep breath, she lunged for the safety of the boardwalk, falling full length on the rough pine floor of the bridge.

Heart pounding with the reaction of her near miss, she came to her feet and raced across the bridge. As she drew closer, Will sensed her movement and looked up. Breathlessly, she pointed to the mouth of the tunnel.

'They're coming!' she cried. And now, the reflected glow of light from within the tunnel was revealed to be the flare of several burning torches as a small group of figures emerged. They paused at the tunnel mouth, pointing and shouting as they saw the flames reaching high above the bridge. She counted six of them, and from their shambling, clumsy gait, she recognised them as Wargals.

The Wargals began to run towards the bridge. They were just over fifty metres away, but covering the ground quickly. And she knew there must be more behind them.

'Let's get out of here!' she said, grabbing at Will's sleeve. But he shook her hand off, grim-faced. He was already scooping up his bow and quiver, slinging the quiver over his shoulder and checking that the bowstring was firmly anchored.

'You get back!' he told her. 'I'll stay and hold them off.'

Almost as he spoke, he nocked an arrow to the string and, barely seeming to aim, sent it hissing towards the lead

Wargal. The arrow took in the chest and it fell, crying out once, then lay silent.

His companions halted in their tracks, seeing the arrow. They looked warily around them, trying to see where it had come from. Perhaps this was a trap, their primitive, single track minds told them. As yet, they couldn't see the small figure at the end of the bridge. And even as they looked, another three arrows came hissing out of the darkness. The steel heads of two of the arrows struck sparks as they smashed into the rocks. The third took one of the Wargals at the rear of the party in the lower arm. He cried out in pain and fell to his knees.

The Wargals hesitated uncertainly. Seeing the light and smoke of the fire above the hill that separated their camp area from the bridge, they had come to investigate. Now unseen archers were firing at them. Coming to a decision, and with no one to order them forward, they retreated quickly to the shelter of the tunnel mouth.

'They're going back!' Evanlyn told Will. But he'd already seen the movement and he was on his knees again, trying to frantically rebuild the fire.

'We'll have to reset the whole thing!' he muttered. Evanlyn dropped to her knees beside him and began shaping the half-burnt strips and heavier pieces into a conical pyre.

'You watch the Wargals!' she said. 'I'll look after this.'

Will hesitated. After all, this was the fire she had set in the first place. He had a moment of doubt as he wondered if she'd done the job correctly. Then he looked up to the tunnel mouth, saw movement there once again and realised she was right. Grabbing his bow, he started to move towards the cover of some rocks nearby, but she stopped him.

'Your knife!' she said. 'Leave it with me.'

He didn't ask why. He slid the saxe from its scabbard and dropped it onto the planking beside her. Then he moved to the rocks. As he left the bridge, he felt it tremble again as the right-hand cable gave a little more. Silently, he cursed the caprice of wind that had fanned one fire and extinguished the other.

Encouraged by the lack of arrows whistling around their ears in the past few minutes, the four remaining Wargals had emerged from the tunnel again and were moving cautiously forward. Without any real intelligent leadership, and with a false sense of their own superiority, they stayed grouped together, an easy target. Will fired three times, carefully aimed shots.

Each one found its mark. The surviving Wargal looked at his fallen comrades, then lumbered into the cover of the rocks. Will sent another arrow skating off the granite directly above his head, to encourage him to stay where he was.

He checked his quiver. There were sixteen arrows left. Not a lot if the Wargals had sent for reinforcements. He glanced at Evanlyn. She seemed to be maddeningly slow with her efforts to rebuild the fire. He wanted to yell at her to hurry, but realised he would only distract her and slow her down if he did. He looked back to the tunnel, his fingers clenching and unclenching on the bow.

Four more figures emerged, running fast and fanning out so that they weren't grouped together. Will brought the bow up, sighted quickly and released at the one furthest to the right. He let go a little cry of exasperation as the arrow flew behind the running figure. Then he was obscured by the rocks.

Blessing the weeks and months of practice that Halt had insisted on, Will had another arrow out of the quiver and ready nocked, without even looking at it. But the other three runners had gone to ground as well.

Now one of them rose in the middle of the line and darted forward. Will's snapshot cleaved the air above his head as he dived for cover. Then another was moving on the left, dropping into cover before Will could fire. His heart was beating rapidly as they made their quick rushes and he forced himself to breathe deeply and think calmly. The time to shoot would be in the last thirty metres, where there was less cover and where the arrows, with a shorter distance to cover, would be travelling faster and so be harder to dodge. Will's heart hammered inside his ribs. He was remembering the last time — only a few weeks ago — when fear had made his shots go wide. His face hardened as he determined that it would not happen again.

'Stay calm,' he told himself, trying to hear Halt's voice saying the words. Another of the figures made a short rush and this time, as the firelight illuminated him more clearly, Will held his fire as his eyes confirmed what he had begun to suspect.

The newcomers weren't Wargals. They were Skandians.

Twenty-one

Gilan slept like a log for six hours, totally exhausted, in the tent where Halt had taken him. Throughout that time, he didn't stir once. His mind and body were shut down, drawing new strength from total rest.

Then, after those six hours, his subconscious mind stirred and began to function, and he began to dream. He dreamt of Will and Horace and the girl Evanlyn. But the dream was wild and confused and he saw them as captives of the Wargals, tied together while the two robbers Bart and Carney stood by and laughed.

Gilan rolled onto one side, muttering in his sleep. Halt, sitting nearby repairing the fletching on his arrows, glanced up. He saw that the young Ranger was still asleep and went back to his routine task. Gilan muttered again, then fell silent.

In his dream, he saw the servant Evanlyn as the King had described her – with her hair long and uncropped, masses of it flowing down her back, thick and lustrous and red.

And then he sat up, wide awake.

'My God!' he said to a startled Halt. 'It's not her!'

Halt swore as he spilled the thick, viscous glue that he was using to attach the goose feather vanes to the arrow shaft. Gilan's sudden movement had caught him by surprise. Now he mopped up the sticky liquid and turned with some irritation to his friend.

'Could you give a bit of warning when you're going to start shouting like that?' he said peevishly. But Gilan was already out of the camp bed and hauling on his breeches and shirt.

'I've got to see the King!' he said urgently. Halt stood warily, not altogether sure that Gilan wasn't sleepwalking. The young Ranger shoved past him, dashing out into the night, and tucking his shirt into his trousers as he went. Reluctantly, Halt followed him.

There was a slight delay as they reached the King's pavilion. The guard had changed several hours before and the new sentries didn't know Gilan by sight. Halt smoothed things over, but not before Gilan had convinced him that it was vital for him to see King Duncan, even if it meant waking him from a well-deserved sleep.

As it turned out, in spite of the late hour, the King wasn't sleeping. He and his supreme army commander were discussing possible reasons for the raids into Celtica when Gilan, barefoot, rumple-haired and with several buttons still askew on his shirt front, was allowed into the pavilion. Sir David looked up in alarm at the sight his son presented.

'Gilan! What on earth are you doing here?' he demanded, but Gilan held up a hand to stop him.

'Just a moment, Father,' he said. Then, he continued, facing the King, 'Sir, when you described the maid Evanlyn earlier, did you say "red" hair?'

Sir David looked to Halt for an explanation. The older Ranger shrugged and Sir David turned back to his son, anger clearly showing on his face.

'What difference does that make?' he began. But again Gilan cut him off, still addressing the King.

'The girl who called herself Evanlyn was blonde, sir,' he said simply. This time, it was King Duncan who held out a hand to silence his angry Battlemaster.

'Blonde?' he asked.

'Blonde, sir. She'd cut it short, as I said, but it was blonde, like your own. And she had green eyes,' Gilan told him, watching Duncan carefully, and sensing the importance of what he was telling him. The King hesitated a moment, covering his face with one hand. Then he spoke, the hope growing in his voice.

'And her build? Slight, was she? Small of stature?'

Gilan nodded eagerly. 'As I said, sir, for a moment, we could have taken her for a boy. She must have used her maid's identity because she thought it was safer if she remained incognito.' Now, he understood those slight hesitations in Evanlyn's speech, and why she had a broader grasp of politics and strategy than most servants would be expected to have.

Slowly, Halt and Sir David began to realise the import of what was being said. The King looked from Gilan to Halt to David, then back to Gilan again.

'My daughter is alive,' he said quietly. There was a long silence. It was finally broken by Sir David.

'Gilan, how far behind you were the two apprentices and the girl?'

Gilan hesitated. 'Possibly two days' ride, Father,' he estimated, following his father to the map table and indicating the furthest point that he thought Will and the others might have reached by now. Sir David took instant charge, sending messengers running to rouse the commander of the cavalry wing and have him prepare a company of light cavalry to leave camp immediately.

'We'll send a company of the Fifth Lancers to bring them in, sir,' he told the King. 'If they leave within the hour and ride through the night, they should make contact sometime around noon tomorrow.'

'I'll guide them,' Gilan offered immediately and his father nodded assent.

'I'd hoped you'd say that.' He seized the King's arm, smiling with genuine pleasure at the relief on the tall man's face. 'I can't tell you how pleased I am for you, sir,' he said. The King looked at him, a little bemused. So recently, he had been privately mourning the loss of his beloved daughter Cassandra. Now, miraculously, she had been restored to life.

'My daughter is alive,' he said once more. 'She's safe.'

Evanlyn crouched over the pile of wood beside the bridge railing. From time to time, she heard the dull thrum of Will's bow as he fired at the approaching enemy, but she forced herself not to look up, concentrating on the job in hand. She knew they had one last chance to get the fire going properly. If she got it wrong this time, it would mean disaster for the Kingdom. So she carefully stacked and placed the wood, making sure there was sufficient air space between the pieces to allow a good draft. She had none of the shavings left to use for tinder this time, but only a few metres away, she had a perfect source of fire. The right-hand cable was still blazing fiercely.

Satisfied that the wood was stacked properly, she took Will's saxe and cut several one-metre lengths of tarred rope from the bridge railing — thinner lengths, not the massive cable itself. It would have been almost impossible to hack through that in time.

Taking the rope lengths, she came to her feet and darted across the bridge to the blazing fire on the other side. It was a simple matter to get the lengths of tarred rope burning, then she ran back to her fire pile and draped the burning rope around the base, trailing it through the gaps she had left in the wood. The flames licked at her fingers as she pushed the rope in between pieces of wood. She bit her lip, ignoring the pain as she made sure the fire was burning freely.

The tar-fed flames crackled at the wood, flickered, then took. She fanned them for a few seconds as they became established, until the lighter kindling strips were burning fiercely, then the heavier planks began to take fire as well. The handrail caught in several places and now tongues of flame were shooting up to the cable, beginning to lick at it, feeding on the tar, then running up to where it joined the wooden pylon structure.

Only now did she take the time to glance up at Will. Her eyes were dazzled by the fire and she could see him only as a dull blur, five metres away, behind a rock outcrop.

As she looked, he rose to a standing position and fired an arrow. She looked into the surrounding darkness but could see no sign of their attackers.

The bridge gave another convulsive jerk beneath her feet and the roadway tilted to an alarming degree as the second of the three strands of the right-hand cable burnt through and the structure sagged further to that side. They wouldn't have much time to get back across to where Horace and Tug waited. She had to warn Will.

Saxe knife in hand, she ran full pelt to where he crouched behind the rocks, his eyes searching the darkness for movement. He glanced quickly at her as she arrived.

'The other side's burning,' she said. 'Let's get out of here.'

Grimly, he shook his head, then pointed with his chin to a jumble of rocks barely thirty metres from where they crouched.

'Can't risk it,' he told her. 'One of them has got behind those rocks. If we go now, he might have time to save the bridge.'

Out of the corner of her eye, she saw a quick, darting movement to their left and pointed quickly.

'There's one!' she said. Will nodded.

'I see him,' he replied evenly. 'He's trying to draw my fire. As soon as I shoot at him, the one closer to us will have a chance. I have to wait for him to show himself before I can shoot.'

She looked at him, horrified, as she realised the significance of what he was saying. 'But that means the others can close in on us,' she said. This time, Will said nothing. The incipient panic he had felt was now replaced by a calm sense of resolution. Deep in his heart, a part of him was glad — glad that he hadn't failed Halt and glad that he had repaid the faith that the older Ranger had placed in him when he chose him as an apprentice.

He glanced at Evanlyn for a long moment and she realised he was willing to be captured if it kept the enemy away from the bridge just a few minutes longer.

Captured or killed, she amended.

Behind them, there was a groaning crash and she turned to see the first cable finally give way in a shower of flame and sparks. It took the burnt-through upper half of its pylon with it. That was the result they had wanted. They had discussed the idea of simply cutting the main cables, but that would have left the major structure of the bridge untouched. The pylons themselves had to be destroyed. Now the entire bridge was hanging, suspended by the left-hand cable, and flames were already eating their way through that. In a few more minutes, she knew, the bridge would be gone. The Fissure would be impassable once more.

Will tried to give her a reassuring smile. It wasn't a very successful attempt. 'You can't do much more here,' he told her. 'Get across the bridge while you've still got time.'

She hesitated, desperately wanting to go but unwilling to leave him on his own. He was only a boy, she realised, but he was willing to sacrifice himself for her and the rest of the Kingdom.

'Go!' he said, turning to her and shoving at her. And now she thought she could see the glitter of tears in his eyes. Her own eyes filled and she couldn't see him clearly. She blinked to clear her vision, just in time to see a jagged rock curving down out of the firelit night.

'Will!' she shouted, but she was too late. The rock took him in the side of the head and he grunted in surprise, then his eyes rolled up and he fell at her feet, dark blood already welling from his scalp. She heard a rush of feet from several directions and she tossed the saxe knife aside and scrabbled in the dirt for Will's bow. Then she found it and was trying to nock an arrow when rough hands grabbed her, knocking the bow from her grasp and pinning her arms to her sides. The Skandian held her in a bear hug, her face pressed into the rough sheepskin of his vest, smelling of grease and smoke and sweat and all but suffocating her. She kicked out, lashing with her feet and tossing her head, trying to butt the man who was holding her, but to no avail.

Beside her, Will lay unmoving in the dust. She began to sob in frustration and anger and sadness and she heard the Skandians laughing. Then another sound came and they stopped. The arms holding her released a little and she was able to see.

It was a drawn out, creaking groan and it came from the bridge. The right-hand support was gone, and the left-hand side, already weakened by the fire, was now holding the entire structure. It was never meant for such a load, even in perfect condition. With a final sharp SNAP! the pylon shattered at its halfway point and, cables and all, the bridge collapsed slowly into the depths of the Fissure, trailing a bright shower of sparks behind it in the darkness.

Twenty-two

Gilan watched impatiently as the company of cavalrymen remounted after a fifteen-minute break. He was itching to be away, but he knew that both horses and men needed rest if they were to continue at the killing pace he had set them. They had been travelling for half a day and he estimated that they should meet Will's party sometime in the early afternoon.

Checking that all the troopers were mounted, he turned to the captain beside him.

'All right, Captain,' he said. 'Let's get them moving.'

The captain had actually drawn breath to bellow his command when there was a call from the lead troop.

'Horseman coming!'

An expectant buzz ran through the cavalrymen. Most of them had no idea what their mission was about. They'd been roused out of bed in the early dawn and told to mount and ride. Gilan stood in his stirrups, shading his eyes against the midday glare, and peered in the direction the trooper had indicated.

They hadn't reached the Celtic border yet, and here the terrain was open grasslands, with occasional thickets of trees. To the south-west, Gilan's keen eyes could make out a small cloud of dust, with a galloping figure at the head of it.

'Whoever he is, he's in a hurry,' the captain observed. Then the forward scout called more information.

'Three horsemen!' came the shout. But already Gilan could see that the report wasn't quite correct. There were three horses, but only one rider. He experienced a sinking feeling in the pit of his stomach.

'Should we send out an intercept party, sir?' the captain asked him. In times like these, it wasn't always wise to let a stranger ride full pelt into the middle of a group. But now that the rider was closer, Gilan could recognise him. More to the point, he could recognise one of the horses he was riding: small, shaggy, barrel-chested. It was Will's horse, Tug. But it wasn't Will riding him.

The lead troop had already fanned out to stop the rider's progress. Gilan said quietly to the captain: 'Tell them to let him through.'

The captain repeated the order with considerably more volume and the troopers separated, leaving a path for Horace. He saw the small group of officers around the company banner and headed for them, bringing the shaggy little Ranger horse to a halt in front of them. The other horses, which Gilan now recognised as Horace's and the pack pony that Evanlyn had ridden, were following behind Tug on a rope rein.

'They've got Will!' the boy shouted hoarsely, recognising Gilan among the group of officers. 'They've got Will and Evanlyn!'

Gilan closed his eyes briefly, feeling a lance of pain in his heart. Then, knowing the answer before he asked, he said: 'Wargals?'

'Skandians!' he replied. 'They took them at the bridge. They . . .'

Gilan flinched in surprise at the word. Surprise and horror.

'Bridge?' he said urgently. 'What bridge?'

Horace was breathing heavily from his exertions. He'd alternated between the three horses, switching from one to the other, but not resting himself at any stage. He paused now to get his breath, realising he should start from the beginning.

'Across the Fissure,' he said. 'That's why Morgarath took the Celts. They were building a huge bridge for him to bring his army across. They'd almost got it finished when we got there.'

The captain beside Gilan had turned pale. 'You mean there's a bridge across the Fissure?' he asked. The implications of such a fact were horrendous.

'Not anymore,' Horace replied, his breathing steadier and his voice a little more under control now. 'Will burnt it. Will and Evanlyn. But they stayed on the other side to keep the Skandians back and —'

'Skandians!' said Gilan. 'What the devil are Skandians doing on the plateau?' Horace made an impatient gesture at his interruption.

'They were the advance party for a force that's coming

up the southern cliffs. The Skandians were going to join forces with the Wargals, cross the bridge and attack the army in the rear.'

The group of cavalry officers exchanged looks. Professional soldiers, all of them could imagine how disastrous that could have been for the royal forces.

'As well the bridge is gone then,' said a lieutenant. Horace swung his tormented gaze on the officer — a young man barely a few years older than himself.

'But they've got Will!' he cried, his eyes welling with tears as he thought of how he had stood by and watched helplessly as his friend was knocked out, then carried away.

'And the girl,' added Gilan, but Horace dismissed her.

'Yes! Of course they got her!' he said. 'And I'm sorry she's been caught. But Will was my friend!'

'You're sorry she's been caught? Do you know who . . .' the captain interrupted indignantly, for he was one of the few who knew the true nature of their task. But Gilan stopped him before he could say more.

'That's enough, Captain!' he said crisply. The officer looked at him angrily and Gilan leaned forward, speaking so that only he could hear.

'The fewer people who know the girl's name now, the better,' he said, and understanding dawned in the officer's eyes. If Morgarath knew that his men held the King's daughter hostage, he would have a powerful tool to bargain with. He looked back to Horace. 'Horace, is there any way they might be able to repair this bridge?' he asked and the muscular youth shook his head vehemently. He was devastated at the loss of his friend but his pride in Will's accomplishment was obvious as he described it.

'No way at all,' he replied. 'It's gone, well and truly. Will made sure that nothing remained on the far side. That's why he was caught. He wanted to make sure.' He paused and added: 'They might get a small rope bridge across, of course.'

That decided Gilan. He turned to the captain.

'Captain, you'll continue with the company and make sure no bridge of any kind is thrown across the Fissure. We don't want any of Morgarath's forces, no matter how small, coming across. Get Horace to show you the location on a map. Hold the west side of the Fissure until you're relieved, and send out patrols to locate any other possible crossing points. There won't be many of those,' he added. 'Horace, you'll come with me and report to the King. Now.' He stopped abruptly as he realised that Horace was waiting for a chance to say something. He nodded for the apprentice to go ahead.

'The Skandians,' said Horace. 'They're not just on the plateau. They're sending a force north of the Thorntree Forest as well.'

There was another buzz of comment from the officers as they realised how close their army had come to disaster. Two unexpected forces, attacking from the rear, would have left the King's men very hard-pressed indeed.

'You're sure of this?' Gilan asked and Horace nodded several times.

'Will overheard them talking about it,' he said. 'Their forces on the beach and in the fens are a feint. The real attack was always going to come from behind.'

'Then we don't have a moment to waste,' said Gilan. 'That force in the north-west could still be a big problem if the King doesn't know about it.' He turned to the company commander. 'Captain, you have your orders. Get your men to the Fissure as soon as you can.'

The captain saluted briefly and issued a few crisp orders to his officers. They galloped off to their troops and, after a quick conference while Horace pointed out the site of the fallen bridge on a map of the area, the entire company was on the move, heading at a brisk canter for the Fissure.

Gilan turned to Horace. 'Let's go,' he said simply. Wearily, the young warrior nodded, then turned back to mount his own horse. Tug hesitated, pawing the ground as he watched the cavalry ride away — back towards where he had last seen his master. He trotted a few uncertain paces after the troop then, at a word from Gilan, he reluctantly fell in behind the tall Ranger.

Twenty-three

Will's head ached abominably. He could feel a constant, rhythmic thudding that pounded through his skull, setting flashes off behind his tight closed eyes.

He forced his eyes open and found himself staring at close range at a sheepskin vest and the back of a pair of leather-bound woollen leggings. The world was upside down and he realised he was being carried over someone's shoulder. The thudding was the thud of the man's feet as he jogged along. Will wished he would walk.

He groaned aloud and the jogging stopped.

'Erak!' the man carrying him called. ''E's awake.'

And so saying, the Skandian lowered him to the ground. Will tried to take a pace, but his knees gave out and he sank to his haunches. Erak, the leader of the group, leaned down now and examined him. One thick thumb caught hold of his eyelid and he felt his eye being opened wide. The man wasn't cruel. But he was none too gentle either. Will recognised him now as the Skandian who had come so close to discovering him when he was eavesdropping by their camp fire in the valley.

'Hmmm,' he said thoughtfully. 'Concussed, most likely. That was a good throw with that rock, Nordel,' he said to one of the others. The Skandian he'd spoken to, a giant of a man with his blond hair in two tightly plaited braids that were greased so they swept upwards like horns, smiled at the praise.

'Grew up hunting seals and penguins that way, I did,' he said, with some satisfaction.

Erak released Will's eyelid and moved away. Now Will felt a gentler touch on his face and, opening his eyes again, found himself looking into Evanlyn's eyes. She stroked his forehead gently, trying to clean away the dried, matted blood there.

'Are you all right?' she said and he nodded, then realised that was not a good idea.

'Fine,' he managed, fighting back a wave of nausea. 'They got you as well?' he added, unnecessarily, and she nodded. 'Horace?' he said softly and she put a finger to her lips.

'He got away,' she said softly. 'I saw him running when the bridge collapsed.'

Will sighed with relief. 'We did it then? We got the bridge?'

This time it was Evanlyn's turn to nod. A smile even touched her lips at the memory of the bridge crashing into the depths of the Fissure.

'It's gone,' she said. 'Well and truly.'

Erak heard the last few words. He shook his head at them.

'And no thanks you'll get from Morgarath for that,' he told them. Will felt a small chill of fear at the mention of the Lord of Rain and Night's name. Here on the plateau, it seemed somehow more ominous, more dangerous, altogether more malevolent. The Skandian glanced at the sun.

'We'll take a break,' he said. 'Maybe our friend here will be up to walking in an hour or so.'

The Skandians opened their packs and produced food and drink. They tossed a water bottle and a small loaf of bread to Will and Evanlyn and the two ate hungrily. Evanlyn began to say something but Will raised a hand to hush her. He was listening to the Skandians' conversation.

'So what do we do now?' asked the one called Nordel. Erak chewed a piece of dried cod, washed it down with a gulp of the fiery liquor he carried in a leather bottle and shrugged.

'For mine, we get out of here as fast as we can,' he said. 'We only came for the booty and there's going to be precious little of that now the bridge is gone.'

'Morgarath won't like it if we pull out,' warned a short, heavily built member of the party. Erak simply shrugged.

'Horak, I'm not here to help Morgarath take over Araluen,' he replied. 'Neither are you. We fight for profit, and when there's no profit to be had, I say we go.'

Horak looked down at the ground between his feet and scratched in the dust with his fingers. He didn't look up when he spoke again. 'What about those two?' he said, and Will heard a sharp intake of breath from Evanlyn as she realised the Skandian meant her and Will.

'We take 'em with us,' said Erak and this time Horak looked up from the dust, where he was drawing senseless patterns.

'What good are they to us? Why shouldn't we just hand 'em over to the Wargals?' he asked, and the others mumbled their agreement. It was obviously a question which had been on their minds. They'd simply been waiting for someone else to bring it up.

'I'll tell you,' said Erak. 'I'll tell you what good they are to us. First and foremost, they're hostages, aren't they?'

'Hostages!' snorted the fourth member of the group, the one who so far hadn't spoken. Erak rounded upon him.

'That's right, Svengal,' he told him. 'They're hostages. Now I've been on more raids and in more campaigns than any of you and I don't like the way this one's shaping up. Seems to me like Morgarath's been getting too clever for his own good. All this leaking false plans and building secret tunnels and planning surprise attacks with Horth and his men coming around Thorntree Forest – it's too complicated. And complicated isn't the way to go when you're facing people like the Araluans.'

'Horth can still attack around the Thorntree,' said Svengal stubbornly, but Erak was shaking his head.

'He can. But he won't know that the bridge is gone, will he? He'll be expecting support that will never come. I'll wager Morgarath won't hurry to tell him. He knows Horth would give it all away if he found out. Let me tell you, it'll be the toss of a coin to see which way that battle goes. That's the problem with these clever-clever plans! You take away one element and the whole thing can come crashing down.'

There was a short silence while the other Skandians thought about what he had said. A few heads nodded in agreement and Erak continued.

'I'll tell you, boys, I don't like the way things are shaping and I say we should take the chance to get to Horth's ships through the fens.'

'Why not go back the way we came?' asked Svengal, but his leader shook his head emphatically.

'And try to get down those cliffs again, with Morgarath after us?' he asked. 'No thank you. I don't think he'd take too kindly to deserters. We'll go along with him as far as Three Step Pass, then once we're in the open, we'll head east for the coast.' He paused to let this sink in. 'And we'll have these two as hostages in case the Araluans try to stop us,' he added.

'They're kids!' said Nordel derisively. 'What use are they as hostages?'

'Didn't you see that oakleaf amulet the boy was wearing?' Erak asked and, instinctively, Will's hand went to the oak leaf on the thong around his neck.

'That's the Rangers' symbol,' Erak continued. 'He's one of them. Maybe some kind of trainee. And they look after their own.'

'What about the girl?' said Svengal. 'She's no Ranger.'

'That's right,' Erak agreed. 'She's just a girl. But I'm not handing any girl over to the Wargals. You've seen what they're like. They're worse than animals, that lot. No. She comes with us.'

There was another moment's silence as the others considered his words. Then Horak spoke. 'Fair enough,' he agreed. Erak looked around the others, and saw that

Horak had spoken for them all. The Skandians were warriors, and hard men. But they weren't totally ruthless.

'Good,' he said. 'Now let's get on the road again.'

He rose and moved towards Will and Evanlyn while the other Skandians repacked the remains of the brief meal.

'Can you walk?' he asked Will. 'Or does Nordel have to carry you again?'

Will flushed angrily and rose quickly to his feet. Instantly he wished he hadn't. The ground heaved and his head swam. He staggered and only Evanlyn's firm hand on his arm prevented him from falling. But he was determined not to show weakness in front of his captors. He steadied himself, then glared defiantly at Erak.

'I'll walk,' he managed to say and the big Skandian studied him for a moment, an appraising look in his eye.

'Yes,' he said finally. 'I daresay you will.'

Twenty-four

Battlemaster David chewed the ends of his moustache as he frowned at the plan outlined on the sand table.

'I don't know, Halt,' he said doubtfully. 'It's very risky. One of the first principles of warfare is never to split your forces.'

Halt nodded. He knew the knight's criticism was intended to be constructive, not simply negative thinking. It was Sir David's role to find any faults in the plan and weigh them against its possible advantages.

'That's true,' the Ranger replied. 'But it's also true that surprise is a powerful weapon.'

Baron Tyler walked around the table, considering the plan from another viewpoint. He pointed with his dagger at the mass of green that represented the Thorntree Forest.

'You're sure you and Gilan can guide a large cavalry force through the Thorntree? I thought nobody could get through there,' he asked dubiously, and Halt nodded.

'The Rangers have charted and surveyed every inch of the Kingdom for years, my lord,' he told the Baron. 'Especially the parts people think there's no way through. We can surprise this northern force. Then Morgarath will be caught out as well, when no Skandians turn up behind us.'

Tyler continued to pace around the table, staring intently at the designs drawn there and the markers set in place in the sand map.

'All the same,' he said, 'we'll be in a pretty scrape if the Skandians defeat Halt and the cavalry over here in the north. After all, you'll be outnumbered almost two to one.'

Halt nodded agreement again. 'That's true. But we'll catch them in open country, so we'll have the advantage. And don't forget we'll be taking two hundred archer units as well. They should even the numbers a little.'

An archer unit consisted of two men: one archer and one accompanying pikeman, mutually supporting each other. Against lightly armoured infantry, they were a deadly combination. The archers could cut down large numbers of the enemy at a distance. Once the battle got to close quarters, the pikemen took over, allowing the archers to withdraw to safety.

'But,' insisted Baron Tyler, 'let's assume that the Skandians do manage to win through. Then the tables will be turned. We'll be fighting a real enemy in the north-west, with our rear exposed to Morgarath's Wargals coming out of the Pass.'

Arald managed to suppress a sigh. As a strategist, Tyler was notoriously cautious. 'On the other hand,' he said, doing his best to keep the impatience out of his voice, 'if Halt succeeds, it will be his force that Morgarath sees coming round from the north-west. He'll assume it's the Skandians attacking us from that direction and he'll bring his forces out onto the Plains to attack us from behind. And then we'll have him — once and for all.'

The prospect seemed to appeal to him.

'It's still a risk,' Tyler said stubbornly. Halt and Arald exchanged a glance and the Baron's shoulders lifted slightly in a shrug.

Halt said, in a dry tone, 'All warfare has a risk attached to it, sir. Otherwise it would be easy.'

Baron Tyler looked up angrily at him. Halt met his gaze evenly. As the Baron opened his mouth to say something, Sir David forestalled him, smacking one gauntlet into his palm in a decisive gesture.

'All right, Halt,' he said. 'I'll put your plan to the King.'

At the mention of the King, Halt's face softened slightly.

'How is his majesty taking the news?' he asked and Sir David shrugged unhappily.

'Personally, he's devastated, of course. It was the cruellest possible blow to have his hopes raised and then shattered again. But he manages somehow to put his personal life to one side and continue to perform his duties as King. He says he'll mourn later, when this is all over.'

'There may be no need for mourning,' Arald put in, and David smiled sadly at him.

'I've told him that, of course. He says he'd prefer not to have false hopes raised once more.'

There was an awkward silence in the tent. Tyler, Fergus and Sir David felt deep sorrow for their King. Duncan was a popular and just monarch. Halt and Baron Arald, on the other hand, both felt the loss of Will deeply. In a remarkably short time, Will had become an integral part of Castle Redmont. Finally, it was Sir David who broke the silence.

'Gentlemen, perhaps you might begin preparing your orders. I'll take this plan to the King.'

And as he turned away to the inner sections of the pavilion, the barons and Halt left the large tent. Arald, Fergus and Tyler walked quickly away, to prepare movement orders for the army. Halt, seeing a dejected figure in Ranger green and grey waiting by the sentry post, moved down the small hill to talk to his former apprentice.

'I want leave to go across the Fissure after them,' said Gilan.

Halt knew how deeply he felt the hurt of Will's loss. Gilan blamed himself for leaving Will alone in the hills of Celtica. No matter how many times Halt and the other Rangers told him that he had taken the right course, he refused to believe it. Now, Halt knew, it would hurt him even more to be refused. Nevertheless, as Rangers, their first duty was to the Kingdom. He shook his head and answered curtly.

'Not granted. You're needed here. We're to lead a force through the Thorntree to cut off Horth's men. Go to Crowley's tent and get hold of the charts showing the secret ways for this part of the country.'

Gilan hesitated, his jaw set. 'But . . .' he began to protest, and then something in Halt's eyes stopped him as the older Ranger leaned forward.

'Gilan, do you think for one moment that I don't want to tear that plateau apart stone by stone until I find Will?

But you and I took an oath when they gave us these silver oak leaves, and now we have to live up to it.'

Gilan dropped his eyes and nodded. His shoulders slumped as he gave in.

'All right,' he said in a broken voice, and Halt thought he saw traces of tears in his eyes. He turned away hurriedly before Gilan could see the moisture in his own.

'Get the charts,' he said briefly.

Twenty-five

The four Skandians and their prisoners had trudged across the bleak, windswept plateau for the rest of the day and into the evening. It wasn't until several hours after dark that Erak called a halt, and Will and Evanlyn sank gratefully to the rocky ground. The ache in Will's head had receded somewhat through the day, but it still throbbed dully in the background. The dried blood on the wound where the jagged rock had hit him itched abominably, but he knew that if he scratched at the irritation, he would only open the wound and set the blood flowing once more.

At least, thought Will, Erak hadn't kept them tied or restrained in any way. As the Skandian leader put it, there was nowhere for the two prisoners to run.

'This plateau is full of Wargals,' he'd told them roughly. 'You can take your chances with them if you choose.'

So they'd kept their position in the middle of the party, passing bands of Wargals throughout the day, and heading constantly to the north-east, and Three Step Pass. Now, the four Skandians eased their heavy packs to the ground and Nordel began to gather wood for a fire. Svengal tossed a large copper pot at Evanlyn's feet and gestured towards a stream that bubbled through the rocks close by.

'Get some water,' he told her gruffly. For a moment, the girl hesitated, then she shrugged, took up the pot and rose, groaning softly as her tired muscles and joints were called upon once more to take her weight.

'Come on then, Will,' she said casually. 'You can give me a hand.'

Erak was rummaging in his open pack. His head snapped round as she spoke.

'No!' he said sharply, and the entire group turned to look at him. He pointed one blunt forefinger at Evanlyn.

'You, I don't mind wandering off,' he said. 'Because I know you'll come back. But as for that Ranger, he might just take it into his head to make a run for it, in spite of things.'

Will, who had been thinking of doing just that, tried to look surprised.

'I'm no Ranger,' he said. 'I'm just an apprentice.'

Erak gave a short snort of laughter. 'You may say so,' he replied. 'But you dropped them Wargals at the bridge as well as any Ranger might. You stay where I can keep an eye on you.'

Will shrugged, smiled wanly at Evanlyn and sat down again, sighing as he leaned his back against a rock. In a few moments, he knew, it would become hard and knobbly and uncomfortable. But right now, it was bliss.

The Skandians went ahead making camp. In short order, they had a good fire going, and when Evanlyn returned with the pot full of water, Erak and Svengal produced dried provisions which they added to the water as it heated to make a stew. The meal was plain and fairly tasteless, but it was hot and it filled their bellies. Will thought ruefully for a few minutes of the pre-prepared food that came from Master Chubb's kitchen. Sadly, he realised that such thoughts of Master Chubb's kitchen and his times in the forest with Halt were no more than memories now. Images sprang into his mind, unbidden: of Tug, and Gilan and Horace. Of Castle Redmont, seen in the last rays of the setting sun, with its ironstone walls glowing dull red, seeming to hold an inner light. Tears formed behind his eyes, stinging and aching for release. Surreptitiously, he tried to wipe them away with the back of his hand. The meal was suddenly even more tasteless than before.

Evanlyn seemed to sense his deepening sadness. He felt her warm, small hand cover his and he knew she was looking at him. But he couldn't meet those vivid green eyes with his own, feeling the tears welling up in them.

'It'll be all right,' she whispered. He tried to talk, but couldn't form the words. Silently, he shook his head, his eyes downcast, staring intently at the scratched surface of the wooden bowl the Skandians had given him to use.

They were camped some metres from the side of the road, at the top of a slight rise. Erak had stated that he liked to see anyone who might choose to approach. Now, rounding a bend in the road several hundred metres away, came a large group of horsemen, followed by a troop of Wargals, running to keep up with the horses' trot. The sound of the Wargals' chant came to them on the breeze once more and Will felt the hairs on the back of his neck rising.

Erak turned swiftly to the two of them, gesturing them back into the cover of the rocks behind their camp site.

'Quick, you two! Behind them rocks if you value your lives! That's Morgarath himself on the white horse! Nordel, Horak, move into the light to screen them!'

Will and Evanlyn needed no second bidding. Staying low, they scrambled into the cover provided by the rocks. As Erak had commanded, two of the Skandians stood and moved into the glare of the firelight, drawing the attention of the approaching riders away from the two small figures in the half light.

The chant, mingled with the clatter of hooves and the chink of harness and weapons, came closer as Will lay on his stomach, one arm covering Evanlyn in the darkness. As he had done before, he scooped the hood of his cloak over his head, to leave his face in deep shadow. There was a tiny gap between two of the rocks and, knowing he was taking a terrible risk but unable to resist, he pressed his eye to it.

The view was restricted to a few metres of space. Erak stood on the far side of the fire, facing the approaching riders. Will realised that by doing so, he had placed the glare of the firelight between the new arrivals and the spot where he and Evanlyn lay hidden. If any of the Wargals looked in their direction, they would be staring straight into the bright firelight. It was a lesson in tactics he filed away for future reference.

The sounds of horses and men stopped. The Wargal

chant died abruptly. For a second or two, there was silence. Then a voice spoke. A low voice, with a slight, snake-like sibilance to it.

'Captain Erak, where are you bound?'

Will glued his eye to the crack in the rocks, straining to see the speaker. Without a doubt, that cold, malevolent voice had to belong to Morgarath. The sound of it was the sound of ice and hatred. The sound of nails scraping on tile. The blood ran cold to hear it. The hairs on the back of his neck stood up and, beneath his hand, he felt Evanlyn shiver.

If it had a similar effect on Erak, however, he showed no sign of it.

'My correct title is "Jarl", Lord Morgarath,' he said evenly, 'not "Captain".'

'Well then,' replied the cold voice, 'I must try to remember that, in case it is ever of the slightest interest to me. Now . . . Captain,' he said, laying stress on the title this time, 'I repeat, where are you bound?'

There was a jingle of harness and, through the crack in the rocks, Will saw a white horse move forward. Not a glossy-coated, shining white horse such as a gallant knight might ride, but a pale horse without sheen or life to its coat. It was huge, dead white and with wild, rolling eyes. He craned slightly to one side and managed to make out a black gloved hand holding the reins loosely. He could see no more of the rider.

'We thought we'd join your forces at Three Step Pass, my lord,' Erak was saying. 'I assume you will still go ahead with your attack, even though the bridge is down.'

Morgarath swore horribly at the mention of the bridge. Sensing his fury, the white horse sidestepped a few paces and now Will could see the rider.

Immensely tall, but thin, he was dressed all in black. He stooped in the saddle to talk down to the Skandians and the hunched shoulders and his black cloak gave him the look of a vulture.

The face was thin, with a beak of a nose and high cheekbones. The skin on the face was white and pallid, like the horse. The hair above it was long, set to frame a receding hairline, and white-blond in colour. By contrast, the eyes were black pools. He was clean-shaven and his mouth was a thin red slit in the pallor of his face. As Will looked, the Lord of Rain and Night seemed to sense his presence. He looked up, casting his gaze beyond Erak and his three companions, searching into the darkness behind them. Will froze, barely daring to breathe as those black eyes searched the night. But the light of the fire defeated Morgarath and he returned his gaze to Erak.

'Yes,' he replied. 'The attack will go ahead. Now that Duncan has his own forces deployed and in what he thinks is a strong defensive position, he'll allow us to come out onto the Plains before attacking.'

'At which point, Horth will take him in the rear,' Erak put in, with a chuckle, and Morgarath stared at him, head slightly to one side as he considered him. Again, the bird-like pose made Will think of a vulture.

'Exactly,' he agreed. 'It would be preferable if there were two flanking forces as I'd planned originally, but one should be enough.'

'My thoughts too, my lord,' Erak agreed and there was a long moment of silence. Obviously, Morgarath had no interest in whether Erak agreed with him or not.

'Things would be easier if your other countryman had not abandoned us,' Morgarath said eventually. 'I've been told that your compatriot Ovlak has sailed back to Skandia with his men. I had planned that they should come up the southern cliffs to reinforce us.'

Erak shrugged, refusing to take blame for something outside his sphere of influence. 'Ovlak is a mercenary,' he said. 'You can't trust mercenaries. They fight only for profit.'

'And you . . . don't?' the toneless voice said with scorn. Erak squared his shoulders.

'I'll honour any undertaking I've made,' he said stiffly. Morgarath stared at him again for a long, silent moment. The Skandian met his gaze and, finally, it was Morgarath who looked away.

'Chirath told me you took a prisoner at the bridge — a mighty warrior, he said. I don't see him.' Again, Morgarath tried to look through the light into the further gloom. Erak laughed harshly.

'If Chirath was the leader of your Wargals, neither did he,' he replied sarcastically. 'He spent most of his time at the bridge cowering behind a rock and dodging arrows.'

'And the prisoner?' Morgarath asked.

'Dead,' Erak replied. 'We killed him and threw him over the edge.'

'A fact that displeases me intensely,' Morgarath said and Will felt his flesh crawling. 'I would have preferred to make him suffer for interfering in my plans. You should have brought him to me alive.'

'Well, we would have preferred it if he hadn't been whipping arrows around our ears. He could shoot, that's for sure. The only way to take him was to kill him.'

Another silence as Morgarath considered the reply. Apparently, it was not satisfactory to him. 'Be warned for the future. I did not approve of your actions.'

This time, it was Erak who let the silence stretch. He shrugged his shoulders slightly, as if Morgarath's displeasure was a matter of absolutely no interest to him. Eventually, the Lord of Rain and Night gathered his reins and shook them, heeling his horse savagely to turn it away from the camp fire.

'I'll see you at Three Step Pass, Captain,' he said. Then, almost as an afterthought, he turned his horse back. 'And Captain, don't get any ideas about deserting. You'll fight with us to the end.'

Erak nodded. 'I told you, my lord, I'll honour any bargain I've made.'

This time, Morgarath smiled, a thin movement of the red lips in the lifeless white face. 'Be sure of it, Captain,' he said softly.

Then he shook the reins and his horse turned away, springing to a gallop. The Wargals followed, the chant starting up again and ringing through the night. Will realised that, behind the rocks, he'd been holding a giant breath. He let it go now, and heard a corresponding sigh of relief from the Skandians.

'My god of battles,' said Erak, 'he doesn't half give me the creeps, that one.'

'Looks like he's already died and gone to hell,' put in Svengal, and the others nodded. Erak walked round the fire now and stood over where Will and Evanlyn were still crouched behind the rocks.

'You heard that?' he said and Will nodded. Evanlyn remained crouching, face down, behind the rock. Erak stirred her with the toe of his boot.

'And you, missy,' he said. 'You heard too?'

Now she looked up, tears of terror staining tracks in the dust on her face. Wordlessly, she nodded. Erak glanced away, in the direction where Morgarath and his Wargals had gone.

'Then remember it if you plan to escape,' he said. 'That's all that awaits you if you get away from us.'

Twenty-six

The Plains of Uthal formed a wide open space of rolling grasslands. The grass was rich and green. There were few trees, although occasional knolls and low hills served to break the monotony. Some distance behind the position occupied by the Araluan army, the Plains began to rise gradually, to a low ridgeline.

Closer to the fens, where the Wargals were forming up, a creek wound its way. Normally a mere trickle, it had been swollen by the recent spring rains so that the ground ahead of the Wargals was soft and boggy, precluding any possible attack by the Araluan heavy cavalry.

Baron Fergus of Caraway shaded his eyes against the bright noon sun and peered across the Plains to the entrance to Three Step Pass.

'There are a lot of them,' he said mildly.

'And more coming,' Arald of Redmont replied, easing his broadsword a little in its scabbard.

The two barons were slowly walking their battlehorses

across the front of Duncan's drawn-up army. It was good for morale, Arald believed, for the men to see their leaders relaxed and engaging in casual conversation as they watched their enemies emerging from the narrow mountain pass and fanning out onto the Plains. Dimly, they could hear the ominous, rhythmic chant of the Wargals as they jogged into position.

'Damned noise is quite unnerving,' Fergus muttered and Arald nodded agreement. Seemingly casual, he cast his glance over the men behind them. The army was in position, but Battlemaster David had told them to remain at rest. Consequently, the cavalry were dismounted and the infantry and archers were sitting on the grassy slope.

'No sense in wearing them out standing at attention in the sun,' David had said and the others had agreed. By the same token, he had set the various Kitchenmasters the task of keeping the men supplied with cool drinks and fruit. The white-clad servers moved among the army now, carrying baskets and water skins. Arald glanced down and smiled at the portly form of Master Chubb, his chef from Redmont Castle, supervising a group of hapless apprentices as they handed out apples and peaches to the men. As ever, his ladle rose and fell with alarming frequency on the heads of any apprentice he deemed to be moving too slowly.

'Give that Kitchenmaster of yours a mace and he could rout Morgarath's army single-handed,' commented Fergus, and Arald smiled thoughtfully. The men around Chubb and his apprentices, distracted by the fat cook's antics, were taking no notice of the chanting from across the Plains. In other areas, he could see signs of restlessness and evidence that the men were becoming increasingly ill at ease.

Looking around, Arald's eye fell on an infantry captain seated with his company. Their minimal armour, plaid cloaks and two-handed broadswords marked them as belonging to one of the northern fiefs. He beckoned the man over and leaned down from the saddle as he saluted.

'Good morning, Captain,' he said easily.

'Morning, my lord,' replied the officer, his heavy northern accent making the words almost unrecognisable.

'Tell me, Captain, do you have pipers among your men?' the Baron asked, smiling. The officer answered immediately, in a very serious manner.

'Aye, sir. The McDuig and the McForn are with us. And always so when we go to war.'

'Then perhaps you might prevail upon them to give us a reel or two?' the Baron suggested. 'It might be an altogether more pleasant sound than that tuneless grunting from over yonder.'

He inclined his head towards the Wargal forces and now a slow smile spread over the captain's face. He nodded readily.

'Aye, sir. I'll see to it. There's nothing like a skirl or two on the pipes to get a man's blood prancing!' Saluting hurriedly, he turned away towards his men, shouting as he ran: 'McDuig! McForn! Gather your wind and set to the pipes, men! Let's hear "The Feather Crested Bonnet" from ye!'

As the two barons rode on, they heard behind them the preliminary moaning of bagpipes coming to full volume. Fergus winced and Arald grinned at him.

'Nothing like the skirl of the pipes to get the blood prancing,' he quoted.

'In my case, it gets the teeth grinding,' replied his companion, surreptitiously nudging his horse with his heel to move them a little further away from the wild sound of the pipes. But, when he looked at the men behind them, he had to agree that Arald's idea had worked. The pipes were successfully drowning out the dull chanting and, as the two pipers marched and countermarched in front of the army, they held the attention of all the men in their immediate vicinity.

'Good idea,' he said to Arald, then added, 'I can't help wondering if that's an equally good one.'

He gestured across the plain to where the Wargals were emerging from the Pass and taking up their positions. 'All my instincts say we should be hitting them before they have a chance to form up.'

Arald shrugged. This point had been hotly debated by the War Council for the past few days.

'If we hit them as they come out, we simply contain them,' he said. 'If we want to destroy Morgarath's power once and for all, we have to let him commit his forces in the open.'

'And hope that Halt has been successful in stopping Horth's army,' Fergus said. 'I'm getting a nasty crick in my neck from looking over my shoulder to make sure there's no one behind us.'

'Halt has never let us down before,' Arald said mildly.

Fergus nodded unhappily. 'I know that. He's a remarkable man. But there are so many things that could have gone wrong. He could have missed Horth's army altogether. He may still be fighting his way through the Thorntree. Or, worse yet, Horth may have defeated his archers and cavalry.'

'There's nothing we can do about it but wait,' Arald pointed out.

'And keep an eye to the north-west, hoping we don't see battleaxes and horned helmets coming over those hills.'

'There's a comforting thought,' said Arald, trying to make light of the moment. Yet he couldn't resist the temptation to turn in his saddle and peer anxiously towards the hills in the north.

Erak had waited till the last few hundred Wargals were moving down Three Step Pass to the Plains, then forced his small group into the middle of the jogging creatures. There were a few snarls and scowls as the Skandians shoved their way into the living stream that was flowing through the narrow, twisting confines of the Pass, but the heavily armed sea raiders snarled back and handled their double-sided battleaxes with such easy familiarity that the angry Wargals soon backed off and left them alone.

Evanlyn and Will were in the centre of the group, surrounded by the burly Skandians. Will's easily recognisable Ranger cloak had been hidden away in one of the packs and both he and Evanlyn wore sheepskin half capes that were too large for them. Evanlyn's short hair was covered by a woollen cap. So far, none of the Wargals had taken any notice of them, assuming them to be servants or slaves to the small band of sea raiders.

'Just keep your mouths shut and your eyes down!' Erak had told them as they shoved their way into the crowd of jogging Wargals. The narrow confines of the Pass echoed to the tuneless chanting that the Wargals used as a cadence. The sound ebbed and flowed about them as they half-ran with the stream. Erak's plan was to move eastwards as soon as they had cleared the Pass, ostensibly with the purpose of taking up a position on the right flank of the Wargal army. As soon as an opportunity presented itself, the Skandians would break off and escape into the swampy wilderness of the fenlands, travelling through the bogs and grassy islands to the beaches where Horth's fleet lay at anchor.

They shuffled along, twisting and turning with the convolutions of the Pass. The narrow trail led down through the sheer mountains for at least five kilometres and Will could understand why it had always been a barrier to both sides. Morgarath's men couldn't move out in any large numbers unless Duncan held back and allowed them to. Similarly, the King's army couldn't penetrate the Pass to attack Morgarath on the plateau.

Black walls of sheer, glistening-wet rock towered above them on either side. The Pass saw sunlight for less than an hour each day, right on high noon. At any other time, it was cold and damp and shrouded in shadow. All of which served to help conceal the presence of the two younger members of the party from prying eyes.

Will felt the ground beneath his feet beginning to level out and realised they must be in the last extremities of the Pass — down at the level of the Plains. There was no way he could even see the ground ahead of him, trapped in the seething, jostling crowd. They rounded a final bend and a lance of sunlight stabbed into the Pass, forcing him to throw up a hand to shield his eyes. They had reached the entrance, he realised. He felt a shove from his left.

'Get over to the right!' Erak told them and the four Skandians formed a human wedge, forcing their way through the crowd until they were on the extreme right-hand side of the Pass. There were growls and angry grunts from the Wargals they shoved, several of them being sent sprawling and then trampled before they could regain their feet. But the Skandians gave as good as they got in terms of threats and abuse.

The sunlight hit them like a physical barrier as they emerged from the darkness of the Pass and, for a moment, Will and Evanlyn hesitated. Erak shoved them on again, more anxious now as he could hear a familiar voice calling commands for the Wargals to deploy.

Morgarath was here, directing operations.

'Curse him!' muttered Erak. 'I'd hoped he'd be out with the vanguard of the army. Keep moving, you two!' He shoved Will and Evanlyn along a little faster. Will glanced back. Above the heads of the Wargals, he could see the tall, thin form of the Lord of Rain and Night, now clad entirely in black mail armour and surcoat, still seated on his white horse and calling instructions to the milling, chanting Wargals.

Gradually, they were moving into ordered formations, then taking their position with the main army. As Will looked back, the pale face turned towards the group of hurrying Skandians and Morgarath urged his horse towards them, unmindful of the fact that he was trampling through his own men to reach them.

'Captain Erak!' he called. The voice wasn't loud, but it carried, thin and cutting, through the chanting of the Wargals.

'Keep going!' Erak ordered them in a low voice. 'Keep moving.'

'Stop!' Now the voice was raised and the cold anger in it instantly silenced and stilled the Wargals. As they froze in place around them, the Skandians reluctantly did the same, Erak turning to face Morgarath.

The Lord of Rain and Night spurred his horse through the throng, Wargals falling back to make way for him, or being buffeted out of the way if they failed to do so. Slowly, his eyes locked on those of Erak, he dismounted. Even on foot, he towered over the bulky Skandian leader.

'And where might you and your men be bound today, Captain?' he asked in a silky tone. Erak gestured to the right.

'It's normal for me and my men to fight on the right wing,' he said, as casually as he could manage. 'But I'll go wherever you need me if that doesn't suit.'

'Will you?' replied Morgarath with withering sarcasm. 'Will you indeed? How terribly kind of you. You . . .' He broke off, his gaze on the two smaller figures whom the other Skandians had been trying, unsuccessfully, to shield from his gaze.

'Who are they?' he demanded. Erak shrugged.

'Celts,' he said easily. 'We took them prisoner in Celtica and I'm planning to sell them to Oberjarl Ragnak as slaves.'

'Celtica is mine, Captain. Slaves from Celtica are mine as well. They're not for you to take and sell to your barbarian of a king.'

The Skandians surrounding Will and Evanlyn stirred angrily at his words. Morgarath turned his cold eyes on them, then looked away at the thousands of Wargals who surrounded them — every one ready to obey any command of his without question. The message was clear.

Erak tried to bluff his way through the situation.

'Our agreement was we fought for booty and that includes slaves,' he insisted, but Morgarath cut him off.

'If you fought!' he shouted furiously. '*If!* Not if you stood by and let my bridge be destroyed.'

'It was your man Chirath who was in command at the bridge,' Erak flashed back at him. 'It was he who decided no guard was to be left on it. We were the ones who tried to save it while he was hiding behind rocks!'

Morgarath's gaze locked with Erak's once more and now his voice dropped to a low, almost inaudible level.

'I am not spoken to in that fashion, *Captain* Erak,' he spat. 'You will apologise to me at once. And then . . .'

He stopped in mid-sentence. He seemed to possess almost unnatural peripheral senses. Although he had been staring, unblinkingly, into Erak's eyes, he had apparently sensed something off to one side. Those black eyes now turned and trained on Will. One white, bony finger was raised, pointing at the boy's throat.

'What is that?'

Erak looked and felt a sinking sensation in the pit of his stomach.

There was a dull gleam of bronze visible in the gap of Will's open collar. Then Erak felt himself shoved to one side as Morgarath moved, snake-fast, and snatched at the chain around Will's neck.

Will staggered back, horrified at the implacable fury in those dead eyes, and the slight flare of colour above the cheekbones. Beside him, he heard Evanlyn's intake of breath as Morgarath stared down at the small bronze oak leaf in his hand.

'A Ranger!' he raged. 'This is a Ranger! This is their sign!'

'He's a boy . . .' Erak began, but now Morgarath's fury was turned upon him and he swept his hand in a backhanded blow across the Skandian's cheek.

'He is no boy! He is a Ranger!'

The other three Skandians moved forward at the blow, weapons ready. Morgarath didn't even have to speak. He turned those glittering eyes on them and twenty Wargals moved as well, a warning growl in their throats, clubs and iron spears ready.

Erak signalled for his men to settle. The red mark of Morgarath's blow flared on his cheek.

'You knew,' Morgarath accused him. 'You knew.' Then realisation dawned on him. 'This is the one! Arrows, you said! My Wargals were hiding from arrows as the bridge burnt! Ranger weapons! This is the swine who destroyed my bridge!' The voice rose to a shriek of fury as he spoke.

Will's throat was dry and his heart pounded with terror. He knew of Morgarath's legendary hatred for Rangers — all members of the Corps did. Ironically, it was Halt himself who had triggered that hatred when he led the surprise attack on Morgarath's army at Hackham Heath sixteen years previously.

Erak stood before the raging Black Lord and said nothing.

Will felt a small, warm hand creep into his: Evanlyn.

For a moment, he marvelled at the girl's courage, to bond herself to him like this, in the face of Morgarath's implacable fury and hatred.

Then, another horse forced its way through the crowd. On its back was one of Morgarath's Wargal lieutenants, one of those who had learned basic human speech.

'My lord!' he called, in the peculiar, emotionless tones of all Wargals. 'Enemy advancing!'

Morgarath swung to face him and the Wargal continued.

'Their skirmish line moving towards us, my lord. Battle is beginning!'

The Lord of Rain and Night came to a decision. He swung back into the saddle of his horse, his furious gaze now locked on Will, not Erak.

'We will finish this later,' he said. Then he turned to a Wargal sergeant among those who had surrounded the Skandians.

'Hold these prisoners here until I return. On pain of your life.'

The Wargal saluted, one fist to his left breast, then growled a command to his men. They surrounded the Skandian party. The four sea wolves now formed a small circle, facing out, Will and Evanlyn in the middle. They held their weapons ready. It was a stand-off and they were obviously prepared to sell their lives dearly.

'We'll settle this later, Erak,' Morgarath said. 'Try to escape and my men will cut you to pieces.'

And, wheeling his horse, he galloped through the throng once again, scattering soldiers in his path, trampling those who were too slow to move. They heard the thin, nasal voice calling commands to his forces as he disappeared.

Twenty-seven

The first clash of the two armies was inconclusive.

The King's skirmish line, consisting of light infantry accompanied by archers, advanced on Morgarath's left flank in a probing movement, retreating hastily when a battalion of heavy infantry formed up and moved forward to meet them.

The lightly armed skirmishers scampered back to the safety of their own lines, ahead of the slow treading Wargals. Then, as a company of heavy cavalry trotted forward towards the Wargal battalion's left flank, the Wargals re-formed from their column-of-fours marching order into a slower moving, defensive square and withdrew to their own lines.

For the next few hours, that remained the pattern of the battle: small forces would probe the other side's defences. Larger forces would offer to counter and the first attack would melt away. Arald, Fergus and Tyler sat their horses beside the King, on a small knoll in the centre of the royal army. Battlemaster David was with a small group of knights making one of the many forays towards the Wargal army.

'All this toing and froing is getting me down,' Arald said sourly. The King smiled at him. He had one of the most important attributes of a good commander: almost unlimited patience.

'Morgarath is waiting,' he said simply. 'Waiting for Horth's army to show itself in our rear. Then he'll attack, have no doubt.'

'Let's just get on with it ourselves,' growled Fergus, but Duncan shook his head, pointing to the ground immediately to the front of Morgarath's position.

'The land there is soft and boggy,' he said. 'It would reduce the effectiveness of our best weapon — our cavalry. We'll wait till Morgarath comes to us. Then we can fight him on ground that's more to our liking.'

There was an urgent clatter of hooves from the rear, and the royal party turned to watch a courier spurring his horse up the last slope to the knoll where they waited. He hauled on his reins, looked around until he saw the King's blond head, then dug in his spurs again, eventually bringing his horse to a sliding stop beside them. His green surcoat, light mail armour and thin-bladed sword showed him to be a scout.

'Your majesty,' he said breathlessly. 'A report from Sir Vincent.'

Vincent was the leader of the Messenger Corps, a group of soldiers who acted as the King's eyes and ears during a battle, carrying reports and orders to all parts of the battlefield. Duncan nodded acknowledgement, indicating that the man should go ahead and give his message.

The rider swallowed several times and looked anxiously at the King and his three barons. All at once, Arald knew this was not going to be good news.

'Sir,' said the scout hesitantly. 'Sir Vincent's respects, sir, and . . . there appear to be Skandians behind us.'

There were startled exclamations from several of the junior officers surrounding the command group. Fergus swung on them, his brows drawn together in a frown.

'Be quiet!' he stormed and, in an instant, the noise dropped away. The aides looked shamefaced at their lack of discipline.

'Exactly where are these Skandians? And how many are there?' Duncan asked the scout calmly. His unruffled manner seemed to communicate itself to the messenger. This time, he answered with a lot more confidence.

'The first group are visible on the low ridge to the north-west, your majesty. As yet we can see only a hundred or so. Sir Vincent suggests that the best position for you to view the situation would be from the small hill to our left rear.'

The King nodded and turned to one of the younger officers.

'Ranald, perhaps you might ride and advise Sir David of this new development. Tell him we are shifting the command post to the hill Sir Vincent suggested.'

'Yes, my lord!' replied the young knight. He wheeled his horse and set off at a gallop. The King then turned to his companions.

'Gentlemen, let's see about these Skandians, shall we?'

Shading his eyes, Baron Arald peered at the small group of men on the hill behind them. Even at this distance, it was possible to make out the horned helmets and the huge circular shields that the sea raiders carried. A small group had even advanced down the near side of the hill and they were easier to make out.

Just as obvious was their choice of the typical Skandian arrowhead formation as they advanced. He estimated that several hundred of the enemy were now in sight, with who knew how many more hidden on the other side of the hills. He felt a great weight of sadness upon his shoulders. The fact that the Skandians were there meant only one thing: Halt had failed. And knowing Halt as he did, he knew that probably meant that the grizzled Ranger had died in the attempt. He knew Halt would never have surrendered — not when the need to stop the Skandians breaking through to the army's rear was so vital.

Duncan voiced the thoughts of all of them.

'They're Skandians, all right.' He glanced around the hilltop. 'We're going to have to fight a defensive battle, my lords,' he continued. 'I suggest we begin to pull our men into a circle around this hill. It's as good a spot as any to be fighting on both sides.'

They all knew it was only a matter of time now before Morgarath advanced, to crush them between the two jaws of the trap he had set.

'Rider coming!' called one of the aides, pointing. They all turned to face the way he indicated. From a copse of trees at the right-hand end of the ridge, a lone rider burst into sight. Several of the Skandians gave chase, hurling spears and clubs after him. But he was stretched low over his horse's neck, his grey-green cloak streaming behind him in the wind, and he soon outdistanced the pursuit.

'That's Gilan,' Baron Arald muttered, recognising the bay horse he rode. He looked in vain for a second Ranger behind Gilan, hoping against hope that Halt might have somehow survived. But it was not to be. His shoulders sagged a little as he realised that Gilan appeared to be the only survivor of the force that had marched off so boldly into the Thorntree Forest.

Gilan had hit the flat land now and was still riding full pelt towards them. He saw the royal standards flying on the knoll and swerved Blaze towards them. In a few minutes, he drew rein beside them, covered in dust, one sleeve of his tunic ripped and a rough, blood-stained bandage around his head.

'Sir!' he said breathlessly, forgetting the niceties of addressing royalty. 'Halt says can you —'

He got no further as at least four people interrupted him. Baron Fergus's voice, however, was the loudest.

'Halt? He's alive?'

Gilan grinned in reply. 'Oh, yes, sir! Alive and kicking.'

'But the Skandians . . .?' King Duncan began, indicating the lines of men on the far ridge. Gilan's grin widened even further.

'Beaten, sir. We caught them totally by surprise and cut them to pieces. Those men there are our archers, wearing helmets and shields taken from the enemy. It was Halt's idea . . .'

'To what purpose?' Arald asked crisply and Gilan turned to face him, with an apologetic nod of his head to the King.

'To deceive Morgarath, my lord,' he replied. 'He's expecting to see Skandians attack you from the rear, and now he will. That's why they even made a pretence of trying to stop me just now.

'Our own cavalry is just beyond the brow of the ridge. Halt proposes that he should advance with the archers, forcing you to turn and face the rear. Then, with any luck, as Morgarath attacks with his Wargals, both the archers and your main army should open a path through the centre, allowing the hidden cavalry to come through and hit Morgarath when he's in the open.'

'By god, it's a great idea!' said Duncan enthusiastically. 'Odds are that we'll stir up so much dust and confusion that he won't see Halt's cavalry until it's right on top of him.'

'Then, my lord, we can deploy the heavy cavalry from either wing to hit the Wargals in the flanks.' The new speaker was Sir David. He had arrived unnoticed as Gilan was explaining Halt's plan.

King Duncan hesitated for a second or two, tugging at his short beard. Then he nodded decisively.

'We'll do it!' he said. 'Gentlemen, you'd better get to your commands straight away. Fergus, Arald, take a section of the heavy cavalry each to the left and right wings, and stand ready. Tyler, command the infantry in the centre. Make sure they know this is a fake attack. And order them to shout and beat their swords on their shields as the "Skandians" approach. We'll make it sound like a battle as well as look like one. Have them ready to split to the sides at three horn blasts.'

'Three horn blasts. Aye, my lord,' said Tyler. He dug his spurs into his battlehorse's side and galloped away to take command of the infantry. Duncan looked to his remaining commanders.

'Get to it, my lords. We don't have much time.'

From behind, one of his aides called out.

'Sir! The Skandians are moving downhill!'

A second or so later, another man echoed the cry:

'And the Wargals are beginning to move forward!'

Duncan smiled grimly at his commanders.

'I think it's time we gave Morgarath a little surprise,' he said.

Twenty-eight

From his command position at the centre of his army, Morgarath watched the apparent confusion in the King's forces. Horses were galloping back and forth, men were turning where they stood. Shouts and cries drifted across the plain to the army of Rain and Night.

Morgarath stood in his stirrups. In the far distance, he could see movement on the ridge to the north of the Kingdom's army. Men were forming up and moving forward. He strained his eyes to see more clearly. That was the direction from which he expected Horth to appear, but the rising dust kicked up by all the movement made it difficult to see details.

Although the bulk of Morgarath's forces were the Wargals whose minds and bodies had been enslaved to his own will, the Lord of Rain and Night was surrounded by a small coterie of men whom he had allowed to retain their own powers of thought and decision. Renegades, criminals and outcasts, they came from all over the country. Evil always attracts its own and Morgarath's inner circle were, to a man, pitiless, black-hearted and depraved. All, however, were capable warriors and most were cold-blooded killers.

One of them now rode to Morgarath's side.

'My lord!' he cried, a smile opening on his face, 'the barbarians are behind Duncan's forces! They're attacking now!'

Morgarath smiled back at the young man. His eyes were renowned for their keenness. 'You're sure?' he asked, in his thin, flat voice. The black-clad lieutenant nodded confidently.

'I can make out their ridiculous horned helmets and their round shields, my lord. No other warriors carry them.'

This was the truth. While some of the Kingdom's forces did use round bucklers, the Skandians' shields were enormous affairs, made of hardwood studded with metal. They were over a metre in diameter and only the huge Skandians, heavily muscled from rowing their wolfships across the winter seas, could bear such heavy shields in a battle for any length of time.

'Look, my lord!' the young man continued. 'The enemy are turning to face them!'

And so they appeared to be. The front ranks of the army facing them were now milling in confusion and turning about. The shouting and noise rose in pitch. Morgarath looked to his right, and saw the small hill where the King's standard marked the enemy command post. Mounted figures were pointing, facing the north.

He smiled once more. Even without the forces from across the Fissure bridge, his plan would be successful. He had Duncan's forces trapped between the hammer of the Skandians and the anvil of his own Wargals.

'Advance,' he said softly. Then, as the herald beside him didn't hear the words, he turned, his face expressionless, and whipped the man across the face with his leather-covered steel riding crop.

'Sound the advance,' he repeated, no more loudly than before. The Wargal, ignoring the agony of the whip cut, and the blood which poured down his forehead and into his eye, raised a horn to his lips and blew an ascending scale of four notes.

Along the lines of the Wargal army, company commanders stepped forward, one every hundred metres. They raised their curved swords, and called the first few sounds of the Wargal cadence. Like a mindless machine, the entire army took up the chant immediately — this one set at a slow jog pace — and began to move forward.

Morgarath allowed the first half dozen ranks to pass him, then he and his attendants urged their horses forward and moved with the army.

The Lord of Rain and Night felt his breath coming a little faster, his pulse beginning to accelerate. This was the moment he had planned and waited for over the past fifteen years. High in his windy, rainswept mountains, he had expanded his force of Wargals until they formed an army that no infantry could defeat. Without minds of their own, they were almost without fear. They were inexorable. They would suffer losses no other troops would bear and continue to advance.

They had only one weakness and that was facing cavalry. The high mountains were no place for horses and he had been unable to condition their minds to stand against mounted soldiers. He knew that he would lose many of his own troops to Duncan's cavalry but he cared little about that. In a normal confrontation, the King's cavalry would be a decisive factor in their battle. Now, however, split between the Wargals and the attacking Skandians, their numbers would be insufficient to stop him. He accepted the fact that Duncan's cavalry would cause immense losses among his troops without a qualm. He cared nothing for his army, only for his own desires and plans.

The dust rose from the thousands of jogging feet. The chant surrounded him, a primal rhythm of hatred and implacable evil. He began to laugh. Softly at first, then the laughter became increasingly louder and wilder. This was his day. This was his moment. This was his destiny.

Black-hearted, thoroughly evil and pitiless, he was the Lord of Rain and Night. He was also, unmistakably, insane.

'Faster!' he cried, sliding his huge broadsword from its scabbard and wielding it in gigantic circles over his head. The Wargals didn't need to hear the word. They were bound to him in an unbreakable linkage of minds. The cadence of the chant increased and the black army began to move faster and faster.

In front all was confusion. The enemy, first turning to face the Skandians, now saw the new threat developing at their rear. They hesitated, then, for some unaccountable reason, they responded to three horn blasts by drawing to either side, opening a gap in the heart of their line. Morgarath screamed his triumph. He would drive his army into the gap, separating the left and right wings of the army. Once an army's front line was broken, it lost all cohesion and control and was more than halfway defeated. Now, in their panic, the enemy were presenting him with the perfect opportunity to strike deep into their hearts. They had even left the way open to their own command centre — the small group of horsemen standing under the royal standard on a hill.

'To the right!' Morgarath screamed, pointing his sword towards King Duncan's eagle standard. As before, the Wargals heard the words and his thought in their minds. The army wheeled slightly, heading for the gap. And now, through the chanting, Morgarath heard a dull drumming sound. An unexpected sound.

Hoofbeats.

The sudden doubt in his mind communicated instantly to the minds of his army. The advance faltered for a moment. Then, cursing the Wargals, he drove them forward again. But the hoofbeats were still there and now, peering through the clouds of dust raised by the enemy army, he could see movement. He felt a sudden, overpowering surge of fear and again the Wargal army hesitated.

And this time, before he could mentally flail them forward, the curtains of dust seemed to part and a wedge of charging cavalry burst into sight, less than a hundred metres from his army's front line.

There was no time to form into the sort of defensive square that was infantry's only hope against a cavalry attack. The armoured wedge smashed into the extended front line of the Wargals, collapsing the formation and driving into the heart of Morgarath's army. And the further they penetrated, the wider the gap became, as the wedge shape split and separated the Wargals, just as Morgarath had been planning to do to his enemy. Now Morgarath heard one long rising horn blast in the distance. Standing high in the stirrups, he cast his glance left and right, and saw, from either wing of Duncan's army, more cavalry deploying, driving in on his flanks, smashing his formations. Dimly, he realised that he had exposed his army to the worst possible situation that he could have contrived: caught in the open by the full force of Duncan's cavalry.

The Wargals were facing the only sort of force that could strike fear in their hearts. Morgarath felt the flicker of defeat in their dull mind waves. He tried to force them on mentally, but the barrier of fear was too strongly embedded with them. Screaming his fury, he directed them to retreat. Then he wheeled his horse and, with his remaining henchmen, galloped back through his army, clearing a path with his sword as he went.

At Three Step Pass, there was a hopeless tangle as thousands of the rearguard tried to force their way through the narrow gap in the rocks. There would be no escape for him there — but escape was the last thought on his mind. His only wish now was for revenge against the people who had brought his plans crashing into the dust. He drew his remaining troops into a defensive half circle, their backs to the sheer rocks that barred the way to the high plateau.

Seething in fury and frustration, he tried to make sense of what had just happened. The Skandian attack had melted away as if it were never there. And then he realised that it never had been. The soldiers advancing down from the ridge wore Skandian helmets and carried Skandian shields but it had been a ruse to draw him forward. The fact that they had the helmets and shields meant that, somewhere, Horth's forces had been defeated. That could only have been accomplished if someone had led an intercepting force throughout the impenetrable tangle of the Thorntree Forest.

Someone?

Deep in his mind, Morgarath knew who that someone was. He didn't know how he knew. Or why. He knew it had to be a Ranger and there was only one Ranger who would have done it.

Halt.

Dark, bitter hatred surged in his heart. Because of Halt, his fifteen-year dream was crumbling before his eyes. Because of Halt, fully half of his Wargal soldiers were lying broken in the dust of the battlefield.

The day was lost, he knew. But he would have his revenge on Halt. And he was beginning to see the way. He turned to one of his captains.

'Prepare a flag of truce,' he said.

Twenty-nine

The Kingdom's main army advanced slowly across the littered battlefield. The crushing attacks by the cavalry on three sides had given them a decisive victory in the space of a few short minutes.

In the second line of the command party, Horace rode beside Sir Rodney. The Battlemaster had selected Horace as his shield man, riding on his left side, in recognition of his service to the Kingdom. It was a rare honour for someone in his first battle, but Sir Rodney thought the boy had more than deserved it.

Horace viewed the battlefield with mixed emotions. On the one hand, he was vaguely disappointed that, so far, he had not been called upon to play a part. On the other, he felt a profound sense of relief. The reality of battle was far removed from the glamorous dreams he had entertained as a boy. He had pictured a battle like this as a series of carefully co-ordinated, almost choreographed, actions involving skilful warriors performing brave acts of chivalry. Needless to say, in those dreams, the most prominent and chivalrous warrior on the field had been Horace himself.

Instead, he had watched in some horror the stabbing, hacking, shoving brawl of blood and dust and screams that had developed before him. Men and Wargals and horses had all died and their bodies sprawled now in the dust of the Plains of Uthal like so many scattered rag dolls. It had been fast and violent and confused. He glanced now at Sir Rodney. The Battlemaster's grim face told him that it was always this way.

Horace's throat was dry and he tried to ease it by swallowing. He felt a sudden stab of doubt. He wondered, if he were called upon to fight, whether he would simply freeze in fear. For the first time in his life, it had been driven home to him that people actually died in battles. And this time, he could be one of those people. He tried to swallow again. This attempt was no more successful than the last.

Morgarath and his remaining soldiers were in a defensive formation at the base of the cliffs. The soft ground held the cavalry back and there was no option but to take the infantry forward and finish the job in bloody hand-to-hand fighting.

Any normal enemy commander would have seen the inevitable result by now and surrendered to spare the lives of his remaining troops. But this was Morgarath and they knew there would be no negotiating. They steeled themselves for the ugly task ahead of them. It would be a bloody and senseless fight, but there was no alternative. Once and for all, Morgarath's power must be broken.

'Nevertheless,' said Duncan grimly, as his front rank stopped a bare hundred metres from the Wargals' defensive half circle, 'we'll give him the chance to surrender.' He drew breath, about to order his trumpeter to sound the signal for a parley, when there was movement at the front rank of the Wargal army.

'Sir!' said Gilan suddenly. 'They have a flag of truce!'

The Kingdom's leaders looked in surprise as the white flag was unfurled, carried by a Wargal foot soldier. He stepped forward into the clear ground. From deep within the Wargal ranks came a horn signal, five ascending notes – the universal signal that requested a parley. King Duncan made a small gesture of surprise, hesitated, then signalled to his own trumpeter.

'I suppose we'd better hear what he has to say,' he said. 'Give the reply.'

The trumpeter moistened his lips and blew the acceptance in reply – the same notes in reverse order.

'It will be some kind of trick,' said Halt grimly. 'Morgarath will send a herald to talk while he's making his escape. He'll . . .'

His voice tailed off as the Wargal ranks parted once more and a figure rode forward. Immensely tall and thin, clad in black armour and a beaked black helmet, it was, unmistakably, Morgarath himself. Halt's right hand went instinctively to the quiver slung at his back and, within a second, a heavy, armour-piercing arrow was laid on his bowstring.

King Duncan saw the movement.

'Halt,' he said sharply, 'I've agreed to a truce. You'll not cause me to break my word, even to Morgarath.'

The trumpet signal was a pledge of safety and Halt reluctantly returned the arrow to his quiver. Duncan made quick eye contact with Baron Arald, signalling him to keep a close eye on the Ranger. Halt shrugged. If he chose to put an arrow into Morgarath's heart, neither Baron Arald nor anyone else would be quick enough to stop him.

Slowly, the vulturine figure on the white horse paced forward, his Wargal standard bearer before him. A low murmur rose among the Kingdom's army as men saw, for the first time, the man who for the past fifteen years had been a constant threat to their lives and wellbeing. Morgarath stopped a mere thirty metres from their front rank. He could see the royal party where they had moved forward to meet him. His eyes narrowed as he caught sight of the small figure hunched in a grey cloak on a shaggy pony.

'Duncan!' he called, his thin voice carrying through the sudden silence. ' I claim my rights!'

'You have no rights, Morgarath,' the King replied. 'You're a rebel and a traitor and a murderer. Surrender now and your men will be spared. That's the only right I will grant you.'

'I claim the right of trial by single combat!' Morgarath shouted back, ignoring the King's words. Then he continued contemptuously, 'Or are you too cowardly to accept a challenge, Duncan? Will you let thousands more of your men die while you hide behind them? Or will you let fate decide the issue here?'

For a moment, Duncan was caught off guard. Morgarath waited, smiling quietly to himself. He could guess at the thoughts running through the minds of the King and his advisers. He had offered them a course of action that might spare the lives of thousands of their soldiers.

Arald moved his horse alongside the King's and said angrily: 'He has no claim to a knight's privileges. He deserves hanging. Nothing more.' Some of the others muttered agreement.

'And yet . . .' said Halt quietly, and they all turned to look at him. 'This could solve the problem facing us. The Wargals are mind-bound to Morgarath's will. Now that we can't use cavalry, they'll continue to fight as long as he wills them to. And they'll kill thousands of our men in the process. But, if Morgarath were killed in single combat —'

Tyler interrupted, finishing the thought: 'The Wargals would be without direction. Chances are they would simply stop fighting.'

Duncan frowned uncertainly. 'We don't know that . . .' he began.

Sir David of Caraway interrupted. 'Surely, sir, it's worth a try. Morgarath has outsmarted himself here, I think. He knows we can't resist the chance to end this on a single combat. He's thrown the dice today and lost. But he obviously plans to challenge you — to kill you as a final act of revenge.'

'What's your point?' Duncan asked.

'As Royal Battlemaster, I can respond to any challenge made to you, my lord.'

There was a brief murmur at this. Morgarath might be a dangerous opponent, but Sir David was the foremost tournament knight of the Kingdom. Like his son, he had trained with the fabled swordmaster MacNeil, and his skill in single combat was legendary. He continued eagerly.

'Morgarath is using the rules of knighthood to gain a chance to kill you, sir. Obviously, he's overlooked the fact that, as King, you can be represented by a champion. Give him the right to challenge. And then let me accept.'

Duncan considered the idea. He looked to his advisers and saw grudging agreement. Abruptly, he made up his mind.

'All right,' he said finally. 'I'll accept his right to challenge. But nobody, nobody, says anything in acceptance. Only me. Is that clear?'

His council nodded agreement. Once acceptance was made, it was binding. Duncan stood in his stirrups and called to the ominous black figure.

'Morgarath,' Duncan called, 'although we believe you have forfeited any rights you may have had as a knight, go ahead and make your challenge. As you say, let fate decide the issue.'

Now Morgarath allowed the smile to creep over his entire face, no longer trying to conceal it from those who watched him. He felt a quick surge of triumph in his chest, then a cold wash of hatred swept over him as he looked directly at the small, insignificant-looking figure behind the King.

'Then, as is my right before God,' he said carefully, making sure he used the exact, ancient words of challenge, 'and before all here present, I do so make my challenge to prove my cause right and just to . . .' He couldn't help hesitating and savouring the moment for a second. 'Halt the Ranger.'

There was a stunned silence. Then, as Halt urged Abelard forward to respond, Duncan's penetrating cry of 'No!' stopped him. His eyes glittered fiercely.

'I'll take my chance, my lord,' he said grimly. But Duncan threw out an arm to stop him moving forward.

'Halt is not a knight. You cannot challenge him,' he called urgently. Morgarath shrugged.

'Actually, Duncan, I can challenge anyone. And anyone can challenge me. As a knight, I don't have to accept any challenge, unless it is issued by another knight. But I can choose to do so. And I can choose whom I challenge.'

'Halt is forbidden to accept!' Duncan said angrily.

Morgarath laughed thinly. 'Still slinking and hiding then, Halt?' he sneered. 'Like all Rangers. Did I mention that we have one of your Ranger brats as a prisoner?' He knew the Ranger Corps was a close-knit group and he hoped to infuriate Halt with the news that he had captured one of their trainees. 'So small we nearly threw him back. But I've decided to keep him for torture instead. That will make one less sneaking, hiding spy in the future.'

Halt felt the blood draining from his face. There was only one person Morgarath could be talking about. In a fury, he urged Abelard forward.

'You've got Will?' he asked, his voice quiet, but penetrating.

Morgarath felt that shock of triumph again. Even better than he thought! Obviously the Ranger brat was close to Halt. A sudden feeling of elation filled him. Could he possibly be apprenticed to Halt himself? Suddenly, somehow, he knew this was the truth.

'Yes, Will is with us,' he replied. 'But not for long, of course.'

Halt felt a red surge of rage and hatred for the vulture-like figure before him. Hands reached out to stop him but he shoved his horse forward, facing Morgarath.

'Then, Morgarath, yes, I . . .'

'Halt! I command you to stop!' Duncan shouted, drowning him out.

But then all eyes were drawn to a sudden movement from the second rank of the army. A mounted figure burst clear, covering the short distance to Morgarath in a heartbeat. The Lord of Rain and Night reached for his sword, then realised the newcomer's own weapon was sheathed. Instead, his right arm drew back and he hurled his gauntlet into Morgarath's thin face.

'Morgarath!' he yelled, his young voice cracking. 'I challenge you to single combat!'

Then, wheeling his horse a few paces away, Horace waited for Morgarath's reply.

Thirty

ill and Evanlyn never learned what it was that caused the wave of uncertainty in the Wargals who surrounded their small group. In fact, it happened at the moment when Morgarath realised he had been tricked into exposing his army to Duncan's cavalry. The sudden frisson of fear that ran through his mind communicated itself instantly to all of his mind slaves.

The two captives, and the four Skandians, all noticed the sudden uneasiness and hesitancy in the twenty or so Wargal warriors who had been left to guard them. Erak glanced quickly at his men, sensing an opportunity. So far, they had not been disarmed. The odds of four against twenty were too much even for Skandians and the Wargals had only been told to detain them, not disarm them.

'Something's happening,' the Skandian jarl muttered. 'Stay ready, everyone.'

Unobtrusively, the small party made sure their weapons were free and ready for action. Then the moment of uncertainty turned to real, palpable fear among the Wargals. Morgarath had just signalled a general retreat and those at the rear didn't distinguish themselves from the front-line troops for whom the order was intended. Over half of the Wargals guarding them simply ran. One sergeant, however, retained a vestige of independent thought and he growled a warning to his section — eight in total. As their companions struggled and fought to make their way into the jam-packed entrance to Three Step Pass, the remaining eight black-clad troops held their position.

But they were distracted and nervous and Erak decided that the opportunity wouldn't get any better than this.

'Now, lads!' he yelled, and swept his double-headed axe in a low horizontal arc at the sergeant. The Wargal tried to bring his iron spear up in defence but he was a fraction too slow. The heavy axe sheared through his armour and he went down.

As Erak sought another opponent, his men fell on the rest of the Wargal troop. They chose the moment when another mind command went out from Morgarath for his men to withdraw and form a defensive position. The confusing orders in their minds made them easy targets for the Skandians and they fell in short order. The others around them, intent on escaping to Three Step Pass, took no notice of the brief and bloody skirmish.

Erak looked around him with some satisfaction, wiping his axe blade clean on a cloth he'd taken from one of the dead Wargals.

'That's better,' he said heartily. 'I've been wanting to do that for days.'

But the Wargals hadn't left their group unscathed. As he spoke, Nordel staggered and sank slowly to one knee. Bright blood stained the corner of his mouth and he looked hopelessly at his leader. Erak moved to his side and dropped to his knees.

'Nordel!' he cried. 'Where are you wounded?'

But Nordel could barely talk. He was grasping his right side, where the sheepskin vest was already heavily stained with his blood. The heavy sword he favoured as a weapon had fallen from his grip. His eyes wide with fear, he tried to reach it, but it was beyond his grasp. Quickly, Horak scooped up the weapon and put it in his hand. Nordel nodded his thanks, and slowly let himself drop to a sitting position. The fear was gone from his eyes now. Will knew that Skandians believed a man must die with his weapon in hand if his soul were not to wander in torment for eternity. Now that he had his sword firmly in his grasp, Nordel was not afraid to die. Weakly, he waved them away.

'Go!' he said, finally finding his voice. 'I'm . . . finished . . . Get to the ships.'

Erak nodded quickly. 'He's right,' he said, straightening up from beside his friend. 'There's nothing we can do for him.' The others nodded and Erak grabbed first Will and then Evanlyn and shoved them along in front of him.

'Come on, you two,' he said roughly. 'Unless you want to stay here till Morgarath gets back.'

And, moving together in a tight little group, the five of them shoved their way through the milling crowd of Wargals, all trying to move in the opposite direction.

Morgarath was stung by the impact of the heavy leather glove on his face. Furious, he turned to stare at the challenger who had ruined his plan. Then he allowed that thin smile to spread over his face once more.

His challenger was no more than a boy, he realised. Big, certainly, and muscular. But the fresh face under the simple conical helmet couldn't have been more than sixteen years old.

Before the startled members of the King's council could react, he replied swiftly.

'I accept the challenge!'

He was a second ahead of Duncan's furious cry: 'No! I forbid it!' Realising he was too late, he appealed to Morgarath. 'For pity's sake, Morgarath, he's only a boy, as you can see. An apprentice. You can't accept his challenge!'

'On the contrary,' Morgarath replied, 'as I've just pointed out, I have that right. And, as you know, once a challenge is given and accepted, there can be no withdrawal.'

He was right, of course. The strict rules of chivalry and knighthood, by which they had all sworn solemn oaths to be bound, did decree just that. Morgarath smiled now at the boy beside him. He would make short work of him. And the boy's quick death would serve to infuriate Halt even more.

Halt, meanwhile, watched the Lord of Rain and Night through slitted eyes.

'Morgarath, you're already a dead man,' he muttered.

Halt felt a firm hand on his arm and he turned to look into Sir David's grim eyes. The Battlemaster had his sword drawn and resting over his right shoulder.

'The boy will have to take his chances, Halt,' he said.

'His chances? He has no chance!' Halt replied.

Sir David acknowledged the fact sadly. 'Be that as it may. You can't interfere in this combat. I'll stop you if I even think you're going to try. Don't make me do that. We've been friends far too long.'

He held Halt's angry gaze for a few seconds, then the Ranger agreed bitterly. He knew the knight wasn't bluffing. The codes of chivalry meant everything to him.

The byplay hadn't been lost on Morgarath. He was confident that the moment the boy fell, Halt would accept his original challenge, King's orders or no King's orders. And then, at least, Morgarath would know the satisfaction of killing his old, hated enemy before his own world came crashing down around him.

He turned now to Horace.

'What weapons, boy?' he said in an insulting tone. 'How do you choose to fight?'

Horace's face was white and strained with fear. For a moment, his voice was trapped inside his throat. He wasn't sure what had come over him when he'd galloped forward and issued his challenge. It certainly wasn't something he'd planned. A red rage had seemed to overtake him and he had found himself out here in front of the entire army, throwing his gauntlet into Morgarath's startled face. Then he thought of Morgarath's threat to Will, and how he'd been forced to leave his friend at the bridge and he managed, at last, to speak.

'As we are,' he said. Both of them carried swords. In addition, Morgarath's long, kite-shaped shield hung at his saddle and Horace carried his round buckler slung on his back. But Morgarath's sword was a two-handed broad-sword, nearly a foot longer than the standard cavalry sword Horace carried. Morgarath turned now to call once more to Duncan.

'The whelp chooses to fight as we are. You'll stand by the rules of conduct, I assume, Duncan?' he said.

'You'll fight unmolested,' Duncan agreed in a bitter tone. Those were the rules of single combat.

Morgarath nodded and made a mocking bow in the King's direction.

'Just be sure that murderous Ranger Halt understands that,' he said, continuing his plan of driving Halt to a cold fury. 'I know he has little knowledge of the rules of knighthood and chivalry.'

'Morgarath,' said Duncan coldly, 'don't try to pretend that what you're doing has any connection with real chivalry. I ask you one more time, spare the boy's life.'

Morgarath feigned a surprised expression. 'Spare him, your majesty? He's a lump of a boy, big for his age. Who knows, you might be better served asking him to spare me?'

'If you must persist with murder, that's your choice, Morgarath. But save us your sarcasm,' said Duncan. Again Morgarath made that mocking bow. Then he said casually, over his shoulder, to Horace:

'Are you ready, boy?'

Horace swallowed once, then nodded.

'Yes,' he said.

It was Gilan who saw what was coming and managed to shout a warning, just in time. The huge broadsword had snaked out of its scabbard with incredible speed and

Morgarath swung it backhanded at the boy beside him. Warned by the shout, Horace rolled to one side, the blade hissing centimetres above his head.

In the same movement, Morgarath had set spurs to his dead-white horse and was galloping away, reaching for his shield and settling it on his left arm. His mocking laughter carried back to Horace as the boy recovered.

'Then let's get started!' he laughed and Horace felt his throat go dry as he realised he was now fighting for his life.

Thirty-one

Morgarath was wheeling his horse in a wide circle to gain room. Horace knew that he'd swing round soon and charge down on him, using the momentum of his charge as much as the force of his sword to try to strike him from the saddle.

Guiding his horse with his knees, he swung away in the opposite direction, shrugging his buckler round from where it hung on his back and slipping his left arm through the straps. He glanced over his shoulder and saw Morgarath, eighty metres away, spurring his horse forward in a charge. Horace clapped his heels into his own horse's ribs and swung him back to face the black-clad figure.

The two sets of hoofbeats overlapped, merged, then overlapped once more as the riders thundered towards each other. Knowing his opponent had the advantage of reach, Horace determined to let him strike the first blow, then attempt a counterstrike as they passed. They were nearly on each other now and Morgarath suddenly rose in his stirrups and, from his full height, swung an overhand blow at the boy. Horace, expecting the move, threw up his shield.

The power behind Morgarath's blow was devastating. The sword had Morgarath's immense height, the strength of his arm and the momentum of his galloping horse behind it. Timing it to perfection, he had channelled all those separate forces and focused them into his sword as it cleaved down. Horace had never in his life felt such destructive force. Those watching winced at the ringing crash of sword on shield and they saw Horace sway under the mighty stroke, almost knocked clean from his saddle on the first pass.

All thought of a counterstrike was gone now. It was all he could do to regain his saddle as his horse skittered away, dancing sideways as Morgarath's mount, trained for battle, lashed out with its rear hooves.

Horace's left arm, his shield arm, was rendered completely numb by the terrible force of the blow. He shrugged it repeatedly as he rode away, moving the arm in small circles to try to regain some feeling. Finally, he felt a dull ache there that seemed to stretch the entire length of the limb. Now he knew real fear. He knew no way to counter the crushing force of Morgarath's sword strokes. He realised that all his training, all his practice, was nothing compared to Morgarath's years and years of experience.

He wheeled to face Morgarath and rode in again. On the first pass, they had met shield to shield. This time, he saw his opponent was angling to pass on his right side – his sword arm side – and he realised that the next shattering blow would not land on his shield. He would have to parry with his own sword. His mouth was dry as he galloped forward, trying desperately to remember what Gilan had taught him.

But Gilan had never prepared him to face such over-powering strength. He knew he couldn't take the risk of gripping his sword lightly and tightening at the moment of impact. His knuckles whitened on the hilt of his sword and, suddenly, Morgarath was upon him and the massive broadsword swung in a glittering arc at his head. Horace threw up his own sword to parry, just in time.

The mighty crash and slithering scream of steel on steel set the watchers' nerves jangling. Again, Horace reeled in the saddle from the force of the blow. His right arm was numb from fingertip to elbow. He knew that he would have to break out of this cycle of battering blows. But he couldn't think how.

He heard hoofbeats close behind and, turning, realised that this time, Morgarath hadn't gone on to gain ground for another charge. Instead, he had wheeled his horse almost immediately, sacrificing the extra force gained in the charge for the sake of a fast follow-up attack. The broadsword swung back again.

Horace reared his horse onto its hind legs, spinning it in place, and taking Morgarath's sword on his shield once more. This time, the force behind it was a little less devastating, but not by much. Horace cut twice at the black lord, forehand and backhand. His smaller, lighter sword was faster to wield than the mighty broadsword, but his right arm was still numb from the parry and his strokes had little power behind them. Morgarath deflected them easily, almost contemptuously, with his shield then cut again at Horace, overhand this time, standing in his stirrups for extra purchase.

Once again, Horace's shield took the force of the sword stroke. The circular piece of steel was bent almost double by the two massive strokes it had taken. Much more of this and it would be virtually useless to him, he realised. He spurred his horse away from Morgarath, scrambling to remain mounted.

His breath was coming in rapid gasps and sweat covered his face. It was as much the sweat of fear as of exertion, he knew. He shook his head desperately to clear his vision. Morgarath was riding in again. Horace changed his direction at the last moment, dragging his horse's head to the left, taking him across the path of Morgarath's charging horse as he tried to evade that huge sword. Morgarath saw it coming and changed to a backhand stroke, crashing it onto the rim of Horace's shield.

The broadsword bit deep into the steel of the shield, then caught there. Seizing the moment, Horace stood in his stirrups and cut overhand at Morgarath. The black shield came up just a fraction too late and Horace's blow glanced off the black, beaked helmet. He felt the shock of it up his arm but this time, the jarring felt good. He cut again as Morgarath wrenched and heaved to remove his sword.

This time, Morgarath caught the blow on his shield. But for the first time, Horace managed to put some authority behind the stroke and the Lord of Rain and Night grunted as he was rocked in his saddle. His shield dropped fractionally.

Now Horace used the shorter blade of his sword to lunge at the gap that had opened between shield and body and drove the point at Morgarath's ribs. For a moment, those watching felt a brief flare of hope. But the black armour held against the thrust, which was delivered from a cramped position and had little force behind it. Nonetheless, it hurt Morgarath, cracking a rib behind the mail armour, and he cursed in pain and jerked at his caught sword once more.

And then, disaster!

Weakened by the crushing blows Morgarath had struck at it earlier, Horace's shield simply gave way. The huge sword tore free at last, and as it went, it ripped loose the leather straps that held the shield on Horace's arm. The battered, misshapen shield came free and spun away into the air. Horace reeled in the saddle again, desperately trying to retain his balance. Too close to use the full length of his blade, Morgarath slammed the double-handed hilt of the sword into the side of the boy's helmet and the onlookers groaned in dismay as Horace fell from his saddle.

His foot caught in the stirrup and he was dragged for twenty metres or so behind his terrified, galloping horse. Oddly enough, that fact probably saved his life, as he was carried clear of the murderous reach of the broadsword. Finally managing to kick himself free, he rolled in the dust, his sword still grasped in his right hand.

Staggering, he regained his feet, his eyes full of sweat and dust. Dimly, he saw Morgarath bearing down on him again. Gripping his sword with both hands, he blocked the downward cut of the huge sword, but was beaten to his knees by the force of it. A flailing rear hoof took him in the ribs and he went down in the dust again as Morgarath galloped clear.

A hush had fallen over the watchers. The Wargals were unmoved by the spectacle, but the Kingdom's army watched the one-sided contest in silent horror. The end was inevitable, they all knew.

Slowly, painfully, Horace climbed to his feet once more. Morgarath wheeled his horse and set himself for another charge. Horace watched him coming, knowing that this contest could have only one possible result. A desperate idea was forming in his mind as the dead-white battlehorse thundered towards him, heading to his right, leaving Morgarath room to strike down with his sword. Horace had no idea whether or not his armour would protect him from what he had in mind. He could be killed. Then, dully, he laughed at himself. He was going to be killed anyway.

He tensed himself, ready. The horse was almost upon him now, swerving away to his right to leave Morgarath striking room. In the last few metres, Horace hurled himself to the right after it, deliberately throwing himself under the horse's front hooves.

A great, wordless cry went up from the onlookers as, for a moment, the scene was obscured by a cloud of roiling dust. Horace felt a hoof strike him in the back, between the shoulder blades, then saw a brief red flash as another slammed into his helmet, breaking the strap and knocking it from his head. Then he was hit more times than he could count and the world was a blur of pain and dust and, most of all, noise.

Unprepared for his suicidal action, the horse tried desperately to avoid him. Its forelegs crossed and it stumbled, then somersaulted in a tangle of legs and body into the dust. Morgarath, managing to kick clear of the stirrups just in time, was hurled over the horse's neck and crashed to the ground. The broadsword fell from his grasp.

Screaming in rage and fear, the white horse struggled to its feet again. It kicked one more time at the prone figure that had brought it down, then trotted away. Horace grunted with pain and tried to stand. He came to his knees and, vaguely, he heard the swelling cheers of the watching army.

Then the cheers gradually died away as the still, black-clad figure a few metres away also began to move.

Morgarath was winded, nothing more. He dragged in a vast lungful of air and stood. He looked around, saw the broadsword lying half buried in the dust and moved to retrieve it. Horace's heart sank as the tall figure, outlined now against the low afternoon sun, began to advance on him, one long stride at a time. Desperately, Horace retrieved his own sword and scrambled to his feet. Morgarath had discarded his triangular black shield. Holding the sword in a two-handed grip, he advanced. Horace, pain racking every inch of his body, stood firm to meet him.

Again came that nerve-jangling, screeching clash of steel. Morgarath rained blow after blow down on Horace's sword. Desperately, the apprentice warrior parried and blocked. But with each massive blow, his arms were losing their strength. He began to back away but still Morgarath came on, beating down Horace's defence with blow after shattering blow.

And then, as Horace allowed the point of his sword to drop, unable to find the strength to keep it up anymore, Morgarath's huge broadsword whistled down one more time, smashing onto the smaller sword and snapping the blade into two pieces.

He stepped back, a cruel smile on his face, as Horace stared dumbly at the shorn-off blade in his right hand.

'I think we're nearly finished now,' Morgarath said in that soft, toneless voice. Horace still looked at the useless sword. Almost unconsciously, his left hand reached for his dagger and slid it from its sheath. Morgarath saw the movement and laughed.

'I don't think that will do you much good,' he sneered. Then, deliberately, he took the great broadsword up and back for a final, mighty overhand blow that would cleave Horace to the waist.

It was Gilan who realised what was going to happen, a second before it did.

'Oh my God, he's going to . . .' he said slowly and felt a ridiculous surge of hope.

The broadsword began its downward arc, splitting the air. And now Horace, throwing everything into one final effort, stepped forward, crossing the two blades he held, the dagger supporting the shortened sword.

The locked blades took the impact of Morgarath's mighty stroke. But Horace had stepped close to the taller man, and so reduced the leverage of the long blade and the force of the blow. Morgarath's sword clanged into the X formed by the two blades.

Horace's knees buckled then held and, for a moment, Morgarath and he stood locked, chest to chest. Horace could see the puzzled fury on the madman's face as he wondered how this situation had come about. Then the fury turned to surprise and Morgarath felt a deep, burning agony pour through his body as Horace slipped the dagger free and, with every ounce of his strength behind it, drove it through Morgarath's chain mail and up into his heart.

Slowly, the Lord of Rain and Night sagged and crumpled to the ground.

Stunned silence gripped the onlookers for a good ten seconds. Then the cheering started.

Thirty-two

What had, a few minutes before, been a battlefield now became a confusion. The Wargal army, released in an instant from Morgarath's mind control, now milled mindlessly about, waiting for some force to tell them what to do next. All sense of aggression had left them and most of them simply dropped their weapons and wandered off. Others sat down and sang quietly to themselves. Without Morgarath's direction they were like little children.

The group struggling to escape up Three Step Pass now stood mute and unmoving, waiting patiently for those at the front to clear the way.

Duncan surveyed the scene in bewilderment.

'We'll need an army of sheepdogs to round up this lot,' he said to Baron Arald, and his councillor smiled in reply.

'Better that than what we faced, my lord,' he said and Duncan had to agree.

The small inner circle of Morgarath's lieutenants were a different matter. Some had been captured, but others had fled into the wastelands of the fens. Crowley, the Ranger Corps Commandant, shook his head, as he realised that he and his men faced many long hard days in the saddle after this. He would have to assign a Ranger task force to hunt down Morgarath's lieutenants and bring them back to face the King's justice. It was always this way, he thought wryly. While everyone else could sit back and relax, the Rangers' work continued, nonstop.

Horace, bruised, battered and bleeding, had been taken to the King's own tent for treatment. He was badly injured after his insane leap under the Battlehorse's hooves. There were several broken bones and he was bleeding from one ear. But amazingly, none of the injuries were critical and the King's own healer, who had examined him immediately, was confident that he would make a full recovery.

Sir Rodney had hurried up to the litter as the bearers were preparing to carry the boy off the field. His moustache bristled with fury as he stood over his apprentice.

'What the hell did you think you were doing?' he roared, and Horace winced. 'Who told you to challenge Morgarath? You're nothing but an apprentice, boy, and a damned disobedient one at that!'

Horace wondered if the shouting was going to continue for much longer. If it were, he could almost wish to be back facing Morgarath. He was dazed and sick and dizzy and Sir Rodney's angry, red face swam in and out of focus in front of him. The Battlemaster's words seemed to bounce from one side of his skull to the other and back again and he wasn't sure why he was yelling so much. Maybe

Morgarath was still alive, he thought groggily and, as the thought struck him, he tried to get up.

Instantly, Rodney's glare faded and his expression changed to one of concern. He gently stopped the wounded apprentice from rising. Then he reached down and gripped the boy's hand in a firm grasp.

'Rest, boy,' he said. 'You've done enough today. You've done well.'

Meanwhile, Halt shoved his way through the harmless Wargals. They gave way without any resistance or resentment as he searched desperately for Will.

But there was no sign of the boy, nor of the King's daughter. Once they had heard Morgarath's taunt, they had realised that if Will were still alive, there was a chance that Cassandra, as Evanlyn was really called, might have survived as well. The fact that Morgarath hadn't mentioned her indicated that her identity had remained a secret. This, of course, Halt realised, was why she had assumed her maid's name. By doing so, she prevented Morgarath's knowing what a potential lever he had in his hands.

He pushed impatiently through another group of silent Wargals, then stopped as he heard a weak cry from one side.

A Skandian, barely alive, was sitting leaning against the bole of a tree. He had slumped down, his legs stretched straight in front of him in the dust, his head lolling weakly to one side. A huge stain of blood marked the side of his sheepskin vest. A heavy sword lay beside him, his hand too weak to hold it any longer.

He made a feeble scrabbling gesture towards it and his eyes beseeched Halt to help him. Nordel, growing weaker by the moment, had allowed his grasp on the sword to release. Now, weak and almost blinded, he couldn't find it and he knew he was close to death. Halt knelt beside him. He could see there was no potential danger in the man; he was too far gone for any treachery. He took the sword and placed it in the man's lap, putting his hands on the leather-bound hilt.

'Thanks . . . friend . . .' Nordel gasped weakly.

Halt nodded sadly. He admired the Skandians as warriors and it bothered him to see one laid as low as this — so weak that he couldn't maintain his grip on his sword. The Ranger knew what that meant to the sea raiders. He rose slowly and began to turn away, then stopped.

Horace had said that Will and Evanlyn had been taken by a small party of Skandians. Maybe this man knew something. He dropped to one knee again and put a hand on the man's face, turning it towards his own.

'The boy,' he said urgently, knowing he had only a few minutes. 'Where is he?'

Nordel frowned. The words struck a chord in his memory, but everything that had ever happened to him seemed such a long time ago and somehow unimportant.

'Boy,' he repeated thickly and Halt couldn't help himself. He shook the dying man.

'Will!' he said, his face only a few centimetres from the other's. 'A Ranger. A boy. Where is he?'

A small light of understanding and memory burned in Nordel's eyes now as he recalled the boy. He'd admired his courage, he remembered. Admired the way the boy had stood them off at the bridge. Without realising it, he actually said the last three words.

'At the bridge . . .' he whispered and Halt shook him again.

'Yes! The boy at the bridge! Where is he?'

Nordel looked up at him. There was something he had to remember. He knew it was important to this grim-faced stranger and he wanted to help. After all, the stranger had helped him find his sword again. He remembered what it was.

'. . . gone,' he managed finally. He wished the stranger wouldn't shake him. It caused him no pain at all, because he couldn't feel anything. But it kept waking him from the warm, soft sleep he was drifting into. The bearded face was a long way from him now, at the end of a tunnel. The voice echoed down the tunnel to him.

'Gone where?' He listened to the echo. He liked the echo. It reminded him of . . . something from his childhood.

'Where-where-where?' the echo came again and now he remembered.

'The fens,' he said. 'Through the fens to the ships.'

He smiled when he said it. He'd wanted to help the stranger and he had. And this time, when the warm softness crept over him, the stranger didn't shake him. He was glad about that.

Halt stood up from the body of Nordel.

'Thank you, friend,' he said simply. Then he ran to where he'd left Abelard grazing quietly and vaulted into the saddle.

The fens were a tangle of head-high grasses, swamps and winding passages of clear water. To most people, they were impassable. An incautious step could lead to a person sinking quickly into the oozing mire of quicksand that lurked on every side. Once in the featureless marshes, it was easy to become hopelessly lost and to wander until exhaustion overcame you, or the venomous water snakes that thrived here found you unawares.

Wise people avoided the fens. Only two groups knew the secret paths through them: the Rangers and the Skandians, who had been raiding along this coastline for as long as Halt could remember.

Sure-footed as Ranger horses were, once Halt was truly into the tangle of tall grass and swampland, he dismounted and led Abelard. The signs of the safe path were minute and easy to miss and he needed to be close to the ground to follow them. He hadn't been travelling long when he began to see signs that a party had come before him and his spirits lifted. It had to be the rest of the Skandians, with Will and Evanlyn.

He quickened his pace and promptly paid the consequences for doing so, missing a path marker and ending chest deep in a thick mass of bottomless mud. Fortunately, he still had a firm grip on Abelard's reins and, at a word of command, the stocky horse dragged him clear of the danger.

It was another good reason to continue leading the horse behind him, he realised.

He backtracked to the path, found his bearings and set out again. In spite of his seething impatience, he forced himself to go carefully. The marks left by the party in front of him were becoming more and more recent. He knew he was catching them. The question was whether he would catch them in time.

Mosquitoes and marsh flies hummed and whined around him. Without a breath of breeze, it was stiflingly hot in the marshes and he was sweating freely. His clothes were soaked and sodden with stinking mud and he'd lost one boot as Abelard had hauled him out of the quicksand. Nevertheless, he limped on, coming closer and closer to his quarry with every sodden step.

At the same time, he knew, he was coming closer and closer to the end of the fenlands. And that meant the beach where the Skandian ships lay at anchor. He had to find Will before the Skandians reached the beach. Once Will was on one of their wolfships, he would be gone forever, taken back across the Stormwhite Sea to the cold, snow-bound land of the Skandians, where he would be sold as a slave, to lead a life of drudgery and unending labour.

Now, above the rotting smell of the marshes, he caught the fresh scent of salt air. He was close to the sea! He redoubled his efforts, throwing caution to the wind as he chanced everything to catch up with the Skandians before they reached the water.

The grass was thinning in front of him now and the ground beneath his feet became firmer with every step. He was running, the horse trotting behind him, and he burst clear onto the windswept length of the beach.

A small ridge in the dunes in front of him blocked the sea from his sight and he swung up into Abelard's saddle on the run and set the horse to a gallop. They swept over the ridge, the Ranger leaning forward, low on his horse's neck, urging him to greater speed.

There was a wolfship anchored off shore. At the water's edge, a group of people were boarding a small boat and, even at this distance, Halt recognised the small figure in the middle as his apprentice.

'Will!' he shouted but the sea wind snatched the words away. With hands and knees, he urged Abelard onwards.

It was the drumming of hooves that alerted them. Erak, waist deep in water as he and Horak shoved the boat into deeper water, looked over his shoulder and saw the green and grey clad figure on the shaggy horse.

'Hergel's beard!' he shouted. 'Get moving!'

Will, seated beside Evanlyn in the centre of the boat, turned as he spoke and saw Halt, barely two hundred metres away. He stood, precariously trying to keep his balance in the heaving boat.

'Halt!' he yelled, and instantly Svengal's backhanded blow sent him sprawling into the bottom of the little craft.

'Stay down!' he ordered, as Erak and Horak vaulted into the boat and the rowers sent it surging into the first line of waves.

The wind, which had stopped them hearing Halt's cry, carried the boy's thin shout to Halt's ears. Abelard heard it too and found a few more yards of pace, his muscles gathering underneath him and sending him along in huge bounds. Halt was riding without reins now as he unslung the longbow and laid an arrow on the string.

At a full gallop, he sighted and released.

The bow oarsman gave a grunt of surprise and lurched sideways over the gunwale of the boat, as Halt's heavy arrow slammed into him, transfixing his upper arm. The boat began to crab sideways and Erak dashed forward, shoved the man aside and took over the oar.

'Pull like hell!' he ordered them. 'If he gets to close range, we're all dead men.'

Now Halt guided Abelard with his knees, swinging the horse into the sea itself and thrusting forward to try to catch the boat. He fired again but the range was extreme and the target was heaving and tossing on the waves. Added to that was the fact that Halt couldn't shoot near the centre of the boat, for fear of hitting Will or Evanlyn. His best chance was to get close enough for easy shooting and pick off the oarsmen one at a time.

He fired again. The arrow bit deep into the timbers of the boat, barely an inch from Horak's hand, in the stern. He jerked his hand away as if he'd been burnt and yelped in surprise, then flinched as another arrow hissed into the water behind the boat, not a foot away.

But now the boat was gaining, as Abelard, breast deep in the waves, could no longer maintain his speed. The little horse thrust valiantly against the water, but the boat was drawing alongside the wolfship and was still over a hundred metres away. Halt urged the horse a few metres closer, then stopped, defeated, as he saw the figures being hauled up from the boat.

The two smallest passengers were led to the stern steering position. The Skandian crew lined the sides of the ship, standing on the rail to shout their defiance at the small figure who was almost obscured by the rolling grey waves.

On the wolfship, Erak yelled at them, diving for cover behind the solid bulwark.

'Get down, you fools! That's a Ranger!'

He'd seen Halt's bow coming up, then saw his hands

move at incredible speed. His remaining nine arrows were arcing high in the air before the first one struck.

Within the space of two seconds, three of the Skandians lining the rail went down under the arrow storm. Two of them lay groaning in pain. The other was ominously still. The rest of the crew flung themselves flat on the deck as arrows hissed and thudded around them.

Cautiously, Erak raised his head above the bulwark, making sure that Halt was out of arrows.

'Get under way,' he ordered, and took the steering oar. Will, temporarily forgotten, moved to the rail. It was only a few hundred metres and nobody was watching him. He could swim that far, he knew, and he began to reach for the railing. Then he hesitated, thinking of Evanlyn. He knew he couldn't abandon her. Even as he had the thought, Horak's big hand closed over the collar of his jacket and the chance was gone.

As the ship began to gather way, Will stared at the mounted figure in the surf, buffeted by the waves. Halt was so near and yet now so impossibly out of reach. His eyes stung with tears and, faintly, he heard Halt's voice.

'Will! Stay alive! Don't give up! I'll find you wherever they take you!'

Choking on tears, the boy raised his arm in farewell to his friend and mentor.

'Halt!' he croaked but he knew the Ranger would never hear him. He heard the voice again, carrying over the sounds of wind and sea.

'I'll find you, Will!'

Then the wind filled the big, square sail of the wolfship

and she heeled away from the shore, moving faster and faster towards the north-east.

For a long time after she'd dropped below the horizon, the sodden figure sat there, his horse chest deep in the rolling waves, staring after the ship.

And his lips still moved, in a silent promise only he could hear.

ABOUT THE AUTHOR

John Flanagan began his working life in advertising before moving to freelance writing and script editing. He has written TV jingles, brochures, corporate videos and comedy-drama for television, and is one of Australia's more prolific television writers.

John wrote the first book in the *Ranger's Apprentice* series to encourage his twelve-year-old son to enjoy reading. Michael was a small boy, and all his friends were bigger and stronger than he was. John wanted to show him that reading was fun, and heroes weren't necessarily big and muscular. Now in his mid-twenties, Michael is six feet tall, broad-shouldered and powerful — but he still loves *Ranger's Apprentice*.

John lives in the beachside Sydney suburb of Manly, and is currently writing more titles in the *Ranger's Apprentice* series and in his new spin-off series, *Brotherband Chronicles*.

A SPECIAL Q & A WITH JOHN FLANAGAN:

Tell me a little about how you came to write the Ranger's Apprentice *series?*

The driving force behind these books was the original twenty short stories, which I wrote to get my son Michael interested in reading. I wanted to show him that reading could excite you, amuse you, frighten you, make you exultant and transport you to another place and time. I also wanted to create a hero who was small, like Michael. Heroes should come in all shapes and sizes.

The Rangers have mastered the art of moving unseen and unheard. Do you ever wish you could make yourself invisible?

Every time certain people come to visit. No names.

Did you ever learn any kind of martial art or fighting skill, or are the fight scenes wholly from your imagination?

My brother and I dabbled in judo when we were young - learning from books, mainly. Also a little boxing. But since he outweighed my by about forty pounds, I was usually at a disadvantage. Still, the principles were absorbed. Plus I think there are certain similarities in the techniques involved in wielding any hitting object - be it a sword, a tennis racquet, a ball axe or a golf club. Letters from martial arts teachers have told me I'm pretty much on the right track.

Do you remember the moment that Will was formed in your mind? Was he different to how he eventually appeared on the page?

I wish I could say yes. But the answer is no. He was modelled on Michael, my son. Originally, he had blonde hair, as Michael had when he was 15. But the model we chose for the cover photo was dark haired, so I changed that. Similarly, Evanlyn orginally had jet black hair, but the model chosen was a honey blonde, so that had to change as well. I'm often accused of making all my heroines blonde, but it was an accident of casting, believe me.

Do you have a favourite character to write for?

I am rather fond of Horace, and Tug.

Your dialogues are very realistic. Do you try to remember conversations that you overhear, to use in the books?

No. But remember, I spent years writing dialogue for television shows. Thank you for the compliment, by the way.

At one stage, when I was younger, I used to eavesdrop on conversations on the bus or train, to get the feeling of how people speak - their rhythms, inflections and what they didn't say as much as what they said - the way people will switch topics in the middle of a conversation, then swing back to the original. They'll start sentences in the middle. That sort of thing. Ed McBain (Evan Hunter) who wrote the *87th Precinct* series of detective novels, was an absolute master of dialogue.

RANGER'S APPRENTICE

THE ICEBOUND LAND

Will, trust in your friends, we will not let you down.

You have been kidnapped and are trapped on a
ship headed to the icebound land of Skandia.

Your future looks dark, as you face a life of backbreaking
slavery. But you must be strong. Remember your training,
and know that your friends will do anything to rescue you,
even if they have to defy the King.